# Makena was

Shane had done ... ~~ed~~ miserably. The idea ... ht and no-strings with Makena might work if she weren't his best friend's baby sister and a woman he knew would expect more than a few nights of meaningless sex.

She deserved more—deserved better than him.

He worked long hours and traveled all the time. He loved his job with the Corcoran Team, the off-the-books undercover group that took on high-risk rescue jobs for companies and governments. He lived with danger. Thrived on it.

Dragging Makena into that life—no matter how hard it was to forget her face even as he traveled thousands of miles away—would be a mistake.

He needed to watch over her. No kissing. No fun. Just two old friends talking.

Now, if he could only get his brain and body on the same page.

# TAMED

## BY
## HelenKay DIMON

Published in Great Britain 2015
by Mills & Boon, an imprint of Harlequin (UK) Limited,
Eton House, 18-24 Paradise Road, Richmond, Surrey, TW9 1SR

© 2015 HelenKay Dimon

ISBN: 978-0-263-25315-3

46-0815

Harlequin (UK) Limited's policy is to use papers that are natural, renewable and recyclable products and made from wood grown in sustainable forests. The logging and manufacturing processes conform to the legal environmental regulations of the country of origin.

Printed and bound in Spain
by CPI, Barcelona

**HelenKay Dimon**, an award-winning author, spent twelve years in the most unromantic career ever—divorce lawyer. After dedicating all that effort to helping people terminate relationships, she is thrilled to deal in happy endings and write romance novels for a living. Now her days are filled with gardening, writing, reading and spending time with her family in and around San Diego. Stop by her website, www.helenkaydimon.com, and say hello.

To Allison Lyons for her patience, support and editing.
I appreciate everything you do even though
I sometimes forget to say it.

# Chapter One

Makena Kingston had spent most of her life waiting for Shane Baker to wake up and notice her. Tonight she waited for him to pull into the guest parking space so they could have dinner.

She'd called him on a whim. A simple "Come over and we'll eat." It seemed innocent enough. He had a few days off from the Corcoran Team, the undercover squad where he worked with his best friend, her big brother, Holt.

She'd asked this morning, and the hours since had ticked by in painful slowness. Now she glanced out the window over her kitchen sink, looking for Shane. Glanced—as in looked for the five hundredth time.

From this position she could see the steps down to a small lawn area and a much bigger gravel-covered spot. The brightly colored cottages sat in a row, close together, allowing for some privacy but not much. The close quarters and general lack of updating helped her afford the place.

Maybe fifteen feet separated her deck from the one next door. Sometimes she could hear her neighbors, a young married couple, argue. They did that a lot, and about everything. Makena often thought marital longevity might not be on their side.

The night fell over Lannaker Estates, the fancy name for the development of cozy single-level homes perched on a small hill overlooking the Chester River. This part of Maryland, the Eastern Shore, possessed the bucolic feel of a university town, which it was. Small and quaint, close to the Chesapeake Bay and about an hour and a half from Washington, DC. Nothing much happened in Chestertown, and she liked it that way.

For the five hundred and first time, she glanced out back on her Shane watch. This time she saw a dark SUV parked parallel to the neighbor couple's back porch. She couldn't make out the exact color thanks to the fading early fall sunlight. Probably just someone coming to referee the fighting couple's newest argument.

She could make out two people...wearing all black. That struck her as a little much for this time of year. They'd moved out of shorts weather, but the cool breezes hadn't started yet.

Yeah, all black and...she balanced her palms on the counter and leaned in closer. She blinked a few times as she tried to figure out what she was seeing. It was as if the two people—men, she thought from their wide-shouldered builds—stalked the house. They separated. One stopped at a utility box attached to the house and did something. She couldn't quite tell what. The other went to the back door and dropped down on one knee.

Then they raced. Stormed the back of the neighbor's house. She switched from the window at the sink to the one on the side of her house. With her back to the wall, she peeked around the window frame and watched a bulky figure run through the back of the house next door.

Her heartbeat thundered in her ears, and her chest ached from the force of her heavy breathing. When a bang rang out in the quiet night, she gasped. She fought to drag air into her lungs, but her body stopped working. As if the messages from her brain just kept misfiring.

She stood, frozen, as her gaze searched from window to window, looking for any sign of movement. Thoughts jumbled in her muddled brain and she tried to think. It was as if someone had thrown a blanket over her, slowing down every movement and blocking every thought. She needed to do something. She should…the phone.

She patted her back pockets but couldn't feel her cell. She didn't have a landline, so she depended on the cell. Fear clogged her throat and a frantic desperation made her movements jerky. She glanced around and forced her brain to reboot. The family room. That was where she'd left it, so if she could get there she could call out.

A weird sensation washed over her. Her head whipped around and she saw him. A looming figure standing in the window directly across from her. He had the edge of the curtains in his fist. Even with the mask she could feel his furious glare.

Then he was gone.

She took off at a dash. Crossed the threshold and stopped at the fireplace. She threw the stack of magazines on the floor and ran around the coffee table. Laptop. Remote control. No cell.

She heard knocking in her head. A deafening series of thuds. It took her a few seconds to figure out the noise came from outside the cottage, not inside her mind. The back door crashed in. Wood splintered and the glass of the small window at the top of the door cracked.

Footsteps echoed around her. She could barely make

out any sound over the clipped panting escaping her throat. She turned around and slammed her knee into the table but kept moving. Standing still meant death. Holt and Shane had drummed that into her head. Fight back. Scream.

She started to do just that.

"Help!" Her voice cut off when the attacker slammed into her.

She felt the force as if she'd run at high speed into a steel wall. Her teeth rattled and her head snapped back. The breath left her body. No mattered how she fought for balance, her feet slid across the floor.

Arms wrapped around her waist in a crushing band. The room spun as she fell back. She waited for the punishing thump against the floor, but it never came. Her butt bounced against the couch cushion just as the attacker's body came toward her.

Tension choked the room. She went from thinking and feeling to autopilot. Before the attacker could use his weight to press her down, she scrambled. Pivoted to the left and kept going. She reached out to stop her fall, but it was too late. She kept going until she landed with a jolt on her hands and knees.

Something crunched under her leg. She grabbed it as she tried to run. She got maybe a foot before a hand latched on to her calf. A tight hand squeezed her muscle until she cried out in pain.

The aches mixed with the fear as her heartbeat kicked up even higher. She felt the burning in her palm and looked down. She didn't know when she'd found her cell, but she held it.

She kicked out against the grip on her leg. Looked

around for something to throw. Tried to keep her mind engaged as terror took off inside her.

The attacker regained his balance and climbed to his feet, never letting go of her leg. She hopped as she tried to make the call. Her eyes focused long enough for her to see the terrifying message: no signal.

She was on her own.

Dizziness hit her out of nowhere. He yanked on her leg and sent her sprawling backward. This time she missed the couch. The free fall ended with a hard smack against the hardwood floor. Her elbow made contact first and her hand went numb. The useless cell dropped and bounced.

She tried to turn over and he fell on top of her. His legs straddled her sides and his hand tightened on her throat. Seemingly using almost none of his strength, he flipped her over onto her back. Dead black eyes stared down at her.

"Move and you die." He slipped a knife out and flashed it in front of her eyes. "Do not test me."

"I don't have anything." She tried to shake her head, but he kept her locked against the floor. "I work at the university. I don't—"

He tightened his hand. "Shut up."

Survival instinct kicked in. She grabbed for the hand, trying to pry his fingers away as he choked off her breath. Desperate to gain traction, she shifted her hips. Her feet slipped across the floor.

Fear clamped down on her. The adrenaline pumping through her gave her a burst of energy. She slapped against him, against the floor. Her gaze whipped around the room as she looked for something to make into a weapon. Anything.

"It's over." The ominous threat sounded even worse in the attacker's flat tone.

"No." She said the word as much to herself as to him.

She had to stay conscious and clear even as panic bombarded her. It became harder and harder to breathe. He outweighed her. His strength far surpassed hers. Which meant she had to depend on her smarts.

But she was running out of options and air. As her vision darkened around the edges, she remembered the fireplace and the poker. While she wrestled with the hand crushing her windpipe, she shimmied. Moved on her back as he shifted and increased his grip.

With one last surge of energy, she threw her arm out to the side. The move nearly wrenched it out of the socket, but when she didn't touch anything she did it again. This time she knocked over the small vase holding the fireplace tools. The poker hit the back of her hand and rolled. The handle slipped away from her fingers, but she lunged and caught it. Cool metal filled her palm.

She tightened her grip and prepared to swing.

SHANE BAKER ARRIVED in Chestertown an hour before Makena's suggested dinnertime. He broke a few traffic laws getting to her, speeding being one of them. But instead of going in right away, he parked at the opposite end of her cottage complex and walked along the river, trying to clear his head.

Makena was off-limits. He'd done the marriage thing once and failed miserably. The idea of trying something light and no strings with Makena might work if she weren't his best friend's baby sister and a woman he knew would expect more than a few nights of meaningless sex. She deserved more. Deserved better than him.

He worked long hours and traveled all the time. He loved his job with the Corcoran Team, the off-the-books undercover group that took on high-risk rescue jobs for companies and governments. He lived with danger. Thrived on it.

Dragging Makena into that life, no matter how hard it was to forget her face even as he traveled thousands of miles away, would be a mistake. Dinner wasn't even a good idea, but he couldn't say no. Holt was out of town, enjoying some time off with Lindsey, his new girlfriend. Shane rationalized his presence at Makena's back door as he walked toward it. He needed to watch over her. No kissing. No fun. Just two old friends talking.

Now if he could only get his brain and body on the same page.

He rounded the far corner of the complex. Heard the crunch of wood just as he saw Makena's back door implode. Before his mind could process, he took off. He ran along the edge of the hill and sprinted to the porch. Up and inside just as he heard her scream, then voices.

His heart hammered in his chest as he silently hoped he wasn't too late. He shot through the doorway. A series of grunts and thuds greeted him as he glanced around the small space. His eyes finally focused. It took him until then to realize the lights had blinked out. But he had no time to worry about that now. He had to get to her.

With his gun out, he approached in rapid speed. He was about to call out when something flashed through the air. She had something in her hand and swung it in an arc. It connected with the attacker's shoulder.

The guy let out a roar. His big body shuddered, but he didn't fall. Shane took care of that part. He switched his grip on the gun and whacked the guy in the side of the head with all his strength. The attacker dropped in a crumpled heap.

Then Shane focused on Makena. Her eyes wide and glassy. A ripped shirt and her long black hair half-pulled out of her ponytail. He'd never been happier to see her.

He took a step forward and she scooted back on her butt as if fear still held her in its grasp. "Makena, are you okay?"

Some of the haze cleared. She blinked and her shoulders fell. "Shane?"

"Come here, baby." He stepped over the unmoving body to get to her.

In one lift he had her up and in his arms. His hands shook with relief, but that was nothing compared to the trembling moving through her. Much harder and she'd break apart. His palm smoothed over her hair as he scanned the room. He had no idea what was going on, but the guy on the floor wasn't exactly dressed for a social visit.

Once he had them out of the immediate grabbing area if the guy should wake up, Shane pulled back from her. As gently as possible, he lifted her head to look into her eyes. "Did he hurt you?"

"There were two of them." Her voice sounded small and shaky, totally unlike her usual spunky go-get-'em attitude.

The news sent a shot of adrenaline coursing through him. He slipped her behind him and faced the open area. The squeal of tires echoed in the distance. Shane left her only long enough to run to the back door. He caught sight of the back of a dark SUV. No license plate.

When he spun around again, Makena stood right

behind him. She rubbed her hands over her arms. "I didn't want to stay in there with him."

Shane's gaze shot past her to the body on the floor. The guy hadn't moved, but he would, and Shane wanted him tied up and ready for questioning. He took out his cell to call in reinforcements.

She shook her head. "Mine wouldn't work for some reason."

Shane got a signal and sent the emergency code to Cameron Roth, one of his teammates, before turning back to her. "Stay here."

With the order given, Shane headed for the guy. Checked for breathing and was relieved the guy was still alive, because it was tough to question a dead man.

"Zip ties?" He knew she had them, but he asked anyway. No sister of Holt Kingston, leader of the Corcoran traveling team, would have a house without zip ties. The bigger question was why the attacker had stormed in here. He had nailed the door with a determined kick, and Shane wanted to know why. "Did he say anything to you?"

"Barely." She buzzed into the kitchen and came back with the restraints.

"I'm going to need to hear every word." Shane went to work on binding the unconscious man. "I'm guessing he was here to rob you, but with your connection to the Corcoran Team, we can't be too careful."

"He's not here for me. They...he...broke into the house next door." She paced the floor a few feet away from him. "I saw him, he saw me and then he came over here."

The idea of her being a witness brought him some comfort. Wrong place, wrong time. It sucked, but it meant she wasn't the target. That would help him sleep again…someday.

"Here." He handed her his cell. "Call the police. They'll need to check on the neighbors."

"I hate to think about what they'll find over there."

"You're not alone on that." Shane did a quick pocket check of the unconscious guy. He was about to stand up when he touched a piece of paper. Slipped it out of the guy's pocket and read the message. The words on it hit Shane like a kick to the gut.

She froze while pacing back and forth a few feet away. "What is it?"

"Your name and address."

She frowned. "What?"

There was only one explanation, and it chilled him straight to the bone. "The men were here for you."

## *Chapter Two*

Makena tried not to throw up. Shane didn't spook easily. The guy tracked killers and kidnappers for a living. He waded into danger without blinking. But now he was crouched down in her family room, holding that piece of paper with his face turning pale and his mouth flattening into a thin line.

Without saying a word, Shane turned back to the downed man and ripped off the knit cap covering his face. "Do you recognize this guy? Have you ever seen him?"

Those qualified as the questions she could answer without even thinking about it. One look and she knew. "No. Never."

"Did he say anything that could—"

"Why is he here? Why my neighborhood?" That was all she could think to ask even though she knew the questions didn't make sense or even match what Shane was saying.

A guy in a commando outfit storming into your house and holding a gun should raise a whole bunch of questions. None came to her in that moment. Her mind went blank. She chalked it up to some sort of weird self-protection mechanism.

She had no idea what her outward reaction looked like, but it had Shane standing up and reaching for her. His eyes narrowed as he stepped over the motionless body and put a hand on her arm. A touch she couldn't even feel.

"Let's try this," he said as he stood there facing her. "Take a deep breath."

"Okay." He could say anything next. She was willing to do or say whatever would unravel the confusion of the last few minutes.

"Did you tell anyone about Holt or the Corcoran Team?" Shane pitched his voice low as he asked, "Maybe in conversation or by accident? Even a mention of the team's name?"

It took a second for the question to register. She'd expected…something else. "No."

"It's fine if you did. I just need to know."

"I said no," she said, her voice growing louder with each word. She knew better. Corcoran's work depended on secrecy and the ability to move freely without being identified. They worked for governments and corporations, protecting and rescuing. She would never endanger anyone on the team.

And she would never risk Shane's life. Seeing him now, the broad shoulders and fit build that had his T-shirt hugging his biceps and hanging loose over his flat stomach, made her a little breathless. The short light brown hair and that familiar scruff around his chin just begged for her to run a finger over it. He possessed a handsome, almost pretty face that guaranteed an unending stream of teasing from his teammates…and she'd spent years loving him from a distance.

"It's easy to do." Shane shook his head. "More than once I've—"

"Honestly, Shane. No." She'd failed at a lot of things in her life, but not this. The safety of the people she cared about ranked above everything else. She'd never even stepped close to that line.

His gaze searched hers for another second. "I believe you."

"You should." It was almost insulting that he experienced any doubt.

"That leaves very few reasonable options." He stood so close and leaned in as he spoke. "Are you messed up in something?"

The words didn't make any sense at first. It was as if the slam against the floor had rattled her brain. Scrambled whatever up there helped her comprehend simple sentences. "Like what?"

"Something that would bring armed men to your door."

"Are you serious?" She worked at a desk. She read files and sat in on meetings. Nothing about her life shouted excitement...except for one thing. Her secret. The one piece she never shared. The same side work that kept her sane and would make Shane furious if he knew. She couldn't even imagine the warnings and threats he'd issue if he knew.

More body aches sparked to life the longer she stood there. She tried to take a mental inventory. Sore knee. A twinge in her back. That pain when she moved her wrist a certain way. She was going to be one big thumping bruise tomorrow.

"I'm being thorough." He talked slowly, enunciating

each word. "We can't miss anything. Even the smallest bit can sometimes provide the lead."

"I work in college admissions. I can't really imagine a kid or a kid's parents resorting to this sort of revenge for an application rejection." Maybe she could, but that didn't mean they'd be able to find her. Neither her cell nor her address was public record.

But the other thing. She bit her bottom lip as she tried to reason it out. The part of her life, the private part, where she sat at a computer and conducted interviews. Pored through records and looked for lies. Those men could get angry enough to hurt her.

Shane stood over six feet and now he bent down until they stood eye to eye. "What aren't you telling me?"

"Nothing."

His intense stare didn't let up. "We've known each other for too long for me not to pick up on that bobble in your voice."

"I was attacked." But he was right. It had been years. She'd met him through Holt. Shane was her big brother's best friend. The guy with the bad marriage and, eventually, the difficult divorce. The one who made sure Holt came home safe from their assignments. The one who hung around and joked and looked and smelled so good.

For Makena, appreciation and attraction had grown from the second they met. She'd kept her feelings locked inside and pushed them away while he was married. Once he was single again, her gaze started lingering longer on Shane's broad chest. Even when they weren't together, the memory of his deep voice vibrated in her head. She looked forward to seeing him, even if the peek amounted to nothing more than a quick glimpse as Shane dropped Holt off somewhere.

She missed him when he was gone and enjoyed whatever little time they spent together these days. And today she silently thanked him for getting there on time. His entry had made all the difference. Anything could have happened to her if he'd waited a few more minutes to show up.

A groan cut off her mental wanderings. Low and almost a growl, it had her attention zipping to the floor. The attacker didn't move and his eyes didn't open, but the air changed. She felt rather than saw movement.

She shifted so they could both look down. "He's waking up."

"Good." Shane moved her back, just far enough that the attacker's hand no longer rested next to her foot. "I have some questions for him."

Funny, but all she wanted was to see the guy dragged out of her house and locked up. The *why* mattered, but seeing the guy's presence triggered a constant shaking inside her. "Any chance we could handle those at the police station?"

"I want to question this guy without an official report."

That sounded like one of those things Holt said and she tried to ignore because she did not want to know. "I'll pretend I didn't hear that."

Shane took a step in the downed man's direction and his eyes popped open. "You have two minutes to tell me who you are and why you're here." Shane aimed his gun at the attacker. "Or do you need an incentive?"

"Shane, please." The only thing she wanted less than to hear about Shane's work plans was to watch them in action. She understood the need for hard talk—even violence—to combat evil, but she did not want to witness it firsthand. She'd had enough of that tonight.

"Go wait outside for the police." He never broke eye contact with the attacker. They'd launched into a staring contest and neither of them moved.

She wanted Shane safe. She also wanted him to stay out of jail, so she was not leaving, no matter how much relief flooded through her at the thought at being outside in the fresh air and away from the injured attacker. "No way."

Shane shot her a quick glance before returning his attention to the guy on the floor. "I need answers. He has them."

The attacker lifted his head but didn't say anything. His fingers moved on the carpet and sent Shane's gaze bouncing.

He held out a hand in her direction even as his focus remained on the attacker's prone form. "Stay back."

She didn't have any intention of getting closer. The exact opposite, actually. She took one step and backed into a chair. She could add her calf to the list of injured body parts.

She swore as she glanced down. The room started spinning in slow motion. The attacker's foot hooked around hers and he pulled. Her knee buckled as the air whizzed under her. Prone one second, the attacker moved with record speed the next as he jackknifed into a sitting position.

Shane's hand brushed her forearm as he made a grab for her, but the attacker proved to be a second faster. He wrapped an arm around her legs. She fell and her weight came down in a rush. The next time she inhaled, she lay on top of the attacker, her back against his front, with the fire poker balanced on her neck, keeping her locked against him.

"Drop your gun." Those were the first words the attacker had spoken since Shane raced through the back door.

Her breath rushed out of her as her heartbeat thundered in her ears. The shaking inside her morphed into waves of panic. Tension filled the room and seemed to have Shane's arm locked as he pointed the gun just past her head at the attacker.

"I said drop it." The pressure against her neck closed in, choking off what little air moved through her, as the attacker spoke. "Do it or I kill her."

"No." Shane didn't offer anything else. Just that.

The attacker tightened his grip until his knuckles turned white. She could see his skin right by her face. His arms shook as he pulled in. The light began to fade on her.

No way was she going out like this, in her own home while Shane watched. She flailed, shifting her weight and elbowing as she pushed and kicked.

Shane said something, but she couldn't hear him. Couldn't hear anything. Could barely think.

Movement flashed in front of her. Shane went from looming over them to shifting to the side. A bang echoed through the room, right by her face. She felt the attacker shudder behind her. His hold tightened for a fraction of a second, then slipped away.

Her ears rang as Shane reached down and lifted her to her feet. She tried to turn and see what was happening as she rose, but Shane's arm blocked her. Her body came to a halt and her head rested on his shoulder as her leg muscles gave out. She glanced over his arm and spied the blood on the floor around the attacker's head, before she quickly closed her eyes again.

Shane had shot the guy.

The realization hit her and her stomach flipped. The trembling moving through her had her teeth chattering. "Did you…"

His arm tightened around her waist as his hand brushed up and down her back. "Yes."

The soothing gesture threatened to suck her in. She fought off the comfort and pulled back so she could look up at him. "You mean you killed him."

"Yeah."

He didn't deny it or try to pretty up the words. Part of her appreciated the clear voice and the sure way he spoke about his actions, without justification. But part of her hated how easy it all seemed for him.

"Are you okay?" With his hands on her shoulders, he turned her body until his shoulders stood between her and an unwanted view of the death below her.

She didn't see a reason to lie, so she didn't. "Not really."

"He would have killed you." Shane sounded so sure.

His conviction fueled hers. That fast, some of the haze cleared. "I know."

"Makena, I—" He broke eye contact and glanced toward the front of the house.

She heard it, too. "Sirens."

"Now we have a problem." Shane stepped back.

"Now? As opposed to two minutes ago?"

"Don't panic."

That comment almost guaranteed she would. "I doubt that."

"The police are going to come in here and act like I'm the suspect." He offered the explanation as he unloaded his gun.

"What?" She needed Shane right where he was. Not down at a police station. Not in danger. But that wasn't her only concern.

A new wave of panic crashed over her. The police could not go through her house. There were papers, folders and files they could not see. She hadn't done anything wrong, but she'd have to explain, and she couldn't. Not to them. Maybe not even to Shane.

He set his weapon on the table with the bullets next to it. "To be safe I'm going to get on my knees and—"

She grabbed on to his arm and fought to keep him on his feet. "No, I need your help." A frantic clawing ripped through her insides. "There are things here."

The sirens wailed and lights flashed outside the window. She could make out the shadows of people outside, likely neighbors gathered to see what was happening. There would be police and possibly press at some point.

None of this could happen.

Shane's hand went to her shoulder, then up to touch her hair. "Talk to me."

"The police can't go near my safe." She'd locked everything away in anticipation of Shane's visit. Gathered up every shred of evidence and hidden it. She knew if she'd left out even a piece of paper, Shane would sniff it out. She'd been so careful. And now...

His eyes narrowed. "What are you saying?"

"I'll explain later." She had his arm and started pushing and shoving him in the direction of the bedroom. "You just need to keep them away from the safe."

A banging started. Sounded like the side of a hand pounding against her front door. Then the doorbell dinged once, and then a second time. The noise hit a crescendo as her panic rose and whipped up around them.

"I'll keep the focus on me." He motioned toward the front door. "Go let them in."

"What about—"

"You'll explain it all later."

She didn't answer. Didn't have time because the front door crashed in. Chaos exploded around her as uniformed officers piled into her small family room. She turned back around to say something to Shane, but he'd disappeared.

Her glance dropped and she spied him on his knees, right near the body. He had his hands hooked behind his head, but the police kept shouting. They knocked him down on his stomach as they wrenched his arms behind his back.

"No, he's not—" A policeman pulled her back before she could rush in and move everyone off Shane.

Shane turned his head to the side and looked up at her. "Call Connor."

Her brain scrambled. "My cell doesn't work." She shook her head, trying to remember where she put it or why that information even mattered.

"They probably blocked the signal. Try again." He glared, as if willing her to listen. "We need Connor."

Connor Bowen, the owner and head of the Corcoran Team. The man with power and connections. She knew one thing: if Shane needed Connor for reinforcements, they were all in trouble.

# Chapter Three

Shane tried not to stare at her. Being in the same room with Makena always resulted in the same reaction. His heart rate kicked up as fast as his common sense took a nosedive. The black hair, usually pulled back with those sexy curls hanging down by her ears. The dark eyes and hints of the heritage passed down from her Japanese mother.

The long legs and trim body…everything about her set his blood boiling. So beautiful that she tested every vow he'd ever made postdivorce about keeping relationships light and sex only. He wanted her every minute and fought off the attraction with every cell and every muscle.

He tore his attention away from her and watched his team as he stood in the middle of her family room with activity buzzing around him. Cam and Connor had arrived. Connor had walked through the door and immediately started doing what he did best—he ran the whole show. Came in with a cover and ordered people, all while silently wrestling control away from whatever poor schmuck thought he ran the crime scene.

Cam, along with Holt, formed the three-man traveling team for Corcoran. Cam showed up to help because that was what Cam did. No questions asked, he rushed in and provided support. Many times that included flying a helicopter. This time he stood on the other side of Makena, across from Shane, and made sure no one got near her.

Connor broke away from the detective and headed over to the Corcoran semicircle. "We have one dead attacker."

"Thanks to Shane," Cam said.

"You would have done the same thing." Every member of the team would have put his body in front of Makena. Forget about her being innocent, though that counted as a good answer. She was Holt's sister, and no one touched the people the team members cared about.

"Probably." Cam shrugged. "I'm betting I would have used more finesse. Maybe been quicker about it."

Shane knew Cam was joking…or engaging in what Cam thought qualified as joking. Making sly comments meant to break the tension. If Shane hadn't walked in on some guy manhandling Makena, watched as the guy tried to choke the life out of her, he might be more in the mood to be soothed. But not right now.

"The guy intended to kill me." The rough edge to Makena's words was hard to miss.

Cam's smile suggested he didn't. "Then I definitely would have killed him, too."

Shane was about to remind her about Cam's odd sense of humor when Connor broke in. "Now that we have that settled."

An officer behind Makena knocked into her. She jumped. Looked two seconds away from screaming but somehow managed to bite it back.

Shane could not help being impressed. She didn't deal in danger as they did, yet she'd stayed calm. She'd listened to the informal training they gave her and kept fighting no matter what. She never let down her guard. Those smarts and that strength had kept her alive.

She cleared her throat as she visibly brought her nerves back under control. Most signs vanished. All but the way she rubbed her hands together in front of her until her skin turned red. "What about my neighbors?"

No surprise her mind went there. Shane had checked on that first thing. "They weren't home."

Her shoulders fell as she blew out a long breath. "I heard a shot…or I thought I did."

She wouldn't like the answer, but Shane offered it anyway. "Killed the dog."

Cam swore under his breath. "That sucks."

An awful situation, but the death toll could have been so much worse and Shane remained grateful it wasn't. "At least it wasn't a person."

"I like dogs." Cam moved out of the way as the ambulance crew brought in the stretcher.

"Is this what you guys always talk about on a job?" Makena watched every move as the crew lifted the still body and locked the stretcher in place. Her voice shook and a certain sadness moved in her dark eyes.

Shane wanted to make it better. Fought the urge to go to her, put an arm around her…test his control to its very limit. But he would do it for her. Or he would have done it if the audience didn't consist of Cam and Connor and what looked like six police officers filing in and out of the house as the detectives talked in the corner.

Unable to think of the right thing to say, Shane went with the one thing that might help. "He's trying to calm you."

Her eyes narrowed as her head turned and she stared at Cam. "Really?"

"He's terrible at it. Makes you pity Julia, doesn't it?" Julia White, the love of Cam's life. The reason Shane now hesitated when he called in a favor or needed backup as he played a hunch.

"The office is working on background on the attacker." Connor talked over all of them. "Preliminary reports are he had a record. Petty stuff."

"Are we sure that's it?" Shane glanced around, from the discarded fire poker to the magazines strewn all over the floor. Despite the battle, most of the furniture and other stuff in the room remained intact. But the man was still dead. "If so, it looks as if he escalated this time."

Connor nodded as he retrieved his cell from his back pocket. "We need to call Holt."

"No." Makena put her hand over the phone. Looked as though she tried to tug it out of Connor's hands.

Connor pulled it out of reach. "Excuse me?"

Before she said a word, Shane knew where this was going to go. Holt had met Lindsey during a job. She had grown up in a cult but possessed an inner strength. Holt hadn't stood a chance against her. He fell in love in the equivalent of a week. He'd spent two months going back and forth from his house in Maryland to hers in Oregon, but he was on his way back home and bringing Lindsey with him for good this time.

"He needs to stay with Lindsey." Makena spoke slowly, as if she were explaining a big idea to a small child. "The only way he'll do that now is if he doesn't know this happened."

Connor waited until she finished. "That's not an option."

The stretcher rolled by and Shane moved the group to the side to stay out of the way. He also lowered his voice as the rumble of conversation in the room died down. "It actually is."

"This explanation should be interesting," Cam said under his breath.

"Makena can stay with me." Shane ignored Connor's lifted eyebrow and the stunned expression on Makena's face, though he thought she could play her shock down a bit. "For protection."

Cam cleared his throat. "Uh-huh."

"Protection?" Connor asked at the same time.

Shane decided to ignore both of them. "We need to move her to a safe location while we confirm this guy's identity and figure out why he had her contact information, because that suggests more than a burglary gone wrong."

"And you're volunteering to be her bodyguard." Connor hesitated over each word, not bothering to ask it as a question. "You think that's a good idea?"

"I'm standing right here." Makena rolled her eyes. "And I'm a grown-up who should be part of this conversation, in case you gentlemen missed that fact."

Shane could fight his team or Makena, not both. "Someone sent men after you and we need to know why."

"Because of Corcoran, I assume." Connor glanced at the detectives. "I've ordered a lockdown just to be safe."

"That sounds bad." Makena bit her bottom lip.

"My wife is not a fan of the protocol," Connor said. "No one on the team is, since it involves being trapped inside and having the women in our lives skip their regular schedules. Not exactly an easy task since they fight every minute of it."

Makena snorted. "Good for them."

"Easy for you to say." Cam whistled. "Julia is going to be ticked off."

Shane jumped back in before the conversation devolved into an us-versus-them battle. "You guys handle the lockdown and I'll handle Makena."

Her eyebrow lifted. "Oh, really?"

Okay, that was a miscalculation. He knew that tone. Dreaded that tone. "Your safety."

"Right." Cam nodded. "That's what you meant."

Connor shifted just enough to bring everyone's attention snapping back to him. "I'll give you a twenty-four-hour reprieve on calling in Holt."

That was not going to go over well. Shane started a mental countdown. *Ten, nine, eight...*

"Don't I get to decide?" Makena asked.

"No." Connor's smile faded as fast as it came. "In the meantime, I need to go finish my 'Homeland Security is taking over' speech."

"That explains the uniforms." Makena's gaze roamed over Connor's vest.

Shane liked the Homeland ones. There was a certain subtlety to the white lettering on the dark material. Better than the FBI. The team had them all. Whatever the job called for, they were ready.

"I wear this, I flash paperwork and give out a phone number that rings in the office of a very important man, and we control the crime scene. No questions asked, which is what we need right now." From anyone else the comment would have come off more egotistical than realistic. Somehow Connor sold it.

Not that Makena was easy to impress. "That's a lot of power."

"I can be trusted." Connor winked and then walked away, forging a path as policemen shifted out of his way.

Cam waited a second, then followed. "I'm going to watch."

A crowd formed around Connor as he rapid-fired questions. Shane appreciated the distraction. Because it left him alone with Makena at least for a few minutes. Enough time had passed. He wanted answers.

"What's in that safe?" He'd kept the police interest off the bedroom and whatever Makena had locked in there, but he wanted to know.

She shushed him. Actually shushed him. "Not now."

He wanted to insist, but as his mind ran through the events of the past few hours, he couldn't bring himself to put her through one more thing. Not that they could wait long. Not with gunmen on the loose and a dead body being taken to the morgue. "Your time is running out."

Her eyebrow lifted. "Meaning?"

His temper. He'd had enough game playing during his marriage to last him forever.

With a hand on her forearm, he steered her out the front door to the porch. Neighbors milled around the yard, shadowed in the police cars' headlights. Darkness had fallen and a cool breeze carried the smell of the nearby river up to the cottage.

He ignored all of it and concentrated on her, making sure to drop her arm as soon as he could. Touching her just tempted him, and right now they had serious business to figure out. "You are way smarter than I am. You know what I'm saying."

She leaned in and dropped her voice to a low whisper. "Can you get it out of here without raising questions or causing a problem?"

He didn't even know what *it* was. He'd been to the
house many times and didn't remember a safe. That probably meant a small one, which made his task easier. No
way could he load a heavy safe on his back and get it
out of there without questions.

"I'll be able to take the contents out." He made the
distinction but didn't know if she picked up on it or not.
"And when I do I plan on looking through whatever is in
there, so don't even bother arguing about that."

She linked her hand under his elbow. "I should be
able to do something to convince you not to invade my
privacy."

The words skidded across his senses. She didn't
mean…couldn't mean… "Don't do that."

Her dark eyes filled with confusion. "What?"

Doubt kicked him in the gut, but he ignored it. "If
that's the kind of offer I think it is—"

She shot him a frown that suggested she was just
about to kick him. "Oh, please. It was an honest comment."

"Before someone tried to kill you tonight, you would
have just had to ask and I would have left your personal
life alone." That wasn't quite true. His job provided him
with the ability to check out certain details. If he thought
she was in trouble, he would not have hesitated to rush
in and help out. "But now that I know you're in danger
and hiding something, the chance of you winning this
battle is zero."

"You don't play fair." She waved a hand between
them. "Whipping out that whole bodyguard, good-guy
thing."

He had no idea what that meant, so he skipped over
it. "Can we carry the contents?"

"Yes." The answer came quickly and didn't sound all that convincing.

But that didn't change the plan. He only had one real play here, and it depended on keeping Connor away from the usual full-house search. "We grab whatever this is, head to a dark and quiet place I know to get something to eat, and you tell me what the big secret is."

Her mouth dropped open. "You can eat after all that's happened?"

The woman latched on to the damnedest comments. "I can always eat."

"How is that possible?"

Shane couldn't remember the last time a situation had robbed him of his appetite. If it didn't mean more hours in the gym, he'd eat even more during the day. "I'm not exactly small."

She leaned against the porch railing. "Oh, I know."

She did it again. The husky tone. The potentially provocative phrasing. Much more of this and he'd hustle her out of there and do something really stupid. "Makena."

Silence screamed between them. After a few seconds she lifted her hands as if in mock surrender. "Fine. Sneak stuff out, eat and talk. Got it."

He could stick to that plan. He *had* to if he wanted to remain sane. "There, was that so hard?"

"Actually, yes."

A weight lifted off his shoulders. "Well, you better get used to it."

"The bossiness, the need you have to get your way— which?"

"All of it. Because for the next day, I'm all you've got." And for some reason, that made him feel infinitely better.

# Chapter Four

Shane hadn't issued an empty threat. Makena could actually feel the time running out as she sat in a tucked-away corner booth of a diner she'd never heard of. Never mind that they were on her turf. Even with the out-of-control way he drove, he lived more than a half hour away. She spent all of her time in and around Chestertown. Yet he'd driven maybe fifteen miles and found some dive she never even knew existed. Drove right to it, so he definitely knew it was there.

"The owners don't spend a lot on lights." She squinted in the dark, trying to make out the faces of the diners sitting nearby but giving up. The smell of French fries and cheese lured her in. If the food tasted half as good as it smelled, she'd be back.

"It was just paperwork." He leaned an elbow on either side of his plate and ignored his hamburger. "That's what had you all twitchy."

Sounded as if Shane wanted to jump right into work and the safe and her secrets. No. Thank. You.

She held up her sandwich. "It's actually grilled cheese."

He flattened a hand against the fake-wood table. "I know you're thinking you can drag this out, throw off my concentration."

She let the cheese stretch in a string before breaking it off and popping it in her mouth. "I'm hoping."

"No."

Energy pounded off him. Every line of his body suggested he'd nip and pick at this until he got his answers. The intense stare. The stiff shoulders. That determined punch to his voice.

She gave up and dumped the sandwich on her plate. "You do understand this has been a rough night, right?"

He frowned. "I guess. Sort of."

She thought about kicking him under the table but leaned in, dragging her body halfway across the table toward him, instead. "Did you miss the part where a guy died on my floor?"

"That sort of thing is not that out of the ordinary for me."

Scary thing was she knew he wasn't lying. Any sane woman would run. Take off in the opposite direction and not look back. She'd tried that. She honestly had. She'd dated other guys and pretended her heart didn't do triple time whenever she saw him. None of it worked.

The big tough-guy thing, the pretty face and linebacker body all combined to knock her off balance. She'd been attracted to him from the start, and the feelings refused to die. But right now she needed him to be more than the man she wove wild dreams about each night. She needed him to back off on her secrets but stay close in case someone really was after her.

She dropped back against the ripped booth and stared him down. "Your work scares me."

"It's fine." He waved her concerns off without ever breaking eye contact. "Back to our deal. I believe you have something to say to me."

She glanced up, about to tiptoe through the facts, when the words clogged in her throat. She could make out one face in the diner. Wasn't tough, since he walked directly toward her, in a line right behind Shane. Slow and steady steps with a face filled with fury.

A ball of anxiety started spinning in her stomach. She had to sit on her hands to keep from fidgeting. "Were we followed here?"

Shane picked most of the toppings off his burger. "You've been watching too much television."

She couldn't move. All of a sudden her body froze and her mind went blank. The guy could have a gun or… she needed Shane on high alert. "You don't understand."

Shane's expression changed as he shifted in his seat and glanced behind him. "What are you—"

The unwanted guest stopped right at the end of the table and stared at her. "Heard you had some trouble at your place tonight."

He looked far too happy about the idea. He'd also just painted a target on his chest as the lead suspect in her attack. "How would you know that?"

Shane stood up, shoving his way out until he seemed to take up most of the space around the booth. "Who are you?"

"You on a date with her?" Jeff barked out a harsh laugh. "Dude, you should run. This one is—"

"That's enough." Shane didn't even raise his voice. Didn't have to. The vibration of menace would have been tough to miss.

Jeff took a step back. "You going to fight me?"

"You do not want that." Shane shook his head as he eyed Jeff up and down. "Trust me."

The mood in the diner changed. People openly gawked

and the waitress backed away from their table. Blame it on testosterone or whatever, but a battle was brewing and clearly everyone felt the danger. Except Jeff. He didn't back down. He outweighed Shane by at least thirty pounds, but Shane was all lean muscle and lethal fighter.

This would be a bloodbath, and while Jeff deserved to be pounded into the floor, she didn't want to witness it. "Shane, stop."

"Listen to the woman, Shane."

"One more time. Who are you?" Shane's voice dripped with disdain.

"Just one of the men she screwed over." Jeff threw out an arm in her direction, nearly hitting her.

She pulled back just in time. "You can't blame me. You're the liar."

With each word, her anger rose. She seethed with it. This guy had tracked her down, showed up at her house more than once. He'd been in the wrong and now pretended to be the victim. She despised him and everything he stood for.

Jeff's face flushed red and he took a threatening step toward her. He reached his arm out but never touched her. Shane moved with lightning speed to stand between them and pushed the guy back. Kept pushing over Jeff's protests and swearing until his back hit the wall. Shane held Jeff there with a hand around his throat. That was it. One hand had him pinned.

Shane didn't even move as Jeff punched at his arm and moved his whole body, trying to break loose. When two men got up at another table, Shane held up a hand. Didn't say a word, but the gesture was enough to get them sitting back down again.

Makena's heart lodged in her throat and wouldn't slip

back down again. She wanted to stop the madness, but it had spiraled so fast and so furiously and she could only stand there, openmouthed and stunned.

"We seem to be having a miscommunication issue here. Let me be clear." Shane's voice sounded deadly cold and even. "You don't go near her. Not to talk with her or touch her. Ever."

Jeff tried to pry Shane's hand off but failed. "She's been asking for it."

"That is the line said by every abusive male on the planet." Shane's grip tightened. "She dumped you. Move on."

The idea of dating Jeff made her stomach roll. "That's not what this is about."

Jeff scoffed. "As if I would date that piece of—" His words choked off as his eyes bulged.

"Last warning." Shane leaned in closer to Jeff. "If you think I won't rip you apart in front of an audience, you're dead wrong."

"Tough talk from a guy who doesn't even know what's going on."

It was as if Jeff wanted Shane to kill him. She couldn't believe Jeff missed the rage simmering there. That he couldn't see the darkness in Shane's eyes.

After a beat of silence Shane let Jeff go, but not before shoving his head back and knocking it against the wall. "Explain it to me."

Jeff doubled over in a coughing fit. It took him a few minutes to regain his composure. When he did, anger thrummed off him. "Ask your girlfriend. She's the one causing trouble." He scowled at her. "You going to turn on this guy, too?"

She hated being put in the role of bad guy. Jeff took

no responsibility for his bad choices. That shouldn't surprise her, but it did. "Shane's not a liar."

"Makena, don't help," Shane said without moving his gaze away from Jeff.

"That won't work. She's ruthless."

Shane pointed at Jeff. "And you're done talking to her or about her."

He batted the hand away. "You'll find out. Just wait."

Makena watched as Jeff stomped off. Pivoted around the tables, ignoring all the stares and the waitress rooted to the spot with the coffeepot dangling from her hand. The noise of the diner muffled. Makena could hear the creaking of chairs and the clanging of silverware, but it all sounded so distant.

Shane dropped back into his seat and stared at her. "So…"

"I never dated that guy. I would never date someone like him." She wanted that clear from the start.

The waitress darted over and refilled glasses. Shane waited until she left again to start talking. "What's his name? And do not hesitate. Tell me."

She didn't even have to wage an internal debate. It would all spill out now. "Jeff Horvath."

Shane exhaled. "And who is Jeff Horvath to you?"

"That's not exactly an easy question."

He shoved his plate of uneaten food aside and leaned in on his elbows. "Lucky for you, I have all night. All day tomorrow, too. Talk."

"He's a fake SEAL." The words tumbled out of her then. "You were in the military. Others weren't. There are men who pretend to be war heroes, special ops guys, and…they lie. They live their entire lives lying and not caring that real people fought and died doing what the liars claim to have done."

She expected to feel empty and frustrated at having the information pulled out of her, but no. A surge of relief hit her. She'd dealt with this huge weight and all the anger that came along with it for almost a year.

Shane's eyes narrowed and stayed there. "This Jeff is one of those guys?"

"Yes."

"Huh, I should have decked him." Shane dropped his hands to the table. Just inches from hers. "What does any of this have to do with you?"

This was the part he'd hate. She steeled her body for the inevitable yelling. "There's this website called *Wall of Dishonor*. It outs men who are pretending to be war heroes." When he continued to frown, she tried again. "I work for the website. Do research, file Freedom of Information Act requests."

"You work at a college. At a desk." His expression went blank. "Didn't you reiterate that earlier?"

The look on his face didn't fool her. He was winding up. She could feel the tension twisting the air around them. "Yes, but—"

"What, Makena?"

That tone. Not helpful, but she decided not to point that out, since he looked half-ready to strangle her. "I do this on the side."

"You tick off men who lie about military service. Men invested in their lies who have everything to lose when you uncover their deceit." With each word he jammed his fingertip against the table with a thud. "Do you hear the tone of my voice? Can you tell how bad this is?"

"They deserve to be exposed." She believed that to

her core. She'd grown up with a military man. Her father had dedicated his life to his career more than he ever had his family. Early in his service, he'd been stationed in Hawaii and found the perfect military wife who put everything aside for his career. By the time Makena and Holt came along, their parents were entrenched.

Dad was tough and commanding and demanded excellence, something she'd failed at for almost all of her life. Holt had suffered their father's wrath while she'd been spared. She'd been the disappointment. She flailed and tried to find her way, but got something of a pass from her parents, who never expected much of her anyway. Holt went into the army.

She'd gotten a lot of things wrong in her life, but she understood the military mind-set and the sacrifices. She hated the idea of someone claiming to have served who never did. It was an insult, and she'd spent most of her free time for nearly a year hunting these guys down.

"I'm not denying that guys like Jeff should be exposed." Shane shook his head. "He deserves to be shamed."

"Then what's the problem?"

"You…are you…" He wiped a hand over his face. "Does Holt know?"

"No." Her big brother could not know. He would try to control her choices in the name of protecting her.

She understood the tendency, even appreciated the concern, but he had a hard time letting go of his protector mode and realizing she wasn't a kid anymore. The fact that she'd transferred colleges twice until she found the right fit and moved around in jobs until she landed at the college only supported his point that she was not responsible. But she was. She had a career now, paid rent. She had a purpose.

"You didn't tell him because you knew he'd lose his mind. That he'd forbid it."

*Forbid.* The word sliced through her brain, bringing a wave of anger right behind it. "I'm a grown woman. My big brother doesn't control what I do."

This time Shane slammed the side of his hand against the table. "He wants you safe."

There was a difference between safe and coddled. She wasn't convinced Holt, or Shane for that matter, always saw the line. "I get that, but he doesn't get to make choices for me."

Shane's back teeth slammed together. "I want you safe."

*Well...* Her heart sped up and it had nothing to do with the argument. "I thought we were talking about Holt."

"We're talking about danger." Shane closed his eyes as he visibly wrestled to control the anger bouncing around inside him. "That guy talked as if he knew where you live. He was here, a place you said you've never been."

"Which is why I asked if we were followed." She'd checked, looked and thought they were safe...until Jeff walked in the door. The idea of him being so close and staying unseen terrified her.

Shane's mouth dropped open. "You're blaming me?"

That was not what she meant. Not at all. She put a hand over his, letting the warmth of his skin seep into her and wipe away the chill. "I'm admitting that I do this job. On the side."

"In secret."

"It's the only way to do it. The liars cover their tracks."

He opened his hand and let her fingers slide through his. "Let someone else take over."

She had to smile at that. "Says the guy who walks into danger every single day without asking someone to fill in for him."

"I'm trained for it. You're not." He turned her hand over and rubbed a thumb over her palm.

The move, so gentle and sweet, had something fluttering inside her. She forced her mind to focus. "For the most part I sit and look things up. It's completely safe."

"Then why does Jeff Horvath know who you are and how to get to you?"

The diner started spinning. She'd fought so hard to control her life, and one moment months ago had ruined all that.

"Because I messed up." She slipped her hand out from under his. "He was one of the first targets and I—"

"Targets?"

"—confronted him."

"You did what?" Shane's voice stayed flat and emotionless.

She looked away, but she could still see the moment. Filled with indignation and a sense of satisfaction, she'd stepped up to Jeff as he came out of church and told him, right there in front of his fiancée, that he'd been found out and now everyone would know. His business associates, his family, all the people he'd lied to for years, would know.

He'd claimed to be deployed while he played in Europe as a civilian. The tales of getting out early for some heroic act were even more ridiculous. She spewed it all in public instead of letting the website uncover him while she maintained her anonymity. A huge misstep she'd never made again, but the one time with Jeff was enough to keep her on edge.

She glanced at Shane again. Saw the rage bubbling under the surface and knew it was all for her. "Please don't break out into a lecture."

"I can't, because I'm speechless."

"You don't need to exaggerate."

His mouth opened twice before he spit out any words. "Do you have any idea what I'd do if someone hurt you?"

She'd waited forever for him to say something like that, and now he'd said it in a wave of fury. "No. You don't exactly share your feelings. How am I even supposed to know you'd care?"

"I'd care." He nodded toward her plate and the globs of now-cold cheese. "Fuel up, because we're going to spend a lot of hours talking about this."

She didn't hide her wince. "I was afraid you'd say something like that."

"You think fake military guys get angry? Wait until you hear this real retired army guy." He stole a French fry off her plate.

"I should have gone with Cam," she mumbled under her breath as she picked up her sandwich.

"Too bad, because you're stuck with me."

She wanted to hate that idea, but she couldn't.

# Chapter Five

Under the circumstances, Shane thought he'd stayed pretty calm. He somehow choked down a burger and drove them to his house without wrecking the car despite the anger shaking through him.

The idea of Makena putting herself in the middle of so much danger made his head pound. He could feel the thumping through every inch of him and had to clamp his mouth shut to keep from yelling at her. Yelling or kissing…one of those.

"Are you ever going to talk again or is this whole brooding thing as good as I'm going to get this evening?" she asked.

"Excuse me?" She just didn't stop. Anyone should be able to see his nerves ran on the edge. Not her. She pushed and demanded.

He hated to admit it, but her refusal to back down from him was one of the many things he found so sexy about her. The face and how she looked in those jeans ranked pretty high as well.

She paced around the family room of his end-unit town house. The strip of houses sat up on a hill with a view of the Chesapeake Bay. He'd picked it because he could get to the Corcoran Team office in Annapolis quickly but didn't live right on top of the place like some of the other members. He needed a break now and then.

Seeing her there filled him with a strange sense of calm. She'd been there before, but always with other people. For group get-togethers. That had been on purpose, but now it was just the two of them. He tried not to think about the big bed upstairs, waiting.

She turned around and faced him while she rubbed her palms up and down her arms. "I get that you're disappointed in me."

Not that. Not even close. "Wrong word."

He actually viewed her secret work as brave and important. He just wished she didn't do it. The idea of her in danger, of some idiot who thought lying about being a SEAL was a good idea tracking her down and taking his revenge, almost doubled Shane over.

"I'm worried about you being involved in something that could get you hurt." He'd already blown it by saying he cared. He tried to write that off as the usual concern someone would have for his best friend's sister. Nothing more.

He knew better.

She waved a hand and shook her head. Neither seemed all that believable. "I'm fine."

"Yeah, you look fine." She'd paled until her skin looked white. And the way she hugged her body, wrapping her arms tight around her middle, said she'd reached her end. It was the only reason Shane hadn't launched into his mental list of a thousand questions.

"Admittedly, I'm a bit shaky." She sat down hard on the armrest of his couch. The room stayed mostly in shadows. The light over the stove in the kitchen behind her cast her in its glow.

"Getting attacked will do that."

Her leg swung back and forth as she stared at her hands. "And I fear you plan on lecturing me all night."

"We got the time, so why not?" He aimed for a lighter tone, but he felt anything but and the words came out harsher than intended.

She glanced up, pinning him with an intense stare. "I can think of better ways to pass the time."

He backed away until his heel hit the step leading up to the foyer and his front door. When he realized she had him running and jumping, he stopped. This was his house and he was in control. Had to be, and that meant maintaining his hands-off policy. "Don't do that."

"What?"

The smile. She knew. He'd bet money she knew. "Tempt me."

She shrugged. "Didn't know I could."

No way he believed that. She'd caught him staring at her more than once. The way she looked. "Do you own a mirror?"

"Do you?"

He went out of his way to never mention any casual dates with other women when she was around. With his past and his record with women—with his family's experience with marriage—she needed to stay in the hands-off category, but he didn't want to hurt her. No matter how he fought it, the attraction zapping between them went both ways.

"We need some ground rules." Seemed logical to him even though he had no idea what those rules would be except clothes on, no touching.

"Right." She sighed and got up. Walked around to

the bottom of the stairs and stared up. "Are we staying here tonight?"

She made it sound as if they were sharing a bed, and that was not happening. He'd sleep on the floor and stay awake. He'd be sensible.

All good thoughts, but they scrambled in his mind as he walked toward her. One second he stood in safety by the door. The next he waited one step below her with only inches separating them. Not a smart move, but his mind and body seemed to think otherwise.

"You're going to get some rest and then we're going to talk about your side job in the morning." She was going to hate this piece. "We need to fill Connor in and let him look into Jeff."

"Why only me?"

Sometimes she said something and lost him. Left him far behind her, coughing up dirt and trying to put the pieces together. "What?"

"Shouldn't we both rest?" She laid a hand on his shoulder.

He concentrated on the danger and ignored how good the simple touch felt. It burned him through the cotton of his shirt and had him squirming. "I'm assuming you're experiencing adrenaline burn off."

"Are you talking about that sensation of having balls bouncing around my stomach?"

Not really. "Sure."

"I did, but now I feel as if I could sleep for a month." Her fingers moved into his hair.

He somehow managed to swallow. "That's the one."

"Are you going to sleep with me?"

He hit the breaking point right there. They were both adults, but she was so hot and tempting and…forget control. He dragged her off the step and down beside him. Before he could think it through or come to his senses, he lowered his head.

His mouth covered hers, and the ground shifted. He'd thought to wipe out the years of need with a quick kiss. Once and move on. Get back to work.

That backfired.

His mouth crossed over hers in a blinding kiss that had him wrapping his arms around her as his heartbeat hammered in his chest. Heat built between them, and a strange energy pulsed through the room. Forget staying detached and moving on. He fell in deeper. Tasting her, holding her, had every nerve ending zapping to life.

The noises she made went straight to his head. He debated taking her to bed and wondered how much they'd both regret it in the morning. The last thought had him lifting his head. He saw a flash of light off to his right and let go of her while he reached for his closest gun.

She stiffened. "What is it?"

"Visitors." He'd caught the beam from the flashlight, thin and bouncing as the holder walked. His gaze zipped to the front door and he saw another beam right before it blinked out.

Two attackers with enough training to know to come in quietly and simultaneously. This was going to get loud.

Her fingernails dug into his arms. "How is that possible?"

*Good question.* The place didn't trace to him and no one had followed them, so Shane had the same question. But he'd worry about that later. "Go upstairs."

"Shouldn't we run to the car?"

Time to fill her in on the bad news. "The easy ways out are blocked."

"I don't understand."

"I think you do." He didn't have time to explain and she was smart enough to know exactly what was happening. She just didn't want it to be happening...and that made two of them. "Go upstairs and hide in the closet in my room. You'll see an extra weapon in the box on the floor. The bullets are hidden in the opposite corner."

"You keep a weapon in your closet just in case?"

All over the house, but now wasn't the time to go into that. "Go, Makena. Stay in there unless you see or hear me or one of the other members of the team."

"Right."

He grabbed her before she could spin and run up the steps. His hand cupped the side of her face. "I'm serious. Do not be a hero here."

Some of the haze cleared from her eyes and she nodded. "I get it."

The thump of her feet against the stairs echoed as Shane put his back against the wall. He had a knife and two guns within easy grabbing range, and that was just counting what he carried on him. Other weapons sat, hidden, nearby. Whatever he had to do to keep the attackers from getting upstairs and to her, he would do.

After a soft click, the front door opened. That would trip the silent alarm and send a scramble code back to Corcoran headquarters. On cue, the phone started ringing, but Shane waited. Not answering would have Connor moving in reinforcements even faster.

The entire team could come. Shane didn't care. He hoped to have the situation neutralized before then. One peek of a human and he'd shoot.

The crash of the glass from the back door shattering caught him by surprise. He ducked, unsure what had caused the break, a bullet or something else. When he lifted his head again, he spied the man stepping into his house. Shane came off the wall firing. The attacker's shoulder flew back as if he'd been hit, but he kept coming.

They had Kevlar vests on and he didn't, which put him at a distinct disadvantage. Shots rang out as he ducked. A second man came through the front. They had him pinned down and trapped. He couldn't crawl away or bore through the wall. That meant going upstairs. Bringing the fight to her. He hated the idea, but he had to keep moving. Standing still guaranteed he'd be shot.

In a crouch, he spun around the railing and started up the stairs, firing covering shots as he went. A simple mantra kept running through his brain—*aim for the head.*

Plaster kicked up around him and more glass shattered. He reached the top of the stairs just as one of the attackers started up behind him. Shane ducked around the wall for protection and concentrated on the steps. The thudding sound grew closer. He waited until the last possible second, then shifted and fired. Nailed the attacker right in the head and sent him sprawling backward.

Shane's breaths came out in steady pants as he scanned the downstairs, looking for the second attacker. The quiet hit him. The banging had stopped and nothing moved except for a curtain that caught the breeze from the broken window.

Too easy. They'd had him trapped and he got out. No way should that have happened without more bloodshed and a hail of bullets.

He heard a noise behind him in the bedroom and sneaked inside, gun up. His gaze went to the window.

Nothing there. If the attacker had climbed in, he was hiding well. Too well.

The dark hair came first, sticking out around the corner leading to his bathroom and closet. Then Makena's face appeared.

"Are you okay?"

Makena whispered the question, but it echoed in his head loud enough to sound like a scream. With a finger over his lips, he gestured toward the window. He had to get her out, and there was only one way down from here.

He opened the bench under the window and took out the rappelling gear and held it out to her. "Here."

She stared at the rope and the carabiner, the locking mechanism that would secure her to the rope. "Are you kidding?"

"No." He opened the blinds, careful to keep the noise to a minimum, and glanced over the windowsill. The night was still on the ground below. He could see everything thanks to the security light he'd set up.

But they were running out of time. A second gunman roamed the house, and gunfire would bring people running. The police had likely already been called. His cover would hold, but Makena being at a second shooting in only a few hours would raise alarms. She'd be questioned, and Shane could not tolerate the idea of her sitting in a police station where he couldn't watch over her.

"We don't have time to argue." The rope was set up and ready to go, just in case. The sheer drop would be rough on him but impossible for her, so she needed the equipment.

He hooked the rope in position and slid it through the hooks that would hold it steady for her to climb down.

They didn't have time for a sling and instructions. She needed to move.

With one eye focused on the door, he opened the window and shifted her until she sat on the sill.

She shook her head and clamped a hand down on his forearm. "I can't do this."

"Makena—"

She shook her head and her teeth chattered. "It's impossible."

"You can do anything." He glanced at her, quick but deadly serious. "You unmask liars as a hobby. You have more guts than most people I know."

"But I—" Her voice cut off and she ducked as gunfire pinged through the room.

"Hand over hand." He gave her a push. "Down, then run."

Just as her body slid over the edge, he ducked behind the bed. He had limited ammo left but another gun within reach. He could cover her as long as necessary.

Shots rang out for a few more seconds, and then silence. Shane looked up, took in the ripped comforter and shards of glass all over the floor. Dark clothing flashed in the doorway, then footsteps thudded on the steps.

Makena.

Shane raced to the window. She stood at the bottom, staring up. He didn't wait. With one hand on the rope, he dropped out of the window. He held his body weight steady for a second, descending at a rapid pace, then giving up and jumping the rest of the way.

He braced for impact. His knees took most of the brunt. He bit back a groan as he landed. That would hurt later, but he couldn't worry about it now. Snagging her hand, he took off, racing through the open yard at the back of the property to get to the parking lot. There they could duck in between cars and wait.

Their sneakers scrunched in the grass, then tapped across the concrete. Through it all, he never let go of her hand. He tugged, trying to keep the pace doable. She surprised him with her speed. Never complained or questioned, either. The woman impressed him in every way.

They slid to a stop by a truck and bent down. Shane watched for feet as he sent the emergency signal to Cam. Connor could mobilize fast, but Cam tended to beat them all to a site. Shane was about to tell Makena how proud he was when he picked up the shadow. A man moving around the side of the building. He could go one of twenty ways, but he headed for them. Straight for them.

The attackers showing up at her house was one thing. People following them here was another. Impossible, actually. Shane knew subterfuge tactics. He could break a tail. But now this. It was as if they had a homing device in... He looked over his shoulder at Makena. A tracker. The first guy had planted one on her. Shane would bet on it.

He'd handle that, but first he had to take care of the newest threat. He wanted to take the guy alive. Bring him in and let the team question him. But then the guy prepared to fire, and Shane took him down. One shot to the head and he dropped.

But there could be more, so that meant one thing. He looked at Makena and tried to figure out the best way to say it. Then he just blurted it out.

"Strip." Even in the dark he could see her eyes widen. "I can explain, but I need everything off."

"Did you get hit in the head back there?"

Shane lifted his T-shirt over his head and handed it to her. "They're following you."

She took the shirt and held it up to her face. "So?"

A countdown ticked in his head. If a third gunman lurked out here somewhere, he'd be closing in soon. "Someone—I'm betting that first guy—planted a device on you that keeps bringing them to us, so I need you…"

She had his shirt balled in her fists. "What? Just say it."

"Naked."

She balanced on the balls of her feet and stared at him. For a few seconds she didn't say anything. "I thought you'd never ask."

Before he could answer—and he had no idea what he would have said—his cell beeped in his pocket. The noise and slight vibration made no sense until he remembered he'd already called for help.

When her fingers touched the bottom hem of her shirt, he turned away from her. Tried to block out the sound of clothes rustling and not think about what he would see if he looked over his shoulder.

He answered the phone instead. Talked before Cam could. "I need a cleanup crew at my house."

"That's the worst phrase ever." Her voice sounded muffled.

Shane ignored every thought running through his brain. Tried to ignore the fact that Makena stood a few feet away without any clothes on. This moment amounted to both his fantasy and his nightmare all wrapped up in one. "Connor prefers that term."

"And, of course, he knows people who do that work."

Shane could hear the smile in her voice. Let the sound

wash over him. Could stand there for hours except for Cam saying his name on the other end of the line.

That snapped Shane back into reality and got him talking to Cam. "Meet us at the safe house by Foster's."

Cam would know that meant the old mill once owned by the Foster family. They had three neutral places close by they could go to if any team member hit the scramble warning. Connor made sure they always had options. Tonight, like so many times in the past, Shane gave thanks for his boss's compulsive tendencies and called the code for one of the safe houses.

"Is that code for something?" she asked.

This time Shane glanced over and immediately regretted it. The T-shirt hung down to her upper thighs. Not long enough to guarantee his peace of mind or prevent losing control.

The long legs, the way she curled her bare toes into the ground…he was a dead man. "And bring clothes for Makena."

# Chapter Six

Makena took a deep breath as she stood in the bathroom of the safe house. The one-bedroom cottage sat at the end of a long, dark road. From the outside it looked broken-down and in need of repair. A building with fading brown wood and a crooked front porch.

Inside told a different story. Just getting to the front door meant unlocking gates and deactivating alarms. Shane did it all using his watch, and then led them through the door. The cozy interior consisted of a small kitchen and living area with an L-shaped sectional sofa. One door led to the bedroom with the bathroom tucked inside. The other opened into what Shane called an SCIF, a sectioned-off room for receiving and reviewing sensitive information. To her it looked like a bare room with a desk, computer and safe, and no windows.

Smoothing down the borrowed T-shirt, the same one that skimmed over her, and the sweatpants that were too long and puddled on the floor around her feet, she guessed Julia had handed Cam the clothing but decided not to ask. Between the stripping and the kiss, Makena's head still spun.

She stepped into the living area with a smile plastered on her face. Seeing Shane kicked up her heartbeat. Noticing Cam also sitting on the couch calmed her nerves a bit.

Cam looked up at her and smiled. "You look good."

"It was either this or a towel."

His smile deepened. "I'll refrain from saying anything in response to that."

"Good call." Shane sounded anything but happy.

Cam leaned back into the couch cushions. "Hey, you're the one to blame here."

"How do you figure that?"

"Clearly Makena being with you is putting her in danger." Cam frowned at Shane. "Why are you shaking your head?"

"Because you're wrong about that." Makena knew the back and forth could go on forever and decided to jump in. She walked farther into the room and took a seat at the very end of the couch. "This is about me, not Shane."

"You're saying that because of the note the first attacker carried?" Cam exhaled. "Yeah, I get that, but there has to be an explanation."

"Yeah, someone is after her," Shane said.

"Not possible."

Shane nodded. "Totally possible."

They were off again. Somehow she managed not to roll her eyes at the male byplay. As much as she wanted to keep her private life private, she knew that would no longer be possible. Her connection to the side business led to a whole new list of suspects. "I do some work for this website called *Wall of Dishonor*."

Cam's eyes widened. "The SEAL-outing one?"

She took in Cam's show of interest and noted a bit of awe in his tone. The support came as a sharp contrast to Shane's reaction. "You know it?"

"Of course. I check it out now and then, and silently curse the liars who have their photos posted." Cam leaned forward with his elbows balanced on his knees. "You work there?"

"I do research and investigate. Corroborate the charges people lodge with the site about people lying about their service." It was a simplistic explanation, but going into the details about requests from the government for information and all the calls and contacts with people who could confirm the stories, or not, would bore them.

Cam nodded. "Cool."

"No, not cool," Shane barked out.

In case she hoped he'd changed his position, he dashed that. "Shane thinks I'm being irresponsible."

Cam looked at Shane. "Why? Those guys should be dragged out to face those who really did serve. Like you, for instance."

"It's dangerous," Shane said in a growling voice.

Since he'd skipped over Cam's point, she made one of her own. "So is driving."

Not that it had any noticeable impact on Shane. He kept right on talking. "Do you think Holt would like knowing she's doing this?"

"Is this really about Holt?" Cam almost whispered.

Exactly the question she wanted to ask. A man did not kiss like that, hold a woman with that sort of fierce grip, if he didn't think about her. At least she hoped that was true. "I've always liked Cam best."

Shane scoffed. "Get over it."

"Holt is in love with, and planning to spend the rest of his life with, a woman who dedicated the last few years to helping people escape a cult involved in gunrunning.

How could he get upset about his sister having the same sort of bravery?" Cam asked.

For the first time all day Makena felt lighter. Some of the tension dragging her down eased. Hearing Cam give Shane a hard time shifted life back into perspective for her. "Well, Shane?"

"It's different when it's your sister." Shane shifted in his seat, and then did it again. For a man who rarely struggled with nerves, he seemed to be in a battle now.

Cam's eyebrow lifted. "Makena isn't your sister."

"This conversation is over." Shane emphasized his point by standing up. He walked into the kitchen.

She watched because she couldn't *not* watch. Something about the lazy gait that was anything but. "Because he says so."

Cam's amusement hadn't faded one bit. "Apparently."

Just as quickly as he'd left, Shane returned to the living area with a pad of paper in his hand. He scribbled something with his left hand. "We need to look into Jeff Horvath and—"

Cam frowned. "Who?"

"One of the men she exposed." Shane glanced up, but his expression stayed blank. "The same one who knows who she is and where she lives and followed us tonight."

"So he's behind all this?" Cam sounded doubtful.

"I'm not sure yet, but he's angry." Shane lowered the pages in his hand. "Out of control."

She bit her lip while she debated sharing the other part of the story. "He's also a bit of a stalker."

Shane's gaze shot to Cam. "Do you see what I'm saying about her being in danger?"

"You've made your point." And if he used the word *danger* one more time, her head might explode.

"I'll need a list of names of the guys you exposed." Shane flipped through the pages. "And the names of everyone you work with at the site. Work and personal contact information. The usual."

Only in his world did any of this qualify as normal, but she had a bigger problem. "Why?"

Shane didn't look up. "They could be in danger or part of the problem. We won't know until we start digging."

That was the problem. The idea of someone breaching Tyler Cowls's privacy had anxiety jumping around inside her. He would hate it and she could lose her position. "There's one guy, but he's really secretive."

Shane's head shot up. "I don't care."

"What kind of answer is that?" Not the one she'd expected and not reasonable under the circumstances. At least not to her.

"What's his name?" Shane asked, refusing to back down.

She tried a different approach. One even he couldn't argue with, in theory. "Let me talk with him and—"

"It's better not to tip him off, since we're going to see him tomorrow."

Apparently he could argue just fine. What a surprise. "Because you say so?"

"Yes."

Cam groaned as he stood up. "On that note, I should head out." He looked at Shane. "I need to talk with you for a second."

SHANE SERIOUSLY CONSIDERED refusing to go out on the porch. He sensed some sort of man-to-man talk coming and wanted to avoid it. "What's up?"

Cam leaned against the porch post and stared out into the darkness beyond. "You're blowing this."

"What are you talking about?" But Shane knew. He and Cam had talked about Makena before. All those years of thinking he hid his attraction proved wrong. Cam knew. He insisted they all knew, even Holt.

But wanting her and being right for her were two different things. Shane could not seem to get Cam to understand that.

"Nope." Cam shook his head as he glanced at his shoes. "You can't sell that level of denial. It's not believable."

He would never let this go, no matter how much Shane wanted that to happen. "You should go home and get some sleep and—"

Cam pushed away from the post. "Do you really think her working for the site is irresponsible?"

He loved her for it. That was what shook Shane so hard. How much everything she did resonated with him and how devastating it would be to lose her for good. "It's dangerous."

"So you've said. Repeatedly, which is annoying, by the way."

Maybe he needed to find a new word, because that one wasn't convincing anyone of anything. "Go ahead. Make your point."

"You care about her, and it's coloring everything you say and do."

Shane had figured that out long ago. "She's Holt's sister and we need—"

Cam groaned. "Stop."

"I'm not the marrying kind. Not anymore." He'd tried it once and it suffocated him. They had grown apart almost as soon as they walked down the aisle. Disappointment and hurt feelings led to a nasty divorce when it should have been easy. Shane remembered every soul-crushing moment. Remembered every vow he'd made not to travel down that road again.

"Who is talking marriage?" Cam didn't use the word *idiot*, but it hovered in the background.

"You think we could just fool around?" The idea sounded so good in Shane's head until he thought about the aftermath and how uncomfortable parties and every other group meeting could get.

"Maybe you should be asking her that, not me." Cam blew out a long breath. "Look, I know your marriage was a disaster."

"No worse than a few of my father's." Shane thought about the weddings…all four of them. His father didn't take much seriously, including marriage. He fooled around, lied, got laid off and basically ruined everything he touched. Shane fought hard not to become the man who had raised him, but the worry lingered out there.

"You're not him," Cam said, as if he'd heard the worry running through Shane's mind. "I know how this feels. You lose control and someone starts to matter more than anything else in your life. You make mistakes and bumble your way through them. I've been there."

Shane thought back to those early days in Cam's relationship with Julia. Cam, one of the most competent men on the planet, had turned into a complete mess. Shane didn't want any part of that. "Just because you and every other member of the team have paired off doesn't mean I intend to."

"She's not going to wait for you forever."

"She should be dating. Other guys, I mean." It hurt to say the words. He got them out over the sharp pain in his gut. Just the idea of her with someone else ripped him to shreds. He half expected to see blood on the floor. "I have to be careful how I deal with her."

"You could start with being supportive."

Shane closed his eyes. Just for a second to try to regain perspective and wipe the memory of that stupid kiss from his mind. "I don't want her working there."

"How do you think she feels about you walking into danger every day?"

Shane refused to think about that, because his job wasn't up for debate. He could handle it. He'd been trained.

"That's different." Though for a second he wondered if it really was. He fought for what he believed in. She claimed to be doing the same thing.

Cam shook his head. "You're headed for a tough fall."

"What does that mean?"

"You'll figure it out." Cam started down the porch steps. "Have a good night."

Shane stood there, watching the taillights disappear down the long drive. He wanted his mind to go blank and to have a moment without thinking or feeling. But the door creaked open behind him. He smelled the scent of her shampoo the second before she stepped out onto the porch.

"Did Cam leave?" She held on to the edge of the door as she peeked out.

Not ready for a civilized conversation, Shane tried to shut this one down. "I'll send him the list of contacts."

"I guess I should go write it, then."

He did that to her. Shut her down. Sucked the life and energy out of her voice. Acted like a jerk.

"Makena." He looked at her, drinking in the sight of her postshower. Dressed but still breaking his concentration. "You know I'm impressed with the work you're doing at the website, right? I'm just worried about your safety."

"I could tell from the way you were yelling and gritting your teeth together."

She had him there. "I could have handled this better. Not…you're not irresponsible. You're the exact opposite, actually."

Her head tilted to the side and her hair fell over her shoulder. "I've wasted a lot of time in my life doing stuff just because, being unfocused. Being a failure."

He didn't even know how to respond to that. That's not how he viewed her at all. "You're only twenty-six."

"I need to do this."

He knew all about need. He'd been driven to join the army for financial reasons and because he wanted a place of his own. "Maybe this isn't a risk worth taking."

"I have enough of those in my life."

She meant him. He got it. "I don't want to fight with you."

"What do you want?"

She couldn't ask that kind of question. It would open doors and send them down the wrong path. Being thrown together in close quarters would be hard enough without adding a new level of sexual tension into the mix.

"I don't know." The first time he'd ever lied to her. Right there.

"When you figure it out, let me know." Without another word, she turned and walked into the house.

It took every ounce of his willpower and strength not to follow her.

# *Chapter Seven*

Frustration still ran through Makena the next morning, making her movements jerky and her head pound with a ceaseless headache. It had been a restless night. She'd taken the bed and Shane had switched off between the chair next to her and disappearing into the living room. Each time he left the room, she let out a breath of relief. Not because she wanted him gone but because having him so close and not touching him made her nuts.

"We sure he's home?" Shane stared at the green house on the quiet tree-lined Annapolis street.

"The house always looks like this."

"Empty?"

Makena couldn't exactly argue with Shane's point. The small house consisted of two floors. Had sort of a cozy dollhouse feel to it. Not what she'd expected the first time she met Tyler Cowls, retired navy guy and the owner of the *Wall of Dishonor* website. The bottom floor had a family room at the front and kitchen at the back, with a small room in between that Tyler used as a bedroom.

Upstairs housed the website office. An open space filled with files, computers and boxes. The neighbors would never know what happened inside from looking at the cute space with the white curtains.

"He's a secretive guy." They watched from across the street and down a few houses. Shane had insisted they approach with caution after she'd called Tyler's unlisted number and hadn't gotten an answer, something that never happened with Tyler. He was on call all the time.

Shane raised a small lens and looked through it. "I wonder if Jeff Horvath knows where Tyler lives."

She wondered how Shane would like to swallow that lens. "I've already admitted I messed up with Horvath."

Shane dropped the glass and stared at her. "I know. That wasn't a shot."

*Yeah, right.* "Are you sure?"

Standing there made her twitchy. She wanted to argue with Shane and get him to open up about last night, to admit the kiss had meant something to him. But that line of conversation only led to heartache, and she needed clear focus now.

Talking to Tyler might help. Clearing this up and finding out if he'd been threatened could give them a lead to follow.

Shane grabbed her arm and pulled her back. "Hold up."

"Do you see something?" If so, that made one of them.

"Nothing."

"Okay, you lost me." Not for the first time and she doubted it would be the last, but it would be nice to have some idea what drove him.

"No movement at all." Shane glanced up and down the street. "You said he works from home and rarely leaves, yet there's no car in the driveway or out front. No shadows or signs of life in the house."

"He didn't answer my calls, either." Dread fell over her. Either Shane's question-everything personality had rubbed off on her or something was wrong. She hoped for the former. "We should go in."

"Me." He pointed at her. "You wait here and be ready to call nine-one-one."

She let Shane take two steps before delivering the news. "Tyler will never let you in. He doesn't trust anyone."

"Sounds like a nice guy." Shane took out his gun. "I'll depend on this to convince him."

"You think he doesn't have his own weapon?" With any other guy that might work, but Tyler would shoot first and not care enough to ask any questions later.

He suffered from a serious case of paranoia. He assumed most people lied. After serving in the navy and returning from Iraq with an injury, he believed in service and country and not much more. Getting him to trust her had taken a long time and many hours of drinking coffee at the shop near where she worked.

Shane swore under his breath. "Fine, but you follow my lead. We're also going to have a talk about your friends at some point."

Because that wasn't annoying or anything. "You want to be in charge of picking those, too?"

He actually smiled. "I probably shouldn't answer that."

She decided he was joking, or pretended he was, and started across the street at his side. They approached the house from the left with Shane constantly scanning the area. He didn't talk, but his intensity vibrated around them. By the time they got to the front porch, he had her nervous and doubting and worried. Something about having him on guard all the time sucked all the calm out of her.

She stepped up to the front door and dialed Tyler's number one more time, thinking to give him warning that she was about to ring the doorbell. She glanced over at Shane, expecting to see him inspecting the doorjamb for booby traps or something, but he wasn't standing there. Her hand dropped and she turned around. It didn't take long to pick him out. He paced the front lawn and stopped in front of one of the windows.

"We have a problem." He delivered the comment the way other people would read a grocery list, in an even tone. No panic.

That was fine, since she sensed she was about to panic enough for both of them. "Another one?"

"Is Tyler messy?"

The question didn't make any sense. "I don't understand—"

"Yeah, we have company." Shane raced past her, taking the porch steps two at a time and rammed his shoulder into the door. The wood cracked and the hinges creaked. On the second hit, the door flew open.

He stormed in and she followed. As soon as she stepped into the family room, her body froze. Ripped sofa cushions, smashed lamps. Someone had torn this place apart.

A bang sounded in the back of the house. She could see through to the kitchen and the open back door. Before she could yell to Shane, he was off. Her heartbeat sped up and fear clogged every pore. Oddly, she'd grown accustomed to the sensation—the rough breathing and anxiety slamming through her—and that scared her. She'd spent her entire life avoiding violence, and now it kept landing right in front of her.

She made it to the back door and stopped with her hands balanced against either side of the doorjamb. The backyard was empty except for the garage, and that looked to be locked. She needed some sign of Shane. To see his hair or those shoulders, anything to confirm he was fine.

But nothing bounced back to her but the usual sounds of a neighborhood. Cars in the distance and music playing in the house a few doors down. At least no gunfire. She winced and waited for it, but it never came.

"He's gone."

At the sound of Shane's voice behind her, she spun around. He stood in the open front door with his gun down by his side. Not winded, but the severe frown suggested he wasn't happy he'd lost the guy he was chasing.

"Did you see him?" she asked as soon as her ability to speak returned.

"Dark clothes. Male build." Shane closed the door and came the whole way inside. "Nothing else."

She glanced around at the open kitchen cabinets and shredded books and papers all over the floor. It looked as if a hurricane had moved through, but they had a bigger problem than bad housekeeping. "Where's Tyler?"

"Good question." Shane's gaze went to the stairs. "What's up there?"

"Everything."

"I'm not sure what that means, but I'll check it out." Shane's sneaker hit the bottom step just as the back door flew open.

Makena felt the punch of warm air at her back. She meant to pivot, but an arm wrapped around her neck and yanked her body back. A gun appeared right by her head and aimed at Shane. Not that it shook him. He maintained a fighting stance only a few feet away, as if daring the attacker to shoot.

"Who are you?"

The male voice whizzed by Makena's ear and she nearly collapsed in relief. She recognized their guest, only he wasn't that. "You're okay."

Shane didn't even twitch. "Let her go or I will put you down."

The band around her throat eased, but she didn't step away. Not until she made sure Shane didn't put a hole in the guy. It was his house after all. "Shane, it's fine."

Tyler frowned. "Who are you?"

"The guy who is going to shoot you if you don't stand away from Makena."

There were too many armed men in the room. Last thing she needed was to step into the middle of a battle between these two. She held up both hands. "Okay, let's all calm down."

Tyler stared at Shane for another second before turning to her. "He's a friend of yours?"

That struck her as the wrong word, but now was not the time for that debate. "Yes. Tyler, this is Shane. Shane, this is the guy we're looking for."

Tyler finally lowered his gun. "No one should be looking for me."

Shane didn't reciprocate. "Too late."

SHANE HATED TYLER COWLS on sight.

Shane had expected an older man, an off-the-grid oddball type. Instead, he got a guy in the suburbs. Not some wild-haired conspiracy guy. No, Tyler was about Shane's age. Probably considered objectively good-looking with a serious staring problem, because his gaze followed Makena wherever she went.

Much more of that and Shane would punch the guy.

"Did you recognize the attackers?" Tyler circled his kitchen table and handed a water bottle to Makena before putting one in front of Shane.

"Thank you." She shook her head. "But no."

Shane continued to size up the other man. He had a name and now could start the team on a full investigation. If Tyler had a secret, Shane would find it.

In the meantime, they had a series of kidnappings and break-ins to resolve. "Petty criminal types."

Tyler stopped staring at Makena long enough to turn to Shane. "Tell me what you do again."

Shane really didn't like this guy. "I never told you the first time."

"Shane." The chair screeched across the floor as Makena pulled it closer to the table.

He bit back the wince when her heel slammed down on his foot. Fine. Message received. He could play nice on the surface while he ripped the guy's life apart behind the scenes.

"Recon work." He glared at Makena, letting her know that move wouldn't always work, before turning back to Tyler. "You're not asking about the break-in here. You don't even seem concerned."

"I saw the attacker coming, locked away what I could and escaped out the window." Tyler pulled out a tablet and swiped his finger across the screen a few times. He turned it and laid it in front of Shane. "I like to be prepared."

Shane stared at the screen with reluctant admiration. Tyler had a security system that rivaled Corcoran's. Interesting choice for a guy who used to fly planes. "This is quite a setup."

"The people we expose are not happy to be found out." Tyler drew out the moment by taking a long drink of water and leaning back in his chair. "So I'm careful."

Makena lifted her hand. "Don't say it."

That was where Shane's mind had gone. Here Tyler sat in his house, all locked up with escape contingencies ready and a surveillance system that prepared him for the worst. Makena had a dead bolt on the door. Little did she understand how easy it was to break one of those.

But that was a discussion for another time…and they would have it. No way would he stand for her living without protection from now on. He didn't know what he wanted to install, but he'd figure out something.

"Which brings us back to the attacks on Makena." That was Shane's main concern. His only one, actually. If Tyler wanted to wallow in danger, fine, but he could not drag her down with him.

Tyler sneaked the hundredth peek at Makena. "I'd look at Jeff Horvath. Frank might have some other ideas."

Frank? Sounded like someone Makena had forgotten to mention. Another thing Shane planned to talk to her about later. "Who is Frank?"

She twisted the lid on and off her water bottle. "Frank Jay."

That triggered a memory, but Shane couldn't place it. "Why do I recognize the name?"

She didn't give him eye contact. Not while she picked at the label and otherwise attacked the poor water bottle from every direction. "He's on the site."

Shane grabbed the bottle out of her hands and set it on the table. "He's one of guys you exposed?"

Now he had her attention. She wore a wait-until-we-get-home scowl. "Yes, but he's redeemed."

Forget Jeff and Tyler. Shane's attention zoomed right to this newest information. They'd uncovered the truth about someone…then made friends with him? The shift didn't make any sense. "I doubt that."

"I've been skeptical, too, but he's done good work for us." When Makena finished her water, Tyler passed her his and kept right on talking. "Came clean and is making amends."

"That makes your website sound like a twelve-step program." Shane said the first thing to pop into his head. It was either that or smash water bottles together. Tyler and Makena looked comfortable at the table. There was a quiet intimacy between them, as if they spent a lot of time together.

One more thing Shane hated.

"I think that's where he learned about amends." Tyler's eyebrow lifted as he talked. "I can put a list of other possibles together for you."

"Clearly this leads back to the site." Makena reached for Tyler's water bottle, then stopped. "The attacks on me. The break-in here."

Shane slid his bottle over to her while he talked to Tyler. Didn't even try to be subtle about the choice he offered her. "Who else knows about your connection to the site and where you live?"

"No one except Makena," Tyler said.

She froze. "Wait a minute."

"No, I'm saying the list of people should be really short." He turned the tablet back around and started typing.

"Maybe someone followed me here last week?" She looked at Shane as she grabbed his bottle and took a sip.

"Possible." He tried to ignore the satisfaction surging through him and the quick glance Tyler took in her direction as she drank. "But why go after the two of you now?"

Tyler shrugged. "Someone finally put the pieces together and traced the site back to me. Then used Makena."

Not good enough. It all seemed too coincidental for Shane's taste. All the big security measures failing at one time? Unlikely. This was about something bigger led by someone with access to money and resources. Hiring criminals wasn't impossible, but the ones who'd attacked Makena had had skills. That took some knowledge.

"What happens now?" Shane knew how he intended to proceed with Makena's protection, but Tyler was the wild card. He could go somewhere or do something that unraveled everything.

Tyler glanced up from whatever he was doing on the tablet. "With what?"

Seemed obvious to Shane, but he spelled it out anyway. "Your address is known. Do you shut down the site and—"

"No." Anger seeped into the other man's voice for the first time since he'd lowered the gun. "I have other places to go."

And an unlimited supply of money, apparently. "Where?"

When Shane had Connor and the team check into Tyler, his finances would be on the list. A nice house in a good neighborhood, no full-time job other than the website, according to Makena, and now a safe house somewhere. Those kinds of preparations cost money. Connor had payments from their missions to set up what they needed. Big checks from big companies. Shane doubted Tyler had that sort of access to money.

Tyler smiled. "You'll understand why I'm not sharing that information."

Either this guy thought he was a Rambo type or he really was. Neither option made Shane feel any better about him. "We'll need a way to contact you."

"I'll give it to you. But that means the only people who know will be you. If something else happens…" Tyler stopped and cleared his throat. Even shrugged. There was nothing subtle about any of the gestures.

Makena's eyes narrowed. "What?"

But Shane got the point. Hard not to. "You think I'm behind this?"

"I don't know you," Tyler said.

"Funny, but I was thinking the same thing about you." But Shane would. Within twenty-four hours he'd know everything about Tyler Cowls, and then they'd talk again.

# Chapter Eight

Makena waited while Shane did his usual visual and physical check of the safe house. He looked under and over everything. Checked the traps he'd laid at the doors and windows to see if anyone had tripped a wire or moved a crumb.

He came back into the living area, tucking his gun away and dropping his keys on the kitchen table. Those long strides and the determined look on his face suggested he had a lecture just waiting on his tongue to be delivered.

She loved to watch him move, all lethal and stealthy. He stalked like a panther and rarely lost focus. But that didn't mean she was in the mood to hear him complain about whatever was on his mind. Not when she had a point of her own to make.

"You hated him." She meant Tyler, but she guessed Shane knew that.

He exhaled, long and loud, before lifting his head to stare at her. "Yep."

The force of his gaze almost knocked her backward. They stood on either side of the table with the furniture between them as a shield of sorts. She couldn't help but think they stood on the edge of a verbal war, though she did not know why.

"You didn't exactly hide it." Which touched off a bit of an angry fire inside her. That website meant a lot to her. Having Shane wave the work off as if it meant nothing put a bigger wedge between them than the table.

"Neither did he."

Something in his tone grabbed her attention. The words didn't sound right. "Meaning?"

Shane rested his palms on the chair in front of him. "He wanted to climb all over you."

A hiss escaped her lips at the ridiculous comment before she could stop it. "What are you talking about?"

His eyes widened and his mouth dropped. "Do you really not know this Tyler guy has a thing for you?"

But they were…he'd never… Her mind started spinning as the memories of all their meetings flipped past in her head. Talking over coffee. Meeting for dinner at his house. But she'd kept it professional.

Tyler had a boy-you-crushed-on-in-high-school look to him. Very cute. Friendly and charming. But she didn't feel anything more than respect for him. The older she got, the more she loved Shane. That had started blocking out her attraction to anyone else, making it impossible for her to move on. But Tyler didn't know that, and now she wondered about the signals she'd sent.

Guilt smacked into her. On top of the fear and adrenaline spikes of the past twenty-four hours, she could not handle one more emotion. So she packed it away to deal with later. And she would. She and Tyler. She'd make him understand.

"We work together. He's never made a move." All true, but now she wondered about the little things. The way he remembered her coffee order and made sure she ate. The glances he threw her. Why hadn't she seen it?

"Yet." Shane leaned harder against the chair. The wooden legs creaked and his hands balled into fists. "When he does make a move, what will you do?"

"We're not talking about this." Opening up about her love life with Shane could not happen. She needed to preserve some dignity.

He pushed off the chair and walked around the table toward her. "Are you interested in him?"

*No, no, no.* "Shane, you can't be this clueless."

"So, you're not."

*Totally clueless.* "Obviously not, as you should know."

"You're talking about the kiss."

She couldn't breathe. Could barely draw in enough air to speak. "It didn't mean anything to you."

"Did I say that?"

For every step he took, she took two in the opposite direction. They were all but ringing the table. She needed to leave. That was the answer. He could play this game on his own. She headed for the door.

"Where are you going?"

His question stopped her. She turned around to face him with her hands behind her, locked on the doorknob. "I need a walk."

"It doesn't work that way, Makena." Then he was right there. In front of her and so close. "I stay here. You stay here."

"You're the one I want to get away from." The words shot out of her before she could call them back.

Instead of being offended, he smiled. His hand caressed her cheek and he moved in closer. "Am I?"

She had no idea what this was or how to react. She knew what she wanted to do but went with dropping her head back against the door. "You've made it clear you're not interested."

"Now who's clueless?" His hands rested on either side of her waist, and his stance widened until his legs straddled hers.

"You practically ran out after we kissed." The comment came out as a whisper as she searched his eyes for some explanation of his sudden interest.

"That's not true." His fingers tightened on her waist. "But you are Holt's sister."

She'd known his name would come up. She could almost see the moment when Shane remembered his best friend and began the emotional push away from her. "Don't use him as the excuse."

"Fine." Shane put a hand against the door right by her head. Wrapped her in his warmth without touching her. "You're the commitment type and I'm a failure at that. What's the plan? We have sex a few times and then go back to acting like nothing ever happened?"

His words touched something deep inside her. She could hear the pain he hid underneath the sensible sentiment. He wasn't a man who failed at anything, but he viewed his private life as a war zone. His father failed at everything and ran through marriages. For some reason, Shane lumped himself in with the man who'd spent a lifetime ignoring him.

She put her hand against his chest and felt the thudding of his heartbeat. "Why do you think you're a failure at commitment?"

"I'm still paying off my divorce lawyer."

"Shane, no." When he started to pull away, she grabbed on to his forearms and held him still. He could have thrown off her hold, but he didn't. He stayed, and she took that as a good sign that he was at least willing to listen. "You guys were all wrong for each other. That needed to end."

Makena knew she walked a fine line. Patty had never wanted to be a military wife and resented every minute. Shane acted true to who he was, and this pulled them apart, to the extent that were ever really together. Makena wasn't convinced. She'd never seen a spark and he'd never talked about having a wife as anything more than a convenience...until it became very inconvenient.

"I made her promises about leaving the army and didn't." He exhaled. "I messed up."

She refused to let him take all the blame. Not after the whispers she'd heard from Holt about how difficult Patty could be. "You both did."

Shane shook his head. "How did we get on this topic?"

Because his marriage colored everything and talking about it was inevitable. The question was whether they could pivot and talk about them without him bolting. "You seem to think I need a ring."

His thumb traced over her lips. "I'm trying to be responsible here."

*Wrong answer.* "Maybe I don't want you to be."

"Makena." He said her name like a plea.

"I am a grown woman." She wrapped her arms around his neck and pulled him in tighter against her. "This isn't about my brother or your ex or even your dad. This is about us. What we feel for each other."

His hands rubbed up and down her back. "If we start down this road—"

"Kiss me." Enough talking. They could talk this to death and never get anywhere. She was done with that.

His chest moved in harsh breaths now. "I won't stop."

"I don't want you to."

That was all it took. His mouth covered hers in a blinding kiss. The type that whipped around and shattered all control. She held on through the smack of heat while need pummeled her.

Her fingers slipped into his hair as she wrapped her body around his. The blood drained from her head, and a wave of dizziness hit her. With an arm around her waist, he lifted her off the floor. She didn't fight the need to get closer, to burrow in deeper. She wrapped her legs around his thighs and held on.

He lifted his head. "Bedroom."

She couldn't say anything, so she nodded. Anything to hold on to the feeling and keep him from breaking away. She feared his brain would kick in and he'd go on the defensive. Shove her away. But none of that happened. He carried her through the small house, pushing the bedroom door open with his shoulder and carrying her inside.

Desire took off in a wild frenzy inside her. She held on because she never wanted to let go.

The room spun and her back hit the mattress. When she opened her eyes, he loomed above her, balancing on his elbow. She ran a fingertip over his eyebrow and across his cheek. Down to his mouth, then over that sexy scruff on his chin. "I love this."

He treated her to a husky chuckle. "That almost guarantees I won't shave it off."

The sound of his voice skimmed over her like a caress. The way he looked, who he was…she loved it all. "Good."

"Be sure."

She could feel his erection against her thigh and sensed the control it took for him to hold back and wait.

But there was no need. She wanted this, wanted him. Had for what felt like forever. "I am."

He nodded and started to get up.

"What are you doing?" She grabbed him and tried to pull him back on top of her.

His smile remained as he leaned down and kissed her. A lingering kiss that left her breathless after he lifted his head again. "Condom."

In her haste she'd ignored the precautions. She was on the pill, but that wasn't the point. Heat hit her cheeks. "Right."

He winked. "The blush is cute."

He left the bed but only for a few seconds. She watched his back as she heard him root around in his bag, then he turned around again. He stripped off his shirt as his knee hit the bed. The mattress dipped and she rolled against him. Then he was on top of her, his hands everywhere at once. His leg slipped between hers as his hands snaked up under her shirt. When his palms touched the bare skin of her stomach, she almost jack-knifed off the bed. When they ventured higher, right to the band of her bra, she stopped breathing.

His hands cupped her breasts, massaging and caressing before he lowered his head. He used his teeth to pull the shirt out of the way. One second she wore it and the next her hands rose and he drew it off her and threw it on the floor.

A mixture of want and need bombarded her. A warm breath blew over her as he peeled the material of her bra down and put his mouth on her. His tongue, those lips. It all hit her like a jolt to her senses. Her fingers slid through his hair and held his head tight against her.

Their legs tangled and her hands traveled down his

back to his belt. She couldn't see, but she heard the clank of the buckle as she opened it. The tick of the zipper came next. He lifted his body off hers long enough to kick off his jeans. When he reached for his gray boxer briefs, she stopped him. Put a hand over his and guided her fingers to his erection. Cupping him, holding him, she tested every inch. Smoothed over his length.

He went wild. He shoved the briefs down and kicked them off. She had seconds to drink in the sight of him before he covered her again. His weight pressed her into the mattress as her hands ran over his skin.

When his mouth started traveling down to her stomach, she struggled out of her bra. By the time she rested her back on the mattress again, he was tugging on her pants. He'd gotten them open and now they slid down her legs. With the material gone, his mouth touched bare skin. He pressed a long line of kisses up her legs to her upper thighs. Between her legs. On her.

Her head fell back and her hands wrapped in the sheets as his tongue went to work. He licked and enticed. With each pass something inside her tightened. Those tiny internal muscles clamped down as her breath morphed into panting.

"Shane." She thought she said his name once, but it echoed in her head until she couldn't tell if the chant was real or imagined.

He kept kissing her, touching her, until her body felt inches from going up in flames. His hands pushed her legs farther apart. He slipped up, between them, until she cradled him. She heard a ripping sound and knew he'd found the condom packet where he dropped it on the bed.

He pressed against her, slowly sliding inside her, inch by inch. She blew out long breaths as her body adjusted to his. Then he was moving, pressing in and pulling out. The steady rhythm hypnotized her. The bed shook. The friction of their bodies sent her control crashing.

They touched everywhere. His mouth met hers as his body plunged inside her. When his hand slipped between their bodies, the tightness inside her snapped. Her body bucked and her legs clamped against him.

Her whole body shook as the orgasm overtook her. She lost all sense of time and felt the energy pulse through her. Heat rolled over them as sweat beaded on his shoulders. The waves of pleasure had just started to die down when his body stiffened and his head dropped down. He buried his face in her shoulder as he whispered her name.

It could have been minutes or seconds later when his weight pressed harder against her. He lay still as she threw back her head and struggled to regain her breathing. Slow and steady in, but it kept shuddering out of her. And she couldn't stop touching him. Her hands roamed over his shoulders and one skimmed up his arm.

He lifted his head and stared down at her. "Wow."

"Eloquent." She tried to bite back the laugh, but it crept out. She laughed until her whole body shook. When it finally died down, the amusement in his eyes matched the lightness running through her.

"No regrets?"

She shook her head as well as she could on the pillow. "None."

She waited for him to say something and ruin the moment. Ground her back teeth together as the dread hit her.

"Good."

Relief flooded her. "I think so."

He lifted off her and shifted his weight to her side, but their bodies never lost contact. He ran his fingertips across her collarbone and over her neck. The gentle touch had her nerve endings firing back to life. He'd exhausted her, wrung every ounce of energy from her, but could still bring her to want more.

But her eyes had different ideas. They started to close and she didn't fight it. She snuggled closer into his side and let the warmth of his body lure her in. "You feel so good."

"I was just about to say that to you." He pressed a kiss on her forehead. "Go to sleep."

She didn't have the strength to answer him. She thought she groaned, but she didn't know. Her muscles weighed her down and her bones refused to move. No body part responded to a signal from her brain. She took that as a sign it was time to sleep. After all the death and panic, her body gave in and she drifted.

She could feel him drag the covers over them. Smell his skin. She was just about to fall under when she heard him whisper.

"I can't fail at this."

Her eyes popped open, but she didn't move. Didn't want him to know she heard the fear. But she had, and now she had to figure out how to fix it.

# Chapter Nine

Frank Jay had his orders. He'd gone from living one lie to another. Getting caught pretending to be a SEAL was just the start to his trouble. It led to the news story, then his friends turned on him and the two job offers on the table were rescinded. The interest from the senator who wanted a real-life hero on staff disappeared as fast as it had come.

No one wanted to be seen with him or associated with his name. Anyone who tried got an anonymous email directing them to *Wall of Dishonor*. The mistake refused to die.

His life had flipped upside down, and he took responsibility for that. That damn website also played a role, but he had created the problem. But what came after wasn't his fault. He'd apologized and gone to rehab. He'd been through the program and stayed clean. Hadn't had a drop of liquor in seven months. Seven long months.

Getting swept up in the rest had been an accident.

He thought about that as he sat in the coffee shop. His drink had long turned cold as he turned the file over in his hands. He'd picked it up ten minutes ago as ordered in the set drop location. Protocol demanded he finish the drink, get up and go, but he didn't. Not today. What else could they do to him?

He opened the fastener on the back of the folder and peeked inside. Photographs and paperwork. The usual. Digging deeper, he saw Makena Kingston's picture and a police report about a break-in at her house. He dropped the documents back inside, not needing to read more or wanting them to be seen. He'd been tied to enough conspiracies and trouble without adding more.

The bigger issue was what came next. He balanced an elbow on the table and stared blankly out the shop's window as he tried to reason it all out. He knew what the contents of the folder meant without reading closer. The boss wanted Makena dead.

Whatever she'd said or stumbled over put her on the firing line, and now... Frank shook his head. He liked her. After he'd gotten done hating her, which he had at first. The smug face and the way she'd scolded. But she'd been the first to believe him. She'd given him a second chance. And now she'd call and ask for help. Seek information. He'd give it to her, tying the string tighter. Then she would be gone and whatever secrets she had would get buried with her.

He took out his phone and stared at the screen. He was in countdown mode now. Soon his debt would be paid...but not soon enough to save Makena.

CAM ARRIVED EARLY the next morning. Too early. He used the alarm codes and buzzed through the layers of protection and walked in.

Makena stood in the kitchen wearing only Shane's tee. On her it worked like a minidress. Not that it fooled anyone. Shane could tell from Cam's smile and the knowing look in his eyes that he had figured out exactly what had happened here last night.

Shane cursed his unexpected need to sleep in. He rarely rested for long periods of time. With his history, short bursts of sleep with a hand on the weapon proved to be the answer. Not this morning. She'd wiped him out. The first time, the second... He'd finally fallen into an exhausted dream around three. Before that he couldn't leave her alone.

Makena unstuck from the floor as her gaze traveled from Cam to Shane and back again. "I should probably... yeah, my clothes."

"Subtle," Shane mumbled under his breath, knowing no amount of subterfuge would help now.

"You're not exactly helping." She let her gaze drop to his briefs as she walked by.

Wearing only a T-shirt and briefs early in the morning wasn't odd, but wearing the outfit on a formal body-guard assignment when Corcoran kept all kinds of gear and clothing there was. "Cam knows when to shut up."

"Let's hope so." She didn't turn around again as she headed for the bedroom.

Cam opened his mouth to say something, likely something smart, but Shane held up a hand. He gestured toward the front door. Shane got there first and did a check before opening it.

Instead of going out, he lounged in the doorway and crossed his arms in front of him. Waited for the comments he knew were headed his way. "Go ahead."

Cam nodded as he pretended to scan the horizon. "I'm just wondering if there's anything we need to talk about."

That was enough to answer. "No."

Cam glanced inside, toward the kitchen. With the

door open, they could look from one end of the house to the other. That was the point of the safe house. It had to be easy to lock down and protect. All seven hundred square feet of this qualified.

He nodded in the direction of the closed bedroom door. "That looked pretty cozy."

Shane let his arms drop to his sides. "Do you want to die?"

"That's what I thought." Cam stepped around Shane and out onto the porch.

Puffy clouds rolled along the clear blue sky. The weather had warmed and the sun heated the porch. Shane ignored it all as he stood there in his bare feet. He'd never been ashamed of having sex and he wasn't about to start now. Not when it had been so good, so freeing.

Not when the nagging voice in his head told him he'd messed up. He didn't regret sleeping with Makena or holding her through the night. It was the way she'd looked at him this morning, all full of hope and renewed energy. As if she believed they could make something work, which was just the ultimate fairy tale.

He'd watched the male members of his family marry and then blow up every relationship in record time. They took advantage, lost jobs, drank too much. Shane had spent his entire life on the run so that his genes wouldn't catch up with him. The one time he'd tried to buck the trend, had found a woman who wanted out of her small town and tried to make a go of it, they'd both ended up miserable.

He couldn't do that to Makena and he sure owed more than that to Holt.

"You folded in about two days." Cam looked at his watch. "That could be a record."

Shane wasn't going to ask. He refused to ask. But… "What are you talking about now?"

"Only that it doesn't take a genius to figure out you stopped keeping your distance."

Shane's gaze zipped to the bedroom door. Still closed. He lowered his voice anyway. "Do I look like I want to talk about this?"

"You look like you got hit by a truck." Cam smiled, as he'd been doing since he walked in the door. "Good news is Connor is giving you a few more days."

"What are you talking about?" Shane wasn't leaving until the case was done. He didn't care what other assignments waited. He wasn't leaving Makena or dumping her off on another team member. The personal stuff had him reeling, but he'd see the other through. She would not be injured on his watch.

"Before he contacts Holt. He knows Holt is going to be ticked off for keeping the danger to Makena quiet, but Connor is willing to take the heat."

"Having her big brother rush back into town and take over won't help." That trip would certainly make Shane's life more difficult. He'd been messing up things just fine without help, so, no, thanks. "We don't need to throw more people at this thing."

Biting down on his lip, Cam looked as if he was trying not to smile…and failing miserably. "Good argument."

Time for a topic change. That qualified as the easiest road out of this unwanted discussion. "Do you have information for me?"

"Yes." Cam hit a few buttons on his phone and then turned it around so Shane could see the photos on the screen. "You were right. There was a tracker in her pants pocket. Connor is tracing it."

Shane glanced at the photo and cursed himself for not checking for one the second after the first attack. He'd led her into danger by skipping steps. That was what he did around her. Work and safety and common sense all took a backseat to blinding need. And spending the night with her had not eased the burning inside him. He wanted her as much as—more than—he had before.

Sex never worked like that with him. He met a woman, stayed around for a few days, then moved on. But then this was not the usual sex.

"I'm guessing Connor is having Joel look into all of this," Shane said. Joel Kidd, the tech genius of the group, was Cam's best friend. The guy worked magic with surveillance and had an eerie ability to find anything.

"The Jeff Horvath information is disturbing." Cam scrolled through whatever file he'd downloaded to the phone or whatever notes he had on there. "The guy lost everything when his face appeared on the site. Got fired. Fiancée left. Family isn't talking to him."

Not a surprise. Jeff had the angry-guy thing down. He threatened and postured and refused to back down even when common sense demanded it. "Sounds like motive."

"In worse news, he has skills. Has taken a bunch of survivalist courses and can definitely shoot."

That qualified as terrible news. Jeff had skills, and that, combined with the anger festering inside him, made him very dangerous. "It would have been easier if he actually went into the military instead of pretending to."

"Point is, Makena picked a bad guy to make an enemy."

Apparently she possessed a knack for that. When Shane talked to her about everything else once this case ended, he'd bring up that point, too. He'd never be able to survive knowing she lived her life without taking precautions. The website or no, she was Holt's sister and had ties to Corcoran, which made her safety a constant concern.

So did the men she knew, but Shane vowed to handle that part. "There's more."

That headache came roaring back to life. "You mean the other guys on the site?"

"Look closely at a guy named Frank Jay." He was a wild card for Shane. He didn't get the relationship or how the man had gone from foe to friend, but he'd figure it out. But he was not the main target. No, Shane reserved that space for someone else. "You should also do an in-depth search on the site's owner, Tyler Cowls."

Cam's eyebrow lifted. "I take it your meeting with him didn't go well."

"There's something about him." Shane actually didn't like anything about the guy, but the investigation would tell him what he needed to know.

"Anything specific?"

Shane heard the shower and knew Makena had dropped the tee and stepped under the spray. He tried to block the thought of her naked. "Tyler is in love with Makena."

Cam whistled. "That's a problem."

"No kidding." She protected the guy and he'd all but drooled over her. That made Shane the outsider, and he hated the sensation.

"I meant a problem for you." This time Cam laughed. "Did you tell him there's no room for him since you're already in love with her?"

And then there was that. The needling he'd get from his friends as more and more information about this case came out. Forget Holt—the other guys could handle the verbal battle just fine in his absence.

Since Shane didn't want Makena shutting off the water and overhearing something annoying, he tried one more time to get control of the conversation. "Keep your voice down."

"That's not a denial."

Shane hadn't even realized that had whizzed by him until it was too late. Probably better that way, as the idea of standing there insisting he felt nothing for her made something twist in his gut. "Just do the intensive background checks."

Some of the amusement faded from Cam's face. "We also need to know what case she's working on now, or just worked on. Someone tipped someone off and this exploded. I'm betting she's getting close to a piece of information someone doesn't want revealed."

Shane had been so lost in trying to stay away from her that he'd missed an easy check. Her work touched a lot of lives. The idea of a recent case setting this off sounded the most rational of all possibilities. "Makes sense."

"Of course it does." Cam slipped his phone back into his pocket. "You look awful, by the way."

The mix of no sleep and a whack of guilt did that to a guy. "Did I ask?"

"It's much more fun just to tell you."

Not for Shane. Nothing about this case or his time with Makena ran smoothly. He felt two steps behind and half out of it. A terrible combination for someone on bodyguard duty.

Not that he thought she was in danger around him. She wasn't. He'd dive in front of her if he had to, but his concentration kept getting tugged and pulled. Combine that with the confusing pieces of the case and the high risk of danger, and the worries of not being prepared kept pounding him.

He tried to put it all into words. "I have this feeling."

"Your instincts are usually pretty good, so what kind?"

He could pretty it up, but he didn't try. With Cam he didn't have to. They'd been through everything as a team, and Shane didn't play games with duty and team. Still, spitting it out meant giving life to the fear, and he hated to do that.

Cam's eyes narrowed. "Shane? What feeling?"

"That this is not going to end well." And it grew stronger every single day.

# Chapter Ten

Makena thought meeting Frank in the park seemed a bit extreme, but he'd insisted on privacy and quiet. Shot down every suggestion that would have allowed them to sit down inside. No, he wanted out in the open, a fact that had Shane delivering an unending lecture for the entire drive over.

"Remember what I said." He slammed the door and stared at her over the top of the car.

"Don't wander, stay out of Frank's grabbing range and listen to you." Even she heard her dry tone. "Got it."

"This isn't a game." Shane came around the hood of the car and slipped his hand under her elbow. He didn't grab on, but his fingers didn't just skim her skin, either.

She didn't love it when this side of his personality came out. Protective and a bit controlling? Fine, she could handle those. Talking down to her? No. That was never going to be okay, and he hovered right on the line right now. It had to do with wanting her safe and worrying about her. She got that, but still.

"You think I don't know that?"

"This guy, Frank, pretended to be something he wasn't." Shane guided her through the parked cars and past the group of preteen boys debating which one of them possessed the better bike. "You can see where I might not believe his sudden change and claims of regret."

"You could try meeting him before judging him." Seemed obvious enough to her.

He stopped walking and brought her with him. There, under the lush canopy of trees with kids squealing in the distance, he stared her down. "I've met guys like Frank before. They rarely change."

The stiffness in his tone and stance bugged her. She refused to back down. Shane might bark and scare other people, but not her. She'd been standing up to him from the moment they met. He said he liked that about her. Well, they would see.

"What is your problem?" When he threw her a blank expression, she widened her eyes and stared right back with an *I'm waiting* look.

He glanced around, his gaze scanning the entire area before hesitating on a picnic table off to her left and then traveling back to her. "You are in danger and it makes me nuts."

No way could she hold on to her anger after that. "Oh."

His expression morphed from blank to frustrated. "*Oh?* That's your response?"

"Yeah. It's sweet." She knew she'd said the wrong thing as soon as the words slipped out.

"You're driving me…" He shook his head as the words cut off.

From the way he kept grinding his teeth together, she guessed the last word wasn't going to be good. She almost felt sorry for him. Almost, but not really, because he'd just admitted how much he cared. She knew he had a she's-my-friend's-sister loyalty, but this went deeper. The way he'd held her and kissed her, the way he protected her and reined in his temper even when he could have blown. It all told her she mattered. He might fight hard and play hard, but with her he took his time, and she wanted that to mean something important.

"Where is he?" Shane asked.

The question hit her from out of nowhere. She'd been thinking about him and them and what could be if he unclenched about the Holt issue and trusted her enough to believe in them together...and his mind was on the job. That summed up their relationship. Rarely on the same page except when kissing or in bed. Apparently talking was their issue.

"Frank." Shane nodded in the direction of the nearby picnic table, the one near the parking lot and about thirty feet away. "Is that him?"

She followed his gaze. Frank sat there wearing blue jeans and a baseball cap pulled low. "Yes."

Shane frowned but didn't start walking again. "He looks young."

"He is."

His hand slipped to her back. "Give me the details before we get over there."

She wanted to point out that they should have had this conversation in the car on the way over, but Shane didn't look open to discussing his decision-making, so she just answered, "Twenty-six. An all-American Midwestern-boy type. He was an army supply clerk who injured his back in a locker room but claimed to have fought on the front lines in Afghanistan."

Shane swore under his breath. "How did he get caught in the lie?"

"An anonymous tip to the website started me checking on his history. His claims all over social media didn't match up with the reports from anyone he served with." She remembered how easy his case had been. Her third and the one she celebrated the hardest because she'd done it alone. "His story unraveled from there and his hometown newspaper did a story."

Shane exhaled. "How do these guys think they can get away with it?"

"Some of them do." She lowered his voice. "Or they do unless the site or someone else exposes them."

They walked a few more steps in silence. They'd almost hit the edge of the table when he whispered one more thing. "You do good work."

The shock still gripped her when Frank looked up. She stuttered a few times before forcing out a greeting. "Thanks for coming."

He tipped his head back and stared up at Shane. "Who are you?"

Shane shook his head. "Not important."

"It is to me."

"He's with me." Makena slid onto the bench across from Frank and waited until Shane sat next to her to start talking to Frank again. "As I said on the phone, we need to ask you a few questions."

Frank shot a quick glance in Shane's direction before focusing on Makena. He reached a hand across the table. "I heard about your house. Are you okay?"

She folded her hands together on her lap. No way was she giving this guy mixed signals.

Shane jumped in and asked, "How?"

Frank frowned. "What?"

"How did you hear about the attack?" Nothing in

Shane's tone suggested he had an ounce of patience left. His words came out in staccato bursts and he looked half-ready to lunge across the table and pounce. Probably would have done so if kids weren't playing on a swing set in the distance.

She decided to step in before she witnessed another bloodbath. "Frank, please. We need you to answer these questions."

He finally nodded. "There's an online group. Men who have been targets by the *Wall of Dishonor* website. They talk and someone mentioned you were in trouble."

"Trouble?"

Frank swallowed. "Attacked."

Her stomach fell. She could have sworn she heard it thud against the ground. A sick shaking moved through her as she tried to imagine the conversation and information these men shared. "So they all know where I live?"

"Not before the police were called in." He winced. "They do now."

She didn't realize her foot had started tapping until Shane put a hand over her knee. The touch should have soothed her. At any other time, it would have. But not now.

She knew these men and how desperately they held on to their lies. How they viewed themselves as victims and took zero responsibility for their behavior. Except for Frank. He'd stepped up, but now that she knew about the loop and his involvement… She kept her mouth closed because she feared she'd start throwing up any second.

Shane gave her knee a gentle squeeze. "Did you know about the group?"

She could only shake her head. She'd almost regained the ability to form words when a wall of indignation smacked into her. The mix of fury and frustration pounded off Shane. Sitting so close, she could practically feel the fire burning inside him.

"Holding back information, Frank? I thought you were all about making amends." Shane didn't move, but he looked bigger, more formidable. Somehow his body expanded and all the air around them stopped, as if suspended. "You understand how guilty that makes you look."

"I wouldn't be here if that were true." Frank's jaw tightened along with his fists. Only the slight bobble in his voice gave him away.

And Shane didn't back down. If anything, he leaned in. "I'm not so sure."

"Who are you, again?"

Shane ignored the question. "Is anyone on this loop taking credit for the attack?"

"No." Frank held up his hands as if he thought he could hold back the flood of anger shooting at him. "No, I would have said something. There was no warning. No one is admitting anything."

She almost hated to ask but had to. "Is anyone celebrating it?"

Frank nodded. "Everyone."

She really was going to be sick, right there where little kids played. She wanted to get up, pace around…move across the country. Somehow she stayed in her seat. Clamping on to Shane's hand with both of hers helped. Feeling his strength fed her. Helped her focus the rage and panic coursing through her at backbreaking speed.

"Except you, of course." Shane's voice dipped lower.

Makena knew that meant trouble. When his tone went soft, he hovered on the brink of explosion. This time she didn't plan to stop him.

"I'm trying to help here. I came when called. I've provided information on other men." Frank jerked in his seat when a dog started barking.

"Then give me what I need to look in on this loop." Shane took out his cell phone and swiped the keyboard.

The move seemed so normal, so every day, but something grabbed her attention. He didn't enter a lock code. She concentrated, studying the black rectangle in his hands. Yeah, that wasn't his phone. She had no idea where it had come from or why he had two, but now was not the time to ask.

"You can't just sit in or read along. This is a private loop and these guys guard all the information on there very closely." Frank's fidgeting ratcheted up. He looked around and leaned in. His hands kept moving.

Shane didn't show one sign of nerves. "I probably can, but just in case give me your log-in information."

"I…just…" Frank's mouth dropped open, and then he turned to her. "This is a dangerous game."

She got that now. Maybe at the beginning this had been an adventure. Never a game, because she took the work seriously, but she'd been excited about the research and uncovering information. The whole thing had given her a thrill. Now she knew how far some men would go to hold on to the lie they'd built, and it scared her.

"I'm the one people tried to kill. I'm well aware how dangerous this all is." She doubted she'd ever forget. She wondered if she could continue doing the work or take pride in any of it from now on.

Frank played with his hat, then scratched his neck. "Fine."

"Why are you so nervous?" Shane's eyes narrowed as he asked.

The question pulled her attention from the numerous little things and made her focus on the bigger picture. Frank looked ready to crawl out of his skin.

"You're not exactly the friendliest guy," Frank said.

No, it was more than that. Something bigger. She'd seen this guy at his worst, right after being found out. Over time, he'd changed. He got sober. He told people the truth. He delivered information, maybe even some of it from that private loop.

"He's actually being pretty civilized." And she wasn't kidding. Shane led with his fists. He'd been trained to ferret out the truth and punish liars.

She knew fury brewed and built inside Shane. The fact that he held it back and stayed coherent amounted to a pretty positive step forward.

"I'm not killing you for lying about being a big-time war hero, so you should consider this a good day." Shane spun the phone around and pointed to the blank notes section. "You're lucky, but I can't guarantee that will last if you don't cooperate and do it right now before I really get ticked off."

*Well said.* "Listen to him."

Frank coughed up the information. He typed it into the notes section, grumbling under his breath the entire time. He shoved the phone at Shane. "Here. Are you happy?"

Shane scoffed. "No."

"It's a start," she said at the same time.

"You should know there is a guy…" Frank wiped a hand over his mouth as he blew out a long breath.

"Get to it," Shane said as his voice sharpened around the edges.

She knew pushing too hard would stop the flow of information, so she trod a bit more carefully. After rubbing her fingers over the back of Shane's hand, she let go. Put her hand on the table in what she hoped came off as a supportive gesture. "Tell me."

"The owner of the group is a guy named Jeff Horvath." Frank gave one final look around before dropping his voice to a near whisper. "Be careful of him."

She talked over whatever Shane was going to say. "Why?"

"There's a core group of really angry guys, and he's their leader." Frank stared at his hands for a few seconds before looking up again. "He doesn't try to hide his dislike of you."

Not a surprise. He never had done so to her face, either. Still, hearing Jeff's name sent a shiver of fear racing through her. "Okay."

"What else do we need to know?" Shane asked.

Frank started talking before Shane finished. "Nothing."

"That better be accurate." Shane put both elbows on the table and eyed up Frank. "You know why?"

"I don't—"

"Because I know where you live." Shane didn't even blink. "So, if anything happens to her, if someone comes near her, I'm going to assume you knew and didn't warn her. That for some reason you made the decision not to choke up the intel for me."

Frank shook his head. "That's not—"

"Then I'm going to choke you." Shane made it sound like a promise.

That was probably enough. She rushed in to get the conversation back on track. "Shane—"

Frank stood up. "I don't have to listen to this."

Shane rose, slow and deliberate, with each inch seeming to take a year. "Yeah, you do. That's the price you pay for what you did."

The nervous tics drained away, leaving behind only anger. A wall of it, from the angry red blush on Frank's face to his ramrod-straight back and stiffness in every muscle. "And just how long do you think I should pay for my mistake?"

*Mistake?* Makena couldn't believe the lack of self-awareness in that word.

"Forever."

She liked Shane's clear answer, so she didn't add one of her own. She stood up, ready to march back to the car with Shane. He'd launch into a lecture at some point, and in light of the information they'd just learned, she thought she might deserve one.

But they had to get out of there. Well, she did. If she looked at Frank for one more second, she might punch him just on principle.

"We should leave." She wrapped a hand around Shane's arm and tugged.

He didn't move. "Do you understand me, Frank?"

"Fine." He had taken two steps when the crack echoed through the trees.

Makena didn't understand what she was hearing, but it sounded wrong. As she turned toward the parking lot, where she thought the sound had come from, a pounding weight nailed her in the back. The world flashed in front of her as her body went down. She put out her hands and waited for the ground to smash into her face. But she felt a tug and turned in midair. Not by choice. Something moved her. It took a second for her to realize Shane had wrapped his body around hers.

She landed with a bounce against his chest. He groaned

but didn't stop moving. He rolled her under him, pressing her back into the freshly cut grass and her face into his chest. She was about to ask him what was happening when the screaming registered. She heard voices and crying. Glanced up and saw people running. Then Shane's weight lifted.

"Do not move." He issued the order as he went.

She followed the flash of his body. In a few steps he hit Frank and knocked him to the ground. They both went down with Frank falling under Shane and neither man moving.

Tires squealed and sirens wailed in the distance. It took her brain another few seconds to kick into gear. A shooting. Someone had fired at her or Shane or Frank. Maybe at all of them. She doubted this was a coincidence and they'd just happened to be in the wrong place at the wrong time. Someone knew they were there or followed them…maybe Frank had been lying all along. The long list of possibilities made her dizzy.

Her gaze flicked to him. He lay on his stomach with his arms folded over his head. His whole body bucked as he said something she couldn't make out. Tears. The man was in a full-blown panicked cry. She sympathized. She also doubted a shooting mastermind would act like that.

Then Shane was by her side. He slid to his knees and pulled her up in his arms. His hands rubbed up and down her back as he rocked her. "Are you okay?"

"Is it over?" she stammered. She'd never tripped over her words before the attacks. Now she spent half her time trying to find the right word and spit it out.

"Makena?" Shane ran his hands over her. "Any injuries?"

Just from where he'd clunked her against the ground,

but she didn't care about that. She snuggled closer into his chest. "I'm fine."

He held her for a few more seconds, mumbling soft words to her that made no sense but managed to soothe her. And she held on. Grabbed on to him with a death grip and refused to let go.

He finally let go, not seeming to notice she didn't. "I need to check on everyone."

"Don't leave me." She knew her answer came off as selfish and maybe a bit crazed, but she didn't care. Irrational was all she had right then.

"It's okay." Each word he uttered sounded measured and calm.

"No." That was all she could get out as she sat there all tucked and hiding from the world.

He slid that new phone out of his pocket and pushed a button. "Cam is on the line. Talk to him while I do a quick look."

He got away from her that time. Shifted to a crouch as he scanned the area.

"You could be killed." And that would destroy her. She'd lost control of her life, and the world kept spinning around her, but she knew that much. Losing him would rip her open until she'd never be whole again.

"The police are coming. Do you hear the sirens?" He caressed her cheek. "They are on the way, which would have made the shooter run."

Logical. Made sense. Unfortunately, she wasn't able to process common sense at the moment. But she tried. "You better be right."

"I am." He leaned in and kissed her. A soft peck on her forehead, more calming than heating.

He got up and went to a lady hiding under a picnic

table nearby. Makena watched until Frank blocked her view. He scrambled over to her with a pale face and a drip of blood running down from a cut over his eye.

She knew she should rush to help, but all the energy had drained out of her. She sat there unable to move. "You're bleeding."

Frank touched his fingers to his head and stared at the red on the tips. "From the guy knocking me down."

The words lit something inside her. This man had pretended to rescue. Shane actually did. "He saved you."

"I know. I was frozen." His voice sounded far away and stilted. "Could only stand there."

Realizing he wasn't arguing with her or blaming Shane sucked the rage right back out of her. "Me, too."

Some of the haze cleared from Frank's eyes. "Is that what happened to you the other night?"

She shivered at the memory and the new one that would haunt her for days…maybe longer. "Close."

"So this is all about the website."

Last week she might have let the comment pass. Not today. "No, Frank, it's about the men who lied and got called out on the website. One or more of them did this. Blame the right thing."

"We don't know that for sure."

"I do." She did. Knew it to her soul. She'd brought this danger into her life. She'd put Shane in peril. Shane and everyone in the park. Anyone who came near her. "And this time when they get caught, the punishment will be way more than public humiliation."

Frank's body froze. "What do you plan to do?"

That was easy. "Stop them for good."

# *Chapter Eleven*

Shane couldn't shake the rage that threatened to plow him under. The men in Makena's life had her teetering on the edge of danger. He'd stepped out to give her space. To keep the need inside him from spilling out. The logic had made sense back then, but now he wondered if distance had done anything but cause more trouble.

He still wanted her. Kissing her, touching her, sleeping with her. It all had been so easy and felt so right. Then the bullets started flying and danger signs flashed and he fell back on the only way he knew to operate—he backed away. The cycle was making him nuts.

He blew out a long breath as he paced the parking lot. After the gunfire ended he'd performed a quick injury check of the people standing nearby. Most were shaken up, but none were injured.

Satisfied, he'd headed out here. Even now, police sirens echoed in the distance as they raced to the scene. Between the noise and calls from potential victims, an entire crowd of law enforcement should show up within minutes. Pretty soon he'd see the lights and then he'd lose control. If there was some piece of evidence to find, he needed to do it now.

Another glance in Makena's direction eased some

of the anxiety slamming into him. She sat on the picnic table bench and watched over Frank and a few of the other people who roamed around, waiting for the police to arrive.

Frank... Shane couldn't place that wild card. The guy claimed to have some renewed sense of purpose after being exposed for the fraud he was. He acted as if he'd found a pool of integrity, but he possessed all the nervous tics of a man two inches from being caught in a lie. Not a good sign.

Shane vowed to wait and see what Connor's investigation turned up, but Frank had moved up on Shane's list of suspects. He did not trust the guy and certainly did not want him near Makena. Now was fine because Frank sat with his head down and looked ready to drop out of fear or guilt or whatever else was jumping around inside him.

Two Good Samaritans had the parking lot blocked off and were stopping new cars from pulling in. Shane had given them the directions and was relieved they followed them without question. Speaking with authority tended to work in these situations. Trouble made some people more willing to follow law-and-order commands. Brought out an inner protective streak Shane leaned on right now to keep the parking lot emptied out.

That allowed him to search. He kept up his pacing, up one line of cars and down the other. He wasn't clear about what he was looking for—evidence of the shooting or an idea of exactly where the guy had stood. He had an idea but would need Cam to come in and work some trajectories to be sure.

He got to the approximate spot. Cars took up most of the spaces, which made it a good place for a shooter to aim and then duck without a high risk of being seen. That didn't answer the questions about why here, out in the open, and who had been the target. Shane assumed Makena, but it could have been him or even Frank. Someone was intent on hiding something in this case, and who knew how far he or she would go to make that happen?

The scrape of a shoe against loose gravel had him turning. A footstep. Just one and then nothing, as if the person froze or dropped. Shane looked from one side to the other. Listened for any sound as he tried to pick up a sign of who else might be out there. That hadn't been a trick of his mind. He'd heard something. Someone close by.

Without making a sound, he crouched down. He didn't move so much as a pebble as he ducked beside the car and scanned the ground. He spied the visitor immediately.

Sneakers. Two rows over and one car down. He could see the blue jeans and the untied shoe. He waited a second longer to see if the guy shifted his weight or made a move, but nothing happened. He had the advantage, but he had to move fast.

Under or over. He debated for a second, only ruling out around because that would waste time and he could shift to one side while this person in hiding went the other way. Shane made the choice and moved. Slipped right over the top of the nearest hood and saw a head pop up. He made out the build and the hair as the guy took off toward the back of the parking lot and picnic area.

He swerved and wove as he moved. Shane went for the straight line. He didn't run through lines of cars, he vaulted over them, taking a row at a time until he ran right behind the guy. Two more steps…one more… Shane reached out and grabbed the guy's shirt. Got two fists full and jerked. Threw his weight behind it.

The guy lost his balance. Thanks to forward momentum, Shane crashed into the runner, causing him to stumble. With his grip secured and the advantage on his side, Shane heaved the man into the side of the nearest car and pinned him there. Nailed the guy across the shoulders and separated his legs with a kick.

Adrenaline rushed through Shane, fueling every move and giving him strength. He felt alive and on fire as he searched the guy for weapons. The energy continued to thrum even though he didn't find a gun. That probably meant he'd dumped the weapon, which was smart.

When Shane flipped the guy over and held him against the car with nothing more than a hand wrapped around his neck, his control almost snapped. He should have been surprised at the guy's identity, but for some reason he wasn't.

"Jeff Horvath." Shane didn't have to search his memory to call up the name, because this guy was also high on his list of suspects. Never mind that Frank had just pointed a finger at him. Shane hadn't liked this Jeff guy from the beginning.

"Let go of me." He squirmed and shifted all around.

Shane braced his arm across Jeff's throat and fought off the urge to press in hard. "Shut up."

The guy's eyes bulged as his fingers clawed at Shane's arm. "Stop."

"Calm down." When Jeff nodded, Shane eased up. He wanted to keep the guy slammed against the car but knew he had to back up. Actually doing that took another few seconds.

The minute Shane let go, Jeff doubled over, coughing and hacking. The display went on for what felt like forever. When he finally straightened up again, fury colored his features and he looked braced for a fight...until his gaze went to the gun in Shane's hand.

Amazing how a loaded weapon changed the balance of power. Not that it was all that level to begin with, but Jeff could pretend about that, too, if he wanted. The guy excelled at pretending.

"Let's try this again." Shane backed up a step just in case this guy was dumb enough to dive for the gun, thinking they could wrestle. Shane wanted to question him, not shoot him, but he would if he had to. "Why are you here?"

"It's a public park." Being the kind of guy he was, Jeff didn't back away quietly. He grew indignant and scowled.

One nowhere near his house, but Shane sailed over that detail. "Try again."

"I don't have to answer your questions."

Shane's gaze bounced down to his gun, then back up again. "This says you do."

Lights flashed as three police cars passed through the gate a few hundred feet away. The roar of the sirens grew louder, drawing everyone's attention. Everyone but Shane. He stood his ground and waited for an answer to the only question he cared about right now. "Why are you following Makena?"

Jeff glanced in the direction of the police cars. "I wasn't."

"They aren't going to help you." They actually would, because the diversion and their presence would stop Shane from going wild on the guy to get information, but Jeff didn't need to know that. "No one is."

The guy kept leaving a trail. He knew where she lived. He showed up after each incident. He'd made threats of a sort. If he'd wanted to paint a bull's-eye on his chest, he was doing a great job of it. And that was what didn't make any sense to Shane. It was too easy to tie the attacks right back to Jeff. He might not be a professional, but the file Makena had on him suggested he wasn't an idiot, either.

The whole thing smelled wrong and Shane couldn't figure out why. But he had a new problem, because she was heading right for them.

She didn't stop until she stood almost on top of them. "It was you? First my house and now you come here." She shook her head with a mouth twisted up in obvious disgust. "You could have hurt a kid or someone just walking by. What is wrong with you?"

She made good points, but this could explode. In addition to that, Shane didn't want her anywhere near Jeff or any other guy associated with the website. "Go back to the picnic area and—"

"We should turn him over to the police," she said as she moved away from Jeff to stand by Shane's side. "End this once and for all so I can get back to work and he can get the punishment he deserves."

"Woman, you just never stop." Jeff's hatred came out in the harshness of his voice and how he almost spit out the words.

"Do not talk to her." Shane shoved against the other guy's shoulder. "Ever."

"Not that it's any of your business, but I got a call to come to the park." Jeff sneaked another peek in the direction of the police. "I didn't ask for any of this."

The police parked on the far side of the lot, and the

doors started banging as they got out of their vehicles. Shane started a mental countdown in his head. He couldn't be seen waving a gun around or he'd become a suspect.

He needed Connor to step in and get the place secured. He also wanted Jeff hauled away but knew that wasn't going to happen. The police might question him, but he should be able to squirm out of that cross-examination.

"We're supposed to believe you?" she asked.

"I don't care what you believe." Jeff tried to take a step toward her.

"Enough." Shane slammed the guy back against the car again. "Explain without the drama and bullying."

"Look at my phone." The guy looked in the general direction of his front pants pocket. "I got a text. Probably from her. This smells like a setup."

"You should continue to not talk unless I ask you a direct question." Shane slipped the cell out, scrolled through the messages until Jeff tried to grab the phone back, then concentrated on the texts.

The message was there from an unknown number. No name or identifying information. A simple statement and no reply from Jeff.

But that didn't make it authentic. Things could be faked. Alibis built on nothing.

"The message sounded cryptic, so I came." His gaze shot to Makena. "Just like you wanted me to. This was your plan, right? It all makes sense now."

She rolled her eyes. "You're forgetting that I was the one who was shot at ten minutes ago."

"And I'm sure you intend to blame that on me, too."

"No more talking." Shane's head might explode if this kept up for much longer. Every word Jeff uttered inched him closer to a punch in the face. "For the record, you lied about your military service. Be a man and own that."

"You don't know what you're talking about." Jeff's denial stayed strong, but some of the heat had left his voice.

"You're still denying?" Makena sounded stunned at the idea.

The idea didn't make much sense to Shane, either. He'd seen the evidence that Jeff had lied. No question about it. But getting him to grow up and take responsibility was not going to happen.

"I tried." Shane stepped back and gestured for Jeff to leave.

"Wait, what are you doing?" Makena grabbed Shane's arm.

"Letting him go." They needed evidence and they all had to get through the newest round of questioning headed their way. Once, maybe twice, Makena could sell the idea of being in the wrong place at the wrong time. Much more of this and the police's focus would shift to her. Shane needed to postpone that—hopefully avoid it, if possible. This case belonged to the Corcoran Team and it needed to stay there.

Jeff rubbed a hand over his neck. "I'm innocent."

"You're not, but if I find out you just shot at us, you will be dead." Shane put his gun away and made a mental note to check the parking lot for the shooter's gun since Jeff didn't have one on him. "Got that?"

"You don't scare me."

Maybe the guy wasn't as smart as Shane thought. "I should."

MAKENA HAD NO IDEA how she made it through the next hour. All those police questions. The sapping of her strength when she saw Jeff leave the lot. He'd been there, in the middle of her life…again. She didn't believe his phone or his story. She'd wanted to spill it all to the police and let them take him in, but Shane had said no. Then Connor arrived and backed up Shane.

She'd had just about enough of the Corcoran Team for one day.

After Shane did his usual search of the safe house before entering, she stepped through the doorway and kept going. She wasn't in the mood for mindless chit-chat. She wanted a hot shower. Anything to wipe away the memory of the morning. Anything for a few minutes of quiet when no one tried to kill her. Seemed simple enough to her.

"What you do is important," he said in a determined whisper.

Shane's voice stopped her steps. It broke into the silence and dragged her back to the present. Had her spinning around. "What?"

"The work you do on the website." Shane dropped his keys on the table next to the small couch. "It matters."

This from the man who'd tried to talk her into leaving and had insisted she'd been foolish to help out there in the first place. She tried to put all the pieces together in her head and balance them against his comments now, and none of it made any sense.

"I don't understand what's happening." She stood frozen to the floor, staring at him.

"When you told me I wasn't supportive, you were right." He sat on the armrest. "I should have been, and I messed up. Meeting these guys…" Shane shook his head. "They're jerks and they should be exposed. They deserve whatever fallout comes to them and should not be able to just walk around as if nothing happened. You make sure that happens. You."

The heartfelt apology tugged at her. After everything that had happened and the exhaustion threatening to suck her under, she knew she should accept his words and duck into the other room. Get a little perspective and tighten the control. Rebuild the walls that held her back from saying too much. Her life kept rolling out in front of her, and now it included fear and danger, and she couldn't catch up no matter how fast she ran.

"I've spent my whole life trying to live up to Holt." The words spilled out and there was no way to call them back.

Shane frowned. "What does that mean?"

"He's always known what he wanted to do. He fights bad guys. He's not afraid or unclear." She loved Holt. He was a great big brother, but his greatness only served to highlight her flailing and years of uncertainty. "I'm the opposite. I bounced around colleges and jobs. I've never known what I wanted or how to get it. A path is so clear for other people, but not me."

"Not for everyone."

She noticed he didn't exclude himself. She got that. The military had been an escape hatch for him. His marriage had been about hope, not love. He viewed himself as so complex, but she saw through it all. She'd spent so much time deciphering him and his actions that little surprised her now.

But she knew her life, her choices, weren't as understandable to him. "The website was just one piece, and with it my life started falling into place."

Shane stood up and walked over until he stopped in

front of her. "These insecurities you have. No one else sees you this way."

He refused to see the flaws, but she didn't have that luxury. "Ask my parents."

"They are of a different generation. They have whatever baggage they have." His hands rubbed up and down her arms. "Forget all that."

If only the looks of disappointment and constant reminders about all she'd failed to do with her life were that easy to ignore. But she tried to pretend. "Fine."

"You are this amazing woman. Beautiful, smart and focused." One hand went to her shoulder, then into her hair. "The idea that you can't see all you are and all you have to offer makes me want to shake some sense into you."

"I need you to see me as more than Holt's little sister." The sentence summed up her fears. That he would always look at her and see braces. See someone younger who followed him around with this crush instead of a woman who loved him for who he was, the scary parts as well as the good ones.

"It's a rough habit to break, but believe me when I say that is not how I view you anymore. Not the only way." His hand went to the base of her neck and pulled her in closer.

"I need you to see me as a woman." Her head dropped back, cradled in his hand. "Living, breathing, feeling woman."

He didn't hesitate. "I do."

Relief had her gulping in breath. "I should have handled the website better. Protected my privacy and weighed the risks. I know I rushed in."

"You wanted to help." His gaze searched her face. "That is not a bad thing."

Every word he said, every touch, drove her feelings for him even deeper. She'd fought for acceptance her entire life. Her difficult parents had given up expecting things from her. Holt thought their overbearing nature was the worst, but their not even caring enough to fight about it ranked as the worst.

But Shane stood there, so open and loving, and told her she mattered. He accepted who she was, the uncertain parts and the focused ones. He didn't judge. Unless the other night had been an aberration, he didn't let any part of her past color how much he wanted her now. The words were freeing, and she grabbed on to them. Wrapped herself in that warm look he kept throwing her.

That only left one thing. "Any chance you're going to kiss me again?"

The corner of his mouth kicked up. "All night."

Her heart did a little twist. She felt the lightness and then excitement. They spun through her, wiping out every inch of darkness. "Really? I figured you'd do the that-was-fun-but-a-mistake thing."

She worried he would. Before he'd seemed to be looking for excuses to run away. He brought up Holt and the baby-sister thing all the time. But he wasn't using that excuse or any other now.

She was about to point out the change when he lowered his mouth to hers. His mouth touched hers, and a spike of heat hit her. Hands roamed her back, and lips covered hers. The kiss rolled on and her control faded. When he did that thing with his tongue, her knees buckled.

The touches lingered. Her body slid against his in

excellent friction as she fought the urge to jump on top of him. Fought and only barely won.

When the blinding kiss threatened to go to her head and wipe out every sensible thought, she lifted her head. "Take me to bed."

He treated her to a full smile this time. "I thought you'd never ask."

# *Chapter Twelve*

Frank paced around his apartment. That had been too close.

No one had told him to expect gunfire. He'd known something big was coming, something having to do with Makena and this new guy. He hadn't expected to be stuck in the middle of it.

Whatever clock kept ticking out there, it seemed to be winding faster. The tension rose along with the stakes. He couldn't handle any of it. He hadn't signed up for this. Yeah, he'd made a mistake, and he'd paid for it. Well, he thought so. Others didn't.

Ask his siblings or his friends, the few he still had. They all looked at him differently now. No one believed anything he said. Even when things did go well at the start of a new job, someone would find the website. They'd insist they'd stumbled over it, and another door would shut.

He deserved to feel bad about what he'd said. He didn't deserve to lose every piece of his life. No one asked for the kind of pressure being applied now. Despite what Makena and her cohorts thought, no one deserved this type of scrutiny. It was time to move on and for his name to come down so his life could move forward.

He sat down on the barstool at his breakfast bar, then stood back up again. Unsure how much longer his legs would carry him, he dumped back on the cushion again.

A strange ticking noise filled the room. He glanced around, looking for the cause. He'd never heard it before and if he didn't track it down, it would drive him nuts.

His foot slipped off the footrest on the stool, and the noise ceased. Didn't wind down. It stopped. He glanced down and watched his leg. Realized it bounced up and down. His nerves were running on edge and the outward signs were tough to miss.

He put his foot back up on the rest, and the noise started all over again. The subconscious tapping made the far end of the footrest move up and down. Just a little, but enough to create the annoying sound. That was what his life had become, a series of random actions and weird noises.

He got up and started pacing again. He'd had two jobs today—give just enough information to get Makena worried about her safety and gather the requested information.

On cue his cell beeped. He reached for it on the counter and almost knocked it to the floor. The thing went sliding and he caught it just in time. Unlocked it and read the text. Didn't take long.

The number?

The main part of his assignment. Deliver the number. Frank had memorized it just to be safe. Shane and Makena had driven in and he'd watched. Sat at the picnic table close enough to get a good look. Good thing he'd done it at the beginning and repeated it over and over in his mind to memorize, because once the shooting started he'd been useless.

But having it and handing it over without knowing what the faceless person on the other end of the phone intended to do with it were two different things. He closed his eyes and when he opened them again nothing had changed. The text question was right there, taunting him.

From memory, he typed the series of letters and numbers in and then turned the screen off again. Now he needed to forget the number.

Because there was no reason for him to know Shane's license-plate number.

NONE OF THE BACKGROUND checks led to real information. Shane expected that of the men who lied about their military service. Many of them fabricated intricate stories, sometimes based on actual people's lives. Borrowed details and inserted themselves inside. And went to great lengths to sell the tales. There were personal sites and photos. A mountain of false information to comb through.

Connor had given Makena credit just that morning for wanting to do the work. Unraveling the information and finding corroboration and evidence refuting the claims of service could be a full-time job. Maybe that explained why Tyler didn't appear to hold any other positions or do any other work. It didn't explain why the under-the-table background investigation on him didn't check out. Some of the tales Tyler told appeared to be just that…fiction.

Tyler kept his life secret. He didn't advertise his service record on the website or anywhere else that Connor and the team could find. He had medals, because Makena had seen them. She'd also seen paperwork regarding deployments and other relocations. Problem was, Connor couldn't find the backup to support the stories or a way to replicate any of them. No witnesses. No government files. Nothing.

For a man who did a lot of finger-pointing, albeit behind a wall of security without his identity being known, he didn't appear to possess a clean record of his own. On the surface, yes. Routine searches, even some more advanced ones, held up. But nothing about Corcoran could be considered routine, and Connor's access to information he shouldn't have, the internal security systems he shouldn't even know about, tended to stun them all.

The problem for Tyler was that Corcoran had intel it shouldn't have. That someone with something to hide would count on Corcoran not having. But the team did. It made lying to any team member tough, and it looked as if Tyler had done just that.

Standing in the middle of Tyler's small first floor, Shane was tempted to ask a bunch of questions. At the very least, go searching through the stacks of papers around here for information. But Makena stood next to him and he didn't sense she'd take either option very well.

Shane hadn't filled her in on his newest concerns. Not yet. He worried she'd have a hard time keeping cover. Or that was the excuse he told himself. He really worried she'd blame him for putting a microscope to Tyler's story. In the end he feared that if she had to pick sides, she'd go with Tyler.

"Are you okay?" Makena moved in next to him with her arm wrapped around his as she crowded against his side.

Not that he minded the closeness, because he didn't.

The smell of her shampoo. Her touch. The way she smiled up at him one minute and frowned at him the next. It all worked for him, and every single day his feelings grew deeper.

He pushed all that aside and focused on the problem in front of him. "Sure. Why?"

"You're standing in the middle of the room not saying anything." Amusement filled her voice.

He glanced around and didn't see Tyler. Didn't hear him, either. The small house stayed deadly quiet. "Where is your boss?"

"Upstairs…getting the information you wanted on Frank and Jeff." This time she did frown. "What's going on with you? You seem a million miles away."

He'd clearly missed part of a conversation. The lag had her worrying and him wondering what he'd missed. Rather than try to catch up, he pivoted to the conversation he wanted to have. "What case were you working on when all this started?"

"None."

The answer made no sense. He'd seen files and she'd been doing background work and fielding calls even now, over his objection, with all the danger bubbling up around her. "Are you afraid to leak confidential information to me?"

"Of course not."

"Really?"

"I thought you meant new work." She waved off the concern. "I have a few cases going on at the same time. Always do. One ended and I was about to look into another anonymous tip, add to the caseload."

Sounded fairly routine. Since the interest in shutting her down had seemed to arise all of a sudden and switched to relentless mode, he thought there must be a new case that had someone nervous. Sounded like no, but he decided to double-check. "Which name is that?"

She blinked a few times. "What does that mean?"

This conversation needed help. One of them still lagged behind, and he feared it was him. "On the list you gave Connor."

"I didn't." Before Shane could butt in, she rambled right over him. "I mean, the name would have been on Tyler's list. He took over the investigation. Said I needed a break."

Shane still wasn't sure he'd heard an answer, and now he really wanted one. "Do you remember the name?"

"I have it written down."

That was all he wanted. He didn't need to tiptoe around the conversation or worry about tipping anyone off. "I want it when we go back to the house."

Her eyebrow lifted. "Or we could just ask Tyler."

For whatever reason, Shane knew that was the wrong answer. "No."

Footsteps thudded on the stairs. The box appeared first, a good-size one that covered most of Tyler's body. He peeked around it as he walked into the room. "This is all yours. Everything I have on the men uncovered since Makena started working with me, including information on Frank and Jeff."

He dropped the box with a thud. Makena immediately went to it and started paging through the files. Shane took a break from the mental analysis for just a second and watched her. As she scanned every page, looked inside and touched each one, excitement lit her gaze. The work touched off something inside her.

He hated to hear her talk about herself as if her life

hadn't amounted to anything or lacked some level of excitement, since neither point was correct. She had people who loved her. She held down a job and made a difference through her work on the site. She gave back by ensuring that only those who deserved to be were called heroes.

He admired everything about her. That drive she thought didn't exist, her compassion and charm. She looked like that and acted with integrity. He'd fought off his feelings for so long, pushed them back and hid behind a crappy marriage that never should have happened. He'd found excuse after excuse. Even made bets with the team and insisted anything other than sex was off the table.

He wanted all of it to be true. He hated the idea of being sucked in and having someone depend on him, only to leave her as he walked into danger. That was who he was, and that wouldn't change. It made relationships impossible. Apparently it didn't make falling in love impossible, because he had fallen. With her.

It couldn't happen and the odds made it impossible, but there it was. He loved her. Maybe he always had. He sat down hard on the kitchen table.

She rushed to his side. "Shane? All the color just left your face. Are you okay?"

No, he was very far from okay. "Sure."

"I don't—"

Time to dodge the question and get some answers. Shane looked at Tyler. "Who do you think is behind all this?"

"Jeff." Tyler shook his head as he grabbed the back of one of the other chairs. "You said he showed up while you guys were eating in that diner. He was at the park just now. I don't even know what to say about this loop with the other men that he told you about. That's news to me, but the lengths they'll go to sound pretty scary."

Clearly Makena had been busy filling her boss in. Shane understood why she thought that was okay, but he had a strange feeling it wasn't. Something about the guy didn't sit right.

Shane wasn't alone. No one on the team thought this was a straightforward case. Their collective experience and wisdom pointed to more than one person. Last thing Shane wanted was an entire group of liars with gun habits to battle, but the theory made sense.

Connor hadn't reached out to Holt to fill him in, but Shane knew their time was running out. That meant his time in bed with Makena likely was running out as well. If this couldn't go anywhere, they had to be realistic. Having fun when it was just them was one thing. They could keep that private. Rubbing Holt's nose in it once he got back did not sit well with Shane.

"What chatter are you picking up now?" Shane asked.

Tyler's grip tightened on the chair. "Chatter?"

"Reports about new cases." Makena smiled. "I think he's kind of asking how the work gets to us."

Shane did love her smarts. Tyler's blank stare was not a favorite. "You get leads all the time, right?"

"Yes."

"Are those drying up? Where is the business right now?" Shane knew most of this information from Tyler's financial records. The same ones that showed a sizable inheritance, which allowed him to spend his life chasing the liars on his site.

The questions weren't about scaring Tyler. Shane needed to assess the guy's truthfulness. Would he embellish or underplay? Would he even admit to knowing anything? Shane could get the information he needed or run into a wall that raised a red flag. For whatever reason, he sensed one of those outcomes was on the near horizon.

"I'm not sure I'm comfortable with this line of questions." The chair creaked as Tyler released the back and walked into the kitchen.

"He's asking for the case." Makena turned around in her chair. "This is all about the attacks. He's not going to steal your bank-account information."

"That's just the thing." Tyler walked back into the room with a water bottle in his hand. "We're assuming this is about you and this website, but from what I've seen of Shane I'm thinking he has some contacts that might be a problem for you."

Blame shifting. Shane knew that was rarely a good sign. "I need to rule everything out."

"I understand, but my financial life is not part of this." Tyler twisted the lid off the bottle with a loud crack. "These men are not adding to my bottom line. I don't get paid by the number of people we expose."

Tyler seemed determined to make that line of questioning into a dead end. Shane decided to let him. But now the team could rip this guy's life apart and Shane would not feel one ounce of guilt over it.

"Of course." He stood up and grabbed the box. "We should head out. It's been a rough few days."

Tyler almost looked relieved to know they were leaving. "No kidding."

Shane waited until the last minute to drop one more bomb. "Are you still staying here, or should we get in touch with you somewhere else?"

"No, here is fine." Tyler's smile didn't reach his eyes.

And that really didn't make sense. The guy had sensitive information stored at his house. No one was supposed to know who he was, and he was desperate to maintain that anonymity. Yet when someone broke in, he didn't ask for help. He didn't pull up stakes or, at the very least, move the boxes somewhere else.

For a guy who supposedly felt as if he were in the firing line, he didn't act like it. He didn't show much emotion at all except maybe panic.

But Shane had gotten the response he'd expected, so he nodded. Put on his best we're-all-friends-here smile and headed for the front door. "We'll talk soon."

They had gotten out the front door and down the porch steps to the car before Makena whispered under her breath, "What was that about?"

"What do you mean?" No way was Shane answering that while still standing in the middle of danger territory. He'd taken a burner phone to the park as a precaution. He didn't want his cloned or lost, so he went with a fake one. It was just as likely he could be overheard. He had no idea what toys Tyler possessed, though he did intend to find out.

"Makena?" Tyler called out from the front doorway. "I need to see you on one more work issue."

Of course he did. So predictable.

Shane nodded in Tyler's general direction. "He wants you alone."

"Don't be so impressed with yourself. You are as transparent as he is." She leaned in closer. "I know you're up to something. I can see the wheels turning in your head."

He would tell her later. Away from here. She'd yell

and kick and scream, all while defending Tyler. So long as she didn't call him a hero, Shane could stomach whatever she said. "And you're wanted. Better find out why."

Shane would bet all the cash in his checking account that he knew what the topic of this conversation would be. Tyler had concerns. Tyler needed to talk.

And Shane knew it was about him.

# Chapter Thirteen

Makena was not in the mood for a lecture, no matter who delivered it. Shane spent a lot of time giving her his opinion. Last night his words had lightened the guilt that had been weighing her down ever since people started dying in front of her.

Sure, she hadn't killed anyone and most of the men needed to be stopped, but the situation in the park could have ended differently. Violently. And every drop of blood tied back to her decision to take on her research work for the website. It was a lot to take in and almost more than she could handle. From the look on Tyler's face, he planned to give her even more to think about.

Tyler gestured for her to join him at the front door then put his back to the walkway and Shane standing twenty feet away by the street. "You doing okay?"

"Sure." But she knew that wasn't the question Tyler intended to ask. Not that she planned to make it easy. Nope. If he wanted to pry, he needed to go ahead and do it and risk her wrath if he went too far.

"This guy…"

She had to give him credit for jumping right to it, but her position hadn't changed. "Yes?"

Tyler shifted his weight from foot to foot. His gaze

kept bouncing to the front door as if he expected Shane to come barging in. "How much do you know about him?"

She didn't need to ask for specifics. She knew Tyler was talking about Shane. "Everything."

Tyler's eyes narrowed. "Excuse me?"

No way was she spelling that out. "I've known him for years."

"Known, as in…" When she just stood there, Tyler's fidgeting increased. Much more of this and he'd be dancing down the street. "You two aren't together?"

Interesting phrasing. "Why are you asking?"

"I'm concerned."

"Why?"

Tyler smacked his lips together and glanced off to his left. He acted as if he tasted each word before he said it. "He's a bit rough for you."

She had no idea what that meant. Wasn't sure she wanted to know. "My feelings for Shane are personal."

"But you do have feelings for him?"

She didn't see a reason to lie. Even Shane knew about this at some level. "Yes."

Tyler shook his head, then did it again. Didn't say anything for a few seconds.

She touched her hand to his arm. "I appreciate that you worry about me."

"Of course I do."

Just what she needed, another man in her life who wanted to tuck her away in a closet to keep her safe. Maybe a week ago she would have been grateful. Now the overabundance of caution insulted her a little. She'd faced tragedy and death over the past few days and hadn't folded. She was stronger than any of them knew. Stronger than she'd ever known.

Only Shane seemed to get it. He didn't try to pack her away or send her to Holt. He kept her by his side and claimed to understand she needed space, but she also needed to see her decision about working on the website through to the end.

"Shane and I…" She fought to find the right words. "We get each other. He'll keep you safe."

Tyler slid a hand over hers. "I can keep me and you safe."

The vibe changed and her comfort level dropped. She'd worked side by side with this man for a year. They shared information and jokes, talked via text and on the computer. They spent far less time together because of her full-time work schedule, but they had shared meals.

To her it all related to business and a friendship. Now she wondered if Shane was right and if, for Tyler, all those times together amounted to something more.

Guilt knocked into her. A different kind, personal and twisting. She'd never meant to lead him on. Shane had her heart, even if he hadn't shown any signs until recently of even wanting it.

She slipped her hand out from under his and dropped her arms to her sides. "I'm good with Shane."

"You should—"

"Are you ready to go?" Shane stalked up the walkway toward them and the front door. "It's not a great idea to be standing out here in the open after the days you've had."

Such a subtle guy. She'd bet he'd been listening to every word. His skills appeared to be endless. Superhearing could easily be one of them.

"We were talking about work." She lied only to save

Tyler from any embarrassment. Maybe men didn't work that way, but she didn't want to test the issue.

Shane smiled as he walked up the steps to join them. "I figured."

"We have some work we need to get done," Tyler said. "You could come back or I could drop her off at—"

"No," Shane answered right before she could give the same response.

Tyler's sudden possessiveness creeped her out. She suspected the feelings were new and innocent, but something about his energy felt off. After all those lunches together, she didn't want to be alone with him, and they certainly didn't have work. If he expected to spend a few hours berating Shane, Tyler had the wrong audience.

"I think Makena should get to make that decision." Tyler crossed his arms in front of him, looking far more confident in his position than he should have.

"Right. Good point." Shane turned to her, the amusement obvious in the way his mouth inched up at the edges. "Makena, you pick which one of us you want to be with."

Talk about a loaded comment. Not that her answer was in question. This, their relationship, only played out one way. She loved Shane. He was her forever. If he didn't figure that out soon, she'd have to move on and settle for less than she wanted. The idea of that happening hollowed out her stomach, leaving her raw and twitchy.

Her gaze zipped between the two men in front of her. One with the ego she didn't want to bruise and the other who needed to stop taking her for granted. Not that there was really any contest. "I'm leaving with Shane."

Tyler shook his head. "But we need—"

"You heard her." Shane winked at her. "Ready to go?"

For a second she wished she could love someone else. Someone easier. "We'll let you know what we hear about the park and anything we uncover."

Makena didn't look at Tyler again as she walked with Shane. They'd parked a short distance away just to be safe and the silence made the walk back feel even longer. She waited until Shane stood beside her near the front of the car to whisper, "You don't have to be a jerk to Tyler."

"He's alive, ain't he?"

He sounded far too amused for her liking. "Why do I think you actually believe that's an answer?"

"Because we know each other so well." He followed her to her side of the car and opened the door for her. "Isn't that what you told him? We get each other?"

"You were listening." Not a question, because she didn't need to ask. She knew and had expected all along.

"Do you blame me?"

She slid into the seat and glanced up at him. "Your ego will be unbearable now."

He leaned in with a wide smile plastered on his face. "Blame yourself."

TWENTY MINUTES LATER, Shane understood Makena was not amused. She hadn't said a word since they pulled away from the curb at Tyler's house. Just stared out the window, tracing a finger over the glass, humming now and then. Not talking to him or even looking at him, which he found annoying.

Shane decided to put it out there. State what ate at him. Not Tyler's murky past or questionable choices. Not how his story fell apart if you dissected it. "He has a thing for you."

She kept her focus out the window and off him. "I know."

That was news to Shane. "You do? Since when? I swear you denied it when I suggested it earlier."

She turned and shot him a don't-be-dumb look. "He all but told me to dump you because you're all wrong for me."

And now Shane had other reasons to hate the guy. "Not happening."

"I wouldn't." She smiled. "Because you're the perfect bodyguard."

That response didn't sit right with him. They'd had sex. He'd held her and kissed her. They spent time together and… Shane cut off his thoughts. He'd been the one insisting they keep their relationship on a friendship level and now he was getting all wrapped up over another man wanting her. Talk about sending mixed messages. Not his style at all, but when it came to her, his feelings and common sense, and what he should do versus what he wanted to do, got all tangled up.

"I don't trust him." Shane offered the explanation without fanfare.

"He performs an important service."

Shane wasn't as convinced. Yes, the site exposed men who deserved to be exposed, but he couldn't help thinking Tyler had a hidden agenda. Of course, every man associated with the site struck him that way. Maybe his paranoia was running on high.

"You don't think he's a little too good to be true?" That was as far as he'd go…for now.

"You don't trust anyone."

She wasn't wrong. "I trust you."

"Because you like me, even though you fight it."

Makena's hand balled into a fist against the door. "I hate this part of the drive."

Shane focused on the road and the narrow bridge ahead instead of her throwaway comment. The span skimmed over the water for half a mile. He understood the concern. Sometimes the sun's reflection bounced off the water and blinded drivers. "I've driven it a million times."

"Your skills aren't what has me concerned. Death by drowning is the main thing on my mind." She seemed to brace her feet against the floor as she stared ahead.

Shane looked at her and did a double take. They'd driven to Tyler's house via a longer route from another part of the county, avoiding the bridge. "I can turn around."

She shook her head. "I'm fine."

She didn't look it. She'd been shot at and looked less fatigued. Shane decided right then that he would never understand her. "The death grip on the door gives you away."

"Just drive. The faster you go, the sooner this will be over."

He admired her spunk. That and about a hundred other things.

The tires crossed the bridge entry with a thump. With the low sides, they could see the open water. It flashed by on both sides, and cables scaled above them. A few other cars passed in the opposite direction, but the road stayed clear.

A quick look in his rearview mirror showed a vehicle coming up behind him. It moved too fast, which suggested a kid or a driver confused about the concept of defensive driving. Shane kept watch, stealing peeks.

Then the mood changed. The truck, big and black, lined up behind him, way too close. He took in the large grille on the truck and the tinted windows. He couldn't make out the driver, but this guy was playing games.

Shane glanced over at Makena. She hadn't picked up on the tension. She sat there, fiddling with the radio. His gaze shot to her seat belt.

The revving of the engine had his attention zipping back to the mirror. He tapped the brakes, trying to back the guy off. If this was innocent, he should get the hint, but Shane sensed this was deliberate. Someone wanted to make a point. A very dangerous one.

"Hold on." He knew that didn't mean much, but he said it anyway.

She looked at him, confusion written all over her face. "What?"

He couldn't hide the facts. She needed to be ready. "We have company."

She shifted in her seat and turned around as the truck tapped their bumper. The move sent her flying forward. "What is he doing?"

"Letting us know we're not wanted around here." When the truck drifted in again, Shane turned the wheel and swerved the car into the empty oncoming lane.

The truck surged, then fell back. This was a game of chicken played out in three-thousand-pound car and a massive seven-thousand-pound truck. Not exactly Shane's idea of a good afternoon, especially since the size advantage was not on his side.

He shifted in his seat, sitting up higher as he started weaving from one lane to the other. The move would steal some of his speed but make him a harder target to hit.

His luck held out and the oncoming lane stayed empty. Shane just had to get them across. He hit the gas, thinking to outrun the larger vehicle in a race. But the truck wasn't ready to give in. He shot forward and smacked into the car's tail end. The move had the vehicle bobbling and tires screeching.

Makena grabbed the dashboard with stiff arms. Shane shouted for her to get down just as the truck ran alongside the car. Not even, but Shane could see the truck's heavy front out of his peripheral vision. See the make and the dark metal. Then the truck slammed into them, crashing them into the guardrail and snapping their bodies forward as far as the seat belts would allow.

The crunch of metal against concrete. The deafening screech as the car scraped against the wall. Shane kept his white-knuckle grip on the steering wheel, forcing the wheels straight and willing the car to stay on the bridge. The water seemed to get closer. It could have splashed up over the side and he wouldn't have been surprised.

With another slam, the car teetered and the wheel shimmied under his hands. He felt the front give and Makena's side ram into the concrete. They bounced and the world spun around them. The tires squealed and the smell of burned rubber and gasoline filled the air.

He could hear Makena's screaming as the force of the blow had her bouncing around in her seat, even with the seat belt. Shane fought against the skid and struggled to hold on to control. His heartbeat hammered in his ears as the car's back end crashed into something. The hit jolted his body until his teeth rattled.

A car horn honked and the sounds of skidding ran through his head. The car bounced and rocked on its tires. It left the ground and he waited for them to flip. A crack echoed around him, and then the car shuddered to a halt.

When his breathing slowed and he focused again, steam swirled out from under the hood. His gaze shot to the other side of the car. Makena had been pushed up against the door and rubbed her head as she mumbled.

He wanted to undo his seat belt, but he didn't know where the truck had gone or if they were alone. Still, he needed to know. He reached over and touched her hair. "Baby, are you okay?"

She nodded and blinked a few times. When she finally looked up at him, tears stained her cheeks and her hands shook. "You kept us from going over the edge."

The car felt uneven and pieces of concrete and car parts littered the road. He wasn't sure part of the car didn't hang over the edge of the bridge. Just the thought of that had anxiety punching his gut. "Barely."

He looked up and saw two cars parked ahead of him. People poured out with terror on their faces. He glanced around and realized they'd spun around and now sat on the opposite side of the road, facing the wrong direction. A quick scan sent a pain shooting up his neck. Shane ignored it as he looked for the truck.

He undid the seat belt and reached for his gun. As soon as his hand touched it he dropped his arm again. The people surrounding the car were shouting about the police coming and asking Makena if they were okay.

Friendlies, not hostiles. Someone might have seen something, could possibly identify the driver of the truck. Shane vowed to ask all those important questions once the ache in his side eased. He leaned his head against the seat and said a quick thank-you to the universe for keeping them from going over the edge. He knew how to escape a flooding car, but that didn't mean he wanted to practice the skill.

His head rolled on the headrest and he looked at Makena. "We should have gone the long way."

She reached over and took his hand. "Next time."

He'd spent his entire life thinking he didn't have an ounce of luck. Anything that could go wrong did. He'd had to earn all he possessed the hard way. But he looked at her, felt her warm hand in his and decided he might be lucky after all.

# Chapter Fourteen

Cam grabbed two bottles of water out of the refrigerator and handed one each to Makena and Shane along with pain pills. "You two need to work on the concept of date night."

"We like adventure." Makena appreciated Cam's attempts to lessen the tension. Not that it worked. To be fair, an entire comedy team working round the clock couldn't restore a sense of calm at this moment.

She'd been a shaking mess at the crash site a few hours ago. It had taken two people to shoehorn her out of the car. The slam into the sidewall had caved it in. When the fresh air hit her, she'd thought her control would come whizzing back. Then she'd seen the black skid marks along the bridge walls and realized how close they'd come to being trapped in an underwater grave. It was a miracle she hadn't thrown up her lunch.

Connor and Cam buzzed around the safe house. They'd come with medical supplies. Connor insisted they visit some doctor she'd never heard of. Shane refused. She figured she'd go if he did. And truth was, he'd sustained the most injuries. She'd gotten thrown around and her insides jumbled, but except for the knock to her head and a sore elbow, she was okay. She'd be a bruise from head to toe tomorrow, but now stiffness was the main issue.

From Shane's scowl she guessed he wasn't happy about his injuries. "This isn't funny."

Nothing about the last week rose to the level of funny, but if she didn't laugh she might cry, and she could not tolerate the idea of curling up in the corner. She glanced over at Connor. He hovered over his laptop. Was on his phone. Asked question after question. Seemed like over-kill to her.

"His neck hurts," she said, referring to Shane.

"I'm fine."

"He will be." Connor nodded in her direction. "What about you?"

"Everything aches. I should be one throbbing pain by tomorrow morning."

Cam laughed. "Sounds like fun."

"We need to focus." Shane got off the barstool, prob-ably too fast, because he grimaced the second he moved. "This last attack went too far."

"Getting hit by a car is worse than being shot at?" Not in her book. It all mashed together, making every hour dreary. She watched Shane pace around the small space in front of the stove and realized there had been a few nonawful hours.

Shane scowled at her. "I'm serious."

So was she, but she didn't belabor the point. "Do you think we were followed from Tyler's house? If so, we should let him know."

Silence greeted her question. She'd expected more. A noise of some type. Agreement, maybe. Sure, they didn't know Tyler and Shane clearly didn't like him, but they protected. That was what the Corcoran Team did. They rushed in when others ran away. They didn't leave people behind or put them in harm's way.

Finally Cam spoke up. "Know what?"

"That the people launching these attacks know where he lives." It seemed simple enough to her. Tyler could walk into a trap or be the newest victim of a shooting.

They all looked at each other this time. Men frowning and acting confused—not her favorite thing and certainly not expected.

"Don't we already know that?" Connor shifted in his chair, leaning back as he delivered the question with measured words. "He claims someone broke into his house. You saw the aftermath."

She caught the doubt. Connor's tone never changed, only his word choice. The fact that neither Cam nor Shane jumped in to correct him couldn't be good. "Claims?"

Shane started to shake his head, then winced. "Let this topic go."

She sensed he was talking to Connor, but she didn't care. "I want to know what you guys are thinking."

"You don't," Shane said without giving her eye contact.

She sure did now. Inhaling as much air as possible, she tried to calm her flaring nerves and concentrate. "I have been shot at and almost drowned. The least you guys can do is not treat me like a little kid. I'm in this, so tell me."

Shane glanced at Connor, who nodded. It took another few seconds of silence for Shane to start talking. "His military record doesn't match the story he tells. Nothing he says makes sense."

She sat down hard on the barstool next to Cam. "What?"

"We've been checking into the past of everyone on

the website and all the files Tyler turned over." Connor turned his laptop around to face her. "On the surface, Tyler is clean. On the surface, Jeff is dangerous and Frank is contrite."

Cam took over. "The men you're researching, that the site is researching, are mostly frauds. A few are clean. They embellish their records but nothing so extreme that it's worth calling them out and humiliating them."

She knew most of that, or had guessed it. But the phrase *on the surface* clued her in to bigger trouble. "But?"

"The man who came to your house and started all of this was on the loop with Jeff." Shane exhaled. "In other words, all of these men are connected."

They clearly thought they were saying something, but she could not follow what. "Didn't we know that?"

"Many claim not to know each other." Shane stopped as if weighing how much to say and how to say it. "They don't live near each other or have any public contacts, but there are contacts. Behind the scenes and not through the usual channels, like emails and phone calls."

"So this is some big conspiracy to wipe out the website." She could believe that. Push bad men hard enough and they shoved back. Some of the men who had been uncovered didn't have much left to lose. Going out by taking down the people who unveiled their lies would not be a surprise.

"Normally I would say yes, but there's more than that." Connor glanced at Shane.

He filled in the blank. "Tyler doesn't appear to be who he claims to be."

Anger rose inside her and she clamped it down. Her inclination was to rush to Tyler's defense, get indignant on his behalf. He'd never been anything but good to her. But she looked around and saw the faces of men who cared about her and her brother. Men who wouldn't lie. Men who clearly knew more than she did. "Explain that."

"The suspicions are in pieces. All circumstantial." Connor flipped the computer back to face him. "We can't prove anything."

"Yet," Cam added.

"These guys are passing information back and forth and hiding it. When you peel the layers away, Tyler's past looks more like the men he hunts than the people he purports to respect." Shane visibly swallowed. "I don't want you alone with him."

No matter what she did, grab on to the counter or blink, she could not stop the spinning in her head. The facts swirled. Every word he said ran through her mind and she tried to grab on and analyze each one. She didn't understand why Tyler would lie or how any of this could be true, but Shane's stern expression told her it was.

Tyler was guilty of something, maybe just coloring the truth. She didn't know, but the team would find out, and she would have to deal with the fallout.

"I hate being lied to." That qualified as an understatement.

Shane walked over to her. There, in front of his friends and coworkers, he wrapped his arms around her. "We'll find out that truth."

And she knew he would.

SHANE PUSHED INSIDE her as his muscles trembled and his breath punched out of his lungs. The thin legs of the bed shook and the springs rattled. He ignored every noise except the soft growl coming from the back of Makena's throat. He loved that sound.

Shifting his weight, he plunged again, in and out, slow and steady, until she grabbed on to his shoulders and tugged him closer. "Shane, now."

"I want it to last." He didn't realize he'd said the words out loud until they pulsed in his ears.

"I need to…" She threw her head back. "Please."

Her shoulders rose off the bed and her ankles dug into the back of his thighs. He pressed her into the mattress as she wrapped her body around his. Friction had their bodies rubbing together, ratcheting up the need flowing through him.

It had been this way from the first time. All wild heat and pounding satisfaction. From her soft skin to every impressive curve, he could not get enough. For the first time in his life he wanted to crawl into bed with her and stay there. Forget work and responsibilities. Forget his past and every wrong turn he'd ever taken.

Her fingernails dug into his shoulders. "I can't hold back."

"Don't."

Before he even got the word out, her hips started bucking. Heavy breaths rocked her body as her lips skimmed over his chin. Energy spooled off her and wove its way around him. She clung to him, pressing her legs tighter against him. The tightness, the clenching, watching the orgasm rip through her, all combined to set him off. He wanted to wait, savor each pulse inside her, but his body had other ideas.

The tightness that had been building inside him let go. His muscles stiffened the second before they released. Unable to hold his sore neck up for one more second, he let his head drop. Buried his face in her shoulder and breathed in as the orgasm overtook him.

When his hips stopped moving, he collapsed, careful not to drop his full weight on top of her. Lifting off and out of her qualified as the sweetest torture, but then he was next to her with his arm wrapped around her shoulder and her body curled up against his side.

He dropped an arm over his face and closed his eyes. "That should not be so good." Nothing should feel that good.

She laughed and the sound vibrated against his skin. "Because I'm Holt's sister?"

Shane lifted his arm and stared down into her flushed face. "Because much more of that and I'll need a hospital."

"Challenge accepted." She leaned her head against his chest again.

This he could handle. The hot during and quiet after. He'd never really experienced the combination before. He loved feeling frenetic and out of control, but this, the part where he combed his fingers through her hair and drifted off to sleep, was new.

He never talked about this, but with her the temptation proved stronger than his will to put it all behind him. "Losing my marriage doubled me over."

She stiffened against him. "Do you miss her?"

"That's not what I mean." He didn't know how to explain and worried that even if he managed to put the right words together he might still sound like a jerk. "I liked the *idea* of being married."

She lifted her head and rested her chin on her hand. "I don't get it."

"Marriage meant family and security. It meant I

managed to accomplish something." But he couldn't hold it together. "But I failed, and it knocked me off stride. I kept thinking that the divorce said something about who I was."

"You married the wrong person. That's all." She pressed her other palm against his chest. "You guys both wanted an out, but that's not enough. Marriage as escape can only go so far if there's nothing fundamental holding it up."

"You can't deny that the danger of my job is a huge stumbling block to anything long term and meaningful."

She nodded. "You better tell Connor and his wife. Talk to all the other guys on the team and explain that the love they feel now means nothing and that they should run."

"Okay, I get—"

"And then call my brother and tell him to leave Lindsey on the West Coast." Makena made a face. "He shouldn't waste his time building a life with her."

She made it sound so easy. So did the guys on the team. You fell, you accepted it and you tried to minimize the risks. It helped if you found a woman strong enough and determined enough to stand up and face the danger on her own terms.

"You should have been a lawyer." Because she made it all sound possible.

"I'm happy right here." She kissed his chest. "With you."

"I'm sorry you heard about the Tyler suspicions like that, with Cam and Connor standing right there." He rubbed a thumb over her forehead, then down her nose to her mouth. "I wanted to give you that information in pieces."

"I'm pretty tough, you know." She raked her nails over his nipple, lightly but enough to get the nerves underneath jumping.

He flattened her hand under his. "Toughest woman I know."

"That's probably an overstatement."

"Not at all." He shook his head. "The woman I've been watching has handled every awful thing thrown her way and kept standing. She's overcome her fear and stood up to Jeff, who is a guy no woman should have to deal with."

"We should call Holt."

Shane hadn't been expecting that conversation change. "Really?"

"If I can handle gunmen, I can handle an overprotective brother with a list of questions to ask."

"You're tougher than I am." Shane dreaded Holt's reaction. They knew so much about each other. Shane couldn't hide or smooth over anything. Holt would know exactly what kind of man wanted his sister, and Shane did not see that as a good thing. "But you're right. It's time."

"You're going to admit we've been sharing a bed?" She whistled. "Brave man."

"I think the word *dating* sounds less likely to get me killed." But not by much. Holt had made it clear Makena was off-limits. If Shane wanted to bumble around, sleep with other women and never get serious, Holt was fine with that, but Makena could not be another number.

She wasn't.

Her eyes widened. "Is that what we're doing?"

Good question. He honestly didn't know. "We can use whatever word you want. I just know I don't want it to end."

He'd finally said it. Admitted it to himself and to her. The walls didn't crumble and the earth didn't open up and swallow him. He'd survived the truth, that being a lone wolf grew exhausting as the days passed, and with her he wanted more.

She moved up his body until her lips hovered over his. "Good, because we're not over."

The words shot through him. Instead of running and panicking, he settled in and enjoyed. "I was hoping you'd say that."

Her fingers slipped into his hair. "Why don't you show me how grateful you are?"

"Done."

# Chapter Fifteen

He couldn't do this one more minute.

Frank shut the cover to his laptop and leaned back in his chair. He'd been investigating every avenue, trying to figure out who had blackmailed him and thought they owned his every move. He'd followed instructions, thinking each new order would be the last. But the assignments bombarded him. He read discussions on the loop and picked out secret messages in every one. He had no idea if he'd grown paranoid or if his life really was closing in on him from every direction.

But he couldn't keep doing this. Every day he clicked on a news link, worrying some action he'd put in motion had ended in death. He'd made so many wrong turns, but he could not tolerate the idea of having more blood on his hands.

That meant coming clean. Taking the venom out of the blackmail and telling one last secret. He'd already been chastised and ignored. What else could happen? Begging Tyler to take his name off the site hadn't worked. Telling his blackmailer one assignment after another would be his last didn't threaten anyone.

The address. The license-plate number. The police

contacts. Information on this Shane guy. Frank had done it all, and he was done. Long done.

He picked up his phone and dialed the number. In a half hour it would all be over.

"FRANK WANTS TO see us." Makena almost hated to utter the words. She didn't look up because she could only imagine the scowl on Shane's face.

When he didn't say anything and the silence continued, she glanced across to the other side of the couch. He'd been crouched over the laptop a second ago. Now he sat back and stared at her with a blank expression.

That couldn't be good.

She tried again. It actually didn't matter if he wanted to be convinced or not; they were going. "He sounds desperate."

"Did you talk with him?" Still no readable expression. Just the question.

She had her legs stretched out until her feet touched the side of his leg. She pointed her toes and pushed against him. "He texted."

"How does one sound desperate in a text?" Shane's hand went to her leg.

She didn't know if he even realized he rubbed a hand over her calf as he spoke. The gesture was so comforting. Sprawling on the couch as the rain hammered the roof felt normal and right. "My point is he asked that we meet him immediately."

His hand kept soothing and caressing. "We?"

The heat from his hand seeped through her jeans and touched her skin. She knew that probably grew out of her imagination, but she felt it. She also wondered why he thought she wanted to tackle anything on her own. "Of course."

Shane smiled then. "I like that."

"As if I'd be dumb enough to go into a meeting with any of these guys right now without firepower." She said it as a joke, but it kind of wasn't.

"So romantic." Shane stood up and reached down to her. "Let's go."

"That's it?" She stared at his hand, then looked at his face. His quick agreement minus a lecture stunned her. The guy thrived on lectures. "No arguments about the danger or…I don't know, anything?"

"You mean the part where this is likely a setup to get us both killed." His wiggled his fingers.

She grabbed on and let him lift her to her feet. "I wasn't going to put it that way."

"I'll call Cam and Connor on the way. They can provide backup and be our eyes."

"You didn't ask where we were meeting."

He dropped a quick kiss on her mouth before stepping around the couch on the way to pick up the keys to the loaner car Connor had gotten for him. "Somewhere dangerous and hard to guard, I'm assuming."

"Aren't you hysterical today?" More like lighthearted and calm. The thrum of tension that normally followed him had disappeared. He came off as relaxed yet just as determined as ever.

She had no idea what to make of the change or why it had happened. She half expected him to pretend to bring her along and then dump her off at one of the team members' houses for safekeeping while he rushed into danger. That was the guy she knew.

"Don't let the sarcasm fool you." He picked up his gun. Then a knife.

That was more like it. "This isn't a kinder, gentler Shane?"

"No such thing."

THEY ARRIVED AT the meeting place a half hour later. Not the park and not the diner. Not even the bridge where they'd almost died. They walked up to the marina that sat just a few miles from her house, which she hadn't been back to since the original shooting. Being this close to the scene where it had all started had something jumping around in her stomach. Nerves or panic…something.

She punched in the code Frank had given her and opened the gate to the docks. Shane followed without saying a word. He was armed and ready, and that was all that mattered. But as they made their way down the incline, she did see Shane's point. There were so many places to hide. So many ways to get lost in a maze of docks and ships, and not come out again.

She blew out long breaths as she struggled to maintain some sense of control. Her heartbeat ran off at a gallop and her chest ached from the force of it. She'd get through this. She had to. She had so much to live for, so much hope for the future for the first time in so long. She wouldn't give that up for a website or Jeff or Frank or anyone else.

The water lapped and metal clanked against metal as the boats bobbed in the water. No one was around. She knew Connor played some role in that. Rain or not, people should be milling around. The mist chilled her skin, but the total quiet was what had her ready to jump on top of Shane and demand he take her out of there.

They reached a T and Shane pointed to the right. "This way."

She looked down, mentally reading off the numbers as they passed each one. They needed 280. Of course it wasn't right near the front where the buildings sat. No, she walked beside Shane as the distance between them and land grew.

One final turn and they reached the point farthest away from the opening gate. Just a few more…something made her look up. Probably a hint in the way Shane carried his body or a shift in the breeze. It didn't matter why, but she saw Frank in front of her. Or a version of him. This Frank was disheveled and jerky in panic. He moved around, his gaze touring the distance as he stood there.

"What do you want?" Shane asked without any inflection in his voice. The wind whipped around him and the rain kicked up, but he didn't show any signs of being uncomfortable. He was in his element and in control.

Frank nodded toward the boat in the slip next to him. "We need to go inside."

Makena looked at the hull. The boat was small, and having any kind of conversation likely meant crawling under and into a space they couldn't see right now. Shane had been right about this, too. It was a setup and one they might not survive if they weren't careful. Sure, Connor lurked out there somewhere and Cam was submerged in the water, ready to come up firing. But one mistake, one second too late, and this could be the last shooting in this case.

She thought about her brother and how many good things lay ahead for him. Her mind wandered over all the mistakes and focused on the good times. On the bright moments of the past few days. She glanced at Shane and took in his strength and energy and realized loving him had switched from a desperate state to a happy one.

"There's no way we're getting on that boat." Shane widened his stance. "So talk."

Frank shook his head. "You're not in charge here."

"This says I am." Shane lifted his hand and flashed his gun. Didn't wave it around or make a big show. Just leveled the playing field with one small gesture.

But she needed to avoid whatever harsh thing came next. She also wanted to know why he wanted them here so badly. "Okay, enough." She glared at the man she once believed had turned a corner to a new life. "You called us, Frank."

Whether it was whatever he saw on her face or the gun, something got him talking. He slipped to the side, getting closer to the boat, but he didn't run as he talked. "There's a group. They've banded together to come after you."

The loop. The men who sat around complaining about getting caught. She hated them even more now. "Right."

"How do you know?" Shane asked in a deceptively soft voice.

Frank took another step back. One more and his foot would slip into the small space between the dock and the boat, and he'd fall in the water. "I've been helping them."

Pain shot through her. She'd believed in him. Stood up for him. "So the 'new Frank' thing is a lie."

"It wasn't my fault." He rubbed his hands together as he shifted around. Every movement choreographed the frenzy taking off inside him.

Guilt could do that to a person. She refused to feel bad for him. Not again. She could not be fooled twice.

"You never get tired of saying that, do you?" Shane

took a threatening step forward. "That thing where you shift the blame and pretend you're not at fault."

"I'm being blackmailed," Frank said.

That didn't make any sense. Before he'd been exposed, sure. He'd been a potential target for anyone looking to benefit from people's fake backgrounds. "Everyone knows your worst secret. What can—"

"No." Shane shook his head. "We don't, do we?"

The blows kept coming. Makena could barely find her breath. "What did you do?"

Frank waved his hands in front of him. The haze covering his gaze suggested a battle waged inside him. He tried to spit out a sentence a few times before getting it out. "I hid the secret."

She knew that. Everyone knew that. The whole point was that his story only worked so long as people didn't know the truth. "And?"

"You weren't the first person to figure it out."

The words sliced into her. They sounded so ominous, and he stopped giving eye contact. The guilt practically radiated off him.

She hated to ask, but she had to know. "Who did?"

"He's dead. That doesn't matter right now." Frank visibly shook. "The attack at your house, the one on the bridge, those were me. Well, I caused them by passing on information."

Shane no longer hid the gun. It was up, and the fury pulling at his mouth and carving deep lines into his forehead suggested he planned on using it, and soon. "I'm going to kill you."

Frank held up both hands. "I'm…no…I'm…trying to help."

The stuttering matched the rest of his affect. The

jumpiness and darting gaze made her want to sit him down and tell him to write it all out. Once and for all, let him unburden himself and then see what happened next.

"Tell me everything you know and how you found out." Shane stood there as if daring Frank to say no.

After a brief moment of screeching silence, he nodded. "I got a contact a few days after I joined the loop."

So he had known about it for a long time and had been a participant. She'd never been moved to violence before the past few days. Now all she wanted to do was hit people until they told the truth.

"When?" Shane asked.

Frank's gaze shot to her, then back to Shane. "Months ago."

It took all her willpower not to lunge at him. So much pain and needless waste of life, and all because a bunch of men didn't like that their lies had been uncovered. The whole situation made her feel sick and achy.

She knew Connor and Cam were following along, listening through the device attached to Shane's shirt. They were taking it all down and would investigate. They'd ferret out the truth and make Frank and the others pay. But right now, in this second, it didn't feel like enough vengeance.

Shane somehow kept it together and continued asking questions. "Who contacted you?"

"That's it, I'm not sure."

"Guess," Shane shot back before Frank could finish his comment.

"I think we both know."

"There are a lot of suspects."

"But only one guy in charge." Some of Frank's panic

subsided, as if talking lifted some of his guilt. "I'm sure it's—"

His words cut off as his body collapsed in a heap. One minute he was standing, and the next his body turned boneless and fell down, knocking against the boat and slipping into the water.

"Get down." Shane called out the order as he slammed her against the dock with his body covering hers. He reached over and grabbed for Frank's arm, but his body was already sliding under the surface.

She lifted her arms off her head and tried to focus on the voices. The quiet of the night hadn't broken, but she heard yelling. Familiar voices. She leaned in and heard the yelling in Shane's ear. Then came the footsteps. Pounding down the dock. Shane spun around, putting his body in front of hers as he sat up and aimed.

Connor stopped in midrun. "It's me. Don't shoot."

"Get down." She tried to repeat Connor's order, but her voice barely rose above a whisper.

He must have heard, because he dropped, crawling the last few feet to where they sat, stunned. "Either of you hit?" Connor looked from Makena to Shane.

"What happened?" She still didn't know. She hadn't heard the bang she'd come to expect in a shooting…and how sick was it that she had any expectations?

The gentle thud of the water against the boats turned into whoosh. Cam popped up, fully outfitted with scuba gear. Next her brother would pop out somewhere.

Dizziness hit her then. She leaned against Shane, trying to absorb some of his strength. "I didn't hear the shot."

"Silencer," Connor and Cam said at the same time.

A new word for her to hate. "Convenient."

Connor frowned at her. "How so?"

Shane spoke up then. "That's exactly what the shooter wanted to do to Frank, silence him."

"It worked." Her stomach wouldn't stop flipping. Her insides were scrambled as if she rode a never-ending roller coaster.

Shane put a hand on her lower back. "We'll make sure it doesn't."

For some reason, in that second, she believed him.

# *Chapter Sixteen*

Shane had grown tired of everyone associated with the website. Really fast. He'd been close enough to get hit with blood splatter when Frank got shot. Scrubbing it off didn't wipe the stain clean.

Good guy or bad guy didn't matter. Frank had been young and misguided and had carried a secret that would fell most halfway decent men. Cam had connected the dots in no time. A friend of Frank's had died in an alley after a long night of drinking. The person with him? Frank. The friend had expressed concerns about Frank's stories before he died, and those concerns had died with him.

Shane didn't know what had happened in that alley, but he'd bet an angry confrontation gone wildly off track. A fight that left one friend dead and the other in an alcoholic spiral and now in the morgue. Life had handed Frank one last wallop. Shane just wished Makena hadn't been there to see it.

At least her color had come back. She sat on the couch with her legs crossed in front of her, hugging a pillow to her chest. She listened to Connor and Cam tried to make sense of it all.

"There are long periods of time when none of the

men in the group are logged in to any of their electronics," Cam explained.

She nodded and kept nodding, then asked, "What does that prove?"

"They likely have an alternative source of communicating and were using that at the time," Connor finished, then sat there across from her. No one said anything, not even her, and he started talking again as if he felt the need to break it all down and explain it. "You can see bursts of activity before an event, like the attack at your house, then sustained inactivity during the actual attack."

The pieces made sense to Shane. Sometimes the lack of information proved to be better evidence than something obvious. Since Frank had only provided a piece— and a small one at that, without much detail—they had to fit it all together. Connor said he had the entire team working on the problem.

Makena tightened her hold on the pillow. "This is so much work. If only they used that power for good."

"Men like that never do." Shane had learned that the hard way long ago. He'd hoped his father would change, ease up and actually be there. Never happened. Some men couldn't change. Men like Jeff thought he didn't need to.

"It's more fun to cause trouble," Connor said. "Speaking of which, Holt is on the way home to check on the two of you."

"No surprise there." She eased her grip on the pillow and tucked it next to her. "So, does all this mean we owe Tyler an apology? Can we clear him?"

Shane wasn't ready to go there. He didn't trust anyone involved in this case, and that only worsened with each hour. "No."

She frowned at him. "You sound so sure."

Shane pretended that look was about wanting more information and not about her being tied to Tyler. Shane knew she didn't have romantic feelings for the guy, but if she possessed a sense of loyalty, that could trip her up and make investigating Tyler harder. "It looks as if he lied about his service record. We need to know why and at what cost."

"I don't get it. Why start the site if he had this big lie in his past?"

That part confused Shane, too. There were possible explanations, but none of them sounded especially smart. "Maybe to throw the scent off, or to get to the investigations first and keep any taint away from him."

Shane's money was on one of those. Tyler might just have the bloated ego to think he could be the one to successfully hide his fake past.

"This is so ridiculous." Makena pressed her head back in the couch cushions and wiped a hand over her face. "I was just trying to help."

The tone got to Shane. He sat down next to her and pulled her hand down. "You didn't do anything wrong."

Cam nodded. "The work is good. It's scary that it's necessary, but it is."

"Tell that to all the dead men scattered wherever I walk." She slipped her fingers through his and held on tight.

He moved their joined hands to his lap. "To be fair, I killed most of them."

Cam's eyes widened. "That's how you comfort her?"

Shane never broke eye contact with her. He needed her to believe the way he did. "She's tough. She doesn't need to be coddled."

"Man, Shane." Connor groaned. "This is almost hard to watch."

"You're not very good at this," Cam added.

"You're both wrong." She lifted their hands to her lips and kissed the back of his. "He knows just what to say."

Once again, they were on the same wavelength. People could think whatever they wanted. Maybe he should come up with the perfect line and serve it to her, but truth was, when it came to her he didn't need to embellish. Flowery words were unnecessary. He felt what he felt. It knocked into him, punched him in the gut and had him reeling. Rather than be scared, he welcomed the sensations this time.

"Are you sure he's good at this?" Cam asked. "Because, wow."

"I am not weak." The words rang out strong and loud. She said them as if the comment resonated with her, rose deep from her belly.

Connor scoffed. "Definitely not."

From their reactions it looked as if they all knew. The important thing was she finally got it.

Shane winked at her. "No, you're not."

She stood up without dropping his hand. "Then let's go find Jeff."

There was a topic sure to wipe out his good mood. With one last squeeze, Shane let go of her hand. "That guy is mine."

The smile that crossed her lips could only be described as blinding. "So long as you end this, you can have whatever you want."

He didn't care who heard or how much crap he took for this. "Sold."

JEFF TALKED BIG. Puffed out his chest and delivered a full blowhard recitation, complete with anecdotes about how he'd been wronged. When it came to annoying displays of minimal self-awareness, this ranked right up there.

The scene went on for almost fifteen minutes. Jeff sat at the picnic table in the park that had served as the site of one of the many shootings during the past week. Shane and Makena sat across from him. She had to listen to how he'd been set up and how the charges had been blown out of proportion. She waited for him to spin out the oldie about how he'd worked in covert ops, so no one could know the truth.

Somehow he refrained, but she sensed he had that explanation in his arsenal. He just hadn't whipped it out yet.

When he finally started to wind down, Shane leaned in and stared at him. "You almost done?"

"You asked." Jeff looked back and forth between them with his gaze hesitating on her for an extra beat.

Just long enough for her to start shifting in her seat. The guy ticked her off. Every word he uttered sent her temperature spiking. The way he made himself the victim and tried to sell his hours logged on the gun range as proof his military story was true. His explanation was a convoluted mess, and she doubted she could hear much more.

"Tell me about the loop." Shane held a pen and turned it end over end on the table.

"What?" But Jeff's tone had changed. Just a hint and only for a second, but anyone listening for it would have picked it up. And everyone was listening in.

"You are the leader of a band of misfits who lied about being in the military and being heroes, and now get together to whine." Shane laid it on thick.

She almost cheered. Jeff didn't fear her but he might fear Shane. Or he would if he was smart.

Jeff didn't take the insults well. His skin flushed red and a vein in his forehead popped out. "You don't know what you're talking about."

"It's not as well hidden as you think." Shane passed the pen from one hand to the other. "My people found the loop and we're going over all the transcripts now."

"Who are *your people*?"

"You should be more worried about what we can do." Shane put the pen down with a click.

Something about the smooth move had Jeff's gaze shooting to the pen, then back to Shane's face. "You're bluffing."

"Frank Jay is dead." It hurt her to say the words. Hurt even more to realize he'd turned out to be less than the man she hoped he would be.

Jeff's mouth opened and closed, but that was all the emotion he showed to that announcement. "That group is made up of hardworking men who had their lives turned upside down by—"

She filled in the rest of the sentence. "Their own lies."

Jeff's balled his hands into fists. "She—"

"Discovered your lies, but you are still the liars, and when you get together to plan violence against other people, you are also criminals." Shane held up both hands. "It's simple math."

"Violence." For the first time Jeff's face fell. He stopped the chest puffing and all the other nonsense and sat there with a stunned, openmouthed expression. "What are you talking about?"

For a second she bought it. Got sucked into the look and the stuttering tone. Then she remembered who he was and how well he could sell a story. "You celebrated me getting attacked."

"Someone talked about it." He hesitated between each word. "There are hard feelings, sure, but no one on the loop had anything to do with that."

Shane never took his focus off Jeff. It was as if he was constantly assessing and analyzing. "The evidence suggests otherwise."

Jeff jumped to his feet. "The evidence is wrong."

The drama was back in full force and she was even less impressed this time than she had been during the first round. "Sit down."

"You can't tell me what to do." He muttered something under his breath. Sounded like a nasty name.

"Yeah, she can," Shane said.

Jeff slowly sank until his butt hit the bench again. "I'm being set up."

It was Shane's turn to swear under his breath. "Is that the only excuse you know how to say?"

"You don't understand." Jeff's gaze traveled between them. He threw in the gestures and facial expressions. Seemed determined to convince them of his innocence. "We blow off steam. We talk about how to put our lives back together, to find jobs. To figure out how to take down the website and erase the information that's been spread."

That didn't amount to gunfire, but it had the potential to blow up into that. People could talk in code or get the wrong idea. The dangers of groupthink were especially high when the group had a single sworn enemy. In this case, her. "So you know, nothing about that sounds innocent."

Jeff shifted in her direction. Spoke straight to her. "If something happens to you, the stories get told again. The spotlight will switch from you to us in a matter of minutes, and all the information on the website explodes all over our lives again."

She figured that probably was an accurate description of what would happen. She refused to feel guilty about that. "So?"

"Making you a martyr would make my life hell." Jeff glanced at Shane. "That's the reality. I need you alive and well, and preferably quiet."

"Or would it free you if she were gone?" Shane asked.

"You're wrong." Jeff's shoulders fell. It was as if the air rushed right out of him, deflating him. "Both of you."

With one final exhale, Jeff stood up. Slipped out from the bench and stood next to the table. He scooped his keys off the top and tucked them in his pocket. Didn't say another word as he turned around and started to walk away.

"Where are you going?" Shane asked in a voice that carried a cool chill.

Jeff still didn't turn around. "To find out who is setting me up. You'll see. I'll prove it to you."

She watched him go. The cocky walk was toned down, but the mess he left in his wake remained. "He's a bit too confident, don't you think?"

"He's had a lifetime of practice at lying."

Now, that was the truth. Somewhere along the line, lying had become Jeff's one true skill. The thought of that made her sad.

She rested her arm on the table and turned to face Shane. "So, now what?"

"Easy." He handed her the pen. Legal or not, the one with the microphone that taped every word. "We keep digging."

## Chapter Seventeen

Tyler showed up the next day. Not at her boarded-up house or the picnic area or even at Corcoran headquarters. No, Tyler came to the safe house. Walked right up to the front porch and knocked.

Shane almost shot him through the door.

He'd tracked him as he came up the drive. Watched him ditch the car around a curve and not near the house. Normally it would have been out of the line of sight of the front door and almost impossible to see. The hidden security cameras helped fill in those shadows.

None of that changed the facts. Tyler shouldn't be here. He couldn't be here. The fact that he knew where to track them down, let alone that he'd left his house to travel to them, had Shane itching to fire his weapon. He fought the urge to grab the other man, drag him inside and slam him up against a wall.

He'd ducked questions and responsibility. For a man who spent his life exposing others, his secrets rose to the same level as many of the people he condemned. In Shane's mind, that made Tyler the worst sinner.

Shane let the guy get as far as the open entryway. Didn't invite him to sit down or have a drink. Kept him pinned by the door and within range of the gun tucked by Shane's side. He only got that far because Shane had had warning and could hide the documents and computers before Tyler walked in.

"Why are you here?" Shane asked even though he'd never believe the answer. Not now. Tyler had managed to wave a red flag that had Shane's back teeth grinding together.

Tyler's gaze stayed on Makena. "We need to talk about Jeff."

He could stare wherever he wanted. He likely thought he could win her over. That they still had a certain rapport. Truth was, she'd looked at the newest investigation documents an hour ago, and whatever loyalty she had to the man was waning.

Then there was the part where Shane didn't want Tyler talking to her. It wasn't a jealousy thing. More like Shane's control hovering right on the edge. He was looking for any excuse to take this guy out, and if Tyler said or did the wrong thing to Makena, he would do it.

"I'm more concerned with how you knew to come here." With that move the target shifted to Tyler and stayed there.

"I have some tech skills and I—"

"No." Not a good enough answer. The Corcoran Team had the latest tech. The team didn't fool around when it came to staying undercover. If anyone even performed an internet search using any of their names, a message was transmitted back to headquarters. No way had Tyler just stumbled on some personal information while poking around. "This is not a house you find on a whim."

"I got the license plate off your car and followed you here." Tyler delivered the line as if he expected applause. But his own words kept tripping him up.

Shane wondered if Tyler knew how easy he made it to doubt him. "The same car that isn't actually in the driveway since I'm driving one I just borrowed."

Tyler shrugged. "Why does this matter?"

As subterfuge went, that response wasn't great. Shane let him get away with it anyway. "Because when people randomly show up where they should not be, I grow skeptical."

Tyler shook his head. "I get that you take your job seriously."

Shane ignored the condescension. He had a feeling he'd have to ignore a lot of annoying stuff if he wanted to make it through this conversation without having his head explode. "Which job?"

"As Makena's bodyguard."

She finally moved. Instead of taking on the bodyguard comment or anything else, she homed in on facts that brought the visit into question. "Tyler, you told me you never leave your house. You stick close and limit your contact with the outside world."

"You matter to me. After Frank…" Tyler held up a hand, gave a big show as if he couldn't talk and had to force the words out. "That was too awful."

Makena didn't back down. She tilted her head and kept rattling off the attacks against her. "Someone followed me, us, from your house, or it certainly seems that way."

"I heard about the bridge accident, and there's chatter online," Tyler said even though she hadn't specified which incident. "Jeff is feeling hunted and looking for revenge."

Interesting how he changed the discussion. Shifted

the attention off him and onto Jeff. Made an allegation without actually saying anything negative.

Her eyes narrowed. "You think he'll hurt me?"

"He's on the edge and desperate." Tyler looked at Shane then. "You guys keep talking with him."

Shane guessed that was supposed to be some kind of shot. It would take a lot more than that to knock him off task, and right now the task was to get as much information out of Tyler as he could before putting a bullet in him. "How do you know that?"

"I follow the chatter."

All of a sudden everyone knew about the supposedly private discussions on the loop. "But you didn't bother to tell Makena that the loop existed so that she could be prepared, too. She had to find out through Frank."

"I didn't take it seriously."

Shane really wanted to hit this guy. He had so many reasons—the way he looked at Makena, the fact that he put their safe house at risk and on general principle. "Do you take your position seriously?"

"What does that mean?"

"Your service record doesn't check out." Makena dropped the biggest bomb of all without flinching. The words came out and then she waited.

Tyler did not disappoint. His expression morphed from concern to disappointment to a touch of anger as Shane watched.

"You're reviewing my records?" Tyler glared at both of them this time. "You can't be serious."

"You were never in combat. You didn't serve in Iraq." There was no need to hold back now. Shane wanted to spook the guy, get him to cough up some piece of intel that might make this entire case fall into place. Now he had doubts and gut feelings. Some evidence but not enough.

"I can see where you'd think that, but my files are confidential." Tyler's smile could only be described as smarmy. "You need specific access."

Shane was done playing with this guy. "I have it."

Some of the color drained from Tyler's face.

"Tyler, the facts and times don't line up. People you supposedly served with couldn't identify you." Makena delivered more of the information in a slightly less hostile tone.

Shane had no idea how she managed it. "The records don't show what you think they show."

Tyler shook his head. "You don't understand how this works."

"I've been researching for a year." A thread of anger moved into Makena's voice. "I think I do get it."

"And I'm retired army, so I know I do," Shane said. When all the life ran out of Tyler's face, Shane knew they had him spinning and worrying. "I have contacts. I work for people with endless contacts."

"I can bring you my file."

The last desperate gasp of the lying man. "Oh, I looked at it. All fake."

Tyler's mouth dropped open in mock outrage. "That is not true."

"I'm thinking you started the site to keep the upper hand. You got first crack at any research and could see if anyone was getting close to your lies." It was the only answer that made sense, even though Shane wasn't convinced it did.

"That's ridiculous. Makena, tell him." Tyler shot her

a quick look. Then his gaze came back. His mouth fell even flatter. "You believe him?"

"You taught me to research. I researched your record." She shook her head. "It does not check out."

"This is him." Tyler backed up until his ankle hit the door. He kept pointing at Shane and stumbling as he rushed to say whatever was going on in his head. "He wants you all to himself."

She shrugged. "He has me."

If he hadn't loved her before, he would have right now. Shane decided to congratulate her later for that hit.

The outrage had Tyler sputtering. "I'm leaving."

Shane didn't argue. He'd be too busy packing and hauling Makena to another safe place to stay this afternoon to get sucked into Tyler's strangeness. "Don't you want to tell us why you came by for a visit?"

Tyler grabbed the doorknob. Wrapped his hands around it and held on. "You'll be sorry."

SHE NEEDED A BATH.

Today's meeting with Tyler had done her in. Makena used to like him, respect him. Now she could barely tolerate standing in the same room with him.

The breadth of his actions hit her. This wasn't a one-time thing or something that could be brushed aside, because it amounted to nothing. "He lied about all of it. Every last piece."

"Yeah, I think so, too." Shane exhaled as he looked out the window. Whatever he saw had his attention. She knew Tyler's leaving kicked off that celebration.

"I know that doesn't definitely make him a killer or the guy we're after, but it taints everything." She didn't believe anything Tyler said now and wasn't in the mood for excuses. They'd celebrated victories for the site, and now they all rang hollow.

"I'm sorry." Shane put an arm around her and pulled her close. "All indications are he was average at everything he tried. Not a stellar student. Not much of an athlete. Not very popular. The type who tried to buy friends using the trust money he got when his wealthy parents died in a plane crash." Shane whispered the words into her hair. "Pretending to be a hero might have been what he thought he needed to do to change his life."

"But he's such a loner. Lying about his life isn't getting him anything." She searched her memory but couldn't think of a single time he'd used his tales to soak up attention or win over friends.

Shane winced. "Maybe he thought it would get him you."

She couldn't even process that. Refused to think about it. "I can't believe I was so wrong. I thought I could read people."

Questioning this led her to question so many other things. She wondered if she saw things as she wanted them to be. Maybe she painted her entire life with one broad brush.

"Don't do that." Shane's voice stayed low and soothing. "Don't take on any more guilt."

It was possible she'd miscalculated about Tyler and put her faith in the wrong person. But she wasn't wrong about Shane. She refused to believe that was even possible. Her head rested against his heart, and his hand slipped into her hair. She craved this closeness with him and loved that he granted it to her so freely.

She listened for his heartbeat and relaxed into the gentle thumping sound. The higher-pitched beeping had her head whipping back. She looked up at him. "What's that?"

He frowned as he lifted his arm. "My watch."

The simple black band. All of the Corcoran Team members wore one. It was part of the uniform, to the extent that they had one of those. She'd never seen him not wearing it. The thing could perform miracles. It did so much more than tell time. It functioned as a camera and a computer, and it gave them the ability to tune in to each other at all times through some sort of internal comm.

But she'd never heard it make noise before. "That's an odd sound. Is it an alarm?"

He froze. "We need to get out of the house."

"What?" She pulled back, letting a breath of air separate their bodies as she tried to figure out what put the edge of frustration in his voice. "Why?"

"There's a bomb in here."

The comment didn't make any sense. "The watch?"

"The house, so move." He had her by the elbow. Got her almost to the front door before he stopped. "What did he touch?"

She had no idea what Shane was talking about. In the past few seconds he'd morphed from this solid male who held her to a guy talking in half sentences. She'd ask him why and try to get more information if she even had a clue what to ask. She didn't.

She tried anyway. "Shane, let's sit down and—"

"Do not move." He held a hand out to her to stay put as he stepped closer to the door.

He'd given her the exact opposite order a second ago. Before the tension had clogged the room to the point of suffocation.

He squatted down and stared up at the underside of the knob. "There you are."

It was as if she'd been thrown into a strange survival movie. She'd come to expect the unexpected and go with it, but this tested her resolve. She could handle these trials, but this one she did not understand.

She tried to grab him as he paced around the small area. "Could you slow down and explain?"

"Later." He walked through the house to the bedroom, tugging her behind him. "We need to get out."

They got the whole way to the bedroom before she built up enough strength to turn him around to face her. She caught his head in her hands just as he lifted the window and let the unusually cool air move in. "Shane, look at me."

He covered her hands with his. "Tyler planted a bomb."

The words sat there for a second. Then she got moving. She wanted to race to the front door and run screaming out into the trees. But he had steered them in here and she had to think there was a reason. She helped him open the window. The next minute he was shoving her through it.

"Run and do not stop." He lifted her legs over the sill and helped drop her to the ground outside. They were on the ground floor and didn't need any acrobatics. "I need you to keep moving and not look back. No matter what you hear."

Her feet had just hit the ground when the bang exploded all around her. A wall of heat smacked into her, lifting her up and sending her flying backward. The noise blocked her ears and took her airborne. She finally hit the ground with a jolt, landing half on her butt and half on her elbow.

In her haze she couldn't think about anything but crawling. She took off, slithering across the ground, as unidentifiable charred pieces landed around her. She didn't totally understand what had happened, but she sensed she couldn't stop. If she did, something could hit her, and with debris all around and flames popping up everywhere she looked, she didn't want to take the chance. Her sole focus stayed on survival.

By the time she rolled over on her back and looked behind her, flames were licking up the walls of the house, and black smoke was billowing from every window. Fire rained down all around her. She scooted on her backside to put as much space between her and the inferno as possible.

Rocks and dirt dug into her palms, and the fire burned hot enough to scorch her cheeks. She kept backing up as her mind switched to one concern—Shane. She searched the landscape, looking for his shoulders. For a shape. For some sign of him.

He'd been right there with her. He'd climbed out…or had he? The memory replayed in her mind, and the horror struck her. He was still inside.

She scrambled to her knees. The hard ground bit into her skin, but she was too busy searching for an easy path back into the raging flame and inside the falling-down building to find him. He could not die. She would not allow it.

Her breath hiccupped in her chest and she choked back a sob. Despair threatened to swamp her, but she pushed the dread away. She had to believe. He was the strongest, most competent man she knew. If anyone could beat a fire, it would be him.

She tried to stand up, but her legs didn't hold her. She

crumpled back down in a heap as every muscle turned to jelly. She'd turned boneless and the shock of what had just happened began to settle in. She rotated between hot and cold as she sat there, listening for the sirens and rocking back and forth.

He could not be dead. The words screamed through her head. She wanted with all her soul for them to be true.

A rumble of noise drew her attention. Fire was so loud as it consumed and destroyed. The sound of the flames rolling over everything in their path had taken on a human vibe. Smoke lifted into the sky and settled around her as she tried to figure out what to do next and how to get in there. Her mind went blank and her heart cracked in two at the idea of Shane not getting out.

Then the pity drifted away and determination moved into its place. She could not just sit there. He had to be alive and she had to find him. She looked around, spinning in a circle and adding to her dizziness. This time she had to get up. She balanced on her palms, then lifted herself. Her knees buckled, but she eventually stayed up.

She took two steps before holding an arm over her head to fend off the mix of smoke and heat. But she couldn't wait. She forced her legs to move. Slow and sure, she got closer, but not close enough to break in or for her frantic screams to be heard over the roar of the flames.

She stumbled and her ankle turned. Somehow she managed to stay on her feet. One more step and then a new round of confusion started. The whack to her back had her pitching forward. She put out her hands just in time to keep from landing on her face.

Her knee hit the ground first and then her hands. A

shot of pain moved through her as she tried to figure out what had hit her. A piece of the house or something. The smoke made it hard to see much of anything and kept stealing her breath. With every inhale, she'd double over hacking.

She needed air to fight this fight. Rolling over to her back, she opened her eyes and tried to breathe in semi-fresh air. She saw something. A few blinks and it didn't disappear. There, off to her right, she spied jeans and a man's legs.

Her heart did a grateful flip. *Shane made it out!* Her gaze lifted and she saw that face. The wrong face. Tyler stood there, holding a gun.

"What are you…" It hurt to talk and she doubted he could hear her over the thunder of flames and crackling and falling debris.

He reached down and lifted her to her feet as if she weighed nothing. He brought his face in close to hers.

She tried to focus and listen to whatever he was saying. She picked out one sentence and her blood turned from burning to icy cold.

"This would have been easier if you'd chosen me."

# Chapter Eighteen

The explosion dropped Shane to his knees. The ground shook beneath him, and the walls caved in over his head. He braced his body for the blows to come. The rafters would break and wood would tumble down on him.

But he'd gotten her out. He'd shoved her out the window and heard her scream and the explosion ripping through the small house. Cam and Connor would grab her. They'd find her wandering around and take her in. Shane refused to believe anything other than that. She hadn't been injured and wasn't stuck in harm's way.

With her safely tucked away in his mind, he concentrated on saving himself. He wasn't sure that was even possible. Smoke obscured his vision, and the fall had him doubting which way led to the outside and which led to the flames.

Heat pulsed all around him. He felt his clothing singe and the hot air tear through his throat and lungs. He covered his mouth and kept low, tried to remember all of his fire training. It had been a while and he was rusty, but he looked for light. For any sign of the world outside the burning walls.

Something smashed into his shoulder as he struggled to drop to his stomach so he could crawl. Pain seared his neck and he jerked. Saw a piece of burning wood fall to the floor. That had been on him, and he knew the amount of falling debris would only increase in the next few minutes. If he was going to crawl, he had to do it now.

His face hugged the floor as he fought for the last few breaths of untainted air. Every move hurt, but he kept going. Crawled in the direction where he thought he'd last seen Makena. Noise roared around him in a deafening cadence. He twice fell to the floor when the walls crumbled around him and threatened to flatten him.

He somehow kept going even though he felt as if his progress amounted only to inches. He couldn't draw in enough breath to focus. His strength waned as his last reserves of energy petered out on him.

He kept counting in his head. Concentrated on the image of her face and how good it would be to see her, touch her, again.

Something clamped around his waist and smashed him into the floor. He kicked out and struggled, trying to lift his arms and legs despite the fact that they suddenly seemed to weigh hundreds of pounds each. The battle got away from him. His ability to fight drained from him.

In his smoke-induced stupor he swore he saw Cam's face, filled with concern through the mask. Then his body floated. Shane couldn't explain it and feared he verged on passing out. Hallucinations and sliding into unconsciousness. If those happened together he sensed he'd die.

With one last kick of adrenaline he surged up, thinking to throw himself into the nearest wall. Instead he slammed into something that felt like a body. Arms wrapped around him and pulled. The smoke drifted over him, and then he broke free. He could see the ground and fire.

"Shane, talk to me." Connor's voice washed over him.

He chalked it up to one last strange vision. Connor wasn't exactly the last person Shane thought he'd see before he lost it. Connor held something. Then Shane inhaled and his senses cleared. A mask covered his mouth, and fresh air pumped through him, burning him. He had to throw the mask off to cough.

He doubled over as the painful hacking overtook every muscle. He felt as if he were being sliced and torn from the inside out.

The roughness in his throat made it difficult to swallow. But he was alive. Connor stood in front of him with Cam off to the side, stripping out of a blanket that had been wrapped around him.

They'd gone in after him and yanked him out. Probably never even weighed the risks. Cam had performed the rescue, but Connor had likely choreographed it. Bottom line: without them, he'd be dead. Corcoran had saved him in every way possible, including here and now. The move humbled Shane and he was filled with gratitude, but there was one piece he needed to fit in with the rest. Her.

When he straightened again, he felt weak and exhausted, as if every last ounce of strength had been used up and expired. One thought kept going through his mind. "Where's Makena?"

Cam and Connor glanced at each other as the flames danced all around them. A gnawing sensation started in Shane's gut. A new burst of energy hit him and drowned out everything else.

"Connor, where is she?"

Cam stepped in next to him and they stood there like

an impenetrable wall, blocking his view of anything else and his line to the fire. Anxiety welled inside Shane and he had to fight to keep from tearing down the burning structure with his bare hands.

Connor held up a hand. "We need you to stay calm."

"Where is she?" That was all he wanted to know. He could take another step, another breath, once he knew.

Connor's hand didn't fall. "Listen to me."

"Just show him." Cam stepped to the side and pointed. In the distance, on the other side of the wall of flames, a figure crouched down. Large and male. He lifted something… Shane blinked and tried to get his sore eyes to focus. Makena. Tyler had Makena.

He surged forward, intent on yelling and running. Strong hands held him back. Cam and Connor wrestled with Shane, dragging him to the ground as they covered his mouth and held on. His reduced strength was no match for their combined attack. He struggled to break free, shoving at them and landing more than one punch.

"We have to get her." The words echoed in his brain as desperation washed over him.

Cam held him from behind and Connor knelt in front. Their will pounded into Shane, but he tried to wave it off. There was no other play here. They needed to start shooting and not stop until Tyler dropped to the ground.

"We'll follow," Connor said in a tighter voice than usual.

Not good enough. Shane wanted her away from that guy. He'd walked right into the safe house and planted a bomb. Had done it like a pro. No sweating or panic. In Shane's mind that made the guy some sort of psychopath and put Makena in even bigger danger. "Now, we go now."

"We'd never make it in time thanks to the fire." Connor shook his head. "And we'd put her in the middle of a shootout."

"She'll lead us right to Tyler." Cam said the words right into Shane's ear.

"She is not a decoy. She can't…no." He looked from Connor to Cam. "Would you agree to this for Jana or Julia? No way. This is the same thing." Words tumbled out of him. "And if you don't care about how I feel, think about Holt. He'll kill us all for letting her be in danger for even one second longer than necessary."

They would fight for the women they loved, and so would Shane. Even if it meant knocking out two of his closest friends.

"She's going to be fine. I promise you." Connor sounded so sure, as if he believed every word he said and that by saying them he could make them true.

But Shane knew better. His mind started to clear, and the list of things that could go wrong piled up. "You don't know that. You can't possibly know that."

Connor stood up. "You don't have a choice."

Shane had never felt so desperate or helpless. "Connor, please."

Cam lifted Shane to his feet and stood with Connor. "Let's go."

It hurt to stand up. Hurt to breathe in. Shane vowed to suck it all up and take it if it meant saving her. "If this doesn't work…"

Connor handed Shane a gun. "It will."

TODAY HAD ROLLED out like a nightmare in her head, and it wasn't over yet.

Makena needed a hospital before the dizziness overtook her and she passed out. She also needed some word about Shane. Her insides felt shredded. Panic ran through her like air. Her mind kept zipping back to the moment of the explosion. She tried to remember pulling him out through the window with her, but feared that was wishful thinking. That it had never happened.

If she were anywhere else, if she had minutes to think, she might be able to put the pieces together in her head. Instead she sat at Tyler's kitchen table and played house. He walked around serving coffee, acting normal. Or some version of normal.

"Tyler, please listen to me." She tried to move her arm and bit back a scream when the bindings cut into her skin.

She couldn't move her legs or arms. She tried to wiggle her hands behind her, get a little bit of give in the rope so she could slip a hand through, but they were so bound so tightly her fingers had started going numb.

He sat down across from her and opened his laptop. "We'll go to dinner soon, and then you should go to bed early."

He spoke as if this were their routine instead of some messed-up delusion in his head. He'd suffered some sort of break. No question. The anger he'd had back when Shane confronted him had disappeared. This Tyler acted as if they were locked in a twisted form of domestic tranquility.

She would have ached for him if she could conquer the terror buzzing in her head long enough to think about anything else. She didn't think he would hurt her, but she didn't know. This Tyler was not a man she knew. He'd been pushed to the edge and now he lived in a world she didn't understand. One that had fear crashing through her so hard that she had to fight back tears.

"Could I go to the bathroom?"

Tyler peeked up at her. Fury highlighted his features. One minute he looked ready to tuck her into bed and the next he looked as if he could kill her. This was one of those latter moments. "No."

She wanted to reason with him, bring him back to reality. She didn't even know if that sort of thing was possible. "You can untie me."

"So you can go to him?" Tyler snapped the laptop shut. "No."

*Shane.* She thought about him and sadness rolled over her. She had to fight back the tears and pain, and push through. "We can talk about this."

Tyler shook his head. "You gave me no choice."

Okay, she could handle this. "I did."

His gaze narrowed. "We had something and you threw it away."

She had to assume this was part of the delusion. A piece where he viewed whatever they'd had as more than a working relationship. "I didn't know how you felt. You never told me."

"You knew."

Some part of her sensed that she needed to keep him talking and prolong this as much as possible. It would take forever for the team to discover her missing. And if they were busy mourning Shane...no, no, no. She dragged her thoughts back from that abyss and kept pretending. "How could I?"

The legs of the chair scraped against the floor as he pushed it back and stood up. "That's not possible. I gave you more and more responsibility. I risked everything for you."

"Tell me how." She tried to lure him in while she spent every spare second visually searching the room for a weapon. "What did you do for me?"

"You researched cases that came so close to me. You almost wrecked all I built, but I forgave you." Tyler dumped out his freshly poured coffee in the sink. "I had it handled until that request came through the website. I got them all, but that one slipped through to you."

She remembered the day well. She'd been looking for a response to something else and had seen the request. Stumbled over it, really. "You were in DC doing research."

He smiled at her. "Just my luck."

"Why did that one matter so much?" The subject of the email inquiry had claimed to be Special Forces and a combat veteran. There was talk about sacrificing everything for his men and saving lives. The usual. Nothing exceptional that would have tipped her off or led her back to Tyler.

He shrugged. "We both borrowed the same life story."

The admission, so subtle and delivered without any emotion, left her breathless. He acted as if his deception didn't matter. She didn't know if that was the sickness talking or something evil. "You're saying...what are you saying?"

"The man you were to investigate told a story much like my own because we both knew a man named Roger Culp. We all grew up in the same small town."

The truth hit her then. "But only one of you actually went to war."

"He was a local hero." Tyler leaned back against the

sink and glanced at one of the small monitors attached under the counter. "There was no reason I couldn't enjoy some of those accolades. Outside the town, of course."

The justifications sounded so familiar. She heard them every day from the men they listed on the site. That her own boss, the man who had started the project, was one of them hit her like a sharp kick to the stomach.

He nodded toward the monitor. "We have company."

She followed his gaze, hoping to see Shane ready to storm in, but Tyler didn't show any fear. From this distance she saw a fuzzy figure outlined in black and white hanging around the front door. A man, but not her man.

As if she'd willed him to do it, he lifted his head. Jeff. The man she'd grown to be more and more uncertain of as the attacks kicked up in intensity. He showed up without warning and his anger festered just under the surface. Now she knew why. He was Tyler's contact. Likely his way onto the loop, where he could watch and contain the information passed around.

"Your partner is here." In that moment, she hated them both.

Tyler's eyebrow lifted. "Not mine."

Not what she'd expected him to say at all. With his narcissism she'd waited for some sort of self-congratulations. She got something very different. "What do you mean?"

"Your failure to keep up makes me second-guess my faith in you." Tyler tucked his gun behind his back. "I'll invite him in."

He walked away, out of her line of vision. She tried to turn in the chair, but the rope dug into her and burned her skin. Moving her head from side to side, she tried to pick up some clue. She didn't hear any conversation, just footsteps.

Then Jeff appeared in front of her. His eyes were glazed over with fear and Tyler had a gun pointed at his head. The hold Tyler had on Jeff's arm didn't make any sense. If they were working together…she didn't get it.

"Jeff stopped by to say hello." Tyler smiled as he said the horrible words.

Jeff's gaze traveled around the room, over her. "You tied her to a chair."

"What did you think he would do?" After all the killing and all the attacks, this ending could not be a surprise. It wasn't to her. She'd seen it coming and tried to avoid it, but failed.

"I thought you were working." He let out a startled gasp as Tyler threw him in a chair. "I wanted to talk."

Tyler used his free hand to wrap a rope around Jeff's chest. The movements proved awkward and ineffective, and he finally let the bindings drop to the floor unused. "You won't be alive that long anyway."

"What is going on?" Jeff sounded confused and lost, and both emotions were mirrored in his eyes.

For whatever reason—the fear, the panic—she believed him. "I found out Tyler lied. That he's one of you."

Jeff spun around and stared at the man looming over him. "You weren't in the military."

A crazed look of desperation lit Tyler's face. "Stop talking."

All she needed was a free hand, but she couldn't get one loose, so she kept the men talking, saying anything to avoid a bullet to her heart. "You didn't know?"

"I would have used it against him." Jeff shook his head. "I can't believe this. After all this time—"

"I said stop." Tyler shifted until he stood at the head of the table between them. He slipped a knife out of the block and pointed at one of them, and then the other. "Let me explain what's going to happen. Jeff, you are going to kill Makena in a horrible revenge-filled frenzy."

The color drained from Jeff's face as he tried to slide his chair away from Tyler. "I would never—"

Tyler linked his foot around the chair leg and dragged Jeff closer to the tip of the blade. "Makena, you're going to get one good stab in, and it'll wound poor Jeff here. But I'll deliver the final blow with the gun I keep for protection."

He'd clearly written the sick scene in his head. She'd failed to play her assigned role and now he gave her another one. "Like a hero."

He glared at her. "I am one."

"This will never work." Possible solutions ran through her head. She could crash her chair into him… She ran out after that.

"You had your chance. I wanted you to be my partner."

Her mind flashed on another scenario. One that would save Jeff, too. Her gaze flicked to him. "How did you get here?"

"I followed you."

She hoped that meant the Corcoran Team had as well. "I blamed you." The apology stuck in her throat. She couldn't get it out, not yet.

"He's a liar," Tyler said in a reasonable voice that carried over the mix of shuffling and chair moving happening on the floor.

She tried to pick up each sound and figure out what was happening. Jeff kept looking at her and then staring at Tyler's stomach. She wasn't sure what he wanted her to do, but she sensed she and Jeff were in this one together.

Jeff shot her one last intense stare. "No one will believe it. I'm not a killer."

"Unfortunately for you, I am." Tyler drew back the knife and stabbed it into Jeff's side.

She closed her eyes but not before seeing Jeff's pop open. He groaned and his body doubled over. Blood seeped through his white shirt. The room broke into chaos. The window on the side of the family room shattered and a male figure crashed inside. She turned her head to avoid the flying glass and saw the front door explode off its hinges.

Her eyes refused to focus, but she thought she heard Shane's voice. The yelling ran together with the banging. The last thing she saw was Tyler reaching for his gun, and then a weight knocked into her, sending her and the chair in a free fall to the floor.

Everything happened at once. A drumbeat thundered in her ears and she struggled to loosen her hands, but it was too late. Her body bounced and her head knocked against the hardwood. She heard gunshots as Jeff's heavy breathing echoed in her ears. Then she couldn't see or hear anything at all.

## Chapter Nineteen

Shane had waited a beat too long. He'd wanted to race in the second Tyler shoved Jeff into the chair. Shane saw the two of them as partners. Sick men who deserved whatever happened next. The full wrath of the Corcoran Team could fall on them and Shane would not suffer one minute of regret. He valued life but not their lives.

Then he saw the blade and Tyler's gun and silently declared, "Go time."

The explosives tore the front door apart. Shredded it into sharp pieces and sent them flying. He didn't wait for the smoke to clear or the space to open, or even for Connor's signal. Shane ripped the debris out of his way, ignored the cuts to his hands and marched through the door.

He headed for Tyler and didn't stop. Not when he lifted the gun. Not when he fired at Jeff, who was a blur streaking across the table to cover Makena. Not when Tyler adjusted his aim and the barrel pointed at the general chaos.

He could shoot anyone, looked ready to kill without spending one second thinking about it. He wasn't a man on the edge. He'd gone careening off it at rapid speed.

Shane didn't waste time trying to fix Tyler or reason

with him. They'd passed that point long ago. To whatever extent he'd ever dealt in reason, he didn't now. Shane had no choice but to take him down.

He came in firing over the heads of Jeff and Makena, trying to get them to duck and stay down. He wanted to draw Tyler's fire and keep his mind off the bodies on the floor. In Tyler's obsessive state, anything could trigger him, and Shane didn't want to test him.

But Tyler didn't stick with the plan. He dropped down but kept shooting. He crawled toward Makena, and Shane increased his speed. Breaking every rule and ignoring protocol, he crossed right in front of Cam's line of fire, heedless of the danger and desperate only to get to her. All those hours of practice and drills faded into the background.

Connor swore and Cam yelled. Shane blocked it all. He had to, because she lay tucked and unmoving. Blood covered her, but he couldn't tell if it was hers or Jeff's, as they were piled on top of each other.

"Stay back." Tyler practically screamed the order as he reached for Makena's arm. He pulled, trying to drag her closer.

She shoved away from him. Jeff trapped her in place, leaving her vulnerable to Tyler's whims. The gun in Tyler's hand waved and bobbled. He pointed it in every direction, as if he'd forgotten he even held it.

The man was the ultimate wild card, out of control and raging. He started yelling about his life and all he'd lost. When he spied Shane, his intensity seemed to find a focus.

*Perfect.* That was exactly what Shane wanted. He made himself a target on purpose and planned to keep his body there for as long as possible. Let Connor and

Cam get into position. Let Tyler make a mistake. Anything to take the attention away from Makena and give them all a chance at survival.

But Shane couldn't look at her for long. Her eyes were wild with fear as her mouth dropped open. The combined look of pain and fear killed him. So did the way she glanced around and silently begged Cam to do something when Shane didn't.

But he could. Rather than wait on the defensive, he grabbed a hold of the offensive. Shane held his hands up. "That's right. You want me."

Tyler scrambled to his knees. "You ruined everything."

Shane took a step back, luring Tyler away from the protection of the barricade of the tipped table and pile of fallen chairs. "I did. I went after her when I knew she was yours."

Makena gasped. "Shane, no."

For a second he worried she believed him, but the concern on her face suggested something else. She was smart and strong. She'd know this amounted to a plot meant to ensnare Tyler and drag him down.

When Tyler's gaze slipped back to her, Shane rushed to get it moving again. "I did it on purpose. I didn't want her, but I really didn't want you to have her." He shook his head and pretended to believe the foul words he spit out. "She was a game. I wanted to beat you."

Tyler lifted up a little higher. An inch more and his head would pop up in firing range. "She wanted me first."

Shane didn't even steal a look at her this time. To get through this, he needed to match Tyler's evil with some of his own. The anxiety pinging around inside him threatened to drop him to his knees, but he kept his attention steady. On Tyler and his gun, waiting for the perfect moment to take him out.

"She did want you. She was all in and talking about you. Thinking you were this hero doing all this amazing work." Shane forced the words out. "But I made her want me. Convincing her was tough, but I did it."

Tyler straightened then and Shane did not hesitate. He lowered his hand with exacting speed and fired. Gunshots rang out from three parts of the room and he knew Connor and Cam had taken the advantage, too.

But Shane didn't care about Tyler. Connor could handle him. Shane's mind went to the woman who held his heart. Ignoring the aches and pain and the way his bones creaked after all the abuse they'd endured, he slid across the floor and skidded to a stop beside her. He was vaguely aware of Connor dropping down to check Tyler's pulse and Cam rushing over to lift Jeff.

Shane only saw her.

He grabbed at the ropes binding her to the chair, trying to rip them apart with his bare hands. His strength alone might have done it, but Cam handed over a knife and Shane got busy cutting.

He had her loose in a few seconds and she flew into his arms. Her warmth seeped into him as he fell back against the floor on his butt. He had her cradled on his lap and he rocked back and forth. "I love you. God, I love you."

He could hear her crying and felt the wet tears against his neck. Sirens whirred to life around them, and car doors slammed shut just outside. Guns came up and people talked over each other. Jeff didn't move while Cam clamped a kitchen towel against his side and tried to talk with him.

Police burst through the door and Connor stopped them. He held up his hands and the yelling match started. All the noise faded into the background for Shane. He couldn't help them and didn't want to let go of her. In this moment he needed her. To hold her, to beg her forgiveness. Everything.

"I'm so sorry." He whispered the words over and over, into her hair, then against her forehead. He kissed the patches of skin he could see and brushed her hair out of the way to get to her mouth. He was about to ask her something when her mouth touched his.

She kissed him, deep and desperate. Her fingers clawed at his back and she drew him in closer. "I thought you were dead."

He had to lean down to hear her. "Are you hurt?"

She shook her head but didn't answer. For some reason he needed to hear her voice. "Baby, talk to me."

She looked up at him with tearstained cheeks. "It's Jeff's blood."

The reminder had Shane glancing over his shoulder. The man's eyes were open but glazed over.

"He saved me." A tremble made her voice vibrate.

"I saw." Shane had watched in shock as Jeff played the hero. He'd spent so much of his life lying about being one. In this instance, he'd acted like one, and Shane was humbled by the sacrifice.

"Is he—"

"Cam is working on him." An ambulance crew rushed in a second later.

The small room burst to life. First responders roamed around and Connor acted as traffic guard, moving people here and there. Being in control and running the room. Business as usual.

Makena grabbed a handful of Shane's shirt and brought his head back down to hers. "Get me out of here."

He could do that. He owed her that much. More, actually. Because of him she'd played the role of decoy. He'd put her in direct danger and then almost stepped in too late to save her. It was every nightmare brought to life. He'd stayed away to keep the ugliness of his work out of her life but ended up doing the exact opposite.

"I'm sorry." He said it because he had to. No other words would come out without a push.

Her hand trailed down his cheek. "You're my hero."

"I'm not, but you're alive and that's all that matters."

He stood up and lifted her into his arms. He knew she needed to see a doctor and get checked out. That would all happen, but he needed to hold her for a few seconds first.

She wrapped her arms around his neck and whispered into his neck, "I love you."

The guilt trapped inside him escaped. "You shouldn't."

He'd never meant the words more in his life.


If anyone had told Makena she'd be sitting at the hospital bedside of Jeff Horvath one day, she would have laughed. Maybe not even that. The idea was so ridiculous it didn't even sound like a joke.

She'd taken the position that Jeff had gotten what he deserved. Somewhere she'd forgotten that he was a human being and had tossed his feelings aside. He deserved most of what had happened to him, but his actions at Tyler's house showed that he could be redeemed. That there could be decency inside someone like him. Once guilt stopped punching her, she'd appreciate the lesson.

Until then, here she was, watching the machinery work to keep him alive and get stronger. The room filled with beeps and strange sounds. Something clicked and an automatic blood-pressure monitor spun to life and checked him every few minutes. He had oxygen and tubes connected to him.

He hadn't opened his eyes, but the doctor said he'd survived the worst and was improving. She had no idea how anyone could tell.

She leaned back and continued to stare, willing him to get better and hoping he had the strength to do so. She did it for him and for her. Concentrating on Jeff helped her to forget Shane's last words to her.

*You shouldn't.*

After everything, all the pain and death, the terror and anxiety, he held on to his lone-wolf stance. In her horror-induced stupor, she'd thought she heard him utter the words she longed to hear. She'd told him she loved him, but he'd said it first…or had he? Those moments blurred together in her mind with Tyler's manic tone and Jeff's death rattle as the knife slipped inside him. Thinking about it had her eyes popping open.

"How is he?" Connor asked as he stepped into the room with Shane behind him.

"Better." But she barely heard the question.

Her gaze traveled over Shane. He had a bandage on his arm and neck, and one arm hugged his ribs. Connor had insisted they all take a trip to the hospital. She'd long ago been released. Shane had had to stay overnight and had slept through it all as she switched back and forth from his bedside to Jeff's.

Shane frowned. "That's a miracle."

It all was. Makena couldn't believe any of it. If she tried to explain it—and she had during a telephone call with Holt, who was ripping apart airports on his flights across the country to get to her—it all sounded so fantastical and unrealistic.

So did Jeff's sacrifice. "How could a guy who would lie about who he was step up like that when to do so risked his own life?"

Nothing about what Jeff had done and the choice he'd made fit with the other things she knew about him. He'd spent so much time pretending to be a hero when he had had the instinct for decency inside him all along.

Connor crossed his arms in front of him. "I like to think a lot of people would do the right thing if confronted with the opportunity."

Shane scoffed as he came over to stand beside her chair. "I think Connor is naive."

She kind of agreed. "I owe him."

"Connor repaid him." Shane's hand fell to her shoulder and squeezed.

The touch warmed all the chilled places inside her. She wanted to grab on to his hand and not let go. But now wasn't the time or the place.

Her gaze switched from Shane to Connor. "What did you do?"

"There will be a feature in the news about Jeff, touching a bit on his past for perspective but talking about how he turned his life around and saved you and other people during a wild shootout in a house."

"Connor left out the parts about Jeff stalking you," Shane added.

Connor shrugged. "It didn't fit with the rest of the story."

She gave in and touched her fingers to Shane's. "I'm sort of happy he did stalk me that last time."

He glanced down at her and winked. "Me, too."

With one last look at Jeff, Connor headed for the door. "I'm going to leave you two—"

"No." Shane snapped out the answer before Connor took his next step. Before she could agree.

She dropped her hand to her lap. "No?"

"I need to head out." Shane didn't make eye contact as he spoke. He glanced around as he moved away from her.

After spending so much of his life putting an emotional wall between them, this time he added a physical one. He was running away from her in every way she could imagine, both physically and emotionally. Even Connor stared at him with narrowed eyes as if trying to read his mood.

"Fine." That was all she could muster.

Shane hesitated as he watched her. "I'll call you."

Yeah, she wouldn't sit by the phone and wait for that call. In fact, she was done waiting for Shane at all. If he couldn't see that he could abandon his past and his fears, and be happy with her, she'd give up. They'd been in this highly stressful situation and managed to survive not by staying away from each other but by finally being together.

That left only one thing for her to say. "Goodbye, Shane."

And this time she meant it.

# *Chapter Twenty*

The next day Shane waited outside the hospital for Makena to come out. He stood in the parking lot, leaning against her car. She'd been keeping vigil by Jeff's bedside since the ambulance crew brought him in. She'd called the Corcoran headquarters to let them know Jeff was going to be okay. She'd talked about going to Holt's house to wait for him to get in after a series of canceled flights delayed him.

Shane wanted to see her before Holt did. Wanted to see her…period.

Footsteps sounded beside him, but Shane didn't flinch. He'd seen Connor park nearby and head for him. He'd likely come over to give Makena a break at Jeff's bedside. A decent thing to do. Shane had never thought of it. He'd left her yesterday and stayed away because there was something he needed to do before he talked with her.

Connor took up position beside Shane and stared at the front door of the hospital. "If Holt were here, he'd tell you to stop moping and go get your woman."

Shane turned slightly to face his boss. "What?"

"This, the doubt and guilt." Connor held out a hand

in front of Shane. "I get it. Believe me. I almost lost Jana because I was so worried about *losing Jana*."

Shane had listened to many lectures from Connor during their time at Corcoran. The guy liked to talk and wanted things to be done his way. Shane appreciated the way Connor ran the business and the team. He had no complaints. Except for these talks that didn't make a lot of sense in or out of context.

"Clue me in on what you're talking about." His mind kept zipping back to Makena and all the things he needed to say to her. Talking with Connor just wasn't a priority, no matter how much Shane liked the guy.

Connor sighed. "Man, you're stubborn."

He'd been hearing that his whole life. Since Shane agreed, he didn't bother to deny it. "That's not news."

"I know you're invested in the whole bachelor thing."

*Was.* Before Makena. Before being with her and realizing he didn't want to be without her. "I am?"

"You're not?" Connor wasn't one to miss a clue. He didn't this time, either. "Are you saying—"

"I love her." The words that had once stuck in his throat now freed him. Shane said them and his whole world shifted into position. The failed marriage was behind him. Makena was his future.

Connor laughed. "I know."

"You could have told me." But Shane knew that wasn't fair. Each of the team members had talked about the difference between life on his own and life with a woman who meant everything. They'd tried to sell him on getting involved again and taking the risk. He'd blocked the comments and ignored every word.

"You weren't ready to hear it." Ever the undercover agent, Connor scanned the parking lot. Watching people as they moved in and out. "So, what was the thing with leaving the hospital room yesterday? You have to know that hurt her."

He hadn't, really. Not until after, when Cam had texted to call him an idiot.

But Shane hadn't been playing games or thinking over his options. He knew he loved her and wanted to be with her, no matter the consequences. But he did have responsibilities and tried to meet them. "I needed to talk with Holt. I owed him that and wanted to go to Makena with a clear head and no barriers between us."

Connor smiled. "What if Holt had told you to back off?"

It would have ripped him apart, but Shane's answer didn't change. "I would have ignored him."

"Yep, that's love." Connor pushed off from the car and stood up straight. "Okay, good luck."

That sounded ominous. "Luck?"

"It's cute that you don't think you'll need it." Connor shook his head as he waved and kept walking. "I almost feel bad for you."

MAKENA'S BODY BEGGED for sleep. She was ten seconds away from dropping. She'd dozed on and off in that chair. Talked with the team members and her brother. Checked in and managed to get two of Jeff's relatives to stop by.

Helping that guy could be a full-time job, but she didn't plan to let it get away from her like that. She'd been there for him, providing support. He was recovering well and other people he knew, some from whom he'd been estranged for years, were taking over. Now she could rest.

If only she could close her eyes without seeing Shane's

face swim in front of her. As she was walking across the parking lot, it happened again. She was wide-awake with her eyes open, yet he seemed to be standing there, right next to her car. She blinked a few times, expecting him to disappear. But no.

If he'd picked this moment to tell her they needed to stay friends, she might just curl up in a ball. A woman could only take so much. Her bruises had bruises. Worse, her heart felt shredded. He'd done that when he walked away. Fine—if he wanted to walk, he should just keep going.

She stopped in front of him but didn't say anything. For a second, neither did he. He leaned against her car and watched her. Stared, really. The intense scrutiny had her squirming.

"What do you want?" It came out harsher than she'd intended, but she didn't have anything left in the tank. She couldn't hide her reactions or control her feelings. She wanted to strike out and scream. Life seemed so unfair at the moment.

"You."

He'd said that once before and she'd bought it. Not this time. "We're not sleeping together again."

He frowned. "I hope that's not true."

"Look, Shane." She inhaled a few times as she worked to keep some portion of the emotional wall she'd built against him in place. "I'm not your consolation prize. I'm not a side benefit to your case."

"No, you're not."

"What are you doing?" The last of her energy drained out of her. Her shoulders slumped and she fought to stay on her feet. "I'm not in the mood for games or for—"

He stepped up and leaned in. Before she could blink,

his arms came around her and his lips met hers. He kissed her with a kick of heat and intensity that stole her breath. She held on as his mouth traveled over hers, and her knees buckled.

When he lifted his head again she expected… Actually, she had no idea what to expect. He could have said anything and she would have nodded. Her brain refused to work and every word died in her throat before she could say them.

"I love you."

Her heart jumped. Hope pulsed inside her, but she tamped it down. He was handing her everything, but she feared it meant nothing. She couldn't bring herself to believe, so she shut it all down. "No, you don't."

"You're telling me how I feel?" He sounded amused by the idea.

Nothing about this moment struck her as funny. She shoved against his arms to get him to let go. "Goodbye, Shane."

She fumbled with her keys. They bounced off her fingers and fell to the ground with a clink. Lost and heartsick, she stood there and tipped her head back to stare up at the sky.

"You can leave, but I'll just follow you." His voice came from right behind her. His hands went to her arms, and his face rested against her hair. "I can't let you go."

He said… She couldn't process the words or anything else that was happening. She turned around to face him, letting him see every ounce of pain running through her. "Is this about your ego?"

"It's about loving you." He rubbed his hands up and down her arms. "About realizing that I was wrong and pushing you away when I should have been grabbing on with all my strength."

That sounded good, but her mind couldn't hold on to a single thought. "I don't understand."

"I'm sorry I let fear and old wounds keep us apart." He balanced his forehead against hers. "I will never do that again."

"You love me?" The words didn't even sound right to her.

He lifted his head and stared down at her. There, written on his face, she saw tenderness and hope, a good bit of lust and, yes, love. She had no idea where or why, but the hope finally took hold. She didn't bat it away or downplay it. She held on.

"Almost losing you nearly killed me." He lifted her hand and pressed her fingers to his lips. "I don't want to be away from you."

"You were last night." That piece didn't make any sense in light of all the wonderful things he said now.

The corner of Shane's mouth kicked up in a smile. "I had to tell Holt while I didn't need his permission and wasn't asking for it. I hoped we had it."

"I talked with him." She ran through the conversation in her mind. Now some of Holt's stray comments made sense. "He never said anything."

"I asked him to let me win you back first." Shane shrugged. "For the record, he made me work for it."

As if that would be hard. "I bet."

"I would have done and said anything. Though I have to admit you are the one I want to win over, not him."

She tried to imagine that conversation and how hard a time Holt must have given Shane. The idea that he would go through that, that he'd even thought it was important to take on the challenge of winning Holt over, made her smile.

"I love you." She said it because she needed him to know. She'd thrown it out in the heat of the attack. Now, in the middle of the parking lot with people walking by and nothing on the line, she made the vow again. "With all I am and all I have."

"Good."

The response made her laugh. "That's all you've got to say?"

"Definitely not. I have all sorts of things I want to say and do to you. Some of them in bed. Some against a wall. Some on G-rated dates."

She loved the sound of all of it. "You tell me when and where."

"We're going to do this right." He lifted her off the ground and held her tight. "Start over. Not fast-forward the relationship and skip over the good parts."

She wasn't sure she loved that. "Meaning?"

"We're going to date. Go out to eat and do whatever it is dating people do. You'll probably need to help me with that, because I'm clueless."

"You're doing great."

"And, just so you know, I'm going to kiss you…a lot. Like, all the time. In private and sometimes in parking lots, like here." He followed through by doing just that. Planted a kiss filled with promise and love and every great thing on her. It went on and on, and dragged her under.

When he lifted his head again, all the strain around his eyes had disappeared. She couldn't help running her finger over his eyebrows.

"You're going to know every single day how much

I love you," he said in a husky voice. "How much you mean to me and how you are my future."

Light burst to life inside her, washing away the exhaustion and the doubts. Her head cleared just as her heart sped up. "We should start now."

He laughed. "Are you making a pass?"

"Do I need to?"

"No, because I'm already yours."

Then she kissed him. Parking lot or no, she wanted her life with him to start right now. "Take me home, so you can make up for leaving me yesterday."

He nodded. "I'm willing to spend a lifetime doing that."

FOUR DAYS LATER Shane still hadn't stopped smiling. He'd survived seeing Holt again. Made it through all the doctor checkups and Makena moving into his place. That last one being the best thing to happen to him in...ever.

Every piece of his life had fallen into place.

He'd been the last bachelor in the group. The only one not attached, and he'd held that as a badge of honor for a long time. Something he now saw as ridiculous.

Maybe he hadn't put a ring on Makena's finger or waited for her at the end of an aisle, but he would. And not years from now—soon. Now that he saw his life with her, he wanted more. There was no reason to wait and see. He knew her. Knew them. Knew that life without her wasn't worth much.

Connor walked into the conference room at team headquarters and dropped a file in front of Shane. "You ready to get back to work?"

He glanced around. "Am I the only one on this case?"

"Nah, that's your expense voucher."

Shane opened the file and stared at the pages. He had a check coming his way. Yeah, so what? It didn't mean much to him. "Okay."

Connor leaned back in his chair at the head of the table and grabbed a thick stack of folders off the long desk in front of the line of monitors. "I actually wanted you to look through these."

The pile landed on the table with a thud. Shane had no idea what he was looking at or why. He could scan every page or he could just ask. "What's going on?"

"Potential candidates."

"For?" Shane opened the cover of the top one and glanced inside.

"To be Corcoran Team members." Connor folded his arms in front of him and leaned against the table. "It's time."

They'd been so insular for so long. Connor rarely added new people. He talked about the need for camaraderie and joked that with too many members he risked being overruled. As if that would ever happen. He had their loyalty and trust, and they were not men who gave either easily.

Just so he was clear, he tried again. "We're hiring?"

"I'm thinking we need a West Coast office." Connor shrugged. "That will allow all of you room to pick and choose cases and spend some more time closer to home."

That didn't sound like the tough sharpshooter Shane knew. Sure, Connor had been married to Jana for years and spent his days protecting others and loving her. But making sure the rest of them had stable home lives? Interesting.

"Are you matchmaking?" Shane couldn't even make the idea make sense in his head.

"Blame my wife."

That, Shane got. Something about keeping Makena happy appealed to him. He hated when she so much as frowned. Shane didn't mind the travel or the work. Still, the idea of spending most nights by her side in their big bed didn't exactly stink.

*Thank you, Jana.* "I love your wife."

Connor did what he always did. Spun his wedding ring around on his finger without even realizing he did it. "You are not alone."

"It won't be easy to find qualified men and women who fit in around here." Shane tried to imagine interviewing people and putting them through a series of tests. A daunting but interesting task.

"It takes a certain kind of crazy, I agree."

No question about that. "Do you have people in mind?"

Shane could think of a few. There were folks he'd worked with over the years whom he could see stepping up and assuming the kinds of risks they took for granted. Strong and decent people who needed to find a purpose, which was exactly what he had been. Lost and wandering. Now he had the best friends of his life, a woman he loved and a team that meant everything to him.

Connor nodded in the direction of the high stack. "Right there. I want you all to take a look and offer feedback. Take your time. There's no rush. This is about finding the right people, not speed."

And that summed up why Connor was in charge. Why he inspired so much loyalty. "Sounds good to me."

"Besides that, we need a few bachelors around here." Connor leaned back in his chair. "I thought you'd never go down. And so easy? Man, you're lucky."

He'd never thought so before, but Shane sure thought so now. "Easy?"

"She should have made you beg."

Shane couldn't help smiling. "She does…sometimes."

Connor leaned forward and the legs of his chair hit the floor. "That's probably too much information."

"I'm happy."

"And I'm happy for you." Connor got up and walked around the table. "Now get ready so you can get home to Makena."

Shane would never tire of hearing that. "You got it, boss."

\* \* \* \* \*

## "Don't you trust me?"

"I trust you." She swallowed, and rubbed one hand, palm down, along the side of her thigh. "But I'm not sure I trust myself."

"What do you mean?" He tried to read her expression, but she wasn't giving off clear signals. Was she afraid? Angry? Guilty?

"I'm not the person you think I am," she said.

"How do you know what I think about you?"

"It's what everyone thinks about me—that I'm this quiet, plain, serious woman who never steps out of line. I'm responsible and sober and dependable and I never cause any trouble at all."

"Are you saying you have caused trouble?" he asked.

"More than you can imagine."

# COLORADO
# BODYGUARD

BY
CINDI MYERS

Published in Great Britain 2015
by Mills & Boon, an imprint of Harlequin (UK) Limited,
Eton House, 18-24 Paradise Road, Richmond, Surrey, TW9 1SR

© 2015 Cynthia Myers

ISBN: 978-0-263-25315-3

46-0815

Harlequin (UK) Limited's policy is to use papers that are natural, renewable and recyclable products and made from wood grown in sustainable forests. The logging and manufacturing processes conform to the legal environmental regulations of the country of origin.

Printed and bound in Spain
by CPI, Barcelona

**Cindi Myers** is an author of more than fifty novels. When she's not crafting new romance plots, she enjoys skiing, gardening, cooking, crafting and daydreaming. A lover of small-town life, she lives with her husband and two spoiled dogs in the Colorado mountains.

For Denise

# Chapter One

The canyon tore a deep gash in the open landscape. Sheer rock walls plunged to a river that was invisible below, lost in blackness. Darker red and gray rock painted the chasm walls in fanciful shapes that resembled two warring Chinese dragons, engaged in a battle that had been going on for centuries.

Sophie Montgomery stood at the edge of the overlook, fighting waves of vertigo as she tried to peer down into the canyon's depths. She struggled to imagine her sister, Lauren, standing in this same, desolate spot. Lauren had battled plenty of demons in her life; which one had brought her to this lonely, forbidding place?

*Lauren, where are you?* Sophie sent the silent plea across the canyon, but only wind and the distant hum of traffic answered.

She shivered again, despite the summer heat, and turned away from the overlook and headed back to her car, walking past an RV and a mom and two children posing in front of the canyon while Dad snapped the picture. They all looked thrilled to be here, though Sophie had never understood the attraction of a camping vacation. She and Lauren had always agreed that getaways should involve nice hotels, preferably with swimming pools and room service. One more reason it didn't make sense that Lauren had come to what must be one of the most remote spots in her adopted home state.

Sophie slid back behind the wheel of her rental car and jammed the key into the ignition. She didn't want to be here, but then, she hadn't especially wanted to be any of the other places that looking out for Lauren had taken her over the years. The only difference was that this time felt scarier. More hopeless. Lauren had done some crazy, wild things over the years, but she'd never stayed gone this long before. And she'd never been in a place where Sophie couldn't reach her. Sometimes, when Lauren was going through a really bad spell, Sophie was the only one who *could* reach her.

She backed out of her parking space and turned the car around, headed toward the park entrance. The police in Denver had been kind—sympathetic, even. But they had found no evidence that Lauren had been abducted, and given her recent history, they suspected she'd run away—or worse. "We understand your sister struggled with depression," the detective who had spoken to her said.

"She was handling it," Sophie had told him. "She was under a doctor's care."

His look was full of sympathy and little hope.

She checked the time on her phone. Five minutes until her appointment with a member of the special task force assigned to deal with crimes in the area. This time, she'd be more assertive. She would make the officer understand that Lauren wouldn't have run away. And she wouldn't have taken her own life. She was in trouble and they had to help.

Lauren had no one else to speak for her; it was up

to Sophie to look after her little sister, just as she'd always done.

She turned the car into the gravel lot in front of the portable building that served as headquarters for The Ranger Brigade—the interagency task force focused on fighting crime on public lands in western Colorado. A hot wind blasted her as she exited the car, whipping her shoulder-length brown hair into her eyes and sending a tumbleweed bobbing across her path. She stared at the beach-ball-sized sphere of dried weeds as it bounced across the pavement and into the brush across the road. The whole scene was like something out of a Wild West movie, as foreign from her life back in Madison, Wisconsin, as she could imagine.

As she made her way up a gravel walkway toward the building, a large dog—blond with a black muzzle and tail, like a German shepherd, but smaller—loped from around the side of the building. Sophie froze, heart pounding, struggling to breathe. The dog kept running toward her, tongue lolling, teeth glinting in the bright sun. She closed her eyes, fighting wave after wave of paralyzing fear.

"Lotte! Down!"

Sophie opened her eyes to see the dog immediately stop and lie down. A young man trotted around the side of the building. Tall and muscular, with closely cropped brown hair, he wore tan trousers and a tan long-sleeved shirt. "Don't worry, she's harmless," he called.

Sophie shifted her attention back to the dog, reminding herself to breathe. The dog grinned up at her, tongue hanging out. To most people she probably did look harmless. But Sophie wasn't most people.

"Can I help you?" the man asked as he drew closer.

Green eyes studied her, fine lines fanning from the corners, though she had a sense that he wasn't much older than her own thirty. The buffeting wind and too-bright sun didn't seem to bother him. In fact, he looked right at home against the backdrop of cactus and stunted pinion. He could have been an old-west lawman, with a silver star pinned to his chest, or a cowboy, ready to ride the range—any of those strong, romantic archetypes with the power to make a woman swoon.

Except she hadn't come here to ogle the local stud lawman, she reminded herself. Even if guys like him paid any attention to quiet bookworms like her. "I'm Sophie Montgomery. I have an appointment with the Rangers," she said.

"Right. Officer Rand Knightbridge." He offered his hand. "Come on in and we'll get started."

She took his hand, but released it quickly, focused on the dog who sat quietly at his side. It was a powerful animal, its eyes alert, as if at any moment it might lunge. "I'm afraid of dogs," she said, and took a step back.

He stopped and looked from her to the dog. "Lotte is very well trained," he said. "She won't hurt you, I promise."

"I didn't say it was a rational fear, I said I was afraid." Why did people always want to argue with her about this? No one ever tried to understand.

"Sure. I'll put her inside, in another room."

"All right. I'll wait out here."

He glanced at her again, then turned and snapped his fingers. "Lotte! Come!"

The dog fell into step beside him, gazing up at him adoringly.

She crossed her arms over her chest and tried not to

feel self-conscious. The windows on the Rangers' head-quarters were covered by blinds, but she had a feeling she was being watched. She fought the urge to stick her tongue out at whoever was looking, but that compulsion died when she reminded herself why she was here. She needed for these people to take her concerns seriously.

After a moment, during which she gave up trying to keep the wind from whipping her hair into her eyes, the front door to the trailer opened and Officer Knight-bridge waved to her. "The coast is clear," he said. "It's safe to come in."

She made her way up the walkway and through the door he held open for her. The office itself was Spartan and utilitarian, with industrial carpet and simple fur-nishings. "Let's use the conference room, back here," Knightbridge said, leading her to another open doorway.

A woman at a computer looked up and smiled at her as they passed and two other uniformed officers glanced her way but didn't acknowledge her. In the conference room, Officer Knightbridge pulled out a folding chair at the scarred table, then took a similar chair across from her. "How can I help you, Ms. Montgomery?" he asked.

"My sister, Lauren Starling, has been missing since May twenty-eighth. That's when she left for a week's vacation, but no one's seen or heard from her since. The Denver Police Department suggested I contact you to see how the investigation into her disappearance is pro-gressing."

There was a flicker of confusion in his green eyes. He shifted in his seat. "The Denver Police Department told you we were investigating your sister's disappearance."

"I understand her car was found abandoned very near here."

"Yes, I believe it was."

"And your organization deals with crime in the park?"

"The park and surrounding public lands."

"So, naturally, I assumed you're investigating my sister's disappearance."

As she'd talked, the lines on his forehead had deepened. The metal folding chair squeaked as he shifted position again. "Ms. Montgomery…"

"Please, call me Sophie." She wanted him to trust her, to confide in her, even.

"Ms. Montgomery, a car registered to your sister was found at the Dragon Point overlook in the park. There were no signs of violence, no notes and nothing else that pointed to violence. Park rangers conducted a search for your sister and found nothing. They had the car towed to an impound lot and contacted Denver police, and they also notified us to be on the lookout for her."

"I know all that," she said, trying to quell her impatience. "That's why I'm here. I want to know what you've discovered since then."

His expression grew even more pained. "After you called, I reviewed what little information we have. No one has seen or heard from your sister. The Denver police led us to believe your sister had come here of her own free will."

"She may have come here voluntarily, but she didn't just walk away from her car, her home, her job, her friends and her family." Sophie fought to keep the agitation from her voice. "Something has happened to her."

"The report I read said that your sister has a history of depression."

Here it was, the excuse they all gave for not taking Lauren's disappearance more seriously. "She's recently been diagnosed with bipolar disorder—what people used to call manic depression. She was in treatment, on medication and doing well."

"The report we received said she was recently divorced."

"Yes." Lauren had adored Phil; she'd been crushed when he announced he'd fallen in love with a woman he worked with. She'd had to cope not only with the end of her marriage, but also with the humiliation of his very public infidelity. But she was rallying. "My sister is much stronger than people give her credit for," Sophie said. "I talked to her only two days before she disappeared and she was very upbeat, excited about a new project at work."

"The police report also said she'd been put on probation at the TV station—that she was in danger of losing her job."

"She told me she wasn't worried about that—that this new project would prove how valuable she was."

This seemed to spark some interest in him. "Did she say what the project was?"

"No. She didn't like to talk about things like that until after they were complete. She was superstitious that way."

The frown returned. "Ms. Montgomery...Sophie." He leaned toward her, elbows on the table, hands loosely clasped. "Do you know the number one reason automobiles are abandoned within the park?"

"No." But clearly he was going to tell her. And the expression in his eyes told her she wouldn't like what she heard.

"For whatever reason, national parks are popular places for people to take their own lives. The canyon seems to offer what some perceive as an easy way out. If they don't drive right off the cliff, they park the car and jump. When a Ranger sees a car parked in the same place for days, he knows he may be looking at a possible suicide. And when the missing person is known to have been depressed…" He spread his hands wide, allowing her to fill in the rest of the thought.

But she refused to go there. "So you're telling me you haven't even investigated my sister's disappearance? She's been missing a month and no one is looking for her?"

"You need to prepare yourself." He sat back in his chair, his face calm, eyes still locked to hers. "There's a good chance your sister is no longer alive."

RAND HAD PUT his assessment of her sister's situation as delicately as he knew how, but he could see by the pain and anger in Sophie Montgomery's brown eyes that he'd been too blunt. Despite all the evidence pointing to this conclusion, she didn't believe her sister had committed suicide. Without a body she'd never believe, and unfortunately, the vastness and remoteness of the parklands made finding a body difficult—sometimes impossible. "I'm sorry," he said. "I wish I had better news for you."

And he wished he had more time for her. So much of his job involved dealing with the dregs of society—drug dealers and killers and people who preyed on the innocent. It was nice to sit with a pretty woman who dressed well and had a soft voice and manicured hands, and just talk.

If only their topic of conversation had been more pleasant. And if only he had more time to listen to her soft, educated voice. But everyone on the task force was under pressure to root out the criminals who'd turned a sleepy corner of Colorado into a center for drug dealing, human trafficking and all manner of violent crime. They'd made some arrests and succeeded in slowing the flow of drugs and illegal aliens, but they'd yet to find the person or persons overseeing the whole operation. They were certain someone was in charge, and had ideas about who that might be, but still lacked the evidence they needed.

Meanwhile, perpetual thorn in their side Richard Prentice, a billionaire who'd made a name for himself causing trouble for local, state and federal authorities, continued to harangue about the need to disband the task force altogether. He filed lawsuits claiming the officers harassed him, held press conferences to point out how much taxpayers spent to fund the Rangers and how little they received in return. And all the while, he sat in his mansion on private land adjacent to the park, protected by his money and a team of lawyers. As far as Rand was concerned, Richard Prentice was suspect number one when it came to crime in the area, but as his boss, Captain Graham Ellison, so often reminded him, being a jerk didn't make a man guilty.

And being a jerk wasn't winning Rand any points with Sophie Montgomery. "My sister did not commit suicide," she said. "I don't care how many times you or the police in Denver or anyone else tell me so. I know her better than anyone, and she wouldn't have done that." She opened her purse and took out a small spiral notebook. "I came here today to convince you that Lauren is worth looking for. The least you can do is hear me out."

Her eyes, full of so much determination…and not a little fear, met his. In that moment, he saw all it had taken for her to come here, knowing that pursuing her quest might only lead to the end of all hope for her sister. Her courage moved him, and fueled his growing attraction to this quiet, determined woman. "Of course," he said. "I'll be happy to listen to what you have to say. Would you mind if I brought in my commander and some other officers, as well?"

"No, not at all." Her lower lip trembled, but she quickly brought it under control. "Thank you."

He resisted the urge to cover her hand with his own; she might take his gesture of comfort the wrong way. He left the conference room, shutting the door behind him, and found Graham in his office. "Lauren Starling's sister is here," he said. "She doesn't think Lauren ran away or killed herself. She thinks she might be in real trouble."

Graham, a big man with the imposing demeanor of the US Marine he had once been, looked up from a stack of files. "Does she have any information that would help us find her sister?" he asked.

"I don't know, but I thought we should hear her out."

"All right. Who else is here?"

"Carmen and Simon were in the computer room a little while ago. And Marco is around somewhere."

"Then round them up and ask them to report to the conference room. Maybe one of us will spot something in the sister's story that will help."

Ten minutes later, they all converged on the conference room. Sophie shrank a little as they crowded into the room—a mass of brown uniforms, all male except for Colorado Bureau of Investigations officer Carmen Redhorse. Carmen sat on one side of Sophie. Rand sat across from her; he wanted to be able to see her expressive face as she talked. He often learned more about people from their body language and emotions than their words.

"Ms. Montgomery, I'm Captain Graham Ellison. These are officers Simon Woolridge, Carmen Redhorse and Marco Cruz. I understand you have some information to share with us about your sister, Lauren Starling."

"Yes." She glanced at Rand and he nodded encouragingly. She looked down at her notebook. "I spoke with my sister on May twenty-sixth, and she was very upbeat, excited about a new project she was working on—one she said would prove to the television station that she was too valuable to let go. She'd been to see her doctor recently and she said she was doing really well on her medication. She had been through some hard things recently, but she was looking forward to the future. She wasn't a woman who was despondent, or who wanted to take her life."

"What kind of medication?" Graham asked.

Sophie's face flushed, but she kept her chin up, and met the captain's direct gaze. "About six months ago, Lauren was diagnosed with bipolar disorder. She'd struggled for years, primarily with mania. The stress of the divorce and job pressures made it worse and there had been a couple of…episodes that forced her to take some time off work. But with the proper diagnosis and treatment, she'd been doing much better. And as I said, she was very excited about this project."

"What was the project?" Carmen asked.

"I don't know. But something to do with work, I think."

"She was the prime-time news anchor at Channel Nine in Denver?" Simon, an agent with Immigration and Customs Enforcement, asked.

"Yes. And as I believe you've already learned, she had been told her job was in jeopardy."

"Why was that?" Graham asked.

The worried furrow in her forehead deepened. "She wouldn't say outright, and the station refused to talk to me, but I suspect it was because of her sometimes erratic behavior in the months prior to her diagnosis as bipolar. She missed some work and showed up other times unprepared. But she was doing much better in the weeks before she disappeared. She was happy to know what was going on and was following her doctor's orders and feeling better."

"But that didn't stop the station from threatening to let her go?" Carmen said.

"Ratings had fallen. Lauren told me she was going to do something that would boost ratings."

"Maybe she came here to hide." Marco Cruz, with the DEA, spoke so quietly Rand wasn't sure he'd heard him correctly at first.

"Hide?" Sophie asked. "From what?"

"Maybe she faked her disappearance to draw attention to herself and to the station, and then she planned to emerge after a few weeks in the headlines." Marco shrugged. "People have faked all kinds of things for attention, from gunshot wounds and muggings to their own deaths."

"Lauren isn't faking anything," Sophie said. "She started her career as an investigative reporter. I think she had a lead on a big crime and came here to report on it."

"What kind of crime?" Graham shifted in his chair, the only sign that he was growing impatient.

"I don't know. It would have to be something big, if she was going to boost ratings."

"And she didn't tell you anything?" Carmen spoke slowly, thoughtfully.

"No—just that she was working on a new project that would fix everything."

"And she never said anything about coming to Montrose or Black Canyon Park or anything like that?" Simon snapped off the question, as if interrogating a suspect. Rand knew this was just his way, but Sophie bridled at this approach.

"No," she said, and pressed her lips together, clamming up.

"How often did you talk to her?" Rand asked.

She turned toward him. "Once a week or so. Sometimes more often."

"Anyone else she was close to? A best friend? Neighbors?"

"She still talked to her ex-husband, Phil, occasionally. Have you interviewed him?"

Rand frowned. "Why do you think we should talk to him?"

"Aren't husbands—or ex-husbands—always the first people police suspect when someone disappears?"

"It depends on the case," Graham said. "Did Lauren and Phil Starling have a contentious relationship?"

She flushed. "No. I mean, she wasn't happy about the divorce—he was cheating on her, after all. And he left her to be with the other woman."

"But she'd already granted the divorce, right?" Simon asked. "She didn't put any obstacles in his way."

"No. She even agreed to pay support, since she made more money than he did."

"So he didn't really have any reason to follow her from Denver to Montrose and do her harm," Rand said.

"We don't know that for sure. And you won't know until you talk to him." She looked stubborn, chin up, mouth set in a firm line.

"What about other family members?" he asked. "Brothers, sisters, parents?"

She shook her head. "There's just the two of us. Our parents were killed in a car accident when I was a sophomore in college. Lauren was a senior in high school."

"So you're used to looking after her," he said.

"Yes."

"Maybe she resented that," Simon said. "Maybe she purposely kept things from you."

"I'm sure she kept a great deal from me. Whatever you think, I didn't try to run her life. But I know her. She wouldn't take her own life. And you can quote statistics all day long, but even if—and it's a huge *if* in my mind—even if she wanted to kill herself, why would she travel five hours away from her home to disappear in a national park?"

"Sometimes people choose a place that's meaningful to them," Marco said. "One they associate with memories or special people."

"She'd never been here before. This park meant nothing special to her. She loved the city. She wasn't a hiker or a camper or anything like that."

"So why was she here?" Graham brought them back to the essential question. "What was this story you think she was working on?"

"I don't know, but it must have been something major, if she thought it could save her career."

"If she wanted to report on a major crime, you'd think she'd stay in Denver," Carmen said.

"Except you guys are here." Sophie sat up straighter,

and looked them each in the eye. "Why form a special task force if there isn't something big going on here? I did my homework. I know about the drug busts, the human-trafficking ring and the murder of that pilot. Maybe Lauren had uncovered something to do with all that."

"She never came to us, or to local law enforcement with that information," Graham said.

"Maybe she never had time," Sophie said.

"In the course of your research, did you see the newspaper articles about your sister's disappearance?" Graham asked. "Written by a local reporter who's taken an interest in the story."

"Emma Wade. Yes, I read the stories. I plan to talk to her, but I came to you first."

Rand watched the captain closely. Only those who knew him well would register the slight flush that reddened the tips of his ears at the mention of reporter Emma Wade—soon to be Emma Ellison. Her reporting on Lauren Starling's disappearance had put her at odds with the gruff commander at first, but now they were engaged.

"Ms. Wade came to us with her concerns about your sister and we have followed every lead," Graham said. "But there's nothing there." He slid back his chair and stood. "I'm sorry, Ms. Montgomery, I wish I had better news for you. If you find out something more, don't hesitate to contact us."

The others started moving chairs and rising also. Carmen gave Sophie a sympathetic look and patted her shoulder. Sophie's expression clouded and Rand braced himself for a storm—of tears or anger, he wasn't sure which.

But she was stronger—and more determined—than he'd given her credit for. "Wait," she said. "There's one other thing that might tie her to this area—to your jurisdiction."

Graham paused on his way to the door. "What's that?"

She dug in her purse and held up a small rectangle of white cardboard. "I found this in her apartment. It was tucked into a book beside the bed—the police said they searched her apartment, but they obviously didn't feel this was significant."

Randall took the piece of thin cardboard and stared at the crisp black letters on its glossy finish.

"What is it?" Simon demanded.

"It's a business card." He turned it over and over, then looked up at his coworkers. "A business card for Richard Prentice."

# *Chapter Two*

Sophie tried to read the look that passed between the officers. The business card definitely interested them. "Do you know Richard Prentice?" she asked. "Have you asked him if he knows anything about my sister's disappearance?"

"You don't know Prentice?" Rand Knightbridge asked. "Your sister didn't mention him?"

"She never said anything about him. And I'm not from here, so I don't keep up with local people and events. I looked him up on the internet, but all I learned is that he's a very rich businessman and he has an estate near the park. That seems significant, don't you think? Maybe she came here to see him."

"Where are you from?" Captain Ellison asked.

"Madison, Wisconsin. Tell me about Richard Prentice."

"Like you said, he's a rich guy who owns a mansion near here," Officer Woolridge said, his sour expression making clear his opinion of Prentice.

"We should talk to him," Sophie said. "Maybe he knows why Lauren was here. Maybe she interviewed him for a story."

Again, Rand and the captain exchanged looks. "What is it?" she demanded. "What aren't you telling me?"

"Prentice is an agitator," Woolridge said. "He likes to make a lot of noise in the press and try to provoke a reaction from people he's trying to manipulate."

"What kind of reaction?"

"He wants money," Rand said. "His specialty is buying historically or environmentally sensitive property at rock-bottom prices, then threatening to destroy the property or to use it in some offensive way if the government, or sometimes a private conservation group, doesn't step in and pay the high price he demands."

"That's extortion," she said.

"And perfectly legal," the captain said. "If he owns the property, he's free to do almost anything he wants with it."

"That sounds like a story Lauren would want to cover," she said. "Maybe she came here from Denver to interview him."

"Or maybe he contacted her," Carmen Redhorse said. "He likes to use the press to communicate his demands."

"We need to talk to him," Sophie said again, her agitation rising. They all looked so calm and unconcerned. Couldn't they see how important this was?

"That's not so easy to do," Rand said. "Prentice has a team of lawyers running interference between him and anyone he doesn't want to talk to—in particular, members of this task force. Unless we charge him with a crime, which we have no evidence he's committed, or subpoena him as a witness, the chances of him answering any questions we have for him are slim to none."

More looks passed between them, but these were easier to read. "You may not believe this is worth pursuing, but I do," she said. "My sister did not commit suicide. She wasn't crazy. And if you won't help me find her, I'll find someone who will."

She shoved back from the table and started toward the door. Randall intercepted her. "Don't go," he said. "We'll do what we can to help." He looked at the captain. "Won't we?"

Captain Ellison nodded. "Start by retracing Ms. Starling's steps here in the county," he said. "Do you know where she was staying?"

"I don't," Sophie admitted.

"Canvass the local motels," the captain said. "Rand, you start there."

Sophie had hoped he would assign the woman, Carmen Redhorse, to the case. A woman would be more sensitive, and easier to work with, she thought. Officer Knightbridge, with his frightening dog and gruff manner, was just as likely to scare people away as to persuade them to help. But he wouldn't frighten her. "I want to go with you to talk to them," she said.

"That isn't possible," Rand said. "I can't take a civilian to question potential witnesses."

"Fine. Then I'll start contacting hotels and motels on my own. If I find anything, I'll let you know." It's what she should have done in the first place, as soon as she saw what a low priority the Denver police gave the case.

Once again, Rand stopped her before she reached the door, his tall, muscular frame blocking her path. She tried to duck around him, but he took hold of her arm, his grasp gentle, but firm. "We can charge you with interfering with a police investigation," he said.

"There wouldn't be an investigation if I hadn't come to you," she said, shaking him off. "Can you blame me if I have my doubts about how much trouble you'll go to to find Lauren? Whereas I know I won't stop until I learn the truth."

"Take her with you to the hotels and motels," Captain Ellison said. "The locals may open up to her. But, Ms. Montgomery?"

"Yes?" She turned to face him.

"Officer Knightbridge is in charge. Do what he tells you or we'll have you on a plane back to Wisconsin before you can blink twice."

She glanced at Rand, whose face remained impassive. "All right," she said. She'd play along, but she wouldn't let him stop her from doing what she thought was best for her sister. "When do we start?"

"How about now?" He opened the door and motioned for her to go ahead of him. "The sooner we get this over with, the better."

RAND'S ANNOYANCE WITH Sophie Montgomery was tempered by the undeniably distracting sway of her hips as she crossed the parking lot in front of him. No doubt her nose would be even further out of joint if she knew he was ogling her. Well, she didn't have anything to worry about. She was pretty, but far too prickly. And she was wasting his time. Her sister's connection to Richard Prentice was intriguing, but he doubted it would lead anywhere. Anyone could have a business card—maybe Prentice had sent it with one of his press releases touting his next attention-getting stunt. Lauren might even have had it for years. If it was important, why had she left it back in Denver?

"My vehicle is the FJ Cruiser with the grill between the back and the passenger compartment." He pointed out the black-and-white SUV. "You can wait for me there while I get my gear."

She crossed her arms over her chest. "I should follow you in my car."

"No, you shouldn't. We'll waste too much time trying to keep track of each other. I'll bring you back here when we're done."

She pressed her lips together in a disapproving line, but didn't argue. Even that didn't lessen her attractiveness. She wasn't actress-and-model gorgeous, like her famous sister, but she had a deeper beauty that went beyond the surface, enduring and natural, like the beauty of a wild animal.

And what was he doing wasting time musing on the attractiveness of this woman who clearly found little to like in him? He returned to the headquarters building and retrieved Lotte from the back room, where she'd been napping. As always, the Belgian Malinois greeted him enthusiastically, whipping her tail back and forth and grinning at him. At least here was a female who appreciated him. "Are you ready to go, girl?" he asked.

She responded with a sharp, happy bark. He rubbed her ears and clipped on the leash. Not that she needed it, but since Sophie was clearly skittish around dogs, he'd do what he could to keep her calm.

When Sophie saw them approaching, she turned the color of milk and plastered herself against the vehicle. "What are you doing with that dog?" she asked.

"Lotte is coming with us." He walked the dog past her to the rear of the vehicle.

"Oh, no. I can't ride in a car with a dog."

"She'll be in the back. And she is coming with us.

That's not negotiable. Lotte is as much a part of my gear as my weapon or my radio."

"I told you, I'm afraid of dogs."

She looked miserable, but he wasn't going to back down on this; he and Lotte were a team. "I promise I won't let her hurt you. And she'll be in the back of the cruiser, with a grate between us. You can pretend she isn't there."

She looked from the dog to him and back, then took a deep breath. "All right."

*Good girl.* But he only thought it—she might be insulted if he praised her the same way he did Lotte.

With Lotte safely secured in the back of the vehicle, he climbed into the driver's seat and Sophie buckled into the passenger seat. "Is this your first visit to the Black Canyon?" he asked as they passed the first of the park's eighteen overlooks into the canyon.

"Yes. I've been to Denver a couple of times to see Lauren, but we never left the city." She gazed out at a trio of RVs in the overlook parking lot. "I'm not much of an outdoor person."

"I'll admit the area around the canyon can look a little desolate at first, but there's really a lot of beauty here, once you get to know it," he said. *Just like some people.* "Not just the canyon itself, but the wilderness area around it. The wildflowers are just beginning to bloom, and the sunsets are spectacular."

"If you say so." She angled her body toward him. "No offense, officer, but I'm not here to sightsee. I came here to find my sister."

Right. And clearly she had no intention of getting friendly with the officer involved in the investigation into her sister's disappearance. Message received. "What will you do when you find her?"

"As soon as I'm sure she's safe, I'll go back home to Madison."

"What's in Madison?"

"What do you mean, what's in Madison? My life is in Madison."

"I just meant, what do you do there?"

"I'm an assistant to the city manager."

It sounded like a dull job to him, but he wasn't about to say so. "How long have you lived there?" he asked.

"Five years."

"Are you married? Any children?"

"That is none of your business."

Of course not. He was just trying to make conversation. He focused on driving, both hands gripping the steering wheel. The silence stretched between them.

"I'm not married, and I don't have children. I'm not even dating anyone in particular," she said after a long moment.

"You were right," he said. "It's none of my business."

"What about you, Officer Knightbridge? Are you married?"

Was she asking because she was truly interested, or merely to even the score? "The only woman in my life right now is Lotte." It was a line he'd used before; if the woman he said it to smiled, he figured they might hit it off.

Sophie didn't smile. Instead, she glanced back at the dog, who sat in her usual position, facing forward, ears up, expression eager and alert. He understood that Lotte could be a little intimidating, if you didn't know her. After all, part of her job was to intimidate, even subdue, criminals. "She's really a sweetheart," he said. "And she's had years of training. She'd only hurt someone to protect me."

"I'll keep that in mind." But her grim expression didn't ease.

"Why are you afraid of dogs?" he asked. He knew such people existed, but he didn't understand their fear. He liked all dogs. And Lotte was his best friend, not merely his working partner.

"I was bitten as a child. I had to have plastic surgery." She indicated a faint scar on the side of her face, barely visible alongside her mouth.

He winced. "I can see how that would be traumatic, but I promise, Lotte won't hurt you. Think of her as an overly hairy officer with a tail."

As he'd hoped, the absurd description made her mouth quirk up almost in a smile. "What kind of dog is she?" she asked.

"A Belgian Malinois. A herding dog, like a German shepherd, but smaller. She only weighs sixty pounds."

"She looks huge to me."

"By police-dog standards, she's on the small side, but she's an expert tracker."

"Too bad she can't track down my sister."

"She might be able to, if we knew the right place to look."

She stared out the window at the passing landscape of open rangeland and scrubby trees. "Where do we start?"

"Like the captain said, we'll ask around at the local motels and hotels, see if anyone remembers her."

"Why didn't you do that before?"

A reasonable question from someone to whom the missing person was one of the most important people on earth. "I don't want to sound callous," he said, "but with no sign of foul play and no one pressing us on the matter, your sister's whereabouts weren't a high priority. We've had murders and drug cases and even suspected terrorism to deal with. We only have so many people and so many hours in the day."

"Then I guess it's a good thing I came down here," she said.

"Don't think no one cares about your sister," he said. "Remember, that reporter has been trying to find out what happened to her. But she hasn't come up with any new information, either."

"How do you know she hasn't come up with any new information? Maybe she didn't bother telling you because she thought you wouldn't pay attention."

"Oh, she knows we'd pay attention. She's engaged to the captain. If she found out anything important, she wouldn't give him any peace until he followed up on it." He glanced at her. "So you see, we're on the same side here. And maybe we'll find out something useful today—provided your sister wasn't staying with a friend, or camping out."

"Lauren definitely isn't the camping type, and I couldn't find that she knew anyone here in town—except Mr. Prentice."

"We've been watching his place pretty closely and we haven't seen any sign of your sister there."

She tensed, and leaned toward him. "Why are you watching Mr. Prentice? Is it because he's…what was the word the other officer used—an agitator?"

Prentice liked to agitate all right, but Rand didn't care so much about that. Part of wearing a uniform was knowing some people didn't like you on principle. "Mr. Prentice's estate is an inholding, completely surrounded by public land. It makes sense for us to keep an eye on his place." He hoped that was enough to satisfy Sophie's curiosity. He couldn't tell her they suspected the billionaire was using his wealth for more than investing in real estate and businesses. Their investigations had linked him, albeit tenuously, to everything from drug runners to foreign terrorists. Sooner or later, the Rangers were going to find the evidence they needed to make him pay for his crimes.

"How many motels and hotels are there in the area?" Sophie's question pulled Rand's attention back to her, and today's search for her missing sister.

"A bunch," he said. "But we can narrow the field by focusing on the most likely places for your sister to stay. She strikes me as a classy woman, so we can move the obvious roach motels to the bottom of the list. Where do you think she'd be?"

She considered the question for a moment, brow furrowed and lips pursed. "She'd probably pick the first nice-looking place she came to when she drove into town. She wasn't the type to spend a lot of time driving around, looking."

"That would be either the Country Inn or the Mountain View."

"No chains?" she asked.

"Would your sister prefer a chain? There's a Holiday Inn and a Ramada closer to the center of town."

"No, she wouldn't care about that, as long as the place looked clean."

He drove to the Country Inn first. Red geraniums bloomed in window boxes against rows of white-framed windows trimmed in white shutters. A water wheel turned in a flower-lined pond near the entrance, splashing water that sparkled in the sun. "Lauren would have liked this," Sophie said.

Rand parked, but left the car running, with the air-conditioning on, to avoid overheating the dog. "Lotte, wait here," he said. "We'll be back in a minute."

"You talk to her as if she understands you," Sophie said as they crossed the parking lot.

"Of course she understands me. Do you have a picture of your sister with you?"

"Yes." She took her phone from her purse and flipped to a shot of Lauren Starling seated in a restaurant booth, smiling at the camera and holding up a colorful cocktail. "I took this when she visited Wisconsin for my birthday last year."

He didn't miss the sadness in her voice. "It's a great picture," he said. "We'll need it to show to the clerk."

The lobby of the motel was busy, with a couple flipping through brochures at one end of the counter, a pair of tweens choosing sodas from a machine and a businessman checking in. The clerk behind the counter was probably a college student from the local university, Rand decided. She had long blond hair, dyed bright pink at the ends, and half a dozen earrings in each ear. When she was done with the businessmen, she smiled at them. "May I help you?"

He showed his badge and the clerk's eyes widened. "We're looking for a missing woman," he said. "Lauren Starling. She may have stayed here about a month ago." He nodded to Sophie and she held out the phone to show Lauren's picture.

"I'm her sister," Sophie said. "This is Lauren."

The clerk's eyes widened. "You say she's missing?"

"Yes. Do you remember her, or could you check your records?"

"I don't have to check the records. She was here. I remember."

SOPHIE FUMBLED WITH the phone, almost dropping it. "Lauren was here? Are you sure?" Her voice shook. Rand put his hand on her shoulder, steadying her.

The clerk nodded. "I recognized her from the TV, but she was obviously trying to hide her identity. I mean, she registered as Jane Smith or something like that, and paid cash for the room."

"You didn't think that was suspicious?" Rand asked.

"Well, yeah, but people do weird things all the time, and you learn not to ask questions." She tucked a strand of cotton-candy-colored hair behind one ear. "Then she met up with a guy, and I figured they were having an affair." She shrugged. "It happens."

"A guy?" Sophie leaned across the counter. "Who was the guy? What did he look like?"

Rand squeezed her shoulder to quiet her. She was going to scare off the clerk, who looked alarmed. He double-checked the girl's name badge. "I promise you won't get into any trouble, Marlee. Just tell us what you remember."

She shrugged again. "He was just a real ordinary-looking guy—early forties, maybe. Light brown hair cut short, not too tall, not too big."

"Did he register also?"

She shook her head. "And that's really the only reason I remember him. I was getting off my shift and I saw him standing with Jane Smith outside her room. Then he took a suitcase—one of those little overnight bags—

from his car and went inside with her. That's against the rules—to have someone staying in the room who isn't registered, but it was no skin off my nose, you know? I was in a hurry to get home and I wasn't going to take the trouble to go back inside and report her. Like I said, it happens."

"Why didn't you say anything to the police?" Sophie asked. "Didn't you see the story about Lauren being missing?"

"I knew she wasn't doing the news lately, but they said something about her being on vacation, and then I just kind of forgot. I don't watch a lot of TV and I mean, I wasn't a hundred percent certain it was her, and I didn't want to look stupid—and you're the first people to come around asking questions."

Rand didn't have to look at Sophie to know she was glaring at him. Maybe she was right. Maybe they should have taken her sister's disappearance more seriously and made it a point to ask questions before now, but there was nothing he could do to change the past. All he could do was try to do a better job going forward.

"Had you ever seen the man before?" he asked. "Or have you seen him since?"

Marlee shook her head so hard her earrings jangled. "I don't think so. But like I said, he was nothing special."

"Was it this guy?" He pulled up a website on his phone that featured an article about Richard Prentice and turned the phone so that she could see it.

She squinted at the photo of a man in his late forties, with thick dark hair, graying at the temples. "The guy I saw was younger, with lighter hair. That's not him."

"Thanks." He pocketed the phone once more. "You've been a big help. We might have more questions for you later. In the meantime, could you tell us when Ms. Starling checked out?"

She went to the computer and began typing. "The reservation was prepaid and she did express checkout," she said. "The next morning. So she was only here for the one night."

"Express checkout meaning she left the key in the room and you never saw her?" Rand asked.

"That's right. I wasn't on duty the next morning, but the record shows express checkout."

"We'll want to talk to whoever was on duty that morning."

"That would be Candy. She comes on at three today if you want to come back."

"Someone will stop by. Thanks."

He could tell Sophie wanted to say more, but he ushered her back to the car. "Maybe they have surveillance pictures," she said. "We could ask to see them."

"We could—and we will. But chances are they're on a tape loop that gets wiped every twenty-four to seventy-two hours. Otherwise the databank fills up with hours and hours of images of empty parking lots." He started the car. "Does the man she described sound like anyone you know? A boyfriend of your sister's? Her ex-husband?"

"Her ex was a big blond, and she wasn't dating anyone. She would have told me if she was."

"Maybe not if he was married, or she had some other reason to keep the relationship secret."

"She would have told me."

She sounded so certain. But how could she know another person so well? Then again, he was an only child. Maybe some siblings were closer. "Everybody has secrets," he said.

"Lauren and I don't have secrets from each other. We're the only family we have left, and we've stayed close."

The fervor in her voice struck a faint, almost forgotten longing within him. Growing up as an only child to older parents, he'd often wished for a brother or sister—someone who would share his background and upbringing, and always be there. "I hope if anything ever happens to me, I have someone like you fighting for me." He meant the words. As much as he still thought they were wasting time searching for her sister, who was probably off in Cancún with her boyfriend, he admired Sophie's determination to find and help Lauren.

The soft strains of classical music rose from the floorboard near her feet. "That's my phone," she said, reaching for her purse. She fished out a pink iPhone and glanced at the screen. "I need to get this."

"Go right ahead." He focused on driving the cruiser through heavy traffic near a school zone, but he couldn't help overhearing her side of the conversation.

"Hello?…Yes, this is she…Oh! Thank you for returning my call…Yes…Yes…Well, as I tried to explain in my message…All right…Yes…That would be fine…Yes…Goodbye."

She ended the call and rested the phone in her lap, her expression troubled. "Everything okay?" he asked.

"I think so." She turned to him, her determined expression once more in place. "That was Richard Prentice. He wants to meet with me to talk about Lauren."

# Chapter Three

Sophie clutched the dash to steady herself as Rand swerved the cruiser to the side of the road, tires squealing and gravel popping as they skidded to a stop. He shifted into Park and turned to face her. From the back, the dog let out a bark of protest. "Sorry, girl," he called. He gripped the steering wheel tightly, radiating strength and more than a little anger. "You told us you didn't know Richard Prentice," he said, his voice low, almost a growl. "That you'd never heard of him."

"I don't!" she protested. "I hadn't."

"Then how does he have your cell number?"

"After I found his business card in Lauren's apartment, I called the number and left a message. When he didn't call back after a couple of days, I figured he wasn't interested." She was not going to let him make her feel guilty about something anyone in her position would have done.

"And you conveniently neglected to tell us any of this," he said.

"Because I didn't think it mattered." She retrieved her purse from the floor and stuffed the phone back into it. "Why are you upset, anyway?" she asked. "Now you don't have to trouble yourself to talk to the guy—I'll do it."

"He wants to meet you somewhere?"

"He invited me to his house."

His glower was enough to make her flinch. All right, she'd had second thoughts about meeting a man she didn't know at his home, but she wasn't going to admit that to Rand, who seemed to think he could order her around.

"I'll go with you," he said.

"Excuse me, but you weren't invited."

"It's not a good idea for you to go to his house by yourself."

She sat up straighter, as if physically stiffening her spine would somehow increase her courage. "Why not? He's rich, not a criminal—or are you the one who's not telling me the whole story now?"

He rubbed his hands back and forth along the steering wheel. They were big, powerful hands, the nails cut short, the skin bronzed. They looked like hands that would be equally at home punching a guy or caressing a woman.

Okay, where had that thought come from? Obviously, all the testosterone this guy gave off was affecting her, and not in a good way.

"We have no proof Prentice is involved in any crimes, but he's a very powerful man and we suspect all his money doesn't come from legitimate sources." Rand glanced at her. "And he's a jerk."

That was all he could come up with? "Being a jerk doesn't make him dangerous."

"It doesn't make him safe, either."

"You're going to have to tell me more than that to persuade me he poses any threat."

The muscles along his jaw tightened, and she could hear his teeth grinding. After a few seconds, he released his death grip on the steering wheel. "This goes no further than this vehicle, all right?" he said.

She nodded. "All right."

"Last month, right after your sister disappeared, we broke up an illegal marijuana-growing operation and human-trafficking ring. The guy in charge had once worked for Prentice, though he swore they had no connection now. We think Prentice was overseeing the operation, but we couldn't prove it. Then, shortly after that, a pilot was murdered after he flew a weapon that had been stolen from the US military onto public land near Prentice's place."

"A weapon?"

"I can't elaborate, but Prentice had links to that, too. Again, we didn't have any proof to tie him directly, but if we're right and he's behind these crimes, we're talking about somebody who's proven he won't let anything—or anyone—stop him from getting his way."

"Now you're just trying to frighten me." The tactic was working, too, though she'd never admit it to him.

"You're right. I am trying to frighten you out of meeting with this guy I don't trust as far as I could throw him."

"If I make sure he's aware that other people—the task force—knows I'm meeting him, he won't try anything," she said. "Right?"

Instead of confirming her evaluation of the situation, he leaned forward and switched on his emergency flashers. "Did he say he knew something about your sister's disappearance?" he asked.

"No. He just said he'd be happy to talk with me about Lauren. He acted like he knew her. I mean, he called her Lauren and said she was a lovely person." The way he'd said it—"such a lovely person"—had been a little creepy, but that was probably just Rand's dislike of the guy rubbing off on her.

"When are you supposed to meet with him?"

"Why do you need to know that? So you can crash the meeting and scare him off?" It would be just like him to charge in, his dog barking and lunging, ruining everything.

"I won't scare him off. And I won't crash the meeting. I'll come as your escort."

"You told me yourself he doesn't like law officers. If you come along, he'll clam up and won't tell me anything."

"We won't tell him I'm a cop."

"Then how do I explain this random guy who invited himself along?"

"Tell him I'm your boyfriend and I'm very jealous and overprotective."

The words sent warmth flooding through her. Hormones again. It was getting pretty warm in this car. Maybe she should roll down the window. "That doesn't say much about me, that I'd hang out with a jealous and overprotective guy," she said.

"Just tell him I'm a friend." His expression softened. "Please. I've got good instincts and I don't have a good feeling about this."

The "please" did it—that and the fact that she was beginning to have her own reservations about a private meeting with Richard Prentice. He was probably harmless, and he might not know anything about her sister, but she should cover all the bases by talking to him, and also staying safe. "All right. You can come with me. But you have to not act like a cop."

"What do you mean by that?"

"I mean, no strong-arming the guy, or firing questions at him. Let me do the talking. And the dog has to stay behind."

He glanced at Lotte, clearly torn. "Nothing says cop like a police dog," she said.

"All right," he said. "But if he makes a wrong move, I won't keep quiet about it."

She sighed. And she'd thought questioning Richard Prentice would be the hard part—he'd probably be a piece of cake compared to handling Rand Knightbridge.

THE NEXT MORNING, Rand waited for Sophie in front of the duplex he rented in the south end of Montrose. Marco Cruz lived in the other half of the building, but he wasn't home today to give Rand a hard time about being reduced to wearing civilian clothes and leaving his weapons and his dog behind, like an ordinary civilian. But, given Prentice's animosity toward the Rangers, Rand's only choice was to make this visit incognito.

Sophie had insisted on driving, too, though it had been Rand's idea to have her pick him up at the duplex—just in case Prentice had someone watching Ranger headquarters. He wouldn't put it past the man.

Her rented sedan turned the corner and glided into his drive. He jerked open the door and climbed in even before she came to a full stop. "Hello, Rand." She lowered her sunglasses and looked him up and down.

"Do I pass the test?" he asked, buckling his seat belt. He'd dressed in khakis and a blue sports shirt with a subtle pinstripe. Nothing too fancy.

"You clean up nice, Officer." A smile played across lips outlined in cherry red.

"I could say the same about you." In addition to the red lipstick, she wore careful makeup that accented her big brown eyes and beautiful skin. Her hair was up, with tendrils curling around her temples. Her blue dress, of some silky material, clung in all the right places. She smelled good, too, like something expensive and exotic. She looked elegant and beautiful—the kind of woman who would appeal to a billionaire who could have anything, or anyone, he wanted.

He pushed the thought away. Sophie was too classy to go for a lowlife like Prentice. The man might have more money than kings, but money couldn't buy morals. "Have you thought of what you're going to say to him?" he asked as they headed out of town.

"I lay awake all night thinking about it. To start, I want to know how he knows Lauren, and when was the last time he talked to her. I'll ask if he knows why she was in the area."

"It'll be interesting to find out if he really knows anything."

The entrance to Prentice's estate was unmarked by any sign but, unlike other properties in the area, featured a stone guardhouse set back thirty yards from the road and a heavy iron gate. A guard stepped out to meet them. Sophie lowered her window. "I'm Sophie Montgomery," she said. "I have a meeting with Mr. Prentice."

"Yes, Ms. Montgomery, we've been expecting you." He nodded to Rand. "Who's he?"

"This is my friend Jake Peters." It was the name they'd agreed on, in case Prentice had a roster of the task force. Jacob was Rand's middle name and Peters was his mother's maiden name.

"Mr. Peters is not on our list of authorized guests," the guard said.

"I am a single woman and Mr. Prentice is a stranger to me," she said frostily, also as they'd rehearsed. "He can't expect me to come to his house, in this remote location, alone."

"Wait here a moment." The guard retreated to the stone hut and made a phone call. He was back a moment later. "Someone will be along in a moment to escort you to the main house. Wait here."

"How many houses does he have?" Sophie whispered when the guard had walked away.

"I think there are a couple of places where the help live," Rand said.

A Jeep roared down the road in front of them and slid to a stop inches from the rental car's bumper. The driver, also dressed in desert camo, motioned for them to follow, then turned the Jeep and headed back up the road.

They drove up the gravel drive, around a curve and up a hill. At the top, Sophie gasped and stomped on the brake. "You've got to be kidding," she said.

The place was definitely a castle, but more Disney than Dusseldorf. Constructed of gray stone, it featured crenellated battlements, towers and turrets…even a drawbridge, though there was no moat. "It's like something you'd see in Vegas," she said.

"Being rich obviously doesn't guarantee good taste," Rand said. "But I suspect it's another of his ploys to goad the government into buying him out. He tried to get the feds to buy the land and incorporate it into the national park. When that didn't work, he threatened to build a triple-X theater right at the park entrance, but the county passed an ordinance making such places illegal. Finally, he built this monstrosity. I suspect he thought if he created a big enough eyesore, the public would push for its removal."

"But you can't see the building from the road."

"You get a great view of it from the Pioneer Point overlook in the park, though. It actually blocks a view of the Curecanti Needle, one of the most famous natural rock formations in the country."

She shook her head and drove on.

They parked under an arching portico and a stone-faced servant who looked and acted like a bodyguard ushered them into a great hall reminiscent of a medieval stronghold. "Mr. Prentice will see you in the library," the man said, and led the way to a pair of large wooden doors.

The room in question was indeed filled with books, and with a Native-American pottery collection that, if it was authentic, would command hundreds of thousands of dollars. Rand wondered if any of it was legal, or if Prentice had acquired it from the network of grave robbers who ransacked the pueblos.

"This place is a real fortress," he said, standing close to Sophie in the middle of the room. "I saw at least three guards from the hallway."

"You don't know that they're guards."

"Right. Maybe he's recruiting his own football team. Why does one man need that kind of protection?"

"I imagine someone with a lot of money could be a target."

"Or someone with a lot of enemies."

"So sorry to keep you waiting."

They turned as Richard Prentice approached. He looked small in the massive room, with more gray in his hair than in the pictures Rand had seen and a slight paunch showing in spite of his expertly cut suit. He walked forward to meet them, hand outstretched to Sophie. "Ms. Montgomery, I'm delighted to meet you." He ignored Rand completely, which was fine by him. He had no desire to shake this man's hand.

Rand followed Sophie to a love seat upholstered in butter-colored leather and sat beside her. Prentice took the matching chair opposite. "Your message said you're looking for your sister, Lauren Starling. How can I help you?"

"She's been missing since late May," Sophie said. "Park rangers found her car in Black Canyon of the Gunnison Park, but no one has seen any trace of Lauren. I found your business card in her apartment in Denver and I wondered if she'd been to see you."

"I'd heard of her disappearance, but I'm afraid I can't be of any help to you. I haven't seen Lauren in four or five months, at least."

"How do you know her?" Rand asked.

Sophie shot him a pained look. All right, he'd promised to keep his mouth shut, but honestly, Prentice was so oily and smooth, Rand wanted to put him on edge.

"How did you and Lauren know each other?" Sophie asked, her voice soft, less demanding than Rand's.

"We met at a fund-raiser in Denver earlier this year, to raise money for an orphanage in Guatemala that is a special interest of mine."

Prentice was interested in Guatemala, all right—as a source for the illegal workers he used in his drug and prostitution operations. Some of the victims of the human-trafficking ring the task force had broken up last month had been from Guatemala.

"We ran into each other in the bar after the dinner," Prentice continued. "She'd clearly had a little too much to drink and I was concerned, so I offered to take her for coffee. We ended up talking for quite a while. She confided her troubles to me—the end of her marriage, her recent diagnosis of mental illness and her worries over her job."

He definitely knew a lot about Lauren, though he could have gleaned all that from newspaper accounts of her disappearance. "Did you stay in touch?" Sophie asked. "Have you talked to her since that night?"

"A few times. Just casual phone calls." He leaned forward, one hand on Sophie's knee. "I hope it doesn't distress you to know this, but your sister was a very troubled woman. She tried to keep a positive face on things around the people she loved, but she was able to let her guard down more with me. I urged her to seek professional help, but she resisted the idea."

Sophie shifted slightly and gave Rand a warning look, perhaps sensing that he'd been ready to take Prentice's hand off at the wrist. "Lauren did struggle with depression, especially in the months immediately following her separation and divorce," she said, the words carefully measured. "But recently she was on medication to control her mood swings and was doing very well."

"Perhaps she wanted you to think that."

"When was the last time you spoke with her?" she asked.

His eyes narrowed and he might have frowned, but his forehead remained perfectly smooth—the result of

BOTOX, or merely remarkable self-control? "We spoke briefly on the telephone perhaps a month ago. She called to ask if I knew of any job openings in television. She was convinced she was about to lose her position. She sounded desperate. I wanted to help her, and told her I would ask around. She promised to call me back, but I never heard from her again."

Rand had to bite the inside of his cheek to keep from commenting on the fact that Prentice had failed to tell the Rangers any of this. In fact, he'd denied knowing Lauren Starling at all.

Sophie knotted her hands in her lap. "The last time I talked to her, she said she was working on a new story—something big that would show the station how valuable she was to them. She sounded very excited."

"She never mentioned anything like that to me. What was this story about?"

"She didn't say. I was hoping you'd know."

"I'm afraid I can't help you. I'm sorry." He stood, signaling the meeting was at an end. "I don't mean to rush you, but I have other business I must attend to."

"Of course." Sophie rose also. "I won't keep you. But do you have a powder room I can use? I just need to, um, freshen up."

This was part of their plan, too—to get her into another part of the house to look around while Rand kept an eye on Prentice.

"Certainly. Back into the hallway, and it's the first door on your left."

She crossed the room quickly, leaving them alone. Prentice turned to Rand, his expression hard. "I hope I've satisfied you that I have no designs on Ms. Montgomery's person."

Did this guy rehearse his stilted dialogue in the mirror? Or did everything he knew about acting come from old black-and-white movies? "Sophie is worried about her sister," Rand said, doing quite the acting job of his own, playing the role of mild-mannered innocent boyfriend. "And your wealth and power intimidate her." Maybe flattery would make him lower his guard a little. "You can understand her wanting a little moral support."

"Since you're such good friends with her, perhaps you can persuade her to give up this fruitless search and accept that her sister has most likely succumbed to depression and taken her own life," Prentice said. "That's what the authorities believe, isn't it?"

"That's what they've told her." What he had told her, though her staunch refusal to accept such a verdict—and Prentice's insistence that she do so—was adding to his doubts. "But she says she won't stop until she's tracked down her sister. That's why she's here, tracing Lauren's last known whereabouts."

Something flashed in Prentice's eyes—alarm? But too quickly the expression was gone. "Lauren did not come to the Black Canyon to see me," he said.

"I'm sorry I kept you waiting." Sophie rejoined them. Her voice was bright, but she was paler than before, and when Rand took her arm to escort her out of the house, he felt her trembling.

Outside, she handed him the keys and walked around to the rental car's passenger side. She waited until they were in the car, driving away, before she spoke. "He's lying," she said. "Lauren has been in that house, and recently. Today even."

"Why do you say that?"

"I smelled her perfume. It's a very distinct scent—Mitsouko. Not very many women wear it."

"Maybe he has a girlfriend who does."

"It would be a big coincidence."

"Coincidences happen." Though less than some people liked to believe.

"Lauren was there. I can feel it." Her voice broke and she turned to him, her face a mask of anguish. "We've got to find her and we've got to help her, before it's too late."

# Chapter Four

"Tell me everything, exactly as it happened."

Graham spoke softly, his expression neutral and non-threatening, but Rand thought Sophie looked ready to bolt. They were back at Ranger headquarters, in the conference room with Graham, Carmen and Simon. The rest of the team—border patrol agent Michael Dance and Montrose County sheriff's deputy Lance Carpenter—had joined them. In her blue dress, Sophie looked like a bright bird in a sea of brown uniforms, but he couldn't tell if her obvious agitation was from fear or excitement.

"I already told you," she said. "Prentice said a lot of nonsense about how upset Lauren had been. Then I excused myself to go to the bathroom and I smelled her perfume. She's been in that house recently. Maybe she was even there while I was there." Her lower lip trembled and she fought to control her emotions. "We're wasting time sitting here. We need to go get her."

"Richard Prentice said he'd talked to Lauren on the phone a month ago?" Graham asked.

"He said 'about a month ago,'" Rand confirmed.

"That's the first time he's admitted even knowing her," Michael said.

"He said they met at a charity function for Guatemalan orphans," Sophie said. "He gave me the impression they were good friends."

"Yet she'd never mentioned him to you?" Simon asked. "Who's going to resist dropping the name of a famous billionaire if he's their buddy?"

"Lauren wasn't like that," Sophie said. "She wasn't a snob. She didn't care how much money you had or how powerful you were. She was as likely to have morning coffee with a panhandler she met on the street as with the bank president."

"But are you sure you'd never heard her say anything about Richard Prentice before?" Graham asked.

"I'd never heard of him before I found his business card in her apartment." She gripped the sides of the chair, knuckles white, as if ready to leap up. "What does it matter if she knew him or how? Lauren was in his house. I'm sure of it."

"He said she was very depressed about her divorce, and afraid of losing her job," Rand said.

"Of course he said that," Sophie said. "He wants us to believe she committed suicide." Her voice broke on the last word, and she ducked her head. Rand offered her his handkerchief, wishing he had something more to give her—some proof that her sister was all right. She shook her head, refusing the handkerchief.

"I don't think he was telling the truth, either," Rand said, turning to the others. "He was too glib, as if he'd rehearsed what he would say. And he was volunteering too much. Usually, Prentice plays it closer to the vest."

"When we talk to him, he knows he's talking to a police officer," Carmen said. "He thought you were the jealous boyfriend or whatever."

"Are you sure about the perfume?" Simon asked. "Couldn't it have been air freshener or something?"

"Lauren has worn Mitsouko for years," Sophie said. "It's a very distinctive scent, not like air freshener."

Carmen leaned toward her, her voice gentle. "Sometimes, when we want something very badly, the senses play tricks on us," she said.

Sophie stiffened. "Are you suggesting I hallucinated it?" she asked. "I didn't."

Everyone turned to Rand. He gave Sophie an apologetic look. "I don't have a very good sense of smell," he said. "I leave that to Lotte."

"Then your dog would have recognized this," Sophie said. "Anyone would have."

"Where were you when you smelled the perfume?" Graham asked.

"I was in the guest bathroom, downstairs, just down the hall from the library where Richard Prentice met us."

He nodded. "Did you say anything to Prentice about this?"

"No. I'm not stupid."

"I'm not questioning your intelligence, Ms. Montgomery," Graham said. "I only want to be sure of every detail."

"Why are we wasting all this time?" She shoved back from the table and stood. "All this talking isn't going to help Lauren." She fled from the room, heels striking the tile floor in a rapid cadence, the door slamming behind her.

Carmen started to go after her, but Graham held her back. "Let Rand talk to her," he said. "She's spent more time with him. Meanwhile, we need to discuss what we're going to do with the information she's given us."

Rand hurried after Sophie, hoping to catch her before she drove away. But apparently she hadn't intended to leave. He found her in the gazebo between the Rangers' trailer and park headquarters. She stood with her back against one of the posts that supported the structure, staring out across the canyon. He climbed the steps into the shelter and stood a few feet away, saying nothing, letting the silence seep into him, soothing as the warm sun. No RVs rumbled by on the road out front, no tourists talked excitedly as they gathered around the Ranger station. He and Sophie might have been the only people around.

"I still can't picture my sister here," she said after a moment. "It's so empty and desolate."

"Some people find the solitude peaceful," he said. When he was in the city he felt too crowded, unable to hear his own thoughts for the clamor.

"I think it's intimidating." She turned toward him, arms hugged across her chest. "It's so vast, it reminds me of how insignificant we are. How alone."

"You're not alone." He took a step toward her. "We want to help you. I want to help you."

She nodded. "I know I need your help. And that means working on your timetable, not mine. But it's hard. I've been looking after Lauren by myself for so long—I can't flip a switch and stop feeling responsible."

She spoke about her sister as if she was still a child. "When you say looking after her—do you mean because of her illness?"

"Yes. I know people look at her and see a grown woman with a successful career and everything going for her—but that was just on the surface. Underneath that shell, Lauren was always fragile. She'd be fine for months, even years, and then something would happen to unbalance her. She needed me there to help her through—to be her advocate when she wasn't able to care for herself, to get her the help she needed and just... just to believe in her, when other people didn't. A mental illness isn't like any other chronic condition. If you have diabetes or cancer, people are understanding. They want to help. When it's your mind that has something wrong, most people judge you harshly—as if you'd get better if you'd only try harder."

"In law enforcement, we only see the bad outcomes of mental illness," Rand said. "We get a lot of training that's supposed to help us understand, but I don't know if that's really possible if you haven't experienced it yourself."

"It's been better since she found this new doctor and has been getting the help she needs, but for so long, I've had to be strong enough for both of us."

"Maybe it's time you let someone else be strong." He moved closer, almost—but not quite—touching her. He wanted to put his arms around her and pull her close, to tell her he would protect her, but he wasn't sure how she'd react to that. Maybe she didn't feel the attraction between them that he did. Maybe she was too distraught over her sister to feel anything else.

She looked up into his eyes, and the force of her gaze hit him like a knockout punch. "I believe you want to help," she said. "And I appreciate it. I do. But I'm not used to relying on anyone else."

"You can rely on me." He did put his arms around her then, and she didn't resist, some of the tension easing from her body as he held her. He let his gaze shift to her lips—soft and pink and slightly parted. Lips he wanted very much to kiss…

A flash of red out of the corner of his eye startled him. Sophie took a step back, out of his arms, as a red convertible turned into the parking lot, a woman in dark aviators behind the wheel. Rand regained his composure and nodded toward the new arrival. "That's Emma Wade," he said. "Let's go talk to her."

The captain's fiancée was a tall, curvy redhead who favored formfitting dresses and four-inch heels. She waved to them, then entered Ranger headquarters. Sophie and Rand followed. Inside the trailer, everyone had gathered around Emma, who stood very close to Graham. The captain's normally stern demeanor softened considerably whenever he was around his fiancée, his expression closer to besotted schoolboy than grim commander.

"You must be Sophie." Emma greeted them, both hands extended. "I'm Emma Wade. I've been looking forward to meeting you."

"I'm sorry I didn't return your phone call when you contacted me last month," Sophie said. "I was so upset over Lauren's disappearance, and then I lost your number."

"It's all right. Why don't we sit down and talk?" Emma led the way back into the conference room. The others followed.

"Emma wrote a profile of Richard Prentice for the *Denver Post*," Graham said. "She spent a couple of weeks at his house and followed him at his various businesses. She knows as much about him as anyone."

"Which isn't that much." She made a face. "Prentice

is very skilled at letting people see only what he wants them to see."

"Did he ever mention Lauren to you?" Sophie asked.

Emma shook her head. "No. I know they attended some of the same social functions, but he never said anything about her to me."

"Ms. Montgomery visited Prentice this morning, at his invitation," Graham said. "While she was there, she thought she smelled her sister's perfume. In the downstairs guest bathroom."

Emma's eyes widened and she leaned toward Sophie. "Did your sister own a set of cosmetic bags in a pink-and-gold paisley pattern—three bags, all matching?"

Sophie looked confused. "I don't know. I don't remember ever seeing anything like that, but…"

"These looked new," Emma said. "They were full of cosmetics and hair accessories—mousse, hair gel, a smoothing iron."

"I don't understand," Sophie said. "Where did you see these? Why do you think they belong to Lauren?"

"I thought they belonged to a Venezuelan fashion model, but now I wonder." At Sophie's confused look, Emma patted her arm. "I'm sorry. Let me back up and explain. The last time I visited Richard Prentice's house, about two weeks ago, I went into the downstairs guest bathroom. As you know, it's quite a room—steam shower, double vanities, the works. Being a reporter, I'm naturally nosy, so I looked in all the cabinets. Nothing that interesting, until I came to a cabinet that was locked. I couldn't imagine why he'd feel the need to have a locked cabinet like that, so I picked the lock. Inside were those cosmetic bags. I thought they might belong to a woman he was seeing at the time—the Venezuelan model—but it still seemed odd to keep them locked away. So I took a photograph."

"They might have been Lauren's." Sophie's expression grew more animated. "Can I see the picture? Maybe I'd recognize something."

Emma sat back and sighed. "Unfortunately, I lost my phone and I don't have the picture anymore."

"She 'lost' the phone because someone kidnapped her and threw her down a mine shaft." Graham rested his hand on his fiancée's shoulder, his expression grim. "We can't prove Richard Prentice had anything to do with the abduction, but since it happened on his property, we suspect he was involved."

"Maybe that's what happened to Lauren," Sophie said. "Maybe he kidnapped her and kept her cosmetics as some kind of sick souvenir."

"We don't know," Graham said. "But we intend to find out."

"Why can't you arrest him now?" Sophie asked. "Aren't the perfume and the cosmetics enough to tie him to Lauren?"

"They're not," Graham said. "We need more solid evidence. Right now we have nothing to place Lauren at his house. The cosmetics might not be hers."

"I'm pretty sure Prentice knows I saw them," Emma said. "So they're probably not even there now."

"And you only have my word that I smelled the perfume." Sophie sagged in her chair. "What are we going to do now?"

"We'll start with trying to find the man Lauren met at the Country Inn," Graham said. "We'll take a look at the surveillance video from the motel. Maybe we'll get lucky and find something. We'll ask the clerk to review some photographs, see if she recognizes the man. And we'll need your sister's cell phone number, and the name of her provider, if you know it."

"Of course," Sophie said. "How will that help?"

"We can review her call records in the days before she disappeared. Maybe we'll find a pattern, or someone who knows something about her disappearance."

"What can I do to help?" Sophie asked.

"That's the tough part," Rand said. "You'll need to be patient while we work all the angles. Things seldom happen as quickly as we'd like."

"If you think of anything else that might be significant, call us anytime," Graham said.

She nodded. "I'll do that. And thank you."

"Give Rand a number where we can reach you." Graham turned away.

"I'll be in touch," Emma said. "We can have lunch." She squeezed Sophie's arm, then followed Graham into his office.

"Let me walk you to your car." Rand took her arm.

She hesitated, as if she wanted to stay, but the last thing they needed was her hanging around. Not that he wouldn't appreciate her company, but he didn't need the distraction. Finally, he was able to coax her toward the door. "Where are you staying?" he asked when they reached the parking lot.

"The Ramada. You'll let me know as soon as you find anything?"

"Why don't I stop by tonight and give you an update?" he said. "I might not have much to tell you, but at least you won't have to spend the night wondering what's going on."

"I'd like that." The pinched look left her face. "And thank you. Not just for that, but for all your help."

He put a hand on her shoulder. "Just remember what I said before—you're not in this alone."

Her eyes met his, dark pools that mesmerized him. Her gaze stripped away any mask of bravado he might wear in his everyday life, and seemed to see the real him, the man who wasn't always so sure of himself, but who wanted to be better and stronger, at least for her. She tilted her face up to his, her lips full and slightly parted. It would be so easy to dip his head and kiss her, to find out if the desire that sizzled inside him was something she felt, too...

"I...I'd better go." She stepped back and focused on finding her keys in her purse. She ducked her head so that her hair fell forward, preventing him from gauging her mood, but his own face felt hot.

"I'll call before I stop by," he said.

"Great. Thanks." She moved toward her car and unlocked the door.

"What's that on your windshield?" He moved closer to study the white envelope with *Sophie* inscribed on the front in a looping, feminine hand.

Sophie stared at the missive, her face as white as the paper.

"What is it?" he asked. "What's wrong?"

"Nothing." She snatched the envelope from beneath the windshield wiper. Her eyes widened, and she swayed.

Rand steadied her, his hands on her shoulders. "What is it?" he asked. "Do you know who it's from?"

She covered her mouth with her hand and shook her head, eyes glistening. "It's from Lauren," she whispered. "I'd recognize her handwriting anywhere."

# Chapter Five

Sophie stared at the envelope, her name scrawled across the front in Lauren's exuberant script. How many times had she seen that handwriting—on birthday cards and phone messages and reminder notes? *Sophie.* Six simple letters representing the first word Lauren had ever spoken, calling out to her now from the page.

Rand's arm around her steadied her, brought her back to the present, to the parking lot in the glaring sun, the wind tugging at her clothes and hair. "Let's go inside and see what it says," he said, and urged her toward the office.

She let him lead her inside, where the captain, Emma and the others looked up. "What's wrong?" Carmen asked.

"Someone left an envelope tucked under the wiper blade on Sophie's windshield." Rand led her to a chair and she sat, still gripping the envelope in both hands.

"Did you see who left it?" Graham asked.

Rand shook his head. "We were out there several minutes and we didn't see anyone. Whoever it was, they must have dropped it off while we were all inside."

"It's Lauren's handwriting," Sophie said. "I know it is. I need to see what she said." She started to lift the flap on the envelope, but Rand covered her hand with his own, stopping her.

"Let me," he said. "You don't want to destroy evidence…just in case."

Carmen handed him a pair of gloves, which he slipped on. Then he slid a letter opener under the flap and carefully teased it open. "One sheet of paper," he said, and showed the others. He tipped the envelope, and the paper fluttered onto the table.

Sophie stared at it. "Tell me what it says."

Rand used the letter opener to unfold the paper and smooth it flat. Sophie leaned around his arm to see the words written there. "It's Lauren's handwriting," she said again. "I'm positive."

"What does it say?" Emma asked, moving to stand behind them.

Sophie scanned the words:

Dear Sophie,
Sorry I haven't been in touch but I'm fine. Don't worry. I've met my Mr. Wonderful and you know how happy that makes me. I'll write again when I can. In the meantime, go home and don't worry.
Love, Lauren.

Tears blurred the words; she blinked, trying to clear her vision. When she looked up from the page after reading the words again, she found Rand studying her intently, his expression both sympathetic and wary. "Can I read this to the others?" he asked.

She nodded, and he read the brief message out loud. "What do you make of that?" he asked Sophie when he was done.

She frowned. "It's her writing, and part of it sounds like her, but…something isn't right."

"What's that about Mr. Wonderful?" Emma asked. "Did Lauren mention seeing anyone when you talked to her last?"

"That's the part that bothers me most," Sophie said.

"So she wasn't seeing anyone?" Carmen asked.

"Maybe she met someone after the last time you talked," Rand said.

"It's not that," Sophie said. "It's the choice of words—Mr. Wonderful. She and I had this joke—whenever one of us went out with some guy who was full of himself, we called him Mr. Wonderful. As in he thought he was Mr. Wonderful and women should be falling all over him." They'd had a lot of laughs over that, sisterly love erasing the pain and awkwardness of bad dates they'd each endured.

"So you only used those words sarcastically," Carmen said.

"Exactly. And the next part—'you know how happy that makes me.' It sounds like she's telling me how unhappy she is." Pain squeezed her chest at the thought.

Rand pulled out the chair beside her and sat. "So you think the message is a code?" he asked.

"I guess you could call it that." She studied the letter again, as if she might suddenly see some hidden message that hadn't yet revealed itself.

"And you're sure this is her handwriting, not simply a good forgery?" Graham moved closer to stand over the table.

"How would a forger know about our Mr. Wonderful joke?" Sophie asked.

"She's right," Emma said. "Most people would say

something like 'I've met Mr. Right.' Or 'I've met a great guy.'"

"What about her ex?" Rand asked. "He'd know her handwriting, and he'd know about the 'Mr. Wonderful' phrase, though maybe he took it literally and didn't realize it was an inside joke."

"Have you spoken to Phil?" Sophie asked.

"Not yet," Rand said. "We telephoned his number and left a message, but we haven't heard anything." The ex didn't seem a likely suspect in the disappearance of a wife who'd given him the divorce he wanted and was paying him support.

"Maybe someone forced Lauren to write this note," Carmen said.

"Someone who knew where you'd be this afternoon," Rand said.

"Do you think someone's been following me?" she asked. The thought sent a chill through her, and she hugged her arms across her stomach.

"I haven't noticed anyone," Rand said. "I think I would have."

She nodded. He'd always seemed alert and aware of things going on around them. "If they weren't following me, how did they—whoever they are—know that I was here? Did they just see my car out front and take advantage of the opportunity?"

"Even if they guessed you might come to the park because your sister disappeared here, they're taking a chance, driving around hoping to spot you," Carmen said.

"They didn't necessarily have to physically tail you." Graham looked thoughtful. "Not if they can track you electronically."

"What is he talking about?" Sophie asked Rand.

Rand's mouth tightened into a hard line. "He's talking about a tracking device on your car." He stood and she rose also and followed him, along with the others, out to the parking lot. He dropped to the ground and rolled over on his back and slid under the bumper. A moment later he emerged, a box about the size of a packet of cigarettes in his hand.

Sophie stared at the box, on which two lights blinked green. "That's a tracking device?"

"It has GPS." He turned the box over, examining it. "Anyone with a computer and the right program can see wherever you go."

Anger surged through her. She wanted to snatch the box out of his hand and stomp on it. "Why would someone do that?" she asked. "And has it been there ever since I got to Colorado?"

"Someone could have put it on while your car was parked at your hotel," Carmen said.

"Or one of Prentice's guards could have put this on your car while we were inside talking to him," Rand said.

"Then that means I was right—Lauren was at his house. He's holding her prisoner and he made her write the note, thinking it would make me go away." She gripped his arm. "You have to rescue her."

"We don't know where she is." He looked pained as he said the words.

Was he being purposely dense? "She's at Richard Prentice's estate. This proves it."

"This isn't proof." The captain moved to stand in front of her, his expression stern, but his voice gentle. "This proves that someone is following you," he said. "But we don't know who that is. We'll try to trace the origin of this device, but the chances of linking it to Richard Prentice are slim to none."

"But the note…"

"Even if you're right and your sister wrote it, we don't know how it got to your car," Graham said. "We'll question anyone who may have driven by and ask if they've seen anything, but it's easy enough for someone to park at the Ranger station and slip over here without anyone noticing."

"She was in the house. I smelled her perfume." She'd been that close to Lauren. Why hadn't she stayed there and demanded to see her?

"If we go back there now I can almost guarantee you won't find any trace of that scent," Rand said. "If Richard Prentice does have your sister, he's been doing a good job of hiding that fact for the last month."

She covered her mouth with her hand, fighting for control. Was Lauren imprisoned in a locked room or dungeon, like women she'd read about in the papers or seen on TV who had been held prisoner for years, invisible to everyone who lived and worked around them?

"There must be something you can do," she said after a moment.

"We'll put extra surveillance on Prentice's estate," Graham said.

"He'll love that," Emma said. "He's already suing the Rangers for harassment."

"Can't you get a warrant to search his property?" Sophie asked.

"On what grounds?" Graham asked. "Not to mention a billionaire like Prentice wields a lot of influence."

"And he has a state senator on his side," Rand said.

"The only way to overcome their opposition is to gather convincing evidence and have a solid case. Which we intend to do."

"How will you do that?" she asked.

"We'll start with the hotel clerk," Graham said. "We'll see if she can identify the man who was with your sister. We know it wasn't Richard Prentice, but maybe it was someone who works for him."

"What am I supposed to do?" she asked.

"Follow Lauren's advice and try not to worry," Graham said, though the sympathy in his eyes told her he knew how difficult that would be.

"Let me help you," she said. "There must be something I can do—paperwork, phone calls…" Anything was better than sitting around worrying.

"When you go back to your hotel this afternoon, try to remember everything you can about your last conversations with her," Rand said. "Even something insignificant might help us understand why she came to Montrose and what she hoped to accomplish here."

It wasn't what she wanted, but she could see it was all she had, for now. She nodded. "All right. And you'll let me know if you find out anything at all?"

He nodded. "I'll stop by this evening." He handed the tracking device to Carmen, then took Sophie's arm and guided her back to the driver's side of the car. "I know this is hard," he said. "But try to stay strong, for Lauren's sake. This is a priority now. We'll do everything we can to find her."

"You believe me, don't you?" She studied his face, searching for confirmation that he was on her side. "You believe that I smelled Lauren's perfume and I recognized her handwriting?"

"I believe you."

"You're not just saying it to be nice?"

"I work with a dog who can recognize the faintest scents—ones the human nose can't detect. Why wouldn't you recognize a perfume your sister wore all the time? Scent is one of the most powerful senses, and even though we don't have the ability of dogs, we associate certain smells with specific people and situations."

"Are you comparing me to a dog?" She managed a smile to show she wasn't insulted.

"Hey, I meant it as a compliment. I think a lot of my dog."

"I'll remember that." Though dogs frightened her, she wished she had someone she could feel as close to right now.

"Hang in there." He squeezed her shoulder. "I'll see you this evening. Maybe we can go to dinner. It will do you good to get out of the hotel for a while."

"All right. See you then." She slid into the driver's seat and fit the key into the ignition. She'd do as he suggested and focus on staying strong, for Lauren's sake. But she'd never imagined how hard that would be. Today had been like losing her sister all over again.

"WHAT IF WE'RE looking in the wrong direction, and Prentice doesn't have anything to do with Lauren Starling's disappearance?" Marco Cruz, his expression unreadable behind his dark sunglasses, asked the question as he and Rand and Lotte headed to the Country Inn that afternoon.

"Anything's possible," Rand said. "Maybe it's an incredible coincidence that everything appears to point back to him."

"Prentice knew Lauren," Marco said. "Maybe she even came here to see him. But I don't see any motivation for him to kidnap her."

"Maybe she found out something about his operation that he didn't want getting out."

"In that case, I think he'd kill her. Why keep her around for a month?"

"I don't know, but I hope Sophie's right and Lauren really did write that letter. Wherever she is, I hope she's still alive."

"After all she's been through, the woman deserves a break," Marco said.

"Yeah. She dropped everything to come down here and look for her sister—not many people would do that."

"I was talking about Lauren, but yeah, I can see it's been hard on Sophie, too."

Rand hoped Sophie was able to get some rest at her hotel this afternoon, though he doubted it. She clearly felt responsible for her sister, almost the way a mother might feel about a child. "Do you have any brothers and sisters?" he asked.

"I've got six sisters." Marco folded his arms over his chest. "I'm the youngest."

Rand started to make a joke about the baby of the family, but nothing about the muscular, six-foot, ex–Special Forces DEA agent said "baby." "Do they all still try to look after you?" he asked.

"They do. When I was still in California they were always up in my business, telling me what to do, what to eat, what to wear, who to date. I told them I had one mother, I didn't need six more, but they don't listen."

"I guess that could get to be a little much. But now that you're so far away, do you miss them?"

"Nope." He glanced at Rand. "But if anybody tried to hurt one of them, I'd do whatever it took to find that person and make him pay."

Pity the man—or woman—who had to face Marco's wrath, Rand thought. He signaled for the turn into the motel parking lot. Marco retrieved the tablet with the mug shots they'd put together while Rand let Lotte out of the back and clipped on her leash. She gave a big shake, like an athlete loosening up before a race, then looked up at him, wagging her tail. "I don't have a job for you right now, girl," he said. "Just thought you'd like to stretch your legs."

Marlee and another young woman, shorter and rounder with long blond hair, looked up from behind the registration desk when they entered. "What a gorgeous dog," the other woman said. "What's her name?"

"Her name is Lotte." Rand checked the clerk's name tag. "Hello, Candy."

"Hey, Officer Knightbridge," Marlee said, but her eyes were fixed on Marco. "Who's your friend?"

"Marco Cruz." Marco showed his credentials and both women leaned forward to study them.

"What can we do for you, Officer Cruz?" Marlee asked, a little breathily. Marco often had that effect on women. Rand might as well be invisible.

"We brought some photos for you to look at." Marco switched on the tablet and handed it to Marlee. "We want to see if you recognize any of them as the man Lauren Starling met when she stayed here." The tablet started through a slide show of men's photos they'd pulled from the files of the local police of everyone who matched the description Marlee had given them.

"You mean Jane Smith?" Candy asked. "I knew that had to be a fake name—what do you call it, when someone makes up a name like that?"

"An alias," Marco said.

"Right." Candy's smile broadened. "I knew Jane Smith had to be an alias, but I had no idea she was somebody famous until Marlee told me. And now she's missing? That's wild!"

"Did you see the man she was with?" Rand asked.

Candy shook her head. "Sorry, I didn't." She elbowed her friend. "Usually, night shift is more interesting, but not that day."

"There's a lot of guys here," Marlee said, eyes on the tablet. "So far, nobody rings a bell."

Candy leaned over her shoulder to watch the slide show. "Some shady-looking characters," she said. "I prefer a more clean-cut type myself." She sent Marco a flirtatious look.

"Was anyone else on duty during Ms. Starling's stay here?" Rand asked.

The two young women exchanged glances. "There's Jobie, the handyman," Marlee said doubtfully. "He's always around during the day."

"Is he here now?" Rand asked.

"Somewhere, I guess," Marlee said.

"Could you ask him to come up here, please?"

"I'll call him." Candy moved to the phone.

Marlee began flipping through the photos on the tablet again.

"Take your time," Rand said. "Don't focus so much on what they're wearing or their expression. Try to picture them standing with Lauren that afternoon. Do any of them match your memory of the man she met outside her room?"

"Jobie's on his way up," Candy said, joining them again.

After a few moments a man in his fifties dressed in baggy pants and a University of Denver sweatshirt shambled in. He eyed Marco and Rand warily, but addressed Candy. "You wanted me for something?"

"These gentleman have some questions for you," she said.

"What kind of questions?" He took a step back.

Jobie looked as if he would bolt out the door if either officer took a step toward him. Rand was used to dealing with people who were nervous around cops. He watched the handyman closely out of the corner of his eye, ready for trouble, but kept his tone casual. "Do you remember a woman who was staying here about a month ago, a pretty blonde, registered as Jane Smith?"

"We get a lot of pretty blondes who stay here," Jobie said.

"This one was in 154, on the back side of the building," Candy said. "Very classy."

He shook his head, his eyes half-closed. "Don't remember."

"Maybe a picture will refresh your memory." Marco handed him the photograph of Lauren they'd copied from Sophie's phone.

His eyes opened wider as he studied the picture, but he shook his head as he handed it back. "Don't know."

"Are you sure?" Rand asked. "We think she met a man here. Did you see her with anyone, maybe talking outside her room?"

Jobie looked at Candy. "It's okay," she said. "You're not in any trouble."

"If you saw something, you need to tell us," Rand said. "If we find out later you lied to us, it could cause trouble."

Anger flared in his eyes, and he shoved the picture back at them. "What's it to you, anyway?" he asked.

"This woman might be in trouble," Rand said. "The man she was with might know something that could help us find her."

"Alan don't know nothing," Jobie said. "He stays clear of trouble."

"Alan who?"

Jobie pressed his lips together and gave a single shake of his head.

Candy leaned across the counter toward him. "Do you mean Alan Milbanks?" she asked. "Was he talking to this Jane Smith?"

"Maybe."

"Who's Alan Milbanks?" Rand asked.

"He's just this guy," she said. "He owns the fish place."

"What fish place?" Rand asked.

"Oh, you know—out on the highway, just past the airport? There's a big sign—Fresh Seafood."

"You go there often?" Marco asked.

Candy flushed. "Not often. I just…I have a friend who likes to go there, and sometimes I go with him, that's all." She turned back to Jobie. "Was it Alan?"

"Maybe."

"Alan wasn't the guy I saw." Marlee looked up from her study of the tablet. "Alan is older than the guy I saw, and his hair is darker."

"Jobie, did you see Jane Smith talking to Alan Milbanks here at the motel?" Rand fixed the handyman with a stern gaze.

Jobie shoved his hands in his pockets and nodded. "Yeah. They were standing by his car, parked in front of her room."

"What were they talking about?" Marco asked. "Did you overhear anything?"

"No. I figured they were just making a transaction, you know."

Rand and Marco exchanged a look. "A transaction?"

Jobie squirmed. "Alan does a little dealing on the side sometimes. At least, that's what I hear. I wouldn't know personally."

*I just bet you wouldn't,* Rand thought. He turned to Candy. "Is that right? Does Alan Milbanks deal drugs?"

She flushed. "I've heard rumors that he sometimes has stuff for sale. Just, from time to time, you know. Nothing big."

"But you say the guy you saw wasn't Alan?" Marco asked Marlee.

She shook her head, then glanced down at the tablet once more. "I think he might have been this guy here." She turned the tablet around and pointed to a color mug shot of a thirtysomething man with light brown hair and schoolboy good looks. "I'm pretty sure this is the one."

Candy leaned over to study the photo. "Cute. I think I'd remember him."

"Did you see him?" Rand asked.

Candy shook her head. "Sorry. No."

"Are you sure this is the guy?" Randall asked Marlee.

She nodded. "I remember the way his nose was crooked, and that little dimple in his chin. His hair was a little shorter than in this picture, and he was smiling, but it's the same guy, I'm sure."

"Thanks for your help." Marco took the tablet and switched it off. "We may have more questions later."

"You did great," Rand said. "Thanks." He tugged at Lotte's leash and they headed for the door.

"Come back anytime," Candy called. "It's usually so boring around here."

When they were in the cruiser again, Lotte in her place behind them, Marco consulted his notes. "Sounds like Lauren was a busy woman during her short stay here. Do you think she was buying drugs from Alan Milbanks?"

"Maybe a little self-medication?" Rand shrugged. "Who knows?" He punched some information into his computer. "I'm trying to see what I can find out about Alan Milbanks."

"Sounds like the guy was selling more than fish."

"Oh, yeah." He nodded. "It says here he was charged with dealing drugs out of his seafood shop, but the case was dismissed for lack of evidence."

"When was this?" Marco asked.

"About five months ago." He scrolled down the screen, but found no previous charges or convictions for Milbanks. "What I'm wondering is, does he have any connection to Richard Prentice? And how would a guy like that know Lauren Starling?"

"We need to go ask him." Marco tapped the tablet on his lap. "What about the guy Marlee picked out? Anybody we know?"

"That guy is Phil Starling. Lauren's ex-husband."

"I thought he was in Denver. What was he doing in Montrose?"

Rand started the cruiser and shifted into gear. "That's what we have to find out."

*Chapter Six*

The hotel room might as well have been a prison cell, for all that Sophie was able to relax in it. She kept replaying the scene in Richard Prentice's mansion. What would have happened if, instead of leaving peacefully, she'd demanded to see her sister? Or maybe she should have looked for her on her own, searching the house until Prentice forced her to stop. Had she passed up the chance to save her sister?

A knock on the door interrupted her fretting. Had Rand learned something to tell her already? She hurried to answer it, and was surprised to see not the handsome Ranger, but Emma Wade and another woman.

"We figured you'd be going stir-crazy, stuck here alone in this hotel," Emma said. "This is my friend Abby Stewart. We thought maybe we could take you out for coffee."

"Come in." Sophie opened the door wider and ushered them into her room. "I have been going a little crazy, sitting here worrying about what's going to happen."

"I'm so sorry about your sister." Abby, slim with long, dark blond hair, offered a shy smile. "I remember seeing her on television—she always struck me as so warm and friendly."

"She never met an enemy," Sophie said. "Growing up, she was always outgoing and popular. I was the quiet, bookish sister, but I guess that's why we got along so well. We never competed in the same arena. I rooted for her at cheerleader tryouts and she bragged to everyone she knew when I made the honor society." The memory sharpened the pain around her heart that never really left her these days. Yes, Lauren could be annoying at times, and they'd had their share of sisterly squabbles, but Sophie never thought of those days, only of the good times.

"Abby's a brain, too," Emma said. "She's getting her master's in environmental science or something."

"That's what brought me to the Black Canyon of the Gunnison," Abby said. "I met Michael while I was doing research in the park."

At Sophie's blank look, Emma filled in the details. "Abby's engaged to Michael Dance, one of the other Rangers. And I take it you already figured out I'm seeing Captain Ellison."

"Rand mentioned it, yes." And there was no ignoring the large diamond on the third finger of Emma's left hand.

"You two seem to have hit it off," Emma said. "I was beginning to think the only female he was interested in is his dog."

"Oh, Rand's not… I mean, he's just trying to help me find Lauren." Her face felt hot.

"Still, he's definitely easy on the eyes," Emma said. "I understand he plays lacrosse in his spare time. Those guys always have great legs."

"Um, I hadn't noticed." Well, she had noticed Rand

was good-looking. After all, she wasn't blind. More blushing. Time to change the subject. "Should we go get that coffee? I really would love to get away from this room for a while."

"Sure," Emma said. "There's a really cute bakery and coffee shop downtown, and there are some interesting boutiques nearby we can check out afterward, if you'd like. I always say, there's nothing like a little retail therapy."

"That would be great." Anything to distract her from her worries, at least for a little while.

The coffee shop was every bit as adorable as predicted, with gingham curtains and chicken-shaped salt-and-pepper shakers on every table. Sophie inhaled the scents of fresh-baked bread and roasting coffee and felt some of the tension leave her body.

They ordered lattes and cinnamon muffins, and took a table by the window. "Thank you again for taking such an interest in Lauren's disappearance," Sophie said to Emma. "I understand you've really stayed on the Rangers' case about it."

Emma stirred sugar into her coffee, all her earlier cheerfulness vanished. "My own sister disappeared when I was a freshman in college," she said. "The police didn't take it seriously at first, because she'd run off once before."

"What happened?" Sophie asked.

"She was murdered. They never did catch the person or persons who killed her." She reached across the table and squeezed Sophie's arm. "I'm hoping for a much better outcome for your sister. After all, that note means she's still alive."

Sophie nodded and sipped her coffee, waiting until

she was sure her voice was steady before she spoke. "I don't know what to make of the note," she said. "I mean, did anyone think I'd really fall for that, without seeing Lauren and talking to her, face-to-face?"

"Someone who's used to everyone doing what he wants might believe it," Emma said as she pinched off a piece of muffin and popped it in her mouth.

"Someone like Richard Prentice?" Abby asked.

"You've both lived here awhile, haven't you?" Sophie asked. "What do you know about Prentice? Would he really do something like kidnap my sister? And why?"

"I've only been here a couple of months," Abby said. "All I know about him is that he likes to throw his weight around, he has lots of money and he doesn't like the Rangers one bit."

"I wrote a profile of him for the *Denver Post*," Emma said. "I followed him around for two weeks and he struck me as a pretty typical powerful businessman with a lot of money. He's smart and arrogant and he's made sure a lot of people owe him favors. But I never thought he was a criminal until I was attacked after visiting his ranch one day, thrown down a mine shaft and left to die."

"Richard Prentice did that?" Sophie stared. The captain had mentioned the abduction, but hearing the details from Emma made it sound all the more shocking.

"He wouldn't get his own hands dirty," Emma said. "But I believe he ordered the attack, to keep me from looking further into goings-on at his ranch."

"Then why isn't he in jail?" Sophie wadded a napkin into a ball, frustration overwhelming her once more.

"Because there's no proof linking him to the attack on me or the crimes in the park or anything," Abby said.

"And his lawyers do a good job of keeping the Rangers from getting too close."

"They're going to have to come up with something so damning there's no way he can wiggle out from under the charge," Emma said. "If he is responsible for your sister's disappearance, and the Rangers can make the case against him, it would put him away for a very long time, and probably save a lot of other lives."

"There must be some way to find out the truth," Sophie said.

"If it's there, the Rangers will find the evidence they need," Abby said. "And they'll find Lauren. Believe me, they're putting everything they have into stopping this crime wave. Michael stays up nights, going over and over the evidence they've amassed, trying to find the one thing that will break open the case."

"Graham, too," Emma said. "I used to get frustrated at what I thought was law enforcement dragging their feet. But now I see all the things they do behind the scenes that the public never knows about."

"That must be hard, though," Sophie said. "Being with men who work such dangerous jobs. Don't you worry?"

"We worry," Abby said. "But you can't live your life worrying all the time, so after a while you just put it aside and try not to think about it. This is just your life now and you try to enjoy each day and not angst about the future."

"I need to learn how to do that," Sophie said. For so many years, she'd had to be the strong one in her family, the one who took care of everything, the one Lauren relied on. Even now, when they lived hundreds of miles apart, Lauren would call asking for advice, or for Sophie's help with a problem. She'd made it her job to worry about her sister for so long, she had a hard time letting go of that role, especially now, when Lauren was in real danger.

Emma and Abby filled in Sophie's silence with small talk as they finished their coffee. "I want to check out that boutique next door," Emma said when they were done. "I saw a really cute dress in the window when we walked past."

"You don't mind if we do a little shopping, do you, Sophie?" Abby asked.

"No," she said. "If I see something cute, I might buy it. I didn't bring that many clothes with me."

The boutique did indeed have a number of cute outfits on display, and a large sale section. Soon all three women were combing through the racks, exclaiming over this dress or that shirt, and setting aside clothes to try on. Sophie was debating between two dresses from the sale rack when she glanced up and saw a man by the door, his face turned toward her. Dark glasses hid his eyes, and a ball cap covered most of his hair, but something about him was so familiar, and the menacing set of his mouth sent a shiver up her spine. She took a step back and gave a small cry of alarm.

Emma, who was combing through the rack across from Sophie, looked up. "What's wrong?" she asked. "You've gone gray."

Sophie ducked her head and moved around the rack to Emma's side. "There's a man over there, by the door," she said, keeping her voice low. "He was staring at me. I'm sure of it."

Emma looked toward the door. "There's no one there now."

"But I swear…" She turned, in time to see a man

exiting the shop. "There he goes." She pointed. "I swear he was staring right at me, and he looked so menacing— angry."

Abby moved to join them, in time to hear the last of the conversation. "Is it someone you know?" she asked.

"I don't know." Sophie hugged her arms across the stomach, fighting a chill. "He was wearing a hat and dark glasses, but he almost looked like my brother-in-law. Lauren's ex-husband. Except that Phil is usually so neatly dressed. This guy needed a shave and a haircut, and his clothes were rumpled and sloppy."

"Maybe he's a transient—or a tourist," Emma said. "He could have been looking at someone behind you."

"Maybe," Sophie conceded. "And maybe I'm just extra jumpy because of everything that's happened."

Abby slipped her arm around Sophie. "We'll stick together for the rest of the afternoon, and keep our eyes open. If the guy you saw is following us, we'll call the Rangers right away."

Sophie nodded. "That's a good idea. And thank you. For everything."

From the boutique they moved on to an art gallery, and then a bookstore. Sophie began to relax. Maybe the man had been staring at someone behind her. After all, Rand had removed the bug from her car, so how would anyone even know where she was right now? And Phil Starling was in Denver, with his new girlfriend. He wasn't likely to show up in Montrose.

She was scanning a row of paperbacks, searching for a title that might take her mind off her worries, when Emma sidled up next to her. "Check out the guy by the cash register," she said. "Is that the one you saw in the dress shop?"

Sophie turned her head just enough to see the man, who was studying a display of blown-glass figurines. From this angle, he looked even more like Phil, though a Phil who had let himself go, or who had fallen on hard times. What was he doing in Montrose? "That's him," she whispered. "And I'm sure it's my ex-brother-in-law."

Just then the man turned and looked directly at her, anger radiating from him, as if at any moment he might lash out at her.

But instead of frightening her, his animosity only made her bold. She'd done nothing to deserve his contempt. "I'm going to ask him what he thinks he's doing," she said.

"Sophie, no!" Abby tried to hold her back, but Sophie shook off her hand. She hurried over to the man.

"Phil, what are you doing here?" she demanded. "Are you following me?"

"What are *you* doing here?" The coldness of his glare made her shrink back, but the others had joined her and Abby steadied her with a hand on her arm.

Sophie forced herself to look him in the eye, aware of the stares of other shoppers around them. "I saw you staring at me in the dress shop," she said. "And again just now. If you have something to say to me, say it."

"You need to go home and keep your nose out of other people's business," he growled.

"Does this have something to do with Lauren?" Sophie's voice rose, all the anger and anguish of the past weeks pouring out. It was all she could do to keep from grabbing Phil and shaking him. "Do you know where she is?"

The man began backing to the door. "You're crazy."

He looked at the other shoppers. "I never saw this woman before in my life. She's crazy."

"I'm calling 911." Abby took out her phone.

The man turned and ran out the door. Sophie followed, but already he'd vanished in the crowds on the sidewalk.

The other shoppers avoided her when she returned to the store, as if they believed her accuser when he'd said she was unhinged.

"Michael is on his way," Abby said.

"I think you ladies need to leave now." The man who'd been working behind the counter came up to them. "I can't have you upsetting the other customers."

"That man was following us," Emma said. "He threatened my friend here."

The bookstore manager frowned. "I didn't see him do anything but shop, and all he said was for you to go home and stay out of his business. That doesn't sound like a threat to me."

Sophie felt sick to her stomach. To other people, their encounter with the man probably didn't seem like a threat on his part. They'd been the aggressors, accusing him.

"Come on." Emma took her friends by the arms. "We'll wait outside for Michael. At least we scared the guy off."

"For now," Sophie said. "But we made him angry, too." What would he do next time? Or would he take his anger out on Lauren? Had she blown yet another chance to save her sister?

"I don't know what you're talking about. I never saw this woman." Sweat beaded on Alan Milbanks's high forehead, and his watery blue eyes looked away—at the counter of the fish shop, at the door, anywhere but at the two officers who questioned him. "Anybody who says they saw me with her is lying."

"I think you're the one who's lying." Rand leaned across the counter at the front of the fish store. The air was heavy with the smell of fish, and the cloying scent of Milbanks's cologne. "You met Lauren at her hotel."

"I meet lots of women," he said, suddenly defiant. "I don't remember all their names. One-night stands, you know how it is."

Rand took in the balding, paunchy man before him, with his sagging jowls and sunken eyes. "Lauren Starling was a real beauty queen," he said. "What would she see in a guy like you?"

"Hey! No need to get insulting." He forced a smile. "I have my charms."

"You got in a little trouble a couple of months ago, didn't you?" Rand said. "Arrested for dealing drugs. Seems you were importing more than fish into your little shop here."

"It was bogus," Milbanks said. "They dropped the charges."

"Maybe you had a little help with that—someone powerful who paid for a good attorney. Maybe someone like Richard Prentice."

Milbanks's face went white, then red. "Get out of here," he said. "You can't come in here harassing a guy trying to make an honest living."

"Is it really an honest living?" Marco asked.

"You got no right," Milbanks said. "Your territory is the park and federal land. This shop is in the city limits."

"Lauren Starling's car was found abandoned on parkland," Rand said. "We're investigating her disappearance. You're the last person known to have seen her."

"Did you two have a disagreement about something?" Marco asked. "Maybe you got a little rough with her and it went too far. Did you hurt her?"

"I didn't hurt nobody." Sweat rolled down Milbanks's face. "You need to leave now. I'm going to call my lawyer." He pulled out a cell phone, but his hands shook so badly he could hardly punch in the numbers.

"We'll leave now," Rand said. "But we'll be back—maybe with a warrant for your arrest in connection with the disappearance of Lauren Starling."

Milbanks looked as if he might faint. The two officers left the store, but stood out on the sidewalk, watching their suspect as he completed his phone call.

"Think he's really calling his lawyer?" Marco asked.

"Or Richard Prentice's lawyer." Rand's phone buzzed and he answered it. "Knightbridge."

"Rand, you need to get over to the Montrose Police Station," Carmen said.

"Why? What's going on?"

"It's Sophie Montgomery. She's been arrested."

# Chapter Seven

Sophie didn't know which was worse—enduring the humiliation of being hauled to the police station in handcuffs while a crowd of people, including her former brother-in-law, looked on, or facing Rand when he arrived with Michael Dance and Graham Ellison to retrieve them. "I didn't do anything wrong," she protested when Rand was finally allowed in to see her.

"You're not in trouble," he said. "The guy you were harassing disappeared, and we persuaded the shop owner not to press charges, as long as we agreed to keep you away from his store in the future."

"That guy was Phil Starling—Lauren's ex," she said as she followed Rand and one of the Montrose police officers into the booking area. "He's here in Montrose."

"That explains why we haven't been able to reach him in Denver." He waited while the officer returned Sophie's belongings to her, then took her arm and escorted her outside to the parking lot.

"What about Emma and Abby?" Sophie asked, looking around for her friends.

"They left a few minutes ago with Graham and Michael."

"Thanks for coming to pick me up. I know you didn't

have to do that." Rand didn't have any obligation to her—not like Michael and Graham had to Abby and Emma.

"I wouldn't leave you in the lurch," he said.

His expression was so warm, so caring, that she had to look away. Being with Rand always unsettled her. She was definitely attracted to him, but now was the worst possible time to start a relationship, with Lauren missing and Sophie in town for, she hoped, only a few days, until her sister was found.

He grinned. "Nothing like an arrest to bring couples together."

"Not funny." Sophie slid into the passenger seat of the Cruiser. "Don't you think it's significant that Phil is here in Montrose, and that he was so hostile toward me?"

"What, exactly, did he do that was so hostile?" Rand started the Cruiser.

"He was following me and glaring at me. And he threatened me."

Rand glanced at her sharply. "What kind of threat?"

"He told me to go home and keep my nose out of business that didn't concern me."

"What was he referring to, do you think?"

"I don't know. That's what I was trying to find out when the local police showed up."

"Next time you think some guy is following you, call me," Rand said.

"By the time you showed up, he would have left. The store owner was out of line calling the police. It wasn't as if we started a brawl or something."

"Still, you could have been hurt. It's dangerous to confront someone like that."

"I wanted to know what he was doing. And I wanted

to know if he knew anything about Lauren—if he'd seen her or talked to her. And what he was doing here. The last I'd heard, he lived and worked in Denver."

"What kind of work does he do?" Rand pulled out of the parking lot.

"He's an actor. Quite a good one, I guess. At least, he had regular work with a Denver theater company."

"But Lauren was paying him support?"

"Yes. She made more money than he did, so the court awarded him monthly support payments." She ran her hand up and down the strap of her seat belt. "I told her she should have fought it, but she was so blindsided by Phil's request for the divorce she was too numb to do anything. And he had a shark lawyer who really went after her."

"What about the other woman? What does she do?"

"She's an actor, too. Glenda Pierce. That's how they met—they were in a play together."

"Do you know if she was with him today?"

Sophie shook her head. "I've never met her. But he seemed to be alone."

"We'll try to track him down and question him."

"Maybe he'll know something that will help us find Lauren. But part of me is afraid to hope."

"Hang in there," he said. "We're getting more pieces of the puzzle all the time. All we have to do is put them together the right way to give us the picture we need."

"What have you discovered?" She half turned in her seat to face him.

"We went back to the hotel and talked to both clerks and the maintenance man. They identified one of the men who visited Lauren at the hotel as a guy who runs a local fish shop, Alan Milbanks."

"A fish shop?" She wrinkled her nose. "What was Lauren doing with him?"

"He's suspected of dealing drugs out of the shop, though local police haven't been able to gather enough evidence to convict him."

"Lauren did not take drugs."

"You sure about that? It's not unusual for people with mental illness to self-medicate."

"She wouldn't do that. She had her prescribed medications and she was very good about taking them. She hardly ever even drinks alcohol."

He nodded and tapped his fingers on the steering wheel. "I'm wondering if her meeting with this guy had anything to do with the big story she was working on."

"That's probably it." Excitement made her jittery. "Did you talk to him? What did he say?"

"He says he doesn't know her and the clerk is lying. But he didn't convince me. We're working on getting a warrant to bring him in for questioning."

"Was someone with him when he met Lauren?" she asked. "You said 'men.'"

"That's another interesting thing we learned. The man Marlee saw Lauren with wasn't Alan Milbanks."

"Then who was it?"

"She identified him as Phil Starling."

Her breath caught in her throat. "So you knew he was in town already? When were you going to tell me?"

"I would have told you tonight at dinner, if you hadn't run into him yourself first."

"Have you talked to him? Do you know where he's staying?"

"Negative on both of those, but we've got people working on tracking him down."

She sat back, letting this information sink in as they passed fields of head-high cornstalks and lots lined with combines and corn trailers, awaiting harvest. "Maybe Richard Prentice doesn't have anything to do with Lauren's disappearance at all," she said, thinking out loud. "Maybe Phil is the one behind it. It makes more sense, really. Didn't I read somewhere that most violent crimes are committed by people the victims know?"

"That's generally true," he said. "But Lauren supposedly knew Prentice, too."

"Not as well as she knew Phil. They were married for almost seven years."

"We'll see what he has to say for himself. Meanwhile, did you think of anything else that would help us? Did you remember anything Lauren said to you about this big story?"

She shook her head. "I've racked my brain, but all she said was that she had a big story that was going to prove to the station how valuable she was to them. She wouldn't give me any details."

"We're going to keep working on this. We'll find her."

"Thank you." She faced forward in the seat once more. "And I'm sorry about the things I said earlier, about you not doing your job."

"Believe me, I've heard worse. Now how about that dinner? I know a great Thai place. Or if you like Mexican…"

"Before we do that, I want to see Lauren's car."

"Her car?"

"Yes. You said it's in an impound lot—that's local, right?"

"Yeah, but what's seeing her car going to do?"

"I just want to see it. Humor me."

"All right." He slowed and switched on his blinker, then executed a U-turn. They headed out of town, past the airport. She spotted a sign that said Fresh Fish. "Is that the fish shop you were talking about?" she asked.

"Yes. Promise me you won't go there and talk to the guy on your own."

"I won't," she said. Though maybe she could stop in sometime. Just to see him, not to talk…

"I mean it," Rand said. "It could jeopardize our case if you interfere. And I don't want to have to bail you out of jail again."

"You didn't have to bail me out." But his teasing tone made her smile. "I promise, I won't go near the place—at least not without you."

The impound yard sat off the main highway, rows of cars behind a tall fence and a locked gate. Rand chose a key from the ring he carried and opened the gate, then drove in.

Sophie spotted Lauren's yellow Mustang, a flashy car for a woman who liked to be noticed. It sat at the far end of the lot, a fine film of dust dulling the finish. Rand stopped behind the car and they got out.

"I can check in the office for the key," he said.

"It's all right. It's open." Sophie pulled open the driver's door, then stopped and looked at Rand. "Is it okay if I look inside?"

"Go ahead. The local cops have already been over it."

She slid into the driver's seat and stared out the window, trying to imagine what Lauren had last seen when she sat here. Had she arranged to meet someone at the overlook and left with them? Had she gone willingly, or been dragged away, kicking and screaming?

She put the image out of her mind and focused on

searching the interior of the car. The glove box turned up only the car's manual, a mini flashlight, a pair of sunglasses and the receipt for an oil change dated three months ago. The console was just as uninteresting—a check from a fast-food restaurant, a gas receipt and a tube of lip balm.

A glance at the backseat showed it was empty. Sighing, Sophie sat back and closed her eyes. *Help me out here, Lauren,* she sent the silent message. *Where should I be looking?*

The memory came to her of a trip the two sisters had taken together last year, when they'd driven from Sophie's condo in Madison to the Wisconsin Dells for a weekend getaway. They'd decided to splurge on a spa visit and Lauren had retrieved an envelope from beneath the front floor mat. "Emergency cash," she'd said. "I call it my mad money. If I keep it here, I have it if I need it, but I'm not tempted to spend it, the way I would if it was in my purse."

Sophie bent and pulled up the driver's side floor mat. She had to tug hard, since it was held in place by plastic hooks. Her heart raced when she saw the rectangular white envelope in the center of the space where the mat had been.

"Find something?" Rand opened the door and leaned in.

Sophie picked up the envelope. It felt stiff, as if it contained a piece of cardboard. "I remember Lauren used to hide money beneath the floor mat," she said. "But this doesn't feel like cash."

"Open it, but use the tips of your fingernails, and only touch the edges," he said.

She slid a nail beneath the flap of the envelope, then

shook out a single photograph. Rand leaned in closer, his cheek practically touching hers. She could feel his warm breath on her neck, and smell his clean, masculine scent.

She forced herself to focus on the grainy, black-and-white photo of two men talking to each other, standing beside a car in what looked like a parking lot. "Isn't that Richard Prentice?" she asked, staring at the man on the left.

"It is," Rand said. "And the other man is the fish shop owner, Alan Milbanks. Did Lauren ever mention that name to you?"

She shook her head. "I never heard of him until you mentioned him to me."

"He may have been the last person to see Lauren before she disappeared."

RAND AND SOPHIE returned to Ranger headquarters with the photograph. Graham and Michael Dance met them there. "This photo proves a link between Lauren and Alan Milbanks," Sophie said. "And a link between Alan and Richard Prentice."

"Let's bring him in for questioning," Graham said. He studied the photo. "Where was this taken, I wonder."

"Looks like a parking lot," Rand said. "The photo's grainy enough, it could be a still from a security camera."

Graham passed the photo to Rand. "Give it to Simon—see if he can determine where it came from. In the meantime, you and Michael bring Milbanks in. Let's see if he can tell us more about this picture and his relationship with Richard Prentice and Lauren Starling."

"What can I do while you're gone?" Sophie asked. She

was doing a good job of keeping it together, presenting a calm outer facade, but he sensed her anxiety climbing.

"We have copies of your sister's cell phone records. Get with Carmen and see how many of the numbers you recognize." He squeezed her shoulder. Maybe when he got back with Milbanks, they could have that dinner they'd been putting off. He was looking forward to sitting down with her and having a conversation that didn't focus on police work and her missing sister.

"All right. I'll do that." She turned to Graham. "I'm sorry about the trouble we caused downtown," she said.

"Never mind that." He waved away her apology. "Emma said the store owner overreacted. But I can see I need to keep you three women away from each other. Emma can get into enough trouble by herself. She doesn't need help."

Rand left Sophie at his desk, scanning through the call list from Lauren's cell phone carrier. He loaded Lotte into his cruiser while Michael Dance waited in the passenger seat. Behind them, the dog danced around, panting excitedly. "What's up with her?" Michael asked. "Why is she so antsy?"

"She knows something's up. That she's going to work." He started the vehicle and backed out of his parking space.

"How does she know that?"

"I guess she picks up vibes from me." He shrugged. "Dogs are sensitive. They're attuned to their surroundings in a way we can't even imagine."

Once again, he headed out of the park, back toward town and the fish market. Michael fiddled with the radio, but finally switched it off. Reception was lousy here in the mountains. "So, what do you make of this Sophie chick?" he asked.

Rand stiffened. "What do you mean?"

"Do you think she's on the level, all this stuff about being followed and smelling her sister's perfume and all?"

"Yeah, I think she's telling the truth. Don't you?"

"I was just wondering. I hear sometimes mental problems run in families."

He gripped the steering wheel harder, knuckles whitening. "Yeah, so what's your excuse?"

"Hey, don't be so touchy. I'm just trying to look at this from all angles. Isn't that what we're supposed to do?"

"Sophie's only problem is that she's concerned about her sister, who's been missing a month, and the police have made pretty much zero progress on the case. I don't blame her for being a little upset."

"She got to you pretty quick, didn't she?"

He glared at Michael. "I don't know what you're talking about."

"I'm just saying I recognize the signs. It happened to me that way with Abby—one look and I was a goner."

"But you two had known each other before, over in Afghanistan."

"We met once—and not under the best of circumstances. She wasn't even conscious." Michael had been a pararescuer in the air force's rescue squadron and Abby had been a casualty he'd helped airlift out of a combat zone. When her heart stopped en route, he'd revived her—but she'd remembered none of that until they met again five years later, after she stumbled onto a shooting in the park's backcountry while she was conducting research for her master's thesis.

Rand's relationship with Sophie—if he could even call it a relationship—wasn't on that level. "I feel for Sophie, that's all," he said. "She's had a rough time of it."

"So that's all you feel—sympathy?"

Sympathy. And a strong physical attraction. He admired her courage and her devotion to her sister. He wanted to know more about her and he enjoyed just being with her. What did all that add up to? "Mind your own business," he said.

"Abby likes her, if that makes you feel any better."

"I'd say Abby has good judgment, except she's with you."

"Here's a little unsolicited advice—if you really feel there's something there, don't be afraid to go for it. Let her know how you feel and see what happens."

"When I need your advice I'll ask for it, which is never."

"Right." Smiling, Michael folded his arms across his chest and closed his eyes. "You can thank me at the wedding."

The image of Sophie, in a white gown and veil, jolted him. But not in a bad way. He shook his head, trying to shake off the wave of unsettling emotions. Dogs were much easier to deal with than women. You always knew where you stood with canines; women were much harder to figure out.

Fifteen minutes passed in relative silence, the excited panting of Lotte over his shoulder and the hum of tires on pavement calming his jangled nerves. He signaled for the turn into the fish market parking lot and Michael opened his eyes and sat up straighter. "What's this Milbanks character like?" he asked.

"Nervous and suspicious," Rand said. "He was

sweating buckets and all we were doing was asking a few questions."

"Let's hope he's not trigger-happy."

Theirs was the only vehicle in the parking lot. The store was dark and empty. Michael parked the vehicle around the back of the building, out of sight of the street. He unloaded Lotte and clipped on her leash, then followed Michael around to the front door. "The hours posted on the door say they should be open until six-thirty," Michael said. "It's six thirty-five." He tried the knob and it turned easily in his hand.

One hand on his weapon, Michael slipped inside. Rand followed, a few paces back, alert for any movement within the store. Lotte strained on her leash, ears forward, tail wagging slowly.

Nothing looked out of place. The shelves of seasonings, cookbooks and a few canned goods were orderly. The coolers full of fish hummed away.

"Mr. Milbanks!" Michael called. "Mr. Milbanks, it's the police. We need to talk to you."

No answer. Michael nodded to Rand. "Check out back," he said.

Rand, with Lotte in the lead, hurried outside and around the building. The parking area here was empty, though the back door to the store stood open. Lotte whined, focused on the door. Rand studied her, recognizing her signal for a find, but her hair wasn't standing up; she didn't sense danger. Cautiously, he approached the open door.

He saw the blood first, a pool of dark red leaking into the doorway. A few feet away lay the body of Alan Milbanks.

# Chapter Eight

Rand crouched beside Milbanks's inert body, avoiding the pool of blood. Michael joined him from the front of the store. Rand leaned over and felt for a pulse at the man's throat, already knowing he wouldn't find one. "He hasn't been dead long," he said. "He's still warm."

"I checked the cash register," Michael said. "The drawer is full."

"This doesn't look like a robbery." Rand studied what was left of Milbanks's head. "More like an assassination. Close range. Somebody sending a message."

The jangle of bells made them both start. Rand stood, withdrawing his weapon as he rose. He and Michael took up positions on opposite sides of the room and started toward the front of the store.

"Hello?" a man's voice called. "Alan? Anybody home?"

Rand moved to where he could see through the passage into the front. A disheveled man in baggy cords and a sweatshirt, dirty blond hair falling into his eyes, stood in the middle of the shop. Phil Starling.

Rand stepped into the front room, his weapon fixed on Starling. "Police. Keep your hands where I can see them."

Starling turned the color of sour milk and inched his hands into the air. "Wh-what's going on?"

"I'll need to see some ID." Rand approached slowly. Out of the corner of his eye, he saw Michael moving up on the other side of the room.

"In my right back pocket." Starling stared at Rand's weapon, mesmerized.

"Take it out slowly."

Starling did so and extended the open wallet toward Rand. "I just came in to buy some fish," he said.

"How do you know Alan Milbanks?" Rand checked the ID. Phillip Starling, with a Denver address.

"Who?"

"Alan Milbanks. You called for Alan when you entered the store."

His smile was weak and lopsided. "I didn't know his last name. Just Alan. He…he introduced himself when I was in here last week."

"You buy a lot of fish, do you?" Rand returned the wallet to Starling.

"Yeah, I do. It's good for you, you know."

Starling's sickly pallor and unkempt appearance didn't mark him as a healthy living aficionado. "When was the last time you saw Alan?"

"Last time I bought fish. Maybe, I don't know—a couple of days ago. Why are you asking me all these questions? Is something wrong?"

"Your license has a Denver address. What are you doing in Montrose?"

"I'm here on vacation." He shoved the wallet back into his pocket. "You know, see the Black Canyon, do some hiking, like that."

"Where are you staying?"

"Why do you need to know?" Starling's expression turned surly. "Like I told you, I just came in to buy some fish. I didn't do anything wrong."

"We may need to get in touch with you. Where can we reach you?"

Starling pressed his lips together, in the expression of a pouting child, then heaved a sigh and gave the address of a cheap motel on the west side of town.

"You seem nervous, Mr. Starling," Rand said. "Any reason for that?"

"You're joking, right? I come in to buy some fish for dinner and suddenly I'm being grilled by cops. Who wouldn't be nervous?"

"Are you related to Lauren Starling?" Michael asked the question, startling the actor, who seemed to have forgotten he was there.

"She's my ex-wife," he said.

"When was the last time you saw her?"

"In court, the day we finalized the divorce. Almost three months ago."

"You haven't talked to her since then?"

"No."

"When did you arrive in Montrose?"

He hesitated. Because he resented the question, or because he needed time to think up a lie? "A week, maybe ten days ago. I don't remember."

"You don't remember?"

"It's a vacation, you know. It's not about keeping track of time."

"We'd like you to come down to the station and answer a few questions for us," Rand said.

"I've already been answering your questions."

"Yes, but we have a few more for you, and we'd like to talk to you where we can all sit down and get comfortable."

"No. You don't have any reason to hassle me this way. I just came in here to buy fish and you guys are giving me a hard time." He started to turn and walk away, but Michael was on him in a flash, twisting his arm and bringing him to his knees.

Starling howled and swore. "What do you think you're doing?"

"What do you think you're doing with this?" Rand gingerly pulled a pistol from the back waistband of Starling's cords. The snub-nosed revolver dangled from his index finger. He sniffed the barrel and shook his head. The gun didn't smell to him as though it had been fired recently, but he'd leave the final determination to the experts.

"I got a right to carry that," Starling protested.

"So you have a carry permit?" Michael asked.

"No, but I have a right to protect myself."

"Do you think buying fish is a particularly dangerous activity?" Rand asked.

"In some neighborhoods, it could be. I like to be careful."

"So do we, Mr. Starling, which is why we're going to take you in for questioning and booking."

"You can't arrest me." Starling's voice rose. "I haven't done anything wrong. What are you charging me with?"

"We'll start with carrying an illegal concealed weapon." Rand pulled the actor's arms behind his back and snapped on a pair of cuffs. "From there we might move on to kidnapping, or even murder."

"ALAN MILBANKS IS DEAD?" Sophie stared at Rand, who met her at Ranger headquarters the next morning with the news. She'd planned to spend the morning with Carmen, trying to put names to the rest of the list of numbers Lauren had called in the days before her disappearance. Some of the numbers were easy to identify. Lauren had made calls to her office, her hairdresser, her doctor's office and Sophie. One of the numbers had surprised Sophie. In the days before she'd gone missing, Lauren had spoken to her ex-husband, Phil, three times.

But none of the numbers on Lauren's phone records had a Montrose exchange. The news that one of the few people they knew Lauren had spoken to in town was dead shook her. "Did he have a heart attack or something?"

"He was murdered. Shot in the head."

She took a deep breath, trying to remain calm and take it all in. "Was it a robbery?" she asked. "Or something to do with drugs? You said he might be dealing drugs."

"It could be related to drug activity." Rand spoke softly, his eyes locked to hers. "Or it could be because someone saw us questioning him earlier and didn't want him to tell us what he knew."

"Do you think Richard Prentice did this?" she asked. "Because of the photograph showing him with Mr. Milbanks?"

Rand settled into the chair beside her at the conference table, where they'd retreated to talk privately. "Richard Prentice is hosting a fund-raiser for Senator Mattheson in Denver today." He slid over a copy of the *Denver Post* with a photograph of the senator and the billionaire smiling and shaking hands.

"That doesn't mean he couldn't have ordered some-one else to do his dirty work," Rand said.

"What will you do now?" Sophie asked.

"We're working with the local police to investigate the crime scene. There are no security cameras and ev-erything had been wiped pretty clean, but maybe we'll find something. Someone driving by might have seen something. But we did arrest someone on the scene for questioning."

"Who is that?"

"Your former brother-in-law, Phil Starling."

Her eyes widened. "You think Phil had something to do with Alan Milbanks's murder?"

"He showed up right after we discovered the body. He said he'd come in to buy fish, but he was acting awfully nervous for an innocent shopper, and he knew Milbanks's name before we mentioned it. And he was carrying a gun."

"A gun?" She shook her head. "This is crazy."

"Do you know if he has a history of drug use?" Rand asked. "Did Lauren ever mention anything like that?"

"No. I mean, I may have heard him mention smok-ing a joint a couple of times, but never anything more than that. He liked to have a few drinks—a few too many drinks, sometimes, but drugs?" She shook her head again. "Did you ask him about Lauren?"

"He said he hadn't seen her since the divorce, and that he'd only been in Montrose a week or so. We're following up on that, trying to find out where he's been staying."

"What else did he say?"

"Nothing. As soon as we got him to the station, he demanded to see his lawyer and clammed up. The lawyer will be here later this morning, so we'll talk to him then. He might feel more cooperative after he's spent a night in jail."

Would she feel more comfortable, knowing her former brother-in-law was in jail? "Do you really think Phil had something to do with Lauren's disappearance?" she asked.

"I don't know. He's a hard guy to read. No surprise, I guess, considering he's an actor."

Sophie thought all men were hard to read, even Rand. Was he spending so much time with her because he truly liked her, or merely because she was part of his case? Or maybe the captain had ordered him to keep an eye on her, despite his protestations to the contrary. After all, everyone who had a connection with Lauren was probably a suspect in her disappearance.

All right, enough with the paranoia already, she thought. Instead of wondering about Rand's motives, maybe she should try to get to know him better.

"Why did you want to be a police officer?" she asked.

"I really wanted to be a park ranger," he said. "I like the outdoors, but, at least for national parks, a law enforcement background is helpful. Then I got on with the Bureau of Land Management and it was a good fit— the outdoor lifestyle I wanted, and the chance to make a real difference."

Her own job didn't make a difference to anyone, she thought. "I wanted to be a librarian," she said. "But those jobs are hard to come by. Business seemed a more sensible choice."

"And you're a sensible person."

She looked away.

"Hey." He touched her shoulder lightly. "I didn't mean that as an insult. I think it's a good thing."

"Sure." Again, she didn't know how to read him. "Would you like to, um, get something to eat? I mean, go to lunch?" she asked. They'd never made it to dinner last night, something that had disappointed her more than she liked to admit. Would he think she was coming on to him, or worse—trying to bribe him or something?

"I'd like that. A lot. But can I take a rain check? I have a feeling I'm going to be pulling a long shift today."

"Sure." She stood, almost knocking her chair over in her haste. "I'll just get out of your way and let you get back to work."

"You don't have to rush off." He smiled, that genuine, warm look that made her insides turn to pudding. Or maybe something warmer and sweeter—hot fudge.

"Sophie?"

"Mmm?" She snapped back to attention.

"Are you okay?"

"Sure. I'm great."

"You look a little flushed."

"It's a little warm in here." She fanned herself. "I'll be fine. See you later." The rest of the phone records would have to wait. She turned and ran from the room. *Get a grip,* she scolded herself as she hurried to her car. Lauren would never have lost her cool with a man that way. Even when she'd been devastated by Phil's behavior, she'd never let him see her pain. She knew how to hide her emotions from the people she cared about.

*Oh, Lauren,* Sophie thought. *I always thought you needed me more than anyone else, because I was the only one you could really be yourself with. But now I need you, sister. I'm not as strong as we both thought.*

# Chapter Nine

In the harsh fluorescent lighting of the interrogation room of the Montrose Police Station, Phil Starling looked even sicklier and more disreputable. "You don't have any right to hold me like this," he said, as soon as Rand and Marco entered the interrogation room. "I didn't do anything wrong."

"You were carrying a concealed weapon without a permit," Rand said. He laid a file on the table and pulled out a chair. "We just have a few questions for you."

Starling turned to the man beside him—a white-haired, florid-faced fiftysomething lawyer in a paisley tie and rumpled suit. "Tell them they can't hold me."

"If my client answers your questions, are you willing to strike a deal for his release?" the lawyer asked.

"That's the district attorney's decision, not mine," Rand said.

"I'm sure the DA will consider your opinion in the matter," the attorney said.

"I see you haven't met our DA."

The lawyer frowned. "If you aren't going to make a deal, why should my client cooperate at all?"

"How about in the interest of justice? Or because it's the right thing to do? Or how about this one—we want to find the person who's responsible for several crimes. If that person isn't your client, maybe he should help us figure out who it is."

"What crimes?" Starling asked.

"We'll get to that." Rand sat in the chair across from Starling and his lawyer. "Why were you at the fish store yesterday afternoon?" he asked.

"I told you—I wanted to buy fish."

"What kind of fish?"

"I don't know. Tuna, I guess."

"You weren't there to buy drugs?"

"You don't have to answer that," the lawyer said.

Phil's gaze slid sideways. "No."

"But you were aware that Alan Milbanks sold drugs?"

He hesitated. "I might have heard some things. But that's not why I was there."

"Did your ex-wife buy drugs from Alan Milbanks?"

This question got a surprised snort from him. "Lauren? Is that what she's into now?"

"Do you think your ex-wife takes drugs?"

"Nothing that woman does would surprise me. You know she's crazy, right? Certifiable. She even spent some time in the loony bin."

"The loony bin?"

"The psych ward. Mental hospital. Whatever the politically correct term is these days."

"Was that why you divorced, because of her mental problems?"

"That, and a lot of other things." Another sideways glance.

"When was the last time you saw Lauren Starling?"

"You don't have to answer that one, either," the lawyer said.

"A lot of help you are," Starling said. "I don't have to answer any of these questions." He turned back to Rand. "I told you. In court, when we officially split."

"You haven't seen her since?"

"No."

"How does she make the court-ordered support payments to you?"

He wiped one hand across his face, which was shiny with sweat, and glanced at the lawyer, who shrugged, arms crossed over his chest. Starling sighed and turned back to Rand. "So you know about that, do you?"

"The court ordered Lauren to pay monthly support payments to you as part of the divorce settlement. How did she make those payments?"

He settled back in his chair, as if hunkering down for the long haul. "She mailed a check. Though she wasn't always on time, I can tell you that."

"What happened when the checks were late?"

"I'd call and tell her she'd better get the check to me right away or I'd see her in court."

"But you told us earlier you hadn't talked to your ex-wife since the divorce."

He frowned. "Did I? Well, it's not like we were having a friendly conversation or anything, you know. We just talked about the money."

"What about the money, Mr. Starling? How are you doing financially?"

"That's none of your business," he snapped.

Rand paged through the file he'd brought with him. "You're staying at one of the cheapest motels in town. The manager tells me you're late with this week's payment. And he says you've been there two weeks."

"He'll get his money."

"When was the last time you worked as an actor?"

"I was in a show in the spring. *Barefoot in the Park*. I got great reviews. Right now I'm waiting for a deal we've got going with Hollywood to come through. I thought it would be good to take a little vacation while I had some downtime, because I can see things are going to get really busy here soon."

"But right now you don't have any money coming in?" Rand said.

"I have some savings."

"But your only reliable income is the support payments from your ex-wife."

He snorted again. "I wouldn't call those reliable. She hasn't paid me anything in almost two months."

"You are aware, Mr. Starling, that Lauren Starling has been missing for more than a month."

"I know she hasn't sent me a check and she hasn't bothered to show up for work."

"What do you think happened to her?"

He shrugged. "Like I told you. She's nuts. She probably decided to run off to Baja or join a commune or something. No telling."

"But you haven't heard anything from her?"

"I told you, no!"

Rand leaned across the table and fixed Starling with a cold gaze. "We have a witness who says she saw you and Lauren together at a hotel here in Montrose."

Phil flinched, a reaction so brief anyone who wasn't watching him closely might have missed it. "What—you think we were still sleeping together? Fat chance of that."

"I didn't mention sex," Rand said. "This witness says you were talking. What were you talking about?"

He looked away and said nothing.

"The hotel has security cameras," Rand said. "I'm sure we can find photographs to prove you were there, in addition to the eyewitness." He was sure of no such thing, but he wanted Starling to worry.

"I went by there to talk to her about the support payments," he said, the words coming out in a rush.

"What about the payments?" Rand asked.

"I needed more money." He twisted his hands together on the table in front of him. "She had it good—cushy job with that news station in Denver. Prime-time news anchor, everybody's sweetheart. I got work coming—a big, important role. But everything in Hollywood takes time, so it's gonna be a while before the money comes in. So I figured, she could pay me a little more now, and when the money starts rolling in for me, I'll cancel the payments altogether. If that's not generous, I don't know what is."

"Did Lauren tell you her job at the news station was in jeopardy? That she might be laid off soon?"

"As if that was ever going to happen. That was just an excuse. The station wouldn't dare get rid of her. I mean, she has a disability, right? They fire her, she could sue. Of course, that might not be so bad. Maybe she'd get even more money. Either way, she could afford to share some of the wealth with me."

"But she refused to pay you."

"She did. I even threatened to take her back to court, but she didn't care. She told me she couldn't help and showed me the door."

"How did you feel about that? Especially after you came all this way to plead with her."

"How do you think I felt? I was plenty irate. I told her that wouldn't be the last she heard from me on the issue."

"So the two of you argued. Maybe things got out of hand?" Rand leaned closer, his voice low, confiding. "What happened? Did you hit her? Did she fall and hit her head? Maybe you got scared and decided the best thing to do was to hide the body, drive her car out to the park and make it look like she'd committed suicide?"

Starling stared at Rand, his jaw gone slack, eyes wild with terror. "What are you talking about? I didn't hurt her. I didn't lay a finger on her. I left—told her I'd come back the next day, after she'd had more time to think about my offer. Only when I came back, she wasn't there. I figured she was avoiding me. I haven't seen her since."

"Yet you stayed in town. Why is that?"

"Maybe I like it here."

"And maybe you have people in Denver who are after you to pay money you owe them?"

"Yeah, maybe some of that, too. But I've just been hanging out. I haven't seen a hair of Lauren's since that one day I talked to her."

"What about Lauren's sister, Sophie?" Rand asked.

His eyes narrowed. "What about her?"

"She says you threatened her when you saw her in town yesterday."

"That little mouse? You've met her, right? Can you even believe she's Lauren's sister? The two are nothing alike."

"Why did you tell her to go home and mind her own business?"

"Because she was giving me the stink eye." He drew himself up, indignant. "She never did like me, always treated me like I was something the cat dragged in. The police arrested her for harassing me, remember. I didn't do anything."

"What did she say to you?" Rand asked.

"She accused me of following her. As if I'd waste my time on a nothing like her."

Rand had to fight not to defend Sophie from Starling's disparagement. She was worth far more that all the beautiful, sparkling, empty-headed women he'd ever met. But better to change the subject. "So you didn't know that Lauren knew Alan Milbanks?" he said.

"Lauren and Alan?" He laughed. "He wasn't exactly her type, you know?"

"What do you mean?" Rand asked.

"Lauren might be whacko, but she was hot. She never had trouble attracting good-looking guys. That's why she married me, you know?"

Behind them, Marco coughed. Starling scowled at him but was smart enough not to comment. "So Lauren didn't introduce you to Alan Milbanks?"

"No. I wanted some fish and people told me he had the best fish in town."

Substitute *crack* or *meth* for *fish* and Starling might be telling the truth, Rand thought.

"Do you always carry a gun when you shop for fish, Mr. Starling?" he asked.

"I told you I'd heard rumors about the other business they did at that place. I wasn't taking any chances." He rubbed his hand across his chin, the beard stubble making a rasping noise. "So, what happened—did you finally catch him in the act? Is that why the place was closed?"

"Mr. Milbanks is dead," Rand said.

Starling froze. "Dead? What happened? Did he have a heart attack or something?"

"He was murdered. Do you know anything about that?"

Starling gaped, openmouthed. He certainly appeared shocked by the news, but after all, he was an actor. Rand didn't trust the reactions of someone who was trained to portray emotions. "Do you know anything about the murder of Alan Milbanks?" he asked again.

"No! What kind of guy do you think I am?"

"A guy who carries a gun to buy fish," Rand said drily.

"I never even fired that gun!" Starling protested. "I bought it off a kid in Denver, for self-protection. I'm not a murderer!"

Fortunately for Starling, tests on the weapon backed up this assertion. The little revolver hadn't been fired in a long time, judging by its condition. And the caliber didn't match the bullet that had killed Alan Milbanks. "Do you know anybody who would want Alan Milbanks dead?" Rand asked.

"How the hell should I know? Somebody he sold bad fish to? I hardly knew the guy. He probably had lots of enemies."

"Why do you say that?"

"Who doesn't have enemies, right?"

"Did Lauren have enemies?"

"Lauren?" The hardness around his eyes softened a little. "Nah. Everybody liked Lauren. Even at her wacki-est, she was never mean. Even when she drove you nuts, you couldn't stay mad at her."

"But you could stay mad at her," Rand said. "You

were angry enough to come all the way to Montrose to confront her."

"I told you, that was about the money." He leaned forward, hands clasped, expression earnest. "Listen, I know I was no angel in our marriage. I cheated on her, but you got to understand what it was like being married to her. The big TV star. The beauty queen. Everywhere we went, people fawned on her. If she came to one of my performances, everybody paid attention to her, not me."

"A little hard on the ego," Rand said.

"Exactly. It gets to a guy, you know? And then, I never knew what she was going to be like from day to day. One day she was this dynamo, racing around from one project to another, all happy and energetic, little Miss Positive. The next day she wouldn't even talk to me. She was like this little dark cloud huddled in the apartment. I couldn't depend on her. It drove me crazy. And it drove me into another woman's arms." He shrugged. "So sue me. I'm human. But even after all that, part of me still loves her. I just couldn't live with her."

"The last time you saw Lauren, what was she like?"

"She was fine. As normal as she ever got, anyway."

"Did she seem depressed? Upset about anything?"

"No. Believe me, you couldn't miss one of her black moods. When she and I talked at the motel, she was all business, but not negative."

"Did she say why she was in Montrose?"

"She mentioned something about work—some story she was reporting on—but she didn't go into detail. To tell you the truth, I didn't care. All I wanted was to come to some agreement on the money and leave. She's not really a part of my life anymore, and I always believed in making a clean break, you know?"

"And you never spoke to her again? No phone calls or texts or any other communication?"

"Nope. I called the hotel the next day and they told me she'd checked out. I drove by a couple of times to make sure and her car wasn't in the lot. She didn't answer my texts or calls to her cell. I figured she was on assignment somewhere else and was avoiding me."

"Did that upset you?"

"Do I look like an idiot? Of course it upset me. But I just figured there was no reasoning with the woman. It was time to get out the big guns. I called my lawyer and told him to petition the court for an increase in support. She could afford it, and since I didn't have any income at the moment, I figured I'd get it. She had plenty to spare."

"And did you petition the court?" Rand asked the attorney.

The man started, as if out of a stupor. "Excuse me?"

"Not this guy," Starling said. "My divorce attorney. I just picked this guy out of the phone book. It's not like I've been in trouble with the law before. Well, maybe a DWAI once, but that was years ago."

"I'm sorry to interrupt this lovely chat," the lawyer said, glaring at his client. "But unless you're going to charge my client with something more than this minor weapons violation, I suggest you let him go."

"A weapons violation isn't a minor charge," Rand said. "Your client can go back to his cell and wait until the judge either sets or denies bail at his arraignment tomorrow."

Starling opened his mouth to say something, but a quelling look from the lawyer silenced him. Rand pushed back his chair and stood. "Is there anything else you'd like to tell us about your wife or Alan Milbanks, Mr. Starling?" he asked.

"I hope Lauren's okay," he said. "Really, I do. She has her problems, but she isn't so bad, really. She doesn't deserve any more hard luck in her life. And if you see her, you can tell her I said so."

Rand left the room as a bailiff came to escort Starling back to his cell. Marco followed him out. "What do you think?" Rand asked.

"I don't think he's telling the truth about his relationship to Milbanks," Marco said. "Ten dollars says one of the reasons he's in such financial straits is that he's keeping up a drug habit. I'm guessing one of the reasons he's stayed in Montrose is that Milbanks was a good source."

"Maybe he's hiding out from the dealers he owes in Denver."

"Probably. As for Lauren Starling—I don't know. I can see things getting out of hand with her, especially if she had a history of erratic behavior that pushed his buttons. Things went too far and he killed her. Maybe accidental, but then he covered things up."

"Except that doesn't explain the note on Sophie's car."

"Maybe he learned she was in town and decided this was a chance to elaborate on the fiction that she'd run away. He was married to Lauren, so he knew her handwriting, the things she would say. He's got a big ego, so he's convinced he can pull this off, divert attention from anyone looking for a body."

"Maybe." Marco pulled his keys from his pockets. "Back to headquarters?"

"I'll meet you there later. I think I'm going to nose

around the hotels in town a little more to see if I can find out more about what Starling—and Lauren— might have been up to."

A DAY SPENT alternately watching bad TV and flipping through outdated magazines scavenged from the lobby, while waiting for the phone to ring with word about Lauren, left Sophie on edge. She paced the floor and gnawed at a thumbnail, picking up the phone half a dozen times to call Rand and ask if he had any news, then setting it aside. If he knew anything, he'd call her, wouldn't he?

Frustrated with her own impotence, she sat down at the one small table by the window and opened her notebook. Maybe if she made a list of things she could do to help find Lauren, she'd feel better. She uncapped the pen and wrote *1* Then stared for a long moment, her mind blank.

A knock on the door startled her. She checked the peephole, and her heart gave a lurch when she recognized Rand. He wasn't in uniform this evening, instead dressed in tight, dark jeans, boots and a pin-striped Western shirt that reminded her again of an old-west cowboy—only this one had cleaned up to come to town.

She undid the chain on the door and pulled it open. "Hello, Rand," she said.

"I thought I'd see if I could cash in that rain check on dinner."

"Oh, uh, well…" Having dinner with him didn't feel like the safest way to spend the evening, either. Being near him distracted her from her purpose more than she wanted. Still, she couldn't think of a way to refuse without being rude, and the thought of sitting alone in her room until she was exhausted enough to sleep depressed her.

"I should change," she said, looking down at her rumpled jeans and blouse.

"You look fine," he said. "Great."

She wasn't used to such flattery, but maybe he was just trying to reassure her. "Just give me a minute," she said, and retreated to the bathroom.

She returned a few moments later, wearing a fresh blouse, with her hair combed and lips glossed. "Even better," he said, and opened the door.

As she approached the FJ Cruiser, the dog, Lotte, poked her nose out of the window and gave a low bark. Sophie stumbled back, but Rand caught her, his hands on her shoulders steadying her. "Don't be afraid," he said. "She's just saying hello."

"How do you know? Maybe she doesn't like me."

"Dogs are like people. If you know what to look for, you can read their emotions." He gave her a gentle push. "Go on, get in the car. You two need to get used to each other."

"Why do we need to get used to each other?" she asked, but she made her way to the passenger side of the vehicle, keeping her gaze fixed on the dog. But Lotte ignored her, her attention focused on Rand.

"Lotte and I are a team." He slid into the driver's seat. "She's with me most of the day, and she goes home with me at night."

"She lives with you?" Sophie had thought the dog would stay in a kennel at headquarters when she wasn't working.

"Of course. She's my partner and I have to take care of her. Did you know that she outranks me?"

"What do you mean?"

"She's a sergeant. I'm only a corporal." He showed her the badge clipped to the dog's harness. "They do that on purpose, so the handler is sure to respect the dog. Not that I wouldn't respect Lotte." He scratched the dog behind the ears. She gazed up at him adoringly, mouth open to reveal a lot of gleaming, sharp teeth. Sophie took a step back, her heart racing.

"You sure you don't want to pet her?" Rand asked. "It might help you to see her as a friend."

Sophie shook her head. "I couldn't."

He shrugged, and closed the gate that blocked the dog from the front seat. Only then did Sophie get into the vehicle. "I know you think I'm silly," she said. "Fearing something you love so much."

"Fear isn't always rational," he said. "I get that. But I'd like to help you get over your fear, if I could."

"It might be easier if I started with a smaller dog," she said. "They look less frightening."

"Smaller dogs are more unpredictable than a trained working dog like Lotte."

"Yes, but if a toy poodle bites something, it's less likely to do damage."

"I guess there is that. What do you feel like eating?"

"Anything." She hadn't had much of an appetite since Lauren had disappeared.

They ended up at a Mexican food place not far from her hotel; Lotte settled down in the vehicle to wait while Rand and Sophie went inside. They ordered chips and salsa and enchiladas. She drank a margarita, while he stuck to iced tea. She tried not to be obvious as she studied him across the table.

"Do I pass inspection?" he asked.

She flushed. "You pass." He wasn't movie-star hand-some—he needed a haircut and his nose had been broken once, probably a long time ago. She guessed he was a few years older than her—old enough to have the be-ginnings of fine lines around his eyes. He had the lean, muscular build of an athlete, and an air of competence that probably put most people at ease. She tried to come up with an adjective she would use to describe him to Lauren, but the word that filled her head was *sexy*.

Oh yeah, he was sexy, all right. Forget the badge and the gun and his position of authority. The real reason Rand made her nervous was that he made her feel more like a woman than she had felt in a long time. She wasn't merely a sister or an employee or a neighbor. She was a desirable female who'd been alone too long. Being with Rand made her lose her focus on her mission to find her sister. She forced her mind away from such dangerous thoughts and searched for some safe subject of conver-sation. "Emma told me you play lacrosse," she said.

"Yeah, I got into it in high school."

"What do you like about it?"

"It's a fast, physical game that requires strength, agil-ity and real skill." He crunched a tortilla chip. "Plus, it's just fun. What do you like to do for fun?"

She forced herself not to squirm in her chair. She hated questions like this, because the answer made her sound so lame. "I like going out with friends and read-ing. That probably seems boring to you, I know…"

"No, I like those things, too."

The warmth of his smile made her want to cuddle up next to him. She traced one finger around the rim of her margarita glass. "Why are we here, having dinner to-gether? Did the captain tell you to keep an eye on me?"

"No. I'm here because I want to be."

"Why? Do you think I'm guilty of something? Or do you feel sorry for me?" She had trouble getting the last words out. The last thing she wanted from him was pity.

He leaned toward her and took her hand. "I'm here because I like you and I want to be with you. I think you're a special woman and I want to get to know you better." He brushed his thumb across her knuckles, and a hot tremor passed through her, the heat settling low in her abdomen. She forced herself to meet his gaze, and the desire she found there shook her. Her instinct was to pull away, to run from that kind of intimacy.

He tightened his grip on her hand. "You don't have to be afraid of me," he said.

She ducked her head but didn't pull away, enjoying the warmth of his hand around hers. Enjoying the connection. "I'm not afraid," she said. A little nervous. Attracted. Aroused, even.

"I really like you," he said.

"Too bad we didn't meet under better circumstances." She reluctantly withdrew her hand.

"Do you believe if you don't think about your sister every minute it's going to make a difference?"

"The longer a person stays missing, the less likely there is to be a positive outcome—isn't that what they say?"

"That's generally true, yes."

"Then I feel guilty even sitting here having dinner. We should be out looking for her 24/7 until we find her."

"Random searches aren't very effective. You have to rest and regroup and focus on the most likely locations."

"Then why aren't you searching Richard Prentice's ranch?"

"Believe me, I'd like to go in there and tear the place apart. But we need to build a strong case against him. What if he's innocent?"

"If he's innocent, where is Lauren? Why haven't I heard from her?"

"Try to hold on to the fact that we haven't seen a single indicator of foul play or violence in this case," he said.

They hadn't seen anything, but that didn't mean Lauren hadn't been hurt, or even killed. She pressed her lips tightly together, determined not to break down in front of him. "I think I want to go back to the hotel now," she said. "I'm lousy company and I'm tired."

"Sure." He signaled the waitress to bring their check. She reached for her purse, but he waved her away. "I'll get this."

She said nothing else until he pulled to a stop in front of her hotel room. "Thank you for dinner," she said, fumbling with the seat belt.

"I'll walk you to your door." He came around to her side of the car, then walked with her up the outside stairs to her room. She kept her head down, lost in a fog of worry, but his hand, pulling her to him, brought her to full awareness again. "The door to your room is open," he said softly.

She stared dumbly at the door, which stood open about four inches. "I'm sure I locked it when I left," she said. "Maybe the maid…"

"Wait here." He drew the gun from his holster and approached the room, staying close to the wall. He stopped to listen for a moment, then nudged the door open with his foot. Nothing happened, so after another pause, he entered, gun at the ready. After another few seconds light spilled onto the walkway and he said, "It's okay for you to come in now. Don't touch anything."

She froze just inside the door, heart pounding, not comprehending the scene that lay before her, jagged images registering in her mind, like the reflection in a broken mirror—upended suitcase, covers dragged from the bed to pool on the floor, gray-white stuffing from the slashed pillows spilling across the top of the dresser, dresser drawers smashed and piled in one corner. Her gaze shifted to the mirror over the sink in the little dressing area outside the bathroom. Greasy pink letters a foot high and slanting upward spelled out STAY AWAY IF YOU WANT TO STAY ALIVE.

## *Chapter Ten*

The room tipped and wobbled, and gray clouds rushed to swallow Sophie. Then Rand's arm was around her, supporting her as he led her to the bed and gently pushed her down to sit on the edge of the bare mattress. "Put your head between your knees," he said, pressing on her back until she bent forward and did as he commanded. "Now breathe in, deeply, not too fast. You're going to be all right."

She gripped his hand, aware of how icy she felt, all over. "Who did this?" she asked when she was able to sit upright and breathe again. She kept her eyes fixed on his, avoiding looking at the violence that had been wrought on the room around her.

"I don't know, but we'll find out." He continued to hold her hand, worry making him look older, as if she was glimpsing the man he'd be ten years from now. The idea reassured her, somehow. "Are you all right?" he asked.

She nodded and sat up straighter, forcing herself to release her grip on his hand, though as soon as they broke contact she felt bereft, and colder still. "Why would someone do this…to me?"

He shook his head. "Do you want to wait in the car until the local cops get here?"

"Will you wait with me?"

"Yes."

He led her outside, leaving the door open a few inches, the way they had found it. Lotte whined when Rand slid into the driver's seat, and pressed her nose against the grill. "She knows something's up," he said, and scratched her through the grate. "She wants to get out and go to work."

"Would she be able to track whoever did this?" Sophie forced herself to look at the dog, at the powerful muscles of her legs and shoulders, and the alert, forward tilt of her velvety ears. She was a beautiful animal, one likely to strike fear in the heart of anyone she turned against.

Sophie faced forward once more. Lotte wasn't turned against her. Rand wouldn't let the dog hurt her. She had to remember that.

They heard the police getting closer, sirens wailing. Two black-and-whites sped into the motel lot, one behind the other, and skidded to a halt behind Rand's SUV. Rand opened his door. "I'm going to talk to them, but they'll probably have questions for you, too."

She nodded. "Sure."

The four officers—a woman, two white men and a black man—stood in a huddle outside the door, talking with Rand. Occasionally one of the men glanced her way, but too briefly for her to read his expression. After a moment, all five of them went into the room, where they stayed for what seemed like a long while.

Lotte panted softly, and Sophie sensed the dog's attention focused on the open room door, as well. Was this because Rand was inside, or because Lotte sensed that violence had taken place in there, the kind of violence she was trained to stop?

After half an hour or more, the female officer emerged from the room and walked over to Sophie's side of the vehicle. "Ms. Montgomery? I'm Officer Cagle, with the Montrose Police Department. I need to ask you a few questions."

"Of course." She glanced toward the room, wishing Rand would join them. But that was silly, she silently scolded herself. She was a grown woman, and she didn't have any reason to be afraid of Officer Cagle.

The questions were ordinary and expected: her basic information, why she was in Montrose, what she'd done that day. Officer Cagle made no comment on the fact that she'd had dinner with Rand. "Do you know of anyone—here or back home in Wisconsin—who might want to do something like this?" the officer asked. "A former boyfriend with a grudge? A coworker who is unhappy with you? A stalker?"

"No one." She shook her head emphatically. "I lead a very quiet life. I'm not the kind of person who makes enemies."

"What about the message on the mirror—'stay away if you want to stay alive'? What do you make of that?"

She wet her dry lips, fighting back the fear. "I...I came to town to look for my missing sister. Maybe... maybe someone who has something to do with her disappearance has heard I'm here and...and they don't like it?"

"Any names?"

Richard Prentice? But why would a billionaire even bother with someone like her? Phil Starling? But wasn't he in jail? She shook her head. "I don't know. It just seems so…so random."

Officer Cagle slipped her notebook into her pocket and straightened. "If you think of anything, let us know." She handed over a card. "That's my number, and of course, Officer Knightbridge can put you in touch with us. We're going to need to seal off the room until our investigation is complete, but if you like, you can come in and collect a few personal belongings—just what you'll need for the next day or so."

She nodded, and followed the officer into the room, stepping gingerly around an officer who was photographing the scene, then skirting debris from the rampage to arrive at the bathroom. She collected her makeup bag—minus the tube of rose-pink lipstick she'd bought only the week before, and which now lay broken in the sink. She kneeled in front of the upended suitcase and reached for a pair of underwear, then snatched back her hand as if she'd been slapped and let out a small cry.

"What is it?" Officer Cagle kneeled beside Sophie.

"My clothes…the underwear…" She choked back another cry and pointed a wavering finger at the pile of garments.

With the tip of a pen, Officer Cagle picked up the pair of underwear on top. It was slashed through the middle of the crotch, neatly sliced through satin and cotton. The other clothes were similarly cut, very precisely across the portions of the fabric that would have covered her most intimate parts.

Sophie turned away, feeling sick.

"It's okay. You're going to be all right." Rand's voice, soft in her ear. His arms, strong around her, lifting her. "Come with me."

He led her outside, into the fresh air. She breathed in deep gulps, as if the oxygen could somehow wash away the image of her violated wardrobe. Rand continued to hold her close, until at last her trembling subsided. "I know this feels really personal," he said. "Whoever did this wants you to feel that way. They're playing a psychological game. But you're stronger than they are. You're not going to let them defeat you."

"I don't feel strong."

"You are strong. A weak woman wouldn't have come all this way to help her sister. A weak woman wouldn't have stood up to me and the rest of the Rangers and demanded we help you."

"Then I guess I've used up all my courage on those things. I don't feel like I have any left."

"You just need time to regroup and let it build back up." He took his arm from around her shoulders, but kept his hand resting lightly at her back. "Are you ready to go?"

"Go where?"

"Back to my place. You can rest, and I know you'll be safe there."

She hesitated. "What about my car?"

"I'll have an officer drive it over."

She couldn't impose on him that way. He couldn't assume what was best for her. They didn't have that kind of relationship… She opened her mouth to refuse.

What came out was "Thank you. I'll feel much safer there." In truth, she couldn't think of anywhere she'd rather be right now than with Rand Knightbridge.

RAND DIDN'T SAY anything on the drive back to his duplex. If Sophie didn't feel like talking, he wasn't going to force her. But he kept glancing at her still figure belted into the passenger seat, her face chalky white. Would it be better if she broke down and cried? Maybe releasing her emotions would be more beneficial than this distant, terrifying calm. He gripped the steering wheel so tightly his knuckles ached as he fought a rage against whoever had done this to her. He'd tried to make light of the seriousness of the attack, not wanting to worry her, but the discovery of her slashed underwear and clothing had sent a chill clear through him. They weren't dealing with some random punk out to make trouble. Whoever was responsible for this attack had a hatred of women in general—or of Sophie in particular—that could lead to further violence.

All the more reason to keep Sophie as close as possible, where he could ensure her safety. "Here we are, home, sweet home." He forced a relaxed cheerfulness into his voice that he didn't feel as they pulled into the driveway of the duplex. A quick check of the area revealed nothing out of the ordinary. Marco's half of the driveway was empty; Rand had called and asked him to check in with the Montrose cops, to see what they turned up. The other cars on the street were familiar to him, and lights shone in the neighbors' houses, the yellow of lamplight and the blue glow of televisions.

He let Lotte out of the back of the SUV and she trotted ahead of them into the house. Rand and Sophie followed. Rand flipped on all the lights and led the way toward the kitchen, pausing to kick dirty socks under the sofa and to close an open cabinet door. "Can I get you some coffee or tea, or maybe a drink?" he asked.

"Don't go to any trouble." She looked around her, and he was conscious of the dirty dishes in the sink and the takeout pizza box protruding from the top of the trash can.

"Sorry it's a little messy," he said.

"You don't have to apologize. You weren't expecting company."

"Sit down." She looked ready to fall down. He pulled out a chair at the kitchen table.

She sat and he moved to a cupboard and rummaged around until he unearthed some herbal tea he'd bought in an attempt to self-treat a cold one time, along with honey from the same episode. Hot drinks with sugar—wasn't that what people said was good for shock? He set a pan of water to boil. He was debating what to do next when his phone rang.

"Hey, Marco," he answered. "What's up?"

"We're not getting much out of the hotel room," he said. "CSI is still trying to lift prints, but the perps probably wore gloves. Is Sophie sure nothing was taken?"

He turned to Sophie. "Marco wants to know if anything was taken from your hotel room."

She shook her head. "Nothing. I had my money and my phone with me. I didn't bring a laptop or anything like that. Do they really think this was a robbery attempt?"

"Tossing the suitcase and dresser indicates the perp was looking for something," Rand said. "If nothing is missing, he didn't find what he was looking for."

"I don't think it was robbery," Sophie said. "I think whoever it was wanted to frighten me. And I'd say he succeeded."

"I'm going to put Marco on speaker so you can hear him," Rand said. "Marco, did you get that about nothing missing?"

"Maybe the perp was looking for the photograph," Marco said. "The one of Milbanks and Prentice."

"But I turned that over to you guys," she said.

"Whoever did this may not know that," Rand said.

"What good would the photograph do anyone?" Sophie asked.

"It's the strongest link we have between Prentice and Milbanks," Rand said. It might be the link they needed to finally bring Prentice to justice.

"We're trying to bring Prentice in for questioning," Marco said. "His lawyers are stalling, but Graham hinted he could arrange for the photo to be leaked to the press. I think that's going to persuade them to be more cooperative."

"Let's hope so," Rand said. He said good-night and disconnected the call, but it vibrated again immediately.

"Don't put me on speaker," Marco said. "I don't want Sophie to hear."

"Okay." Rand turned his back and busied himself at the stove. "What's up?"

"One more thing you need to know," Marco said. "Phil Starling was released on bond this afternoon, about four o'clock."

"Gotcha." He hung up and finished making the tea for Sophie, his mind racing. If Phil was out of jail by four, he could easily have driven to Sophie's hotel and trashed her room while they were at dinner. Maybe his feelings for his former sister-in-law went deeper than mere disdain.

Rand fed Lotte her kibble. Sophie watched the dog eat, leaning as far away from the dish as possible without getting up from her chair. "Let's go in the other room," he said. "We'll be more comfortable in there."

He took her elbow and escorted her out of the room, keeping himself between her and the dog. He didn't completely understand her fear of Lotte, but he believed she wasn't faking it. They sat on the sofa, where she perched on the edge of the cushion, hands cupped around the mug of tea balanced on her knee.

"Relax. I won't bite." He kept his voice light, not letting on how much her distance hurt, after the closeness they'd shared not an hour before. Over dinner and even later, after they'd first discovered her trashed hotel room, he'd thought she was letting down her guard with him—enjoying his company, even.

She leaned back against the cushions, though tension still radiated from her.

"Would you like it better if I sat over there?" He motioned to the recliner across the room.

"No. No, this is fine." She sipped her tea, her gaze shifting around the room, looking at anything but him.

"Do you want me to put Lotte in the other room?" The dog had finished eating and lay on a pad beside the recliner, head resting on her front paws.

"I…I'd forgotten she was even in the room."

"Then what is it?" He scooted forward to sit closer to her, almost—but not quite—touching her. "Don't you trust me?"

"I trust you." She swallowed and rubbed one hand, palm down, along the side of her thigh. "But I'm not sure I trust myself."

"What do you mean?" He tried to read her expression, but she wasn't giving off clear signals. Was she afraid? Angry? Guilty?

"I'm not the person you think I am," she said.

"How do you know what I think about you?"

"It's what everyone thinks about me—that I'm this quiet, plain, serious woman who never steps out of line. I'm responsible and sober and dependable and I never cause any trouble at all."

"Are you saying you have caused trouble?" he asked.

"More than you can imagine."

# Chapter Eleven

Sophie waited for some reaction from Rand—shock, disbelief, even argument. But all he did was settle back against the cushions and regard her calmly. "Tell me about it," he said. "I'm not in any hurry. And some people say I'm a good listener."

She sipped the tea, which had grown cold. What would it hurt to tell him? Maybe it would help him understand the things that drove her. She set aside the half-empty mug and hugged a pillow to her chest. "When we were girls, Lauren was always into mischief," she began. "She wasn't a bad child, just more daring than I was, more likely to bend the rules."

Lauren had been beautiful and winsome, even as a toddler, all blond curls and blue eyes and perfect dimples. "She was an angel child, with the personality of an imp," she continued. "Lauren was the one who climbed to the top of the playground gym and jumped off into a mud puddle, or who decided, when she was seven, that she wanted to drive the car and backed it into a tree. She ran away from home when she was thirteen, and again when she was fifteen. She dated the wildest boys, racked up traffic tickets and curfew violations, got caught skipping school and smoking pot and drinking when she was underage. Our parents dragged her to therapists and summer school and extracurricular activities, in a vain effort to curb an exuberance they didn't yet recognize as mania."

"And what were you doing while all this was going on?" Rand asked.

"I suppose to make up for all the trouble she caused, I tried to be better, more responsible," Sophie said. "I was like everyone else—I adored her and let her get away with things. No one could stay angry with her. She was so charming and witty, and really sweet. Not a malicious bone in her body. And maybe we all sensed, even then, that there was something different about her brain that made it impossible for her to fit into the mold everyone else had to conform to."

"How old was she before she was diagnosed with bipolar disorder?" Rand asked.

"Not until this year. Isn't that wild? But she did a good job of masking her worst symptoms, and after a while we all took it for granted that that was her personality. Whenever she did something a little off, we thought she was just being Lauren."

"While you were the good, responsible daughter," he said.

"Yes, but when I was a freshman in college, Lauren was still in high school, and she had the first of what I know now was a major manic episode. She lost control. She ran away and ended up in jail in a town just across the state line, charged with destruction of property and disturbing the peace." The horror of those days still made a knot in the pit of her stomach—hushed conversations between her parents, angry outbursts followed by tears, everyone tiptoeing around, fragile and furious and fearful. "My dad was able to pull strings and hush up the incident. The charges were dropped and Lauren came home and finished school in a private boarding facility. It cost my parents a lot of money—so much that they asked me to take a semester off college."

"Ouch!" Rand said. "That must have hurt."

"Oh, yes. I was furious—not just about having to postpone my schooling, but about all the attention Lauren had taken away from me for all those years. Instead of leaving school and coming home, as my parents asked me to do, I stayed and got a job working at a bar to pay my living expenses. I thought they only wanted me to come home to look after Lauren. They'd expect me to go with her everywhere, to be responsible for her so they didn't have to."

"Had they done that kind of thing before—made you her caretaker?"

"Yes. And I hated it. I wanted a normal sister, one I could have a normal relationship with. And I was tired of always being the responsible one. During that time, I hardly spoke to my parents, and I cut off any contact with Lauren."

"I think that's understandable," he said.

"No, it's not," she said. "I was being a brat. My poor parents. They were losing one daughter to mental illness, they'd practically bankrupted themselves and I was only making things worse with my little temper tantrum."

"You were what—nineteen?" he asked.

"I was. But I should have known better."

"If you say so. But living away from home when you're legally an adult isn't even a minor crime, much less anything you need to ashamed of."

"No, that's not the shameful part. I'm getting to that."

She hugged the pillow to her chest and wished there'd been something stronger than honey in that tea. She could have used a bit of false courage to get through this next part. "While I was working at the bar, I met a man," she said. "He was older, a customer who came in fairly often. He was handsome and charming and I was really attracted to him—more than I'd ever been attracted to anyone before. I'd dated a little before then, but never anything serious, and all those guys seemed like boys compared to this man. He made me feel so special."

"You were starved for attention and he gave that to you."

She glanced at him, then away. She didn't know whether to be impressed or wary, that he could read her so well. "I guess that was it. But at the time I thought I was in love. We'd known each other only a couple of weeks when I moved in with him. I made a point of telling my parents, of course. They were devastated. I thought they were upset because I'd proved they could no longer control me."

"What happened with the guy?" He moved closer, his thigh brushing hers. She sensed the heat of him through the denim, and she fought the urge to lean into him.

"He stopped being so nice once we were living together," she said. "He took my money and accused me of cheating on him—though I found out later he had two other girlfriends. After three months with him I was broke and I'd lost my job at the bar because he'd threatened my boss. I didn't have any choice but to go home to my parents."

"How did they react to that?"

"They seemed thrilled. It was more relief than anything, I suspect. By that time, Lauren had calmed down and I think they were happy to have both of us back under their roof and seemingly stable. But they'd aged terribly in the few months I'd been away—graying hair and sagging skin. I saw what my running away—and that's what I'd done, really, run away—had done to them." She swallowed past the hard knot in her throat that was equal parts unshed tears and an unuttered primal scream, and forced herself to go on. "I hadn't been home even a week when they were both killed in a car accident."

Only the dog's soft snores and the low growl of a big rig out on the highway disturbed the silence that stretched between them. Rand cleared his throat. "Do you really think I'm like that man?" he asked. "The one who used you?"

"No. I'm sure you're not." She turned toward him, her knees bumping into his. This was the scariest part yet, the words she almost couldn't say. "I...I'm attracted to you the same way I was attracted to him," she said. "And I'm not sure of my motives. Are the things I feel when I'm around you real, or are they just because I resent having to once again upset my whole life because of something Lauren did? Am I trying to declare my independence from the needs of my family in the only way I know how?" Articulating these questions only raised more doubts; she'd had so little experience relating to men on anything but the most casual terms since that college disaster that she had no idea what it was like to feel a normal attraction to someone.

"You were a kid then," he said. "The fact that you're even thinking about this shows you've learned a few things."

"I would hope so, but I don't know." She smoothed

both hands down her thighs, her palms clammy. "I just…
I don't trust myself anymore. Especially with everything
in such turmoil with Lauren's disappearance."

"Maybe you're overthinking this." He took one of her
hands in his, cradling it between his palms. "Why can't
we just be two people who enjoy each other's company,
without any expectations?"

"There can't be any expectations." She tried to pull
her hand away, but he wouldn't let her. "I'm only going to
be here a little while," she said. "Until we find Lauren."

"Then you'll go back to Madison." He kept his voice
even, stating a fact.

"Yes…at least I will, unless Lauren needs me." She
hadn't even realized the truth of these words until now.
Whatever happened, she wouldn't desert her sister.

"You've always been there for her," he said.

"She's my sister. And the only family I have left."

"I hope she knows how lucky she is to have you. But
maybe it's time someone was here for you." He leaned
closer, and ducked his head to press his lips against hers.

She stilled, startled by the suddenness of the gesture, yet aware that she'd been waiting for it—wanting it—ever since he'd sat beside her on the sofa. He
squeezed her hand, a gesture of reassurance, and increased the pressure of his lips slightly. She relaxed, and
as the warmth of his nearness engulfed her, she melted
against him, sliding her free hand up his chest and over
his shoulder to cradle his head in her palm and draw
him closer still.

He tilted his head to achieve a better angle and coaxed
her lips apart. She opened to him eagerly, almost desperately, pressing against him, nipples beading against the
hard wall of his chest. The sweep of his tongue inside

her mouth sent little shock waves of pleasure through her that reverberated all the way to her toes. Desire, hot and urgent, flooded her, making her clutch at him when at last he pulled away.

They stared at each other, openmouthed, breath coming in ragged gasps, his gaze a little unfocused, as she was sure hers was. "That was…intense," he said, his voice rough, like sandpaper across sensitive nerve endings.

"Yeah." All she could manage was a whisper. She stared at his lips, wanting him to kiss her again, wondering if she had the nerve to insist on it.

He did kiss her again, more gently, a tender exploration of lips and tongue that was just as dizzying, if less urgent. She rested her palm flat between them, not pushing him away, but keeping herself a little apart from him, trying to keep her wits about her. But it was like trying to fight the tide, the pull of him relentless and so strong…

She was the first to pull away this time, withdrawing her hands and looking away, not wanting him to read the turmoil of her emotions reflected in her eyes. "I don't think I'm very good at this relationship stuff," she said. The best they could hope for, given her circumstances, was a casual affair. A temporary fling. But nothing about her feelings for him felt casual or temporary.

"I don't want to rush you," he said.

No. She was the one who wanted to rush—headlong into the kind of emotional minefield she'd spent years avoiding. She didn't even know herself anymore when she was this close to him.

He stood. "You look exhausted," he said. "Let me show you to the bedroom. You can sleep in one of my old T-shirts, if you want." At her startled look, he chuckled. "Don't worry, I'll sleep on the sofa."

"I feel bad, taking your bed," she said as she followed him to the bedroom.

"It's okay." He left her at the door with a light kiss on the cheek. "Good night. Sleep well."

He sauntered down the hall, humming softly under his breath. She closed the door and leaned against it, eyes squeezed shut and forehead pressed against the wood. She could still feel his lips on hers, the firm curve of his muscular chest, the grip of his hand in hers. He could give her his bed, but she didn't expect she'd sleep much in it, knowing he was spending the night only a few feet away.

SOPHIE WOKE TO BARKING—sharp, percussive explosions of sound that sent panic spiraling up from her stomach to constrict her chest. She sat up and blinked at the gray light filtering behind the blinds. Nothing in the room looked familiar, yet it clearly wasn't a hotel room.

"Lotte, silence!"

The quiet but commanding voice calmed her as well as the dog, and she remembered she was in Rand Knightbridge's duplex—in his bedroom. She eased back down into sheets that carried the faint scent of his cologne. Lying here alone, listening to him and his dog move about, made her feel that much more isolated. Despite her fears to the contrary, exhaustion had overcome anxiety and within minutes of climbing into bed she'd succumbed to a deep, dreamless sleep. But the escape felt like just that—a fleeing from the consequences of the previous night's events.

What would have happened if she'd asked him to

spend the night with her in this bed, instead of sending him to sleep on the sofa? Would things have been awkward between them this morning, or would she have felt more sure of herself, better prepared to face the events of the day?

He tapped on the door. "Sophie? Are you awake?"

She sat up again and pulled the covers up to her neck. "I'm awake," she called.

The door eased open and his face filled the gap. His hair was tousled and he hadn't yet shaved—probably because all his things were in here with her. "Want some coffee?" he asked.

"That would be great."

"If you want, you can grab the shower while I make the coffee.

"Sure. What time is it?" She looked around for a clock.

"Early. Just a little after six."

"Do you always get up this early?"

He grimaced. "Only when I have to. But the captain called and wants us all at the station early."

"Why? Has something happened?" She sat up straighter, more alert.

"I'll tell you at breakfast. See you in a minute." He shut the door before she could question him more.

In the bathroom, she examined Rand's shampoo, toothpaste and soap, noting they preferred the same brand of toothpaste. What did a man's choice of toiletries say about him? Rand's seemed to say that he was an uncomplicated man who stuck to basics. He was well-groomed, but not vain. A woman wouldn't have to compete with him for space in the medicine cabinet.

She showered quickly, resisting the urge to luxuriate in the flow of hot water, then dressed and dried her hair. Only light makeup this morning—a touch of lip gloss and a sweep of mascara would have to do, since she didn't want to keep Rand waiting.

He sat at the table in the kitchen, hunched over a bowl of cereal. "The coffee's ready," he said. "For breakfast, there's toast or cereal. Sorry, but I'm not much of a cook."

"That's okay." She poured coffee into the mug he'd set beside the machine, and sat at the table across from him. "Why do you have to go into the office early?" she asked.

"I'm probably not supposed to tell you."

"Is it something to do with Lauren?" Her hand trembled as she set down her coffee mug. Had they found her sister—or only her body?

"Maybe not."

Which meant that maybe it did. "Then what is it? Don't keep me in suspense like this," she pleaded.

"We're bringing in Richard Prentice for questioning."

Him again? Did a man with everything in the world going for him really have something to do with Lauren's disappearance, much less the other crimes the Rangers seemed to think him guilty of? "Do you think he knows something about Lauren?"

"We don't know, though I'm sure the captain will be asking those questions." He stood and carried his empty cereal bowl to the sink. "I probably won't be in on the questioning."

"What prompted this? Did the investigators find something in my hotel room that pointed to Prentice?"

"No. But the picture you found links him to Alan Milbanks. We want to question him about that, and about

Milbanks's drug-dealing activities, and anything else we can link him to."

"When will this happen?"

"Soon. I have to be at headquarters by seven. I imagine we'll pick him up after that."

"Will he even be awake?"

"All the better if he isn't. Pulling people out of bed is a good way to catch them off guard. And we want to do this before his lawyers are in the office."

"Why?"

"Not because we want to violate his rights, but because lawyers always throw up roadblocks. They'd make it impossible for us to question him at all, even if the answers might completely clear him from suspicion."

"Do you think the photograph of Preston and Milbanks together is what the people who trashed my hotel room were looking for?" she asked.

"Maybe. If they didn't know you'd already turned the picture over to us. Or maybe they only wanted to frighten you."

"They did a good job of that." She hugged her arms across her chest and shivered.

He squeezed her shoulder. "I know it's hard, but hang in there."

"What will I do while you're with Prentice and the other Rangers?" she asked.

"You can stay here. The place has an alarm system. You'll be safe."

More waiting and not knowing what was happening. She didn't know if she could stand it. "What will you do while Prentice is being questioned? Will you search his house?"

"We can't do that without a warrant. We're hoping we'll get something from the questioning that will convince a judge to grant the search warrant."

"His lawyers will try to keep that from happening."

"Yes, they will. But we'll push back as hard as we can. They can't fight us forever." He dropped his hand from her shoulder. "I'm going to take my shower. Don't worry about the dishes. I'll do them when I come home."

He left the house while she was still sitting at the kitchen table, drinking coffee. She wandered into the living room and turned on the television, then turned it off again. She wasn't going to do this. She wasn't going to sit and let others do all the work of looking for her sister. Maybe the police had to wait for a warrant in order to search Richard Prentice's house, but she didn't have to. Now, while she knew he was away, was the best time to find out if Lauren was locked away in some room of that mansion.

She grabbed her keys and hurried to the rental car, and the malaise that had dragged at her vanished. If she got caught in Prentice's house, she'd be in trouble, but she'd make sure she didn't get caught. She'd always been a quiet person, the kind other people didn't notice. She could use that to her advantage now.

# *Chapter Twelve*

Sophie consulted the map in her car and figured out the route to Prentice's ranch. On the drive over, she debated how to deal with the guards at the gate. They'd never let her in, so her best bet was to ditch the car somewhere and hike in, avoiding the guards. She stopped at a convenience store and bought a bottle of water and some energy bars. She wished she had a weapon, then discarded the idea. Her cell phone would be her best weapon. At the first sign of trouble she'd call Rand and alert him.

She drove past the ranch and parked the car behind a telephone-relay building a quarter mile past the gate. It wasn't completely invisible from the road, but she figured someone would have to be specifically looking for her in order to notice the vehicle. With luck, she'd be back to the car before anyone became suspicious.

She hurried along the road, planning to hide behind a tree or dive into the ditch if anyone drove past, but no one did. When she came to the wood rail fence that marked Prentice's property line, she checked the area for security cameras and, seeing none, ducked between the rails and headed across the prairie in the direction she thought the house was situated.

Before long she could make out the narrow gravel

drive that led to the mansion. She kept to the field to the left of it. Dressed in faded jeans and a brown-and-tan blouse, she hoped she blended in with the landscape of drying grasses, cacti and shrubby trees. She wondered what Abby Stewart had found to study in these surroundings. This wasn't exactly desert, but it was close.

The house appeared on the horizon, a gray hulk that looked out of place against the backdrop of distant mountains and turquoise sky, like a Scottish castle set down on the surface of the moon. She stopped to drink some water and study the building, wondering if she should approach from the back.

A cloud of dust rose in the distance, lifting up from the ground in a soft white fog and hovering near the horizon. Then the cloud grew larger…closer. With a start, she realized a car was approaching, barreling down the unpaved road toward her.

She dropped to the ground, flattening herself in the dirt, ignoring the bite of sharp stones into her knees and the tangle of sticks in her hair. She stared at the approaching cloud, too frightened to draw more than shallow breaths.

Then tension eased as she realized the car was headed away from the house, and the two men inside, dressed in brown camouflage fatigues, didn't appear to have noticed her. She wished she had binoculars so she could get a better look at them. Were they leaving, or merely on patrol?

She lay in the grass a long time after they left, shifting after a while to pull out her phone to check the time. If the Rangers had met with Prentice at their headquarters at, say, half past seven at the earliest, the interview had only just begun. She had plenty of time to get up to the house and away again before he was due to return home. All she had to do was find the right opportunity to get closer and seize it.

When the Jeep didn't return after fifteen minutes, she decided it was safe to proceed. She crossed the gravel drive and circled the house, keeping low and avoiding any cameras she saw. She counted two in the front of the house and one in the rear. She decided that if she stayed close to the wall of the house, she'd be out of view of the camera at the rear.

She crept along the side of the house, the rough stone catching and pulling at her clothes. After waiting and listening ten minutes and hearing and seeing nothing and no one, she hurried up the steps and tried the back door, stopping first to wrap her hand in the tail of her shirt. Why hadn't she bothered to bring gloves?

She gasped when the knob turned easily in her hand. Holding her breath, she pushed it open and waited for the blare of an alarm. But maybe that wasn't how security systems worked. Rand had showed her how to punch in the code to his system, but he hadn't told her what would happen if she failed to do so. Maybe the system sent a silent alarm to the police, or to a private security company.

But she hadn't come this far to turn back now, especially because of something she wasn't even sure would happen. Richard Prentice had so many of his own guards and cameras on this place, why would he need to pay for an alarm? Resolute, she slipped into the house, and shut the door softly behind her.

She found herself standing in a mudroom that was larger than her bedroom back in Madison. Through an open doorway she spotted the kitchen, gleaming with marble and stainless steel. A quick check showed this room to be empty, as pristine and undisturbed as a kitchen in a model home, where no one lived or ever cooked.

Walking lightly, one foot placed carefully in front of the other, she traversed the kitchen, a formal dining room and a hallway. The first door she tried in the hallway was locked. She debated trying to open it, but unlike the heroines in television crime dramas, she had no idea how to go about doing so.

She moved on to the stairs. The risers were covered with an Oriental patterned runner, but every so often one let out a creak that sounded as loud as a firecracker in her ears. She stopped at the top of the landing, listening, but the house held the silence and stillness of an unoccupied dwelling.

Staying close to the wall, she moved down the hall, peeking into the open doors that lined the passage: a game room with a pool table and a dartboard that looked as if they'd never been used, a home gym with free weights, a treadmill and a complicated-looking exercise machine with bands and bars and a digital readout. She did a cursory tour through these, then moved on to the end of the hall and an unoccupied bedroom.

This room was furnished with a massive four-poster bed and dresser that both looked antique, but she suspected were expensive reproductions. Layers of silky drapes shrouded the window, over which a black-out shade was drawn. Half a dozen pillows almost obscured the carved headboard, and a check under the brocade comforter revealed sheets heavily trimmed with cotton lace. Did that mean someone was using this room? Or that guests were expected very soon?

Under the bed she found nothing but dust bunnies,

though were those smudges an indication that someone had stood at the edge of the bed, perhaps before climbing in for the night? She moved on to the adjoining bathroom, which gleamed with marble basins and pewter fixtures, the beveled mirror reflecting a tiled steam shower big enough for two. She traced the outline on the counter where a trio of bottles had recently sat. Shampoo? Perfume? Lotion? And who did these things belong to? It wasn't as if Richard Prentice would use this room himself, or any of his guards. As far as she knew, from her own visit and information she'd gleaned from listening to the Rangers talk about the billionaire, he lived in the house alone.

Still puzzling over this, she opened the door to the shower. Fragrant humidity hit her in the face, the smell of lavender and vanilla, a soft, feminine fragrance. A tickle of apprehension danced up her spine. Did Richard Prentice have a girlfriend staying with him? A female relative?

She returned to the bedroom, in time to hear the scrape of metal on wood, like a door slamming. She froze in place as heavy footsteps crossed the downstairs rooms, then started up the stairs.

When whoever it was reached the top of the stairs, Sophie looked around frantically for somewhere to hide. She started for the bed, thinking to dive under, then whirled and dove into the closet instead. She closed the door with a soft click seconds before the footsteps turned into the room.

Choking back a gasp, she pressed her ear to the door, but all she could hear was the thudding of her own frantic pulse. What was going on out there? She didn't dare open the door to look, and no old-fashioned keyhole afforded a peek into the room. The narrow gap at the bottom of the door let in a dim light, but there was no way could she stretch out enough in this small space to look through.

As her eyes adjusted to the darkness, she could make out clothes filling the bar across the back of the closet, with various boxes and bags sitting along the shelf above. But before she could investigate any of these, the bedsprings creaked loudly. What was he doing? She prayed he hadn't decided to take a nap. Maybe she'd been wrong about the room's occupant. Maybe it wasn't a woman at all. She thought the person out there must be male, given the heaviness of his tread.

She needed a weapon. The kind of thing someone might keep in a closet—a baseball bat? Golf club? Dropping into a crouch, she felt along the back wall, then the sides, then the floor. She came up with a shoe—a woman's dark stiletto. It didn't have the weight or heft of a club or bat, but if whoever was out there opened the door, she'd hit him as hard as she could, driving the pointed heel into his face. It would hurt like hell, and maybe give her enough time to get away.

The bed creaked again, and then the footsteps retreated—across the room, down the hall, on the stairs, all the way out the door, which closed with the solid click of the lock catching. Sophie closed her eyes and sagged against the wall, too afraid to give in much to relief. Maybe whoever had been out there had discovered something to make him suspicious and had merely gone for help. She had to get out of here while she still could.

She peered out the door, making sure the coast was clear. The only sign that she hadn't imagined the last ten minutes was the rumpled comforter and the faint impression on the mattress, as if someone heavy had lain there for a short while.

She was halfway across the room before she realized she was still holding the shoe. She couldn't leave it out here, and carrying it across the prairie would be awkward. In the full light, it didn't look like much of a weapon, the heel a thin column wrapped in leather, the upper a network of leather straps, a bow at the instep. The insole bore the name of a designer Sophie recognized as expensive. Lauren had owned several pairs of that particular brand. In fact, she would have loved this shoe. Sophie checked the label again; yes, it was just Lauren's size.

She hurried back to the closet and flicked on the light. More shoes filled boxes on the top shelf, all styles Lauren would have loved, in her favorite brands and her size. She turned her attention to the clothes—a beaded evening gown in the royal blue Lauren favored, also in her size. Sophie pressed her face against the fabric and inhaled deeply. The scent of Mitsouko permeated the silk. The desire to shout for joy warred with the urge to weep. Instead of doing either, she released her hold on the dress and turned her attention to the woman's purse on the shelf. The bag proved to be empty. Disappointed, she started to close it again, then spotted a slip of cardboard peeking out of a small pocket sewn into one side of the lining. She pinched the cardboard between thumb and forefinger and teased it out. *Lauren Starling* was printed in crisp black lettering beneath the image of a stylized bird.

RICHARD PRENTICE WASN'T happy to be at the police station and he let everyone know it. He didn't raise his voice, but his tone was scathing. His lawyers—two of them—were equally imperious. "Keep that beast away from me," one snarled as he followed his client down the hallway, glaring at Lotte, who sat at Rand's side, attention fixed on the new arrivals, with their expensive suits and haughty airs.

"The dog doesn't intimidate me," Prentice said. He strode past Rand and Lotte without a second glance, into the interrogation room, with its gray walls and utilitarian table and chairs. "Let's get this over with. I don't intend for you to waste any more of my time than is absolutely necessary."

They'd chosen not to question him at Ranger headquarters, but at the Montrose police station, which had a proper interrogation room, with recording equipment and cameras. Rand and Marco watched from another room while the captain and Lieutenant Michael Dance handled the questioning.

"Earlier you told us you didn't know Lauren Starling," Graham began, after logging the preliminary information of Prentice's name, address and the date and time. "But you told her sister the two of you were friends. Such good friends that Ms. Starling confided to you her worries about her job."

"That's hearsay," one of the lawyers interjected.

"We're not in court here, counselor." Graham kept his attention focused on Prentice. "Answer the question."

"My friends are none of the government's business." Prentice's tone was clipped, as if he couldn't be bothered wasting breath on their concerns.

"They are when one of the friends has been missing for over a month and you may be the only person she knew here," Michael said.

"You're merely speculating," Prentice said, even before his lawyers could interrupt. "A woman like Lauren Starling, who works in the public arena, knows many people."

"Then you tell us," Graham said. "What was she doing in Montrose?"

"I have no idea."

"She didn't stop by to say hello while she was here?" Michael asked.

"She did not."

"When was the last time you saw her?" Michael continued the questioning, while Graham stood, arms folded, leaning against the wall, glowering at Prentice.

"I haven't seen Lauren for some time. Several months at least."

"How many months?"

"I don't know. It was at a charity function. I can have my secretary research my calendar and get back to you."

"You do that." Michael's voice held a sour note. "When was the last time you talked to her?"

"I don't remember."

"We can subpoena your phone records and find out," Graham said.

"Then maybe you should do that." Tone defiant, eyes hard as stones.

"Are you giving us permission to do so?" Graham asked.

"He is not!" The older of the two lawyers spoke.

"I am not," Prentice agreed.

"This is getting nowhere," Rand said.

"They haven't asked him about Alan Milbanks yet," Marco said.

"What is your relationship with Alan Milbanks?" Graham asked.

"Who?" Prentice looked blank.

Michael slid a piece of paper across the table—Rand assumed it was the photograph.

Prentice studied the image without expression. "Who is that?" he asked.

"It's a picture of you and Alan Milbanks," Rand said.

Prentice leaned over the picture, studying it closely. "I don't know who that is in the picture. It's not me."

"Do you have a twin?" Michael asked.

Prentice merely glared.

"He's a cold one," Rand said. "How can he look the captain in the eye and deny that's him in the photo?"

"Lying is like anything else," Marco said. "You get better with practice."

"Then I'd say Prentice has had a lot of practice," Rand said.

"That is a dark, blurry photo of someone who vaguely resembles my client," the older lawyer said. "My client has already denied it is him, and you have no proof that it is."

"This picture shows a meeting between you and Alan Milbanks." Michael stabbed a finger at the picture. "A known drug dealer who is now dead."

"I don't know anyone named Milbanks and I certainly don't know anything about his death."

"It's interesting to me that people you associate with keep dying." Michael pulled out a chair and sat next to Prentice. "First your pilot, Bobby Pace, and now your friend Milbanks."

"We're done here, gentlemen." The older lawyer stood and the other lawyer and Prentice rose also.

Marco checked his watch. "Twenty minutes. That's longer than I thought we'd get."

"Twenty minutes wasted," Rand said.

"Not necessarily. We showed our hand. Now we see if we made him nervous enough to do something stupid."

"Or maybe this just gives his lawyers more ammunition. We'll get to read in the papers tomorrow about our continued harassment of an innocent man."

They moved back into the hallway in time to see Prentice walking out, flanked by his lawyers. Lotte growled low, under her breath. Rand rubbed behind her ears. "That's right. You know the bad guys when you see them." They joined Graham and Michael in the interrogation room. "What do you think?" Rand asked.

"He's lying about Milbanks," Graham said. "His eyebrow twitches when he's stressed—it's a tell Emma clued me into. It was twitching like crazy when I showed him the photograph."

Rand hadn't picked up on that. "Anything when you asked about Lauren?"

Graham shook his head.

"So what now?" Michael asked.

"CSI towed Lauren's car this morning," Graham said. "They're going to go over it again and see if we turn up anything new. How's her sister?"

"The scene at her hotel room yesterday shook her up some, but she's hanging tough."

"Everything go okay last night?" Graham studied him intently.

"Fine." He'd tossed and turned most of the night, kept awake by the memory of those incredible kisses, torn between the desire to get up and knock on the bedroom door and invite himself in, and worry that she'd reject him. In the end, his responsibility to protect her and help her through this overcame his desire.

"Let her know we aren't giving up," Graham said.

"I will."

His phone rang. He checked the display and felt a catch in his chest. "It's Sophie. She's probably calling to ask how things went with Prentice. How much can I tell her?"

"Tell her we didn't learn anything new, but we're still working on it."

He punched the button to answer the call. "Hello, Sophie."

"Rand, you have to get out to Richard Prentice's ranch right away." She sounded out of breath, her voice an excited whisper.

"Why? What's going on?"

"I'm here now, in an upstairs bedroom. There's a closet with women's clothing and shoes, all in Lauren's size. The dresses smell of her perfume—I'm sure she's been wearing them. And I found a purse with one of her business cards in it."

"Sophie, what are you doing there?" Disbelief and alarm made him speak more loudly than he'd intended, drawing attention from the others.

"I knew he'd be at the station with you, so I thought this would be the perfect opportunity to look around."

"Sophie, you have to get out of there," Rand said, his agitation growing.

"I promise I was careful with everything."

"Sophie, get out of there now." He couldn't believe she was taking such a terrible risk. "Prentice is on his way back there."

"All right. But do you think this is enough to get a

warrant to search the place? Lauren was here, I know it. She may still be here now."

"We'll talk about it when you're safe."

"Maybe I should look around a little longer."

"No!" He almost shouted the word. Taking a deep breath, he tried to calm down. "That isn't safe."

"All right, but… Okay. I have to go. Someone's coming."

"Sophie? Sophie?" The line went dead.

# Chapter Thirteen

Sophie pressed her ear against the closet door, listening to the footsteps approaching. A man's heavy tread. Was it the same guy as before, or someone new? Only one person, she thought, so the first man hadn't gone for help.

The steps headed straight for the bedroom. She held her breath, afraid to even breathe. The bed creaked, then two thunks—had he removed his shoes and dropped them on the floor? The mattress creaked again, and someone sighed. Was he settling in for a nap?

She waited for several minutes, straining to hear, but all was silent. Finally, she wrapped her hand around the doorknob and turned it ever so slowly, then eased it open, easy…easy…

She pressed one eye to the narrow opening and stared out at a bulky man in desert camo, stretched out on his back on the bed, hands folded on his chest like a corpse. Maybe he'd been the one who came into the room before, only a call had forced him to delay his nap. Another call could wake him at any time—especially a call that Prentice was returning to the ranch.

The man on the bed snored, making her jump. She shut the door and leaned her forehead against the smooth wood. *Think!* she silently commanded herself. She had to get out of here. Once Prentice returned, she'd be trapped. She'd probably only been able to get in because the guards had relaxed a little with their boss gone. When he returned, they'd be on their best—and sharpest—behavior.

The snoring continued, heavy and even. The guy was really out of it. This had to be her best chance to get by him.

She eased the door open once more, then slipped out of the closet. The sleeping man's chest rose and fell evenly, his snores like the rumble of a motorbike. On tiptoe, Sophie crossed the room. He'd shut the door, so she had to stop and deal with that. She turned the doorknob and tugged, expecting it to open easily, as all the other doors had. But this one stuck. She tugged again and it opened suddenly, sending her lurching back. Worse, the hinges let out a tortured squeal. Sophie cringed, and started into the hall.

"You there! Stop!" The voice, deep and commanding, had the force of a bullet hitting her back, but she hesitated only a moment before taking off down the hall. No sense worrying about being quiet now; she ran as hard as she could, feet pounding along the hall and down the stairs. Behind her, the guard shouted and raced after her.

She crossed the kitchen, slipping a little on the tile, then regained her balance and hurtled through the mudroom, hitting the back door hard, fumbling for the knob. Behind her a second guard had taken up the pursuit. "Stop, or I'll shoot!"

She stumbled down the steps and darted across the prairie, aiming for the fences and the road in the distance. She'd only gone a few dozen yards when the first bullets whistled past her. She'd read before that it was hard to hit a moving target, but that didn't mean it was impossible, was it?

Her side ached, and every breath was torture, her lungs burning. Why hadn't she kept up her New Year's resolution to go to the gym more? Maybe the bullets wouldn't have to kill her; she'd collapse on the prairie from exhaustion. She glanced over her shoulder and let out a wail when she saw the Jeep barreling toward her. Oh, God, they were going to catch her. What would they do to her?

She tried to run faster, but she stumbled and sprawled forward, the breath knocked from her. She lay facedown in the rocks and bunch grass, trying to breathe, waiting for the shot she was sure would end her life. Tears squeezed from beneath her closed eyes. So much for being brave; her foolishness had cost her everything.

The Jeep stopped somewhere behind her and footsteps approached. "Get up," a man's voice commanded.

She didn't move. Maybe they'd think she was already dead and go away. Or did that only work with bears?

Rough hands grabbed her arms and hauled her to her feet. "Who are you?" the guard—the one who'd been napping on the bed—demanded. Up close, he looked much younger, only in his early twenties, she thought, with a sunburned, unlined face and blond stubble on choirboy rosy cheeks.

She kept her mouth shut. If she didn't say anything, they couldn't use the information against her.

"What are you doing here?" The other guard, older and beefier, like a linebacker, had climbed out of the Jeep and walked toward her.

She looked away and tried to assume a bored expression. She doubted she was fooling anybody, especially since her knees were visibly shaking.

"Were you trying to steal something?" the older guard asked. "Did you take anything?"

"Maybe we should search her." The younger guard leered at her.

If he tried, she'd kick him where it hurt. Wasn't that what they taught in all those female self-defense classes at the Y?

Something behind them distracted them. She followed their gaze and saw the dust plume that indicated an approaching vehicle. "Mr. Prentice is back," the older guard said.

"Come on." The first guard dragged her toward the Jeep. "Let's go talk to him."

"If you let me go, I won't tell him you were napping on the job," she said.

The younger guard gave her a sour look but didn't stop walking. "I don't know what you're talking about," he said.

The older guard shot them a curious look, but he didn't slow down, either. So she'd have to throw herself on Prentice's mercy. He'd been perfectly civil to her when he invited her to his home, but chances were he wouldn't view her return visit so favorably.

The Jeep and Prentice's SUV met in front of the house. The guards hauled her out and brought her to stand in front of Prentice and two men in dark suits. His lawyers, she guessed. All three men regarded her sourly. "Ms. Montgomery," Prentice said. "What are you doing here?"

"I came to see you," she said. "But you weren't at home."

"How did you get past the guards?"

She shrugged. "Maybe they were occupied elsewhere. I didn't see any reason not to come up to the house."

"Oh, you didn't?" Prentice looked her up and down, with the attitude of a man who had ordered a new suit and found it not to his liking. "You have no business on my property. I could have you jailed for trespassing."

"I came to see you. That's not the same as trespassing."

"She was in the house," the younger guard said. "In the upstairs bedroom."

Prentice's scowl deepened.

"I was waiting for you to come home," Sophie said. "You have a very nice house, so I thought I'd look around. I didn't hurt anything. I didn't take anything." Except pictures.

"We should search her, to be sure," the older guard said.

"We should call the police and have her arrested," one of the lawyers said.

"It seems someone has already summoned them." The others followed Prentice's gaze to the vehicles speeding down the drive toward them. Sophie sagged with relief as she recognized the black-and-white FJ Cruisers used by The Ranger Brigade.

The SUVs stopped and Rand and Graham stepped out. They both wore dark sunglasses, so she couldn't read their expressions, but the hard set of their mouths told her they weren't pleased to be here. "We had a report of a trespasser," Rand said.

"Who made the report?" Prentice asked. He showed no sign of recognizing Rand from his previous visit, when he'd posed as Sophie's boyfriend. Maybe the uniform, or Rand's commanding attitude, distracted him. "I didn't call anyone."

"Then someone who works for you must have called us." He moved toward her, long strides covering ground quickly.

"We know how much you value your privacy," Graham said.

Rand wrapped his hand around her upper arm. The touch wasn't gentle, but it reassured her, nonetheless. He might be angry with her, but she trusted him to keep her safe. "We'll take her now," he said. "Do you want to press charges?"

Prentice regarded her coldly for a long moment, as if weighing his options. "No charges," he said. "But I want to know what she is doing here."

"I told you. I wanted to talk to you—about my sister."

"I've already told you everything I know about your sister," Prentice said.

"I was hoping you might have remembered something else. Something that would help us find her."

"Maybe your sister doesn't want to be found," he said. "Maybe she's started a new life and is happy with her new circumstances."

"She knows I only want her to be happy," Sophie said. "Why would she hide that from me?"

"Sometimes the best way to start over is to cut all ties with the past," Prentice said.

"Not with the only family you have," Sophie said. "Lauren wouldn't do that."

"My advice to you is to go back to Wisconsin and get on with your life," he said. "I'm sure Lauren is fine."

"Do you know something we don't?" Rand asked.

"I'm merely being logical. You haven't found a body or anything to indicate that Lauren Starling is dead. She was at a difficult place in her life. Why not make a fresh start, perhaps with a new name, in a new place? It happens more than most people think. There's nothing criminal in it."

"Lauren wouldn't turn her back on me," Sophie said. "I know she wouldn't."

Prentice turned to the Rangers. "Take her away," he said. "Then all of you, get off my property."

She and Rand followed Graham out of the house. "I'll see you at headquarters," Graham said, and climbed into his vehicle.

Rand dragged her toward his FJ Cruiser, where Lotte greeted them with a sharp bark. She hardly noticed the dog, she was so focused on the man beside her. Gone was the gentleness he'd shown her earlier. He held his body rigid, his jaw clenched, as he started the vehicle and pulled away, tires squealing and gravel pinging against the undercarriage. "I'm sorry I upset you," she said when they'd cleared the ranch gates.

"Upset me?" He slammed on the brakes and skidded to the side of the road, so violently she clutched the dashboard to keep from being thrown forward. "Of all the stupid, ill-conceived, foolhardy stunts—you could have been killed." His voice shook with some emotion she couldn't name—anger, frustration…fear?

"But I wasn't killed." She struggled to keep her own voice even. "You showed up at just the right time. And I'm very grateful for that." She'd never been so glad to see anyone in her life.

"Didn't what happened yesterday at your hotel teach

you anything about the kind of people we're dealing with here?" he asked. "I thought you were smart enough to be afraid."

"Of course I'm scared," she said. "But I'm more afraid of what will happen to Lauren if we don't find her soon. I had to do something."

"It's my job to find your sister." The anger had left his voice, and his expression grew gentle again.

"I know you're doing what you can, but it's not enough." She swallowed against the sudden threat of tears. "Maybe what I did wasn't smart, but I got the proof you need to get a warrant to search Prentice's house."

"You obtained the proof illegally. We can't use it in court."

"But you can use it to get your warrant."

"What proof do you have?" he asked a little more calmly.

"I have pictures." She held up her phone and he leaned over to peer at the image.

"What am I looking at?" he asked.

"It's a woman's purse, with a business card inside. Lauren's card. It proves she was in the house—I know it."

RAND DIDN'T KNOW whether to kiss Sophie or shake her. She really thought she'd done the best thing, going into Prentice's house when he wasn't home, but she could have jeopardized their whole case, not to mention her life. He shook his head and put the vehicle in gear again. "We'll talk about it more at headquarters." Maybe the captain could explain it to her better. He was obviously too emotionally involved to view anything she did impartially.

"Are you really arresting me for trespassing?" she

asked when he turned into the lot in front of the Ranger headquarters.

"I ought to." He shut off the engine but made no move to get out of the vehicle. "What you did was incredibly foolish and dangerous." And he broke into a cold sweat, just thinking about it.

"Playing it safe isn't finding Lauren."

She sounded stubborn now. He turned to her. "I don't think you realize that what you did could jeopardize the whole investigation."

"Or it could solve all your problems."

"Your sister's disappearance isn't the only crime we're trying to solve here. If it is a crime."

She stiffened. "What do you mean?"

"What if Lauren is with Prentice—but she's with him voluntarily? What if it's like he said—she's trying to start over and cut ties to the past?"

"She wouldn't do that." Was that doubt in her voice?

"Why not?" he asked. "The man's a billionaire. He's always being photographed with beautiful women, so he must have some charms. His last girlfriend was a Venezuelan fashion model. Maybe Lauren really likes him."

"She wouldn't disappear without telling me."

"Didn't you say she'd dropped out of sight for a while once before?"

"That was before her diagnosis. Now she's being careful, taking her medication…"

"People relapse. I don't know a lot about bipolar, but I've been doing a little reading. Apparently, sometimes people enjoy the manic periods so much they're reluctant to let them go. They go off their medication, believing they can handle themselves this time, but then they fall back into the old cycles. Maybe that's what happened to your sister."

Tears sparkled in her eyes, and he felt like a jerk for causing her such pain. But better that she face facts now than be doubly hurt if he turned out to be right later. "I've read those things, too," she said. "But even when she was sickest, Lauren never stayed out of touch with me this long. And she loved her job."

"She doesn't need a job if Prentice is supporting her."

She looked away, cheeks flushed, mouth set in a stubborn line. "So you have this neat little theory of what happened to her. Does that mean you're going to stop looking?"

"No. We're going to keep looking. But you have to stay out of the way and let us do our jobs." He softened his tone. "I don't want you to get hurt."

She nodded. "I know. And…that means a lot to me." She opened the car door. "Let's go in and see what everyone else has to say."

He released Lotte from the back and the three of them walked up to Ranger headquarters. Sophie didn't shy away from the dog as much now, though she still avoided looking at or touching her. Baby steps, he reminded himself. At least she could be in the same room with the dog now without freaking out.

Most of the other Rangers were gathered around the conference table when they arrived. Carmen, who stood at the head of the table, looked up when they arrived. "The CSI report on the fish shop just came in," she said. She looked at Sophie. "Maybe you should go into another room."

"I don't care about the fish shop," she said. "Besides, I don't have anyone to tell."

"She's okay." Rand steered her to a chair along the back wall. "What's in the report?"

"Drugs," Carmen said. "Lots and lots of drugs. Milbanks had received a shipment of fish from the Gulf of Mexico that morning. One of the investigators cut open a big amberjack and it was full of balloons of heroin. Another contained a bag of cocaine."

"So the local cops were right that the fish shop was just a front for drug smuggling?" Michael asked.

Carmen nodded. "It was a pretty slick operation, from what we can determine. Milbanks owned a fleet of fishing boats. They'd catch the fish, then load them up with drugs, put them on ice and fly them up here. He'd remove the drugs, load them on trucks to be distributed elsewhere, then sell the fish to local restaurants and individuals. He made money on both ventures and looked like a legitimate businessman."

"He could be the guy we've been looking for," Graham said. "The kingpin in charge of the increased activity in the region."

"He had the money and the contacts," Carmen said.

"That doesn't mean Richard Prentice wasn't involved," Rand said. "The picture of him and Milbanks together proves they knew each other."

"Maybe they were working together, or maybe the picture relates to something else," Graham said. "We don't know."

"Whoever killed him left behind all those drugs?" Simon asked.

"Maybe they didn't know about the drugs," Carmen said. "Or they didn't care."

"Did the investigators find anything in the shop to connect Milbanks and Prentice?" Rand asked.

"Nothing," Carmen said. "And nothing to tie Milbanks to Lauren Starling, either. We do think we know where the picture of Milbanks and Prentice together was taken, though."

"Where?" Rand asked.

"Behind the shop," Simon said. "The parking lot has a security camera trained near the door. The video analyst who studied the photograph recognized a pattern in the brick behind the men. She thinks the photograph is probably an enlarged frame from video taken by that camera."

"Milbanks could have gotten the picture from his own security system," Michael said. "Maybe that's what he was giving to Lauren the day he met her at the motel."

"But why give her something like that?" Simon asked.

"There's some indication that Milbanks may have been preparing to leave the country," Carmen said. "The investigators found airline tickets to the Cayman Islands in his desk drawer. He was supposed to fly out yesterday. We believe he may have planned to process this last shipment of drugs and fish, then get out of town before authorities caught up with him again. He probably has money stashed in accounts in the Caymans."

"But someone murdered him before he could leave," Rand said.

"Maybe he was killed because of the photograph," Sophie suggested. They all swiveled to look at her. "Maybe Prentice found out he'd given the photograph to Lauren."

"How would he find out?" Rand asked. "The photograph was still in her car."

"Maybe she told him," Sophie said.

"Right now Lauren Starling is the only one who can

answer these questions," Graham said. "We have to find her."

"The calls we've been making checking on Lauren's background did turn up one interesting fact," Carmen said. She consulted her notes. "She had a one-million-dollar life insurance policy through her employer. The beneficiary is her ex-husband, Phillip Starling."

Michael whistled. "So he had at least one reason to want Lauren out of the picture. Especially if he was having money problems."

"Why wouldn't she have changed the beneficiary on the policy when they divorced?" Rand asked Sophie.

"Lauren wasn't always good about following up on that kind of detail," she said. "And money wasn't really that big a deal to her. She might have even wanted Phil to have the money—part of her still cared about him."

"So Phil is still on our list of suspects," Rand said.

A phone rang. Graham shifted in his chair to pull out his cell. "Hello?"

He listened for a few moments, then ended the call. "Marco is on his way with the warrant to search Richard Prentice's home," he said.

"Then my photographs helped," Sophie said.

"Your photographs, along with the photo of Prentice and Milbanks together, were enough to persuade the judge that we had grounds to investigate further," Graham said.

"I want to go with you," she said.

"No." Rand spoke before anyone else could answer. "You have to stay here." He didn't want her anywhere near Prentice again.

She frowned but had sense enough not to argue. "Then let me go back to my hotel room."

"I can't let you do that, either. It's not safe."

She looked around the utilitarian room. "What am I supposed to do while you're away?"

"You can go back to my place." Could he trust her to stay put this time?

"I've got an idea," Graham said. "Some place she'll be safe and out of trouble, but more comfortable." He took out his phone and punched in a number. "Emma? How would you like some company this afternoon?"

*Chapter Fourteen*

Sophie rode with Rand to Graham and Emma's house. Awkward silence still stretched between them. His anger annoyed her, though she told herself it was merely a sign of how much he cared. But it rankled that he wouldn't give her credit for helping his investigation. As if the work the cops did was the only kind that mattered.

He pulled up to the house and shifted into Park. "I'll call and let you know what we find out," he said, not looking at her.

She nodded and opened the door. But she couldn't leave with this coldness between them. "Be careful," she said softly. "I've already lost one person who's important to me. I don't want to lose another."

She didn't wait for his reaction, but slid from the car and hurried up the walk to the house, where Emma welcomed her. "Come on in," she said, ushering her into the living room.

"Hey." Abby looked up from the sofa, where she was petting a large gray tabby. "We're glad you could come."

"Thanks for having me," Sophie said. "I really didn't want to hang around Ranger headquarters alone." Or at Rand's house. There were too many unanswered questions between them for her to feel comfortable there.

"It's our pleasure," Emma said.

"We're hoping you can fill us in on everything that's going on," Abby said.

Sophie settled onto the sofa opposite Abby. "There's not much to tell. Apparently, Alan Milbanks was smuggling drugs in his fish, and they think he was getting ready to leave the country when he was killed. I found a closet full of women's clothing in an upstairs bedroom at Richard Prentice's ranch. The clothes were Lauren's size, and they smelled of her perfume."

"I can't believe you went out there on your own," Abby said. "Weren't you scared?"

"Yes." She still got shaky, thinking about it. "But my worry about Lauren was stronger than my fear."

"You're lucky the Rangers got to you before Prentice did," Emma said.

"Do you really think he's dangerous?" Sophie asked. The billionaire was stern and grumpy and imperious, but he seemed too urbane to be violent.

"Remember what I told you—the last time I was at his ranch someone drugged me and knocked me out," Emma said. "I was thrown down a mine shaft and left to die."

"It's hard to picture Richard Prentice doing something so violent," Sophie said. The man was so cold and businesslike.

"We don't have any proof, but I think it was one of his guards," Emma said. "The mine was located not far from his land, in the Curecanti wilderness area. Graham rescued me, though he was injured in the process."

"Several people have died who had connections to Prentice," Abby said.

"Then why is he still free?" Sophie asked. It didn't make sense.

"Because he's very rich and very smart," Emma said. "No one's been able to come up with strong proof to tie him to the crimes that are happening all around him."

"What kind of crimes?" Sophie asked.

"All the things the Rangers were formed to investigate and prevent," Abby said. "Last month they broke up a big illegal marijuana-growing and human-trafficking operation within the park. The man who was overseeing that had ties to a Mexican drug cartel, but the Rangers believe he wasn't operating independently, that he had someone local who was financing the operation. The man—Raul Meredes—was shot by a sniper before he could talk to authorities."

"A friend of mine, a pilot who flew for Prentice, was murdered while smuggling a stolen Hellfire missile," Emma said. "He landed in Black Canyon of the Gunnison National Park and was shot by the woman who had hired him for the job—the daughter of the Venezuelan ambassador to the United States."

"Who was also Richard Prentice's girlfriend," Abby said. "She was caught on Prentice's ranch with the missile."

"What did she want with a Hellfire missile?" Sophie asked.

"We're not sure." Emma took up the story again. "Some people believe she planned to pass it along to terrorists in her homeland. In that case, Prentice may have financed the purchase. Or she might have gotten it for Prentice himself, to arm the unmanned drone he's rumored to have purchased."

"That's the problem," Abby said. "All of this is merely

rumors and theory. Prentice may not have known any-thing about the missile. Valentina—the ambassador's daughter—may have just been taking advantage of her connection to him."

"The human-trafficking operation was happening all around him," Emma said. "But no one has proof he knew anything about it. Maybe he's telling the truth and he really is innocent."

"That doesn't explain what women's clothing in Lauren's size, smelling of Lauren's perfume, is doing in a closet in his home," Sophie said. "And he admits he knows her."

"He can't really deny that," Emma said. "They attended the same charity ball in Denver not that long ago. It was in the paper."

"Did they find any luggage in your sister's car when she disappeared?" Abby asked.

Sophie shook her head. "None. Her laptop and phone are missing, too."

"Then maybe she's somewhere hiding?" Abby said, speculating. "Or she's with Prentice voluntarily?"

"That's what Rand suggested, too," Sophie said. "But I don't believe it. She wouldn't hide from me. She has no reason to."

"Families are funny." Abby hugged a pillow to her chest. "Sometimes the people we love the most are the ones we need to get away from the most."

"What do you mean?" Sophie asked.

"I was injured in the war," Abby said. "That's where I got this." She tucked her hair behind one ear and traced the scar along her cheek. "My parents were so worried and upset. They tried hard to protect me and encour-age me at the same time, but all their hovering was too much. I felt like I was smothering. That's one reason I struck out on my own and came here. It wasn't that I didn't love them, just that I needed to figure out things on my own. I needed to live the life I wanted, not the one they wanted for me."

"So you're saying that Lauren might have felt smothered by me?" The words pained her to say them.

"She had a lot to deal with," Abby said. "Her diagnosis, divorce, problems at work. I can see how that would be overwhelming."

"And I've always been the big sister, looking after her." Sophie nodded. "I guess in her place, I might have found that a little smothering, too. But all she had to do was tell me to back off. I would have respected that. She didn't have to cut ties altogether. With everyone."

"Maybe the Rangers will find something at Prentice's ranch today," Emma said. "Maybe they'll even find her and she can tell us herself what's going on."

GRAHAM, MICHAEL, RAND and Lotte pulled up to the gates at the Prentice Ranch a little after three in the afternoon, where Graham presented their search warrant to the guard who walked out to greet them. "Wait here and I'll consult with Mr. Prentice," the guard said, and started to turn away.

"No, we won't wait." Graham shifted the FJ Cruiser into gear. "We'll go on up to the house. Now." He gunned the engine, forcing the guard to jump out of the way or be run over.

"He must have called ahead," Rand said as they neared the house. Prentice, flanked by the two lawyers, waited for them in front of the massive oak door.

"I strongly object to this violation of my client's

privacy." The younger lawyer began speaking before the Rangers were even out of the car.

"Object all you like. We have a legal warrant." Graham held the papers out to Prentice.

The billionaire put his hands behind his back, his face impassive.

Graham opened his hand and let the papers flutter to the ground at Prentice's feet. "Come on." He addressed the others. "We'll start upstairs."

Lotte led the way, trotting up the stairs ahead of them. She stopped and waited on the landing at the top. Rand pulled a handkerchief from his pocket, one he'd scented with the Mitsouko perfume he'd ordered from a department store in Denver two days earlier. *"Sic,"* he commanded, and Lotte hesitated only a moment before heading down the hall.

Rand trotted to keep up with the dog, the others following. Lotte stopped and whined at a closed door. Rand slipped on a pair of gloves, then carefully opened the door. The dog rushed in and stopped again beside an ornate carved bed.

"Does she think Lauren Starling's been in that bed?" Michael asked from behind him.

"Someone wearing this perfume, in any case." He glanced under the bed. Nothing there but dust. "Let's try the closet."

Michael opened the closet door and the three men and the dog crowded around to look in. Lotte whined excitedly, her signal for a find. But the closet was empty. Not so much as a coat hanger disturbed the space.

"Is this the closet Sophie said was full of women's clothes and shoes?" Graham asked.

"According to the diagram she drew for us, yes."

Rand frowned. Even he recognized the scent of the Mitsouko perfume in here, but the space looked as if it had been empty for a while. He ran a finger along the edge of the shelf. It came away dirty—the kind of dust that collected when a space sat unused for a long time.

"Come on, let's see what else is up here." Graham led the way out of the room.

Looking confused, Lotte followed. She kept looking back over the shoulder at Rand, her expression worried. When she found what they were looking for, everyone was supposed to be happy. They weren't supposed to ask her to keep looking. But she obediently sniffed every corner of every room they entered and found nothing.

Downstairs proved just as empty, of anything but Prentice's furniture and books and personal belongings. The longer they searched, the more visibly frustrated Graham grew. Downstairs, Prentice and his duo of dark-suited attorneys followed them from room to room, the billionaire's expression growing more and more smug.

When they had searched every room, even looking into the washer and dryer and every cabinet and closet, Graham snapped off his gloves and stuffed them into his pocket. "We're done here," he said. "Thank you for your cooperation."

"You will be hearing from us," the older attorney said.

Back in the SUV, Graham remained impassive until they were on the road headed back to headquarters. He slammed one hand against the dash, making them jump. "How is it he's always one step ahead of us?" he asked.

"Maybe there's another possibility we need to consider here," Michael said.

"What's that?" Rand asked.

Michael looked away "Maybe Sophie is making all this up."

Rand stiffened. "Lotte alerted on that closet. Even I could smell the perfume in there."

"Maybe because Sophie put it in there. We're only taking her word for it that Lauren even wears that perfume."

"What about the photographs she showed us?" Rand asked. "Those weren't fake."

"They were photographs taken in a closet of some women's clothes and shoes," Michael said. "That could have been any closet. That could have been any purse with a business card in it. There's nothing to show where the pictures were taken. If we tried to introduce them in court, a good lawyer would say the same thing."

Rand shook his head, disoriented. "Why would she do that? Why go to so much trouble to lie to us?"

"Because she wants attention?" Michael shrugged. "Maybe she's as unbalanced as her sister."

Rand's stomach heaved. "No."

"I'm not saying that's what happened," Michael said. "But until we find more evidence to support her claims, we have to consider the possibility."

"No," Rand said again. "I've spent a lot of time with her these last couple of days. She's worried about her sister, sure, but nothing about her struck me as off or unstable."

"Maybe you're letting your feelings for her get in the way of your judgment."

Rand realized he'd curled both hands into fists. He'd never felt so much like punching his friend. He turned to Graham. "What do you think, Captain?"

"Sophie has spent the last three hours with Emma

and Abby," he said. "I think they're both good judges of character. Let's ask them what they think."

BY THE TIME RAND, Graham and Michael joined them at the captain's house, the three women were like old friends. They'd spent the afternoon discussing the wedding plans for Emma and Graham, and Michael and Abby. From there the conversation had moved on to books they'd read, music they enjoyed and jobs they'd held. They were sharing "worst boss ever" stories when the men showed up. Quickly, their attention shifted to the investigation.

"What did you find?" Emma asked, before Graham had even settled onto the sofa beside her.

"Nothing." Graham rubbed the back of his neck with one hand. "We didn't find anything at all incriminating in that house."

"But the closet..." Sophie began.

"The closet was empty," Rand said. His eyes met hers, his expression hard and cold.

"Then he must have cleaned it out as soon as I left," she said. "The guard would have told him I was in that bedroom. He'd have known what I saw, and that I'd tell you."

"Or maybe you were...mistaken," Michael said.

"There was no mistake in what I saw," she said. "And what about the pictures I took?"

He shrugged. "Prentice's attorney would say those pictures could have been taken anywhere. There was nothing to prove they were taken in Prentice's house."

Feeling sick, Sophie turned to Rand. "You believe me, don't you?"

"I want to believe you."

She turned away, not wanting him to see her hurt.

"You all have spent too much time around criminals." Emma's voice cut through the silence. "Sophie isn't lying, any more than I was lying about seeing women's cosmetics in Prentice's bathroom."

"Do you really think Sophie came all this way to stage some elaborate hoax?" Abby asked. She sounded indignant.

"No," Rand said. "I think we're all frustrated at our lack of progress." He glared at Michael.

Michael looked away. "I was just playing devil's advocate," he said. "It's important to look at an investigation from all angles."

"So, what did you find at the house?" Emma asked. "What did Prentice say?"

Graham began describing their visit to the house. Sophie turned away. She wasn't interested in any of this.

"I'm sorry." Rand gripped her shoulder and turned her to face him. "Of course I believe you."

"I wasn't lying," she said. "I didn't stage the photos or make anything up."

"I know that," he said. "Why would you? You want your sister safe. I want that, too."

He opened his arms and she went to him, letting him hold her, her head resting against his chest. She felt bone-weary and discouraged, too exhausted almost to stand. "This must be what it's like for Lauren all the time," she said.

"What do you mean?"

"Having people judge you, second-guess you, question your motives. Her illness has led her to do some ill-advised things in the past, but that doesn't mean everything she does is irrational or because of her illness.

Most of the time she's as rational and ordinary as the rest of us. But a lot of people can't see her that way, because of things that happened when she wasn't well. It must make everything so much harder. It's why she wanted so much to prove herself to her bosses. She wanted to show them that she was still an asset to the station, that she was still a good reporter."

"We have the testimony of the hotel clerk that she met Alan Milbanks there, and we found the photograph in her car of Milbanks with Prentice," Rand said. "Milbanks was involved in drug smuggling and distribution. Maybe Lauren uncovered that and confronted him. That made him angry and he—or someone he hired— decided to silence her."

Sophie shuddered at his words. Not that she hadn't made herself face that her sister might not be alive after all this time, but hearing someone else say as much was hard to bear. "If Milbanks was her target, what did she gain by confronting him at the hotel?" she asked. "Why not just go to the police with whatever evidence she had? Her story would be his arrest and conviction. She had nothing to gain by taunting him."

"Then what was she doing, meeting with him?"

"What if Milbanks promised to cooperate with her by revealing someone higher up the food chain?" Sophie asked. "He gave her the photograph as proof, but then that person—Richard Prentice?—found out."

"That would explain both Lauren's disappearance and Milbanks's murder," Rand said. "Except, so far at least, we don't have any evidence that Prentice is linked to either of those crimes."

"What will you do now?" she asked.

"We'll keep digging. Maybe focus on Milbanks, look

at his financial records, phone records, talk to people who knew him. We'll try to get as complete a picture as possible of how he operated. That may help us figure out how he knew Lauren, and if Prentice is involved at all."

Paperwork. She had no doubt this kind of research was important, but they needed action to rescue her sister. "Meanwhile, Lauren is still out there, missing."

He caressed her shoulder. "I know it's hard. I wish I could do more. We'll keep searching for her, I promise."

"I know she wouldn't go this long without contacting me. And now I'm more sure than ever that Richard Prentice is the 'Mr. Wonderful' she mentioned in her letter. But what has he done with her?"

"I don't know. But I'm ready to listen to any ideas you have."

"Are you, really?" She studied the eyes she couldn't help thinking of as kind, the strong slant of his nose, the firm jut of his chin. He wasn't movie-star handsome, but he had strength and character, and she trusted him not to lie to her. "You don't think I'm being hysterical, or mentally unbalanced, or obsessed?" she asked. "You don't think I'm making things up?"

"No. I believe you care for your sister very much, and you're doing everything you can to see that she's safe."

She glanced toward the others, who had moved to the kitchen and were making sandwiches. "Your coworkers don't feel the same. They think I'm making all this up. Maybe they don't even believe I'm Lauren's sister."

He winced. "Cops are trained to be suspicious. It's a useful trait for an investigator, and sometimes it keeps us alive."

"I believe Lauren is still alive. And after what I saw today, I think she's with Richard Prentice."

"We searched everywhere in that house and we didn't find so much as a hair."

"He's hiding her, then. He moved her and all her things when he knew you all were coming."

"We didn't call ahead and warn him," he said.

"You said yourself, he has contacts everywhere. Someone from the judge's office could have called him. Or he might have figured out what I'd seen and moved her in case I came back."

"Yes, that could have happened. But where would he hide her?"

"Some place close. Probably still on the ranch. Did you search any outbuildings?"

"Our warrant was only for the main house and garage. The property has some other structures on it, everything from housing for his guards to log bunkhouses dating from the late eighteen hundreds."

"Lauren could be in any one of those. How can you get back there to look?"

"I don't think he'd use one of those other buildings and risk her being seen. He knows we fly surveillance over the property occasionally."

"He could put her in a vehicle and drive her to wherever she was going," Sophie said.

"Or he could use a tunnel."

She frowned. "A tunnel?"

"We've heard rumors that he has a tunnel connecting the house to an old mine near the house," Rand said. "We thought he might be using the mine to hide contraband, but we never got a look inside." He took her arm. "Let's run this by the others and see what they think."

When they walked into the kitchen, Emma looked up from spreading mustard on a slice of bread. "Do you two want something to eat?" she asked. "I've got ham and turkey, and a couple of different kinds of cheese."

"Not right now, thanks." He turned to Graham. "Captain, I have an idea where Prentice might be hiding Lauren."

Graham swallowed a bite of sandwich. "What's your idea?"

"Maybe he has her in that mine—the one where we thought he'd stashed the missile? Supposedly there's a tunnel that connects the mine to the house. It would be easy to move a person there from the house without being seen."

"I looked for any kind of secret passage or door when we were in the house today," Michael said. "I didn't find anything."

"It could be a very sophisticated mechanism, one we wouldn't be able to find without special equipment we didn't have with us today," Rand said.

"Even if you're right, I don't know what we can do about it," Graham said. "By this time Prentice is raising so much hell in the press and with every politician he has in his pocket that a judge will never give us another search warrant."

"Then we go in without a warrant. We sneak in at night."

"That's illegal," Graham said. "And it's dangerous. If he is hiding someone—or something—in that mine, he'll have guards watching."

"We'll avoid the guards," Rand said. "Or I could go in alone. No sense risking anyone else."

"I'd go with you," Sophie said.

"Do that and I really will arrest you for trespassing," Graham said.

"Do you think I care about that when my sister could be in danger?"

"Let me go, Captain," Rand said. "If I get caught, you can suspend me and deny any knowledge."

"I wouldn't do that. In this organization, we've always got each other's backs." He pressed his lips together, silent for a moment. Sophie waited, scarcely breathing, the muscles in Rand's arm tense beneath her hand.

"Take Marco with you," Graham said. "You'll have to hike in from federal land."

Rand nodded. "We'll go tonight, about ten. There's no moon, but the weather is supposed to be clear. I'll get with Marco now to start planning."

He turned to Sophie. "You'll be all right here, won't you?"

"Take me back to your place," she said. "Emma has to cover a council meeting tonight for her paper and Graham will be working." She wouldn't be comfortable staying by herself with the gruff captain.

"All right." He patted her hand. "Wish me luck."

"Good luck. And…thank you."

He pulled her close. "I'll do my best to find her."

She nodded, unable to speak. As much as she wanted Lauren safe, what if she lost Rand in the process?

## Chapter Fifteen

Rand and Marco set out in the dark, with backpacks and night-vision goggles. They'd spent the early evening studying the layout of Prentice's ranch, choosing the best approach to the old mine. They'd decided to approach from the rear, over rugged country, reasoning that this section of the ranch would be less heavily patrolled. The guards would expect a threat to come from the front of the ranch, from the road.

The going was tough, scrabbling up loose talus slopes, climbing down into cactus-choked gorges. The two didn't say much, communicating mostly in grunts and hand gestures, focused on the task at hand. They saw the lights from the house long before they could make out the structure itself, the floodlights sending up a pink glow like the light pollution from a small city, blotting out the stars.

When the building itself was in view, Marco thrust out a hand, signaling to stop. He pointed in the distance, and Rand made out the pinpoints of two head-lights. The lights drew closer and closer, the vehicle in no hurry, crawling over the rough terrain. The two men flattened themselves, faces pressed to the ground. Rand could hear the rumble of the Jeep's engine now, and the growl of tires on gravel. The beams of light passed over their heads, and then were gone. Rand crawled closer to Marco. "Did you get a look at them?" he asked.

"Two of Prentice's guards," Marco said. "Regular patrol. They shouldn't be back this way for an hour, at least."

Marco led the way toward the old mine. Iron bars set too close together for anything larger than a pack rat to pass through blocked the entrance, a common safety precaution in a country littered with abandoned shafts. Marco motioned to move around to the side. Two hundred yards farther on they found a second entrance, a dark hole with cool air coming from it. They peered inside and saw a single guard, leaning against the wall, dozing.

Rand nudged Marco. *Bingo.* Why set a guard over an abandoned mine unless there was something inside worth guarding?

Marco motioned that he would go first and Rand should cover. Both men drew their duty weapons. Marco crept along the passage, keeping close to the wall. When he reached the dozing guard, he clamped one hand over his mouth and twisted his arm back and up, forcing him to his knees.

Rand hurried forward and together they tied up and gagged the guard. Rand shouldered the AR-15 the man had carried, and Marco pocketed his pistol. "We don't have long now," Marco said. "They probably have to check in at regular intervals."

They moved on down the passage, which was tall enough for them to walk upright, one behind the other. Rand's heart raced and cold sweat beaded on his forehead. He'd never particularly liked enclosed spaces. He forced himself to take deep, even breaths of the cool, dusty air. "What's that smell?" he asked, wrinkling his nose at the ammonia-tinged odor.

"Bats," Marco said. "They like caves and old mine shafts."

"I wish we had Lotte with us. She'd probably take us right to Lauren if she's here."

"It's harder to be stealthy with a dog," Marco said.

"Lotte can be stealthy, but I thought it would be better to leave her with Sophie."

"I thought she was afraid of dogs."

"She is, but Lotte will protect her."

Sophie had protested when he insisted on leaving the dog, but the memory of the slashed underwear and the menacing message in her hotel room made him adamant. "She won't hurt you," he'd reassured her. "But she will hurt anyone who comes after you."

"There's a light up ahead," Marco said softly.

Rand spotted the faint glow from the side passage. They moved faster toward it, but stopped abruptly when they spotted a second guard. This one was awake, pacing back and forth. Marco's eyes met Rand's. *Rush him*, he mouthed, and Rand nodded.

Guns drawn, the two rushed the guard, and were on him before he could ready his weapon to fire. "What are you guarding, pal?" Rand asked as he bound the man's wrists with plastic zip ties.

"Why should I tell you?"

"Suit yourself." Marco stuffed a gag in the man's mouth and slapped on a strip of duct tape. "Let's go." He jerked his head toward the passage the guard had been watching over.

The room was dimly lit with two lanterns hung from

nails on opposite walls, and set up like a bedroom, complete with a queen-sized bed, a dresser and a fuzzy pink rug beneath their feet. Someone stirred beneath the heap of quilts on the bed, then sat up, staring at them.

"Lauren Starling," Marco said, and she began to scream.

SOPHIE SAT RIGID on the sofa in Rand's duplex, hands clenched tightly in her lap, her breathing shallow. Every few seconds she glanced at the dog who lay on her pad in the corner, mouth open to reveal gleaming white teeth, golden eyes fixed on Sophie.

She'd argued with Rand when he insisted on leaving the dog with her, but he'd been stubborn. "She'll protect you," he'd said.

"I'm afraid of her." Something he would never understand.

"Then now is a good time for you to get to know her, to work on getting over your fear." He squeezed her arm. "I've seen how strong you are. How brave you are. If you can risk Prentice's guards, you can risk spending a few hours with Lotte."

"How is she going to protect me?"

"She'll hear someone coming before you will. And she's trained to defend me with her life. She'll do the same for you."

"Leave me a gun. I can protect myself."

His expression grew skeptical. "How much shooting have you done?

"None."

"Then Lotte will be better protection," he'd concluded.

She looked at the dog again, trying to see her objectively as a beautiful animal. Her fur gleamed in the lamplight, gold with black tips, thick and looking as soft as a Persian rug. Dark hair ringed her eyes, making her appear to be wearing eyeliner, and her lashes were as long and lush as any starlet's. The idea almost made Sophie giggle. She must have made some sound, because Lotte pricked up her ears and cocked her head in a quizzical gesture.

"I'm sure you think I'm crazy," Sophie said. "Why not? Everyone else does. Rand is the only one who—maybe—believes in me."

At Rand's name, Lotte lifted her head higher and began to pant harder. "I want to believe him when he says you won't hurt me," Sophie said. "It's just hard. Not your fault, I know. I think I used to like dogs before… before the accident." She ran her hand along the jaw, where the scars had been, before plastic surgery had rendered them invisible. "It was just so terrifying. I was only a child and it's like an involuntary reaction—I look at a dog and my body remembers."

Lotte sighed and rested her head on her paws, though her gold-brown eyes remained alert and fixed on Sophie. "If Rand and I are ever going to do anything about these feelings between us—whatever those feelings are—then you and I had better learn to get along." Sophie felt a little foolish, talking to the dog, but the conversation soothed her, and Lotte didn't seem to mind. And who else did she have to talk to about these things? "I've never been in love before," she said. "Not real love. So I don't know if this is what it feels like. And I don't even know if the two of us—together—are a good idea. I mean, I live in Madison. A long way from here. And he's here. And then there's Lauren. When they find her—

and I have to believe they'll find her—I have no idea what she's been through. She may need me to focus all my attention on her, and would that be fair to Rand?"

Lotte lifted her head and whined.

"You're right," Sophie said. "It wouldn't be fair. So I shouldn't lead him on. I should just forget about him and go back to Madison when this is over and..." And what? Mope around with a broken heart? That sounded so melodramatic, but if leaving Rand behind didn't break her heart, she knew she'd at least be badly bruised. And for what? Not because she was so devoted to Madison, Wisconsin, and her job there. But because she was a coward. Afraid of getting hurt. Not just physically injured by Rand's dog, but emotionally wounded by his possible rejection. After all, she wasn't like Lauren. She wasn't beautiful and charming and she hadn't been born knowing how to captivate a guy. Sophie was quiet and plain and ordinary. No match for an edgy guy like Rand, with his tattoos and muscles and dangerous job. They weren't a bit alike and shouldn't a couple be at least a little compatible if they were going to build a long-term relationship?

"What do you think?" Sophie asked the dog. "Could Rand really love someone like me?"

Lotte leaped to her feet, every hair on her back standing on end. A deep growl made Sophie feel cold clear through, and when Lotte barked, Sophie screamed and stood on the sofa, looking wildly around for some weapon with which to defend herself.

Lotte rushed toward her, then past her. Weak-kneed and dry-mouthed, Sophie realized the dog was barking at the door. And not just barking, but jumping and pawing at the wood. Muffled voices sounded, their words indistinct.

"Who is it?" Sophie called, still standing on the sofa. "Who's out there?"

The door burst open, slamming hard against the wall. Lotte's barking grew more furious. Sophie was aware of two men rushing into the room. Then someone threw a blanket over her and wrapped strong arms around her. She struggled, kicking with her legs, her arms pinned. The dog's barking almost drowned out the men's shouting and her own muffled screams. A gunshot reverberated and then everything went black as she was dragged away.

MARCO REACHED LAUREN first and put a gloved hand over her mouth to stop her screaming. "It's all right," he said, his soft, deep voice soothing her. "We're here to rescue you."

She nodded, blue eyes wide in her pale face. Marco removed his hand. "Thank God," she said, her eyes wet with unshed tears. "I thought I'd never get out of here."

"You can tell us everything later," Rand said. "We've got to go before someone realizes the guards aren't reporting in." If Marco was right, the first guard had already missed his check-in period. Reinforcements might be on their way already.

Lauren climbed out of the bed and grabbed a robe—a long pink-and-gold brocade affair that looked like something out of a period movie. Something a queen or a movie star would wear. She shoved her feet into kitten-heeled slippers. Marco eyed them skeptically. "Don't you have anything sturdier?"

"Unfortunately, no. Richard won't let me have anything else."

"So, is he your boyfriend or something?" Rand asked.

Marco shot him a warning look and shook his head. But why not get the truth out in the open right away?

"My boyfriend?" Lauren laughed, a sound like bells. "Please, no. Though if you ask him, he calls himself my fiancé. He's convinced if he keeps me here long enough I'll wear down and agree to marry him. He's sick, that's what he is." She sashed the robe tighter and tucked her hand into the crook of Marco's elbow. "Let's get out of here."

"We'll have to go back the way we came." Marco pointed to the door. "How often do the guards change?"

"They work six-hour shifts, I think," she said. "This one just came on a couple of hours ago." She gingerly stepped around the guard's prone figure. "I hope you hit him hard," she said to Marco, her tone conversational. "He was always trying to look down my gown and feel me up every chance he got." She shuddered. "A really foul man. I mean, at least Richard is a gentleman, even if he is delusional."

"We should move him out of the way," Rand said. "If someone comes along, maybe they'll think he deserted his post."

Marco grunted in agreement and grabbed the guard's ankles. Rand took his shoulders and they dragged him some distance to a side passage, the man glaring up at them malevolently the entire time. They left his weapons in a different side passage, then returned to Lauren, who waited at the entrance to her underground bedroom.

Rand studied her closely. He thought he saw some resemblance to Sophie, in the sharpness of her chin and the shape of her nose. But in demeanor the two sisters were nothing alike—Sophie quiet and serious, Lauren sparkling and chatty.

She must have felt his gaze on her. She looked over her shoulder at him and asked, "How did you find me? I was giving up hope."

"Your sister," he said. "Sophie traveled here from Wisconsin and demanded we keep looking for you. She refused to give up."

Tears glistened in her eyes once more. "Sophie has never given up on me," she said.

"Are you doing okay?" Marco asked. "Do you need anything before we head out?"

"I'm fine." Her smile dazzled. Even Marco looked dazed by it. "Richard makes sure I have all my medications. He denies me nothing, except my freedom."

He nodded and took her arm. "Let's go, then."

But just as they prepared to turn into the passage leading toward the exit, they heard someone coming. "That will be the guard coming to check on me," Lauren whispered. "They do a bed check every hour. If I'm not there, they'll raise the alarm."

Marco turned her around and they hurried back to the chamber. "Quick, back under the covers," he said. "Let the guard see you're okay. Then we'll have an hour before the next check—provided they don't discover the missing guard."

"Where will you be?" she asked, crawling into the bed and pulling up the covers.

"Under the bed." He slid under one side, and Rand rolled under the other.

The guard shuffled into the room. "Good evening," Lauren greeted him brightly.

"You're supposed to be asleep," the guard said.

"I'm having trouble sleeping. I sent the other guard to the house to get me my pills."

"He's not supposed to leave you unguarded," he said.

"Oh, it'll be all right. Who's going to find me down here?"

The guard grunted. "It's just as well you're awake. We brought you some company."

"Company?" Lauren sounded puzzled.

"She says she's your sister." Rand, watching from beneath the bed, stared in horror as a second man entered the room, dragging a bound-and-gagged Sophie behind him.

"You two can have a little reunion," the first guard said, and pushed Sophie onto the bed beside Lauren. Then the men left.

As soon as the guards were gone, Rand and Marco rolled from beneath the bed. Lauren was already kneeling beside her sister, struggling with her bonds.

Rand stripped off the tape over Sophie's mouth while Marco cut the ties on her wrists. "Lauren!" she cried, hugging her sister close.

The two women cried and exclaimed, until Marco finally interrupted. "We have to get out of here," he said.

"Are you all right?" Rand put an arm around Sophie, feeling her tremble. "Did they hurt you?"

She shook her head, but tears streamed down her cheeks. "But I'm afraid they shot Lotte. She did what you said she would do. She tried to protect me. But they had guns…"

His chest constricted as he thought of the dog, but he shoved the emotions aside. He had to focus on the situation at hand, on Sophie and Lauren and helping them escape.

They started back the way they had come, but skidded to a stop when they spotted not one, but two guards in the passage ahead. "Is there another way out?" Marco asked.

"There's the passage to the house," Lauren said. "There's no guard there, since the only place it goes is the house."

"Let's go," Rand said. "Once there, we can steal a vehicle and get away faster."

They rushed along the passage Lauren indicated, sacrificing stealth for speed. But one of the guards must have heard them and sounded the alarm. Marco grabbed Lauren's hand and pulled her forward. "Faster!" he commanded.

Sophie grasped Rand's hand and they hurried to keep up, but Lauren and Marco were faster and the two couples soon became separated. "Which way did they go?" Sophie asked.

Rand stopped and studied the dust at their feet. In the dark passageway it was impossible to make out distinct footprints. "Marco!" he shouted.

But the only answer was a deafening explosion that knocked him off his feet, and a shower of boulders crashed down around them.

# Chapter Sixteen

Sophie came to, aching and disoriented in the darkness, choking in the dust. She closed her eyes and rested her head against the stone floor, willing memory to return. Back at Rand's duplex, after she'd been wrapped in the blanket, someone had stuffed her into the backseat of a vehicle while a second person bound her wrists and ankles. They'd driven for some time, then bumped down a rough road. Her captors cut the ties at her ankles so that she could walk, but gagged her and kept her wrapped in the blanket until she stood outside the passage that led to Sophie's room.

Tears streamed down her face as she remembered the shock and delight of seeing her sister at last, and Rand there with her.

Rand! Where was he? She felt all around her in the darkness until she encountered cloth, hard muscle and bone beneath. "Rand!" She curled her fingers around whatever part of the body she held. "Rand, please tell me you're all right."

"Sophie?" He tried to sit up, then fell back, moaning. She felt her way up his body to his head and caressed his face with her hands, then kissed his cheek. "Rand, wake up," she pleaded.

"I'm awake." His voice sounded strained.

"Are you all right?" she asked. "Are you hurt?"

"I got a bump on the head, but I'm okay." He levered himself up on his elbow. "I'm going to roll over. You reach into my pack and get a light so we can see our situation better."

"Okay."

He rolled onto his side and she sat up and felt in the outer pocket of his pack for the mini Maglite he told her she'd find there. When she switched it on she had to look away at first, it was so bright.

She handed the light to Rand and he sat up and shone it around them. They were in one end of a chamber blasted from the rock, the entrance and the other end of the space filled with fallen rock. "What happened?" she asked.

"Maybe the guards set off some kind of charge to collapse the tunnels." He continued to shine the light on the tumble of rock. "Maybe that was the plan."

"You mean Prentice would rather kill Lauren than let her escape?" It sounded like something out of a horror movie or something.

"If she's dead, she can't testify against him," Rand said. "And if she's buried in an old mine, the chances of us finding her are slim to none."

She choked back a sob. "Lauren can't be dead," she said. "Not when we've only just found her."

He gripped her arm. "Don't give up hope yet," he said. "We made it okay. And she's with Marco. He'll look after her."

She clutched his hand, trying to hang on to some of his calm, as well. "What do we do now?" she asked.

He slipped off his pack and pulled his radio from the

belt at his side. "It's too far underground to transmit," he said, "but maybe headquarters can get a ping. They'll realize something has happened and come looking. Meanwhile, let's see if we can find a way out of here."

Together, they moved to the rubble-filled end of the chamber. He used the light to inspect every crevice between the rocks, but none revealed open space beyond. Sophie clawed at the rocks, trying to dislodge them. Maybe they could dig their way out—

Rand put a hand on her arm. "Stop. You're going to hurt yourself." He led her to the other side of the passage and spread his jacket for them to sit on. "The best thing to do is rest and wait."

"Wait for what?" she asked.

"Rescue. Someone will come for us, I'm sure."

"How can you be sure?"

"You heard the captain. We're all in this together. A team. You don't leave a team member behind."

She wanted to believe him, but she had no experience with that kind of loyalty. For so much of her life she and Lauren had only had each other. And Sophie was the dependable one, the sister who almost always came to the rescue. Except that now she was helpless to rescue Lauren, or herself.

"I can't believe Prentice was keeping Lauren prisoner down here," she said. "Why? It's not as if he could expect a big ransom for her or anything."

"Apparently he believed he could make her marry him if he kept her long enough," Rand said.

"But that's insane. And he looks so...so ordinary."

"I guess some sick minds can live under ordinary exteriors. But according to her he didn't mistreat her—he just wouldn't let her leave."

"She looked the same as always. Beautiful."

"I prefer the darker, quieter ones." Rand took her hand and squeezed it.

She smiled, even though he probably couldn't see it in the dark. She knew she wasn't beautiful like Lauren, but Rand made her feel beautiful. Special. She leaned against him, her hand wrapped in his. "If this had to happen, I'm glad I'm with you," she said.

"It's kind of nice to have some time alone with you." He smoothed his hand along her shoulder. "Not exactly the most romantic setting, though."

"I don't know about that." She snuggled closer. "It's dark. And private." He'd propped the flashlight against the rocks so that it cast an indirect golden glow, like a wall sconce, giving just enough light for her to make out his form, without a lot of details.

He turned his face toward hers and she kissed him. What she'd meant as a brief buss transformed into a long, lingering caress—contact that said all the things she could find no words for.

He cradled her face in both hands. "I've never met anyone like you," he said.

"You mean stubborn and afraid and crazy?" She tried to laugh, but the sound came out too shaky, revealing how important his answer was to her.

"I mean determined and brave and loyal. Amazing." He drew her to him in a deep, breath-stealing kiss, his hands sliding down her arms, then up her sides to cup her breasts, which felt swollen and heated at his touch.

She opened her mouth in a gasp and he swallowed the sound, his tongue sweeping over her lips, teasing into her mouth, enticing and erotic. She arched to him, wanting to be closer. Wanting more.

He slid his mouth from hers, and pressed his lips to her temple. "Maybe we should stop now," he said, his voice ragged.

Everything about this was wrong—the location, the timing, their clothes. Making love to Rand had felt inevitable for a while now, but she'd imagined candlelight and crisp sheets, soft music and silk, not rock walls and dirt floors, dusty jeans and dried blood. But being with him was the only good thing she had to hold on to now. Denying each other the one thing they wanted most seemed stupid. They might not have much time left; they might as well use that time for something good.

She unbuttoned the top button of his uniform shirt, resisting the urge to tear it from him. "I want this," she said. "More than I've ever wanted anything."

"I want it, too." He caressed her shoulders. "But you deserve better than this."

"Shhh." She pressed her lips to the triangle of exposed chest her unbuttoning had revealed. He tasted of sweat and dust. "This isn't about what either of us deserves."

He pulled her tight against him and kissed her, a hard, bruising kiss full of longing and regret. She cradled his head in her hands and opened her mouth to him, tangling her tongue with his, letting her need for him fill her and drive out the fear.

He slid both hands beneath her shirt, skimming along her ribs, then pushing her bra out of the way to cup her breasts, squeezing gently. The ridge of his erection pressed against her stomach; she could feel the heat even through the layers of cloth separating them. She reached down and rubbed her hand along the evidence of his desire, eliciting a groan of frustration from him.

He grasped her arms and held them over her head, then tugged off her shirt and bra, leaving her naked from the waist up. Goose bumps formed along her flesh, and she automatically tried to cover herself, but he kept hold of her arms, pulling them away. "You are so beautiful," he said, and bent to kiss the top of one breast, then the other.

She gasped when he drew her nipple into his mouth, the suction pulling between her legs. "Rand," she breathed, but he only suckled harder, leaving her light-headed and trembling.

He lowered the zipper of her jeans and slid his hand in to cup her over her underwear. She fumbled the rest of his shirt buttons loose and pushed the fabric away from his chest, then stilled, staring at what the parted fabric revealed.

He stilled also, and lifted his head, his eyes meeting hers. "I got my first tat when I was nineteen," he said. "I've been adding on ever since."

With one finger, she traced the lines of black ink: mountains and waves following the contours of his muscles, trees and rocks and animals inscribed across his torso and chest in an intricate mural. "It's beautiful," she said. "But not what I expected."

"I'm just full of surprises." He unbuckled his belt. "I can't wait to show you more."

They helped each other out of their clothes, even that mundane activity made sensual by the thrill of hands touching places they hadn't allowed themselves to touch before, revealing flesh they had never seen before. He made a pallet of their clothes on the floor and urged her down beside him. Side by side, they traced the contours of each other's bodies, exploring each peak and valley, discovering a map that was uniquely theirs. He learned she had had an appendectomy when she was twenty-four, and he had fallen while climbing a mountain at nineteen, leaving a jagged scar as a permanent reminder of that adventure.

He surprised her by stopping at one point and retrieving a condom from his pack. "It's not what you think," he said. "They make great temporary canteens."

She laughed. "Sure they do." She lay back and beckoned to him. "I don't care why you have one, just that you have one."

He kneeled beside her and ripped open the package, then sheathed himself. She held her breath as she watched him, her whole body tensed with need for him. When he positioned himself between her legs, she arched to him, all shyness vanished. "Hurry," she whispered.

She was more than ready for him, and the sensation of him filling her almost sent her over the edge. She tightened around him and he shaped his hands to her buttocks and pulled her even closer. "Look at me," he said.

She stared into his eyes, and the grimness of their surroundings, the rock and sand and darkness, receded. She lost herself in those intense brown eyes, and in the waves of desire buffeting her with each powerful thrust of his body. His hands caressed as his body moved, the need within her coiling tighter and tighter. "Don't hold back," he urged, so she didn't, and her climax rocketed through her, stripping away the last fragment of fear and hesitation that had bound her.

She clung to him, stroking his back, his chest, leaning forward to trace her tongue along the line of a tattooed mountain range. As she dragged her tongue across the flat brown nipple half-hidden in the lines of the artwork, he cried out his own release and convulsed against her. She held him tightly, eyes closed, listening to the strong, steady rhythm of his heartbeat, bringing them back to themselves.

They lay in each other's arms, their discarded clothes drawn around them as makeshift bedding. "Is it all right if I switch off the flashlight?" he asked. "We need to save the batteries."

"All right." She closed her own eyes, but even that didn't shut out the depth of the darkness when he switched off the little light. Only the solid feel of his chest against the side of her face, and the hard muscle of his arms pulling her to him, kept her grounded. "What do we do now?" she asked.

"I don't know. I only had the one condom."

She laughed, something she would never have thought she could do, considering the circumstances. "That's disappointing news," she said. "But I meant, what are we going to do about getting out of here?"

"I don't know yet, but we'll figure something out. For now, we need to sleep. We'll think better when we're rested."

"All right." She lay still, sure she'd never be able to relax, but gradually sleep did steal over her. In the security of Rand's arms, she relaxed. Later, they'd think of something. They didn't have any choice.

Sophie woke to a low, groaning noise, like some ancient animal moving in the depths of the cavern. "Rand!" She shook him, hard. "Rand, wake up!"

He shifted beneath her, sitting up, his arm still around her, pulling her up with him. "What is it?" he asked, his voice only a little groggy.

"That noise. What is it?"

They listened, and it came again, a long, low moan, primitive and chilling. Rand switched on the light and began sorting through their clothes. "Get dressed," he said. "Hurry."

She pulled on underwear and pants and reached for her shirt. "What is it?" she asked, his anxious expression feeding her own fear. "Is it some kind of animal?"

"No animal." He buttoned his shirt halfway, then pulled on his pack. "It's the tunnels. Timbers shifting."

"The tunnels? I don't understand." She sat and began pulling on her shoes.

"We need to shelter along the wall, where the rock is thickest." He pulled her to her feet. "I think we might be in for another cave-in."

# Chapter Seventeen

Sophie buried her face against Rand's chest and put her hands over her ears, trying to block out the groan of splintering timbers and crash of falling rock. Only his arms holding her tightly kept the panic at bay. With Rand, she could be strong enough to get through this.

Eerie silence settled over them. "What happened?" she asked. "Did they set off another charge?"

"I don't think so," he said. "I think the timbers will shift and settle for a while after an explosion. It's one of the things that make mine rescue work so dangerous." He coughed and switched on his flashlight. "Hey, take a look at this!"

She didn't want to look, didn't want to see their world reduced even further to a rocked-in tomb. But something in his voice encouraged her to lift her head and peer down the narrow beam of light.

Rather than reducing their world, this latest collapse had opened the way into a new passage. "Is that a light up ahead?" she asked.

"Let's go find out." He took her hand and helped her over the rubble. In a few moments, they stood on the other side of the debris, in a smooth-walled tunnel. "Why does this section look different?" she asked.

"I think this must be the passage leading to the house." He ran his hand over the pale surface of the wall on their right. "It's poured concrete," he said. "Like one of those big highway culverts." He drew his gun. "Stay behind me. In case we run into one of Prentice's guards."

But they met no one in the tunnel, and no one waited at the door at the end. Rand tried the knob, but it wouldn't turn. "Stand back," he told her.

She took two steps back and covered her ears, expecting he'd shoot off the lock, as she'd seen in movies. Instead, he slammed his heel into the lock, collapsing it inward. The door swung open. They waited, but no one emerged. No one shouted. No alarms sounded.

Rand motioned her forward and cautiously, they stepped into what appeared at first to be a closet. He shone the light around the paneled walls until the beam illuminated a steel door.

"It's an elevator," Sophie said.

"Looks like it." He pressed the single lighted button on the wall, and the door slid open. They stepped inside and Rand pressed the number *one*. After a few seconds, the doors silently closed and the car began to rise.

The elevator opened and they faced another door, this one unlocked, and it opened into a coat closet on the mansion's first floor. They passed through the closet, into the deserted front hall of Richard Prentice's mansion. "Where is everyone?" Sophie whispered.

"I hear something down there." Rand motioned with the pistol toward the back of the house. As they walked closer, she could hear a whirring sound and see the light spilling into the corridor.

Richard Prentice stood beside a filing cabinet, pulling out papers, a handful at a time, and depositing them in a whirring shredder. He looked up at their approach and frowned. "I don't have time to talk now, Officer," he said. "I'm very busy."

Rand motioned for Sophie to step back, then addressed the billionaire. "Richard Prentice, you're under arrest for the kidnapping of Lauren Starling."

Prentice inserted another sheaf of papers into the shredder, and raised his voice to be heard over the whirring. "I wouldn't believe anything poor Lauren tells you," he said. "She's crazy, you know. Completely unbalanced."

"Lauren is not crazy." Sophie couldn't keep quiet any longer. If anyone here was unbalanced, it was Richard Prentice. "She certainly didn't lock herself in that mine all these weeks," she said.

Prentice shook his head. "Lauren suffers from severe paranoia. She believed people were trying to kill her. I suppose she's transferred those feelings to me now. She came to me and I tried to help her. I care about her and I thought with time and attention, she'd recover. I see that's impossible now."

He sounded so calm and reasonable. So sane. If she hadn't known better, even Sophie might have believed him. "You were holding her prisoner in a mine," she protested.

"I created that room in the mine to reassure her." He continued shredding documents as he spoke. "She felt safe and protected there, at least at first."

"Liar," Sophie said. "Don't think your money will protect you now."

"You need to come with me, sir," Rand said. "You have the right to remain silent—"

Sophie didn't see the gun in Prentice's hands until it

fired. She screamed as Rand fired his own weapon, but Prentice was already racing toward a door on the other side of the room. Rand shoved Sophie to the floor and fired again, bullets striking the door frame as Prentice jerked it open and threw himself outside.

Rand raced after him, Sophie trailing after. When she burst through the door she spotted a waiting helicopter, Richard Prentice running toward its open door.

"He's getting away!" she shouted as the door to the helicopter slammed shut, and the aircraft rose into a sky streaked pink with the dawn.

A black-and-white Ranger Brigade vehicle raced into the yard and skidded to a halt near where the helicopter had waited. Michael and Graham climbed out of the front seat, while Marco and Lauren exited the back. No longer the elegant newscaster who had smiled from television screens and billboards, Lauren's face was streaked with dirt, her hair long and limp, a sweatshirt and pants hanging on her small frame. But at the sight of her sister, she broke into a smile. "Sophie!" she cried, and held out her arms.

Sophie didn't try to hold back the tears as she embraced Lauren. "I've been so worried about you," she said. "What happened?"

"Marco and I escaped during the explosion," she said. "He found a way out of the mine. Then we went for help. But I was so worried about you."

"I'm fine. But Richard Prentice got away." She looked up, toward the fast-departing silhouette of the helicopter.

"We'll find him," Graham's expression was grim, but determined. "We have more than enough evidence now to charge him with a long list of crimes, thanks to Ms. Starling."

"His lawyers won't pull him out of the fire this time," Rand said. "We'll make sure of that."

Sophie clung tightly to her sister's hand and watched the helicopter until it disappeared over a distant mountain. She wanted to believe justice would be served, and Richard Prentice would be punished for what he'd done, but the memory of him standing before the shredder, explaining away every bit of evidence against him with the assurance of a man who can buy the best lawyers and the best reputation, made her sick to her stomach. Maybe no matter how hard they all tried, he was a man who was truly above the law.

THE DAY AFTER her dramatic rescue, dressed in a new suit, her hair carefully styled and makeup perfected, Lauren Starling stood before two dozen reporters at the Dragon Point overlook in Black Canyon of the Gunnison National Park. Flanked by Captain Graham Ellison and Agent Marco Cruz of The Ranger Brigade, she looked composed and professional, and much calmer than Sophie would have been in her position.

Sophie waited with Rand to one side of the gathering, marveling at her sister's composure. "I want to thank The Ranger Brigade for their tireless efforts to locate and rescue me," Lauren said, in the smooth, modulated tones of a professional broadcaster. "And I especially want to thank my sister, Sophie Montgomery, who put aside everything to come to my aid in my time of need. People talk about the depths of brotherly love, but nothing can match the depths of a sister's devotion." She smiled at Sophie, and dozens of cameras flashed.

Lauren directed that dazzling smile to the reporters in front of her. "And now I'll take a few questions."

"Ms. Starling, what do you say to Richard Prentice's assertion that everything you've told us today is a lie, an elaborate scenario that resulted from your own mental illness?" The reporter, a man in a bow tie whom Sophie didn't recognize, hurled the question like a dagger.

Lauren's smile vanished. Maybe Sophie was the only one who saw the flash of pain in her eyes, the tightening of her fingers on the edge of the podium, the tension in her shoulders. She quickly masked the fear, and replaced it with a stern, but determined look. "Mr. Prentice is facing many years in prison for his crimes, and the complete ruin of his reputation," she said evenly. "He is desperate to blame anyone but himself for his misdeeds. He is the one who is lying."

"But you are mentally ill," the reporter persisted. "You've admitted to a diagnosis of bipolar disorder."

"Yes, I suffer from an illness shared by five-point-seven million people in this country alone," she said. "And as with other illnesses, such as diabetes or asthma, I take medication and have adjusted my lifestyle to control the disease. I was definitely in my right mind when Richard Prentice kidnapped me and held me hostage for six weeks. He's the one who's delusional, if he thinks he can dismiss that behavior as a product of my imagination."

"In the statement he issued this morning, Mr. Prentice says the Rangers have no proof of the other charges against him," another reporter read from a tablet computer. "He says, quote, 'The Ranger Brigade continue their established pattern of harassment and character assassination with these unfounded claims. I have no connection to drug dealers, murders, smuggling and the other crimes they have charged me with.' End quote. What do you say to that?"

"I came to Montrose to interview a witness and obtain photographic proof of Mr. Prentice's ties to drug dealing in the area," she said. "That witness has since been murdered, and Mr. Prentice tried to silence me, but failed. Once he is returned for trial, the world will see we have plenty of proof."

"If he wanted to silence you, why didn't he just kill you?" a female reporter asked.

"That will be explained in the trial." Graham stepped forward. The Rangers' attorney had advised Lauren not to go into Prentice's plan to persuade her to marry him. The scheme was outlandish enough that some in the media might latch on to it as proof of Prentice's claims that Lauren was delusional. After all, the stoic billionaire didn't strike people as the type to obsess over a woman, no matter how beautiful.

"That's all the questions we have time for today," Graham said, and reporters immediately turned their attention to him, firing questions about the Rangers' case against Richard Prentice. Lauren moved to stand beside Marco Cruz. Sophie had noticed her sister seemed to feel safest near the handsome, taciturn officer.

The press conference ended and the reporters and cameramen began to move back toward their cars. But one man, tall and blond and dressed in slacks and a dress shirt, the sleeves carefully folded back to reveal muscular forearms, broke away from the crowd and moved toward Lauren. "Phil!" she said, her expression wary. "I didn't expect to see you here."

He glanced at the officers flanking her and held out his hands, palms up. "I'm not here to cause trouble. I just wanted to say I'm glad you're okay. Despite what other people might think—" again, a look at the officers "—I didn't have anything to do with what happened to you."

"I know you didn't." Lauren's smile would have melted chocolate. "Take care of yourself, Phil."

"I'm trying." He adjusted his collar. "I'm checking into a rehab program in Grand Junction this afternoon."

"That's a good idea," Lauren said.

"Yeah, well, I guess this is goodbye. For now, anyway."

"Goodbye, Phil." Marco took her arm and she turned away, toward his waiting car.

"She did great," Sophie whispered to Rand. "She's so brave."

He took her hand and squeezed it. "You're the one who's brave. I'm proud of you."

She had to look away from the admiration in his eyes, aware of the people crowded around them. Her gaze focused on the dog beside him. "I'm glad Lotte's all right," she said. "I was worried."

"Lucky those guys were terrible shots." Rand scratched the dog behind the ears. Then he put his arm around Sophie. "Let's go for a walk."

He led her down the path to the very edge of the canyon, where she looked out at the figures of the fighting dragons etched in the opposite wall of the chasm. Though composed by nature, they looked like Chinese paintings, the giant figures in red and black crisp against the gray stone walls.

"What will you do now that Lauren is safe?" he asked.

"I don't know. I'm thinking of staying here for a while, to make sure she's all right." Though Lauren hadn't said much about her ordeal, Sophie sensed her sister was still fragile. She'd need support for the long trial—both in the media and in the courtroom—that lay ahead. "I don't really have anything to go back to in Wisconsin. My job stopped challenging me a long time ago, and I could probably find another one here."

"Does that mean you'll stay in Montrose?"

"I'm thinking about it. Lauren plans to stay here. She'll do all she can to see that Richard Prentice is convicted. It's not going to be easy for her. I want to be here to help."

"I'd like it if you stayed."

She met his eyes, searching for the emotions behind his words. Did he mean he'd like it if they got to know each other better, maybe casually dated? Or did he want what she wanted, to continue this deeper connection she felt for him? "Why would you like me to stay?" she asked.

He smoothed his palm down her arm, then caught her hand in his. "I used to joke that Lotte was the only woman I needed in my life," he said. "But I was wrong. I need you. I think I've stayed single until now because I was waiting for you."

"I can't make any promises right now," she said. "Not while things are still so unsettled for Lauren."

"Just say you'll give me a chance—you'll give us a chance." He squeezed her hand.

She squeezed back. "Yes. I want that." She wanted Rand in her life—for a long time to come. Maybe even forever.

Lotte whined. They looked at the dog. "What about Lotte?" he asked. "The two of us are a package deal."

"I've never felt this way about anyone else." She swallowed, her mouth suddenly dry. "I love you, Rand. It scares me a little."

"I love you, too. And we both know you're not going to a let a little fear stop you."

They kissed, a light, brief contact that held the promise of much more. Later, when they were alone.

Lotte whined again, a soft, pleading sound. Sophie put out her hand and stroked the dog's soft head, trembling only a little as she did so. "I'm learning to love Lotte, too," she said. "She risked her life to try to save me. And since she's so important to you, I want her to be important to me, too."

He put his hand over hers and they stood that way for a long moment, man, woman and dog. An unlikely circle of love. Sophie sighed with happiness. She had spent so many years being afraid, when all along she'd had the power—the courage—inside her to save herself. To find the love she deserved, with a man who was truly worthy.

\* \* \* \* \*

# MILLS & BOON®
## INTRIGUE
### Romantic Suspense

**A SEDUCTIVE COMBINATION OF DANGER AND DESIRE**